Praise for

Sleeping with the Fishes

"A zany, amusing fantasy." —*The Best Reviews*

"A hilarious romp with a mermaid, a merman, and a human with a Ph.D. that will have you rolling on the floor in laughter."

—*Romance Reviews Today*

"[Davidson's] sense of humor and imagination know no bounds . . . Pure delight to read from start to finish." —*A Romance Review*

Swimming Without a Net

"An engaging undersea adventure . . . Hang on for a fun-filled ride . . . This is a not-to-be-missed, laugh-out-loud adventure. Believe me, you will love this story!" —*Romance Junkies*

"Fast-paced, enjoyable, and at times downright hilarious."

—*Romance Reviews Today*

"A story that will entertain, delight, and enlighten fans of mermaid Fred . . . Fans of Ms. Davidson, rejoice—Fred is back and as sassy as ever!"

—*Fresh Fiction*

"Another wacky, amusing romp from MaryJanice Davidson, the queen of this subgenre. The story line is fast-paced but loaded with humor."

—*Midwest Book Review*

continued . . .

Fish out of Water

"A swimmingly good finale." —*Booklist*

"Fred is really such a lovable creature . . . Reading about her antics, on land and sea, can make even the most humorless of brutes laugh and cry along with her . . . out-of-this-world craziness. *Fish out of Water* is too good to pass up." —*Bitten by Books*

"The usual zany comedic romantic fantasy that MaryJanice Davidson is renowned for . . . The story line is action-packed on land and under the sea." —*Midwest Book Review*

"It's a great ride . . . Super hilarious—and very satisfying at the end." —*Night Owl Reviews*

Praise for MaryJanice Davidson's
Betsy Taylor, Vampire Queen novels

"What can you say about a vampire whose loyalty can be bought by designer shoes? Can we say, outrageous?" —*The Best Reviews*

Undead and Unfinished

"Humorous . . . Fans of the series will enjoy the latest." —*Midwest Book Review*

"Entertaining . . . Complex . . . Sassy." —*Monsters and Critics*

Undead and Unwelcome

"Twists and turns to keep the readers hooked." —*ParaNormal Romance Reviews*

Undead and Uneasy

"A winner. Told with the irreverent humor Ms. Davidson's fans have come to expect."

—*Fresh Fiction*

Undead and Unpopular

"Think *Sex and the City* . . . with demons and vampires . . . [Davidson] lets the children of the night show their lighter side."

—*Publishers Weekly*

Undead and Unreturnable

"There is never a dull moment in the life (or death!) of Betsy . . . A winner all the way around!"

—*The Road to Romance*

Undead and Unappreciated

"The best vampire chick lit of the year."

—*Detroit Free Press*

Undead and Unemployed

"If you're fans of Sookie Stackhouse and Anita Blake, don't miss Betsy Taylor. She rocks."

—*The Best Reviews*

Undead and Unwed

"Delightful, wicked fun!"

—Christine Feehan

Titles by MaryJanice Davidson

UNDEAD AND UNWED
UNDEAD AND UNEMPLOYED
UNDEAD AND UNAPPRECIATED
UNDEAD AND UNRETURNABLE
UNDEAD AND UNPOPULAR
UNDEAD AND UNEASY
UNDEAD AND UNWORTHY
UNDEAD AND UNWELCOME
UNDEAD AND UNFINISHED
UNDEAD AND UNDERMINED

DERIK'S BANE
WOLF AT THE DOOR

SLEEPING WITH THE FISHES
SWIMMING WITHOUT A NET
FISH OUT OF WATER

Titles by MaryJanice Davidson and Anthony Alongi

JENNIFER SCALES AND THE ANCIENT FURNACE
JENNIFER SCALES AND THE MESSENGER OF LIGHT
THE SILVER MOON ELM: A JENNIFER SCALES NOVEL
SERAPH OF SORROW: A JENNIFER SCALES NOVEL
RISE OF THE POISON MOON: A JENNIFER SCALES NOVEL
EVANGELINA: A JENNIFER SCALES NOVEL

Anthologies

CRAVINGS

(with Laurell K. Hamilton, Rebecca York, Eileen Wilks)

BITE

(with Laurell K. Hamilton, Charlaine Harris, Angela Knight, Vickie Taylor)

KICK ASS

(with Maggie Shayne, Angela Knight, Jacey Ford)

MEN AT WORK

(with Janelle Denison, Nina Bangs)

DEAD AND LOVING IT

SURF'S UP

(with Janelle Denison, Nina Bangs)

MYSTERIA

(with P. C. Cast, Gena Showalter, Susan Grant)

OVER THE MOON

(with Angela Knight, Virginia Kantra, Sunny)

DEMON'S DELIGHT

(with Emma Holly, Vickie Taylor, Catherine Spangler)

DEAD OVER HEELS

MYSTERIA LANE

(with P. C. Cast, Gena Showalter, Susan Grant)

MYSTERIA NIGHTS

(includes Mysteria *and* Mysteria Lane, *with P. C. Cast, Susan Grant, Gena Showalter)*

UNDERWATER LOVE

(includes Sleeping with the Fishes, Swimming Without a Net, *and* Fish out of Water*)*

Underwater Love

MARYJANICE DAVIDSON

BERKLEY SENSATION, NEW YORK

THE BERKLEY PUBLISHING GROUP
Published by the Penguin Group
Penguin Group (USA) Inc.
375 Hudson Street, New York, New York 10014, USA
Penguin Group (Canada), 90 Eglinton Avenue East, Suite 700, Toronto, Ontario M4P 2Y3, Canada
(a division of Pearson Penguin Canada Inc.)
Penguin Books Ltd., 80 Strand, London WC2R 0RL, England
Penguin Group Ireland, 25 St. Stephen's Green, Dublin 2, Ireland (a division of Penguin Books Ltd.)
Penguin Group (Australia), 250 Camberwell Road, Camberwell, Victoria 3124, Australia
(a division of Pearson Australia Group Pty. Ltd.)
Penguin Books India Pvt. Ltd., 11 Community Centre, Panchsheel Park, New Delhi—110 017, India
Penguin Group (NZ), 67 Apollo Drive, Rosedale, Auckland 0632, New Zealand
(a division of Pearson New Zealand Ltd.)
Penguin Books (South Africa) (Pty.) Ltd., 24 Sturdee Avenue, Rosebank, Johannesburg 2196, South Africa

Penguin Books Ltd., Registered Offices: 80 Strand, London WC2R 0RL, England

Cover photo copyright © by Chris A. Crumley/Alamy.
Cover design by Sarah Oberrender.
Interior text design by Kristin del Rosario.

PUBLISHING HISTORY
Berkley Sensation trade paperback edition / February 2012

Library of Congress Cataloging-in-Publication Data

Davidson, MaryJanice.
Underwater love / MaryJanice Davidson.—Berkley Sensation trade paperback ed.
p. cm.
ISBN 978-0-425-24719-8
1. Mermaids—Fiction. 2. Marine biologists I. Title.
PS3604.A949U56 2012
813'.6—dc23

2011043249

PRINTED IN THE UNITED STATES OF AMERICA

10 9 8 7 6 5 4 3 2 1

CONTENTS

Sleeping with the Fishes

For my husband, who did tons of research for this project, who came up with countless ways to turn the mermaid genre on its head, who helped me several steps of the way with this book, who supports me in the good times and bad, and who loves that I make more money than he does.

ACKNOWLEDGMENTS

I knew next to nothing about the things in this book when Fred popped into my head. Oh, sure, I knew about mermaid clichés and stereotypes (Ariel, of Disney-movie fame, yowling on top of a rock in a harbor instantly springs to mind) but nothing about the U.S. Coast Guard, marine biology, sea life, the National Ocean Service, or the New England Aquarium. (I'm from landlocked Minnesota.)

All these places and subjects had extensive books and websites available, which were truly a godsend to this landlubber. And I *did* have my wedding reception at the New England Aquarium years ago, which helped.

Further, I must (again) thank my editor, Cindy Hwang. I made the gross mistake of initially writing Fred the Mermaid in first person—gross because first person should be used sparingly, if at all, and a mistake because Fred ended up sounding like Betsy with fins.

Even worse, it took me two hundred pages to figure that out. So, seconds from my deadline, I ripped the whole thing up and started over: page one, chapter one. Cindy, to her great credit, did not implode, burst into tears, quit, tear up my contract, hire a hit man, smack me upside the head, or even raise her voice. She just cheerfully extended my deadline and asked me to be sure to tell her if I needed anything else.

Little did she know, my grandfather was going to die three weeks later. Again: no weeping (well, there was weeping, but it was all on my end), no threats, nothing but calm condolence and an assurance that the last thing I should worry about is some silly deadline. (She managed to say this without ripping out any of her hair as she pictured the fall line with a big hole where *Sleeping with the Fishes* was going to be.)

Thus, an even later manuscript. (See, see? Unlike most writers, I'll actually admit it: the book was late. It was entirely my fault. I suck.) And, though she must have been sorely tempted, rather than shoot the thing straight to galleys, the same team of editors descended on the book and did their usual stellar job of fixing my mistakes and making me look all, y'know, smart 'n' stuff. These people turned a messy pile of mistake-ridden pages (more than a few, tear-splotched) into a book, the one you're holding in your hands.

It's people like me who give people like her peptic ulcers. I'll get the credit and hardly anyone will know her name: Cindy Hwang. People will wait in line for my autograph and they'll ask her where the bathroom is.

Fair? No. The saving of me? Good God, yes.

AUTHOR'S NOTE

As a landlubber, I could only rely on my imagination so much. Various sources were invaluable. The World Wide Web is truly a wonderful place:

http://www.wellesley.edu/Psychology/Cheek/Narrative/home.html

http://life.bio.sunysb.edu/marinebio/becoming.html

http://oceanlink.island.net/career/career2.html

http://www.uscg.mil/

http://www.uscgboating.org

http://www.legislative.noaa.gov/

This is the part where I write something banal like, "There's no such thing as vampires," or whatever. And I was in the middle of typing, "Of course there's no such thing as mermaids," but after all the research and time put into this book and all the stories I heard and . . . well, I wonder.

Let's just say Fred is one of a kind and leave it at that.

O, train me not, sweet mermaid, with thy note,
To drown me in thy sister's flood of tears:
Sing, siren, for thyself and I will dote:
Spread o'er the silver waves thy golden hairs,
And as a bed I'll take them and there lie.

—WILLIAM SHAKESPEARE, *Comedy of Errors*

In the blue depth of the waters,
Where the wave hath no strife,
Where the wind is a stranger,
And the sea-snake hath life,
Where the Mermaid is decking
Her green hair with shells;
Like the storm on the surface
Came the sound of thy spells.

—LORD BYRON, "Manfred"

At sea once more we had to pass the Sirens, whose sweet singing lures sailors to their doom. I had stopped up the ears of my crew with wax, and I alone listened while lashed to the mast, powerless to steer toward shipwreck.

—Homer, *The Odyssey*

Them sirens loved him up and turned him into a horny toad!

—*O Brother, Where Art Thou?*

Yeah . . . bullshit.

—Fredrika Bimm, hybrid mermaid

One

The unbelievable horror began when Fred walked in on her parents making love on the living room coffee table. Like all children (even when grown), her first muddled impression was that her father was hurting her mother. Or perhaps fixing her back. Her second impression was that the coffee-table books (*Alaska: The Last Frontier*; *Cape Cod: An Explorer's Guide*; *The Black Sea: A History*) must sting like hell on her mother's knees. Her third impression sounded something like this:

"Aaaaeeeiiiiieeee!"

Her mother slipped and National Geographic's *Seals of the Antarctic* flew like a tiddlywink from the coffee table and hit the floor with a thud. Her father flinched but, unfortunately, did not fall off (or out of) her mother.

Fred darted across the room and, before she realized what she was doing, hauled her father off and tossed him over the back of the couch. She then yanked the puke-orange throw from said couch and threw it over her mother.

"Ow," her father groaned from out of sight.

Her mother wriggled under the throw, sat up, and faced her daughter, her normally pale face flushed with wrath. Or something else Fred did not want to think about. "Fredrika Bimm, what do you think you're doing?"

"Freaking out. Losing my mind. Thinking about snapping your husband's spine. Squashing the urge to vomit. Wishing I'd died at childbirth."

"Oh, you say that when you don't get a prize in your Lucky Charms," her mother snapped. "What's your problem, miss? You don't knock anymore?" Her mother, a good-looking blonde with silver streaks and shoulder-length hair (and a disturbingly sweaty face), climbed off the coffee table with remarkable dignity, fastened the blanket to cover her chubby thighs, and went around the couch to help her husband. "You just barge in?"

"I have a key, I didn't barge," Fred pointed out, still revolted but regretting the violence. "And you told me to come over."

"Yesterday. I told you to come over yesterday."

"I was working," Fred tried not to whine, or stare. "I couldn't just ditch all the fish. Although they deserve it, the little bastards. Anyway, I couldn't come."

"Well," her mother retorted, "neither could I."

Fred again tried not to vomit, and succeeded for the moment. She peered over the couch, where her father was groaning and clutching the small of his back. His bald spot was flushed almost purple. His ponytail had come undone. "Sorry, Dad."

"Sorry, hell," he gasped. "I swear, I'll never touch her again."

"Oh, Sam, just stop it."

"Not even if we're married for another thirty years."

Fred flashed a rare smile. "Okay."

"Fred, stop it! You, too, Sam." Mrs. Bimm helped her husband to his feet and hustled him out of the living room. Then she turned on her daughter.

"Fredrika."

"Mom, put yourself in my fins."

"Fredrika Shea Bimm."

"Mom, he was *fucking my mother.* He's a motherfucker! What would you have done?"

"Not tossed him halfway across the room," her mother snapped, then puffed her bangs out of her face. "What in the world is wrong with you? You're almost thirty, for heaven's sake."

"And you're almost fifty! Way too old to be—to be—yech."

Her mother stuck a stubby finger in Fred's face. Everything about Moon Bimm was short and stubby, compared to Fred's long lankiness. Even Fred's nose was long, and while Mrs. Bimm's mouth was permanently turned up in a smile, Fred's everyday expression was a scowl. If Fred hadn't seen the birth certificate, she would have doubted any birth relation to Moon Bimm. "Violence. Language. Manners. All unacceptable."

"I overreacted, okay? I'm sorry, all right?"

"Not to me. To your father. Who is probably icing his back right this minute."

"Hopefully he's put some pants on first."

Fred looked around the small living room, which was artfully decorated in Cape Cod Tourist. "Why here, Mom? Why next to the pleather chair? The La-Z-Boy? Why not anywhere else?" *Why not never? Never ever?* "I mean . . . you've got a bed."

"We are often strongly affected in the living room," her mother said primly, then giggled (giggled! *O gods of all the seas, kill me now and make it snappy*) and marched out, trailing blanket fuzz behind her.

"Oh, fucking gross," Fred muttered, following her mother.

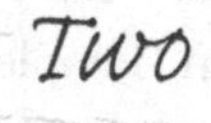

Two

"It's not as bad as you think, Fred," the Defiler of Her Mother said, wincing when he moved the bag of frozen peas to better cover his lower back. He had, thankfully, put on pants. Said frozen peas were stuffed in back of said pants. Fred's mom was still prancing around in the couch blanket, all "nature's never wrong" and "be empowered, not embarrassed" and "you shouldn't cover up God's handiwork."

Is there anything sillier than a grown-up hippie?

"I'm sorry you had to catch us in an intimate moment—"

"Bird-watching Wednesday," her mother said solemnly, then giggled again.

Fred groaned and looked around for a fork or a spoon or a gravy boat to gouge out her eyes. And ears. Because Moon Bimm was referring to the cardinal tattooed on her left butt cheek. Other mothers had laugh lines and wrinkles. Not animal tattoos.

She rested her forehead on her hands, her green hair brushing the table. She stared at the kelp-colored strands and thought, *That's it. I'm running away for sure. Again. Twenty-nine-year-olds run away all the time. It's perfectly normal. It's—*

"Why," she muttered, "did you call me over in the first place?" *And why didn't I come yesterday, when she actually called?*

"Oh, that. Well . . ." Her mother fluttered about the kitchen, strands of the couch blanket making her look like a freaked-out caterpillar. "We believe—your father and I believe—that is, Sam and I believe in full disclosure."

"So I see," Fred sniffed, eyeing the blanket.

"Lies and deception, they're a bad trip, honey. A baaaa—"

"You want to talk bad trips? Cast your mind back, Mom. Your acid-fried mind. Remember ten minutes ago?"

Moon Bimm ignored her daughter's sarcasm; she'd had almost three decades of practice. "Lies and deception, baby. They can make you physically ill. There's science to back this up, hon. People get ulcers and high blood pressure, just from keeping secrets! And—"

"Mom. Will you cut to it, please? I have to go home and Clorox my eyeballs."

"We're going to adopt."

Fred kept staring at her hands.

"Hon? Did you hear me?"

"If you're adopting, why are you fucking?"

"Language," her father said, squirming on the chair and groping for the bag of peas.

Moon "Children Should Be Allowed to Express Themselves However They Wish" Bimm focused on the sentiment, not the verbiage. "So lovemaking is only for procreation?"

"When it's your *mother* and your *father*, yes, lovemaking is only for procreation!" Fred screamed. She longed to toss the kitchen table through the dining room hutch. "I have seen some dark and wicked things, Mom and Dad, take it from me—you would not believe what lurks in the oceans' deep. I have seen a shark barf out another shark and then eat it again. But nothing I've seen was as bad as my mother and father—"

"Except I'm not your father," her father said.

"—as my mother and father—uh—doing dark and wicked things in the ocean. What?"

"Full disclosure," her mother said, dramatically swooping about the kitchen, blanket flapping. "All this paperwork we have to fill out for the adoption, it got me thinking. And it's time you knew the truth. Sam Bimm isn't your biological father."

"Yeah, Mom. I know."

Her mom sat down across from her and took Fred's cold (they were always cold) hands in her warm ones. Even now, Fred took comfort from her mother's touch: how many times had those hands tucked her in, held her, rubbed her back? Her mom was like a walking, talking, jasmine-scented electric blanket.

"I know it'll take some getting used to," she said with touching earnestness. "And I'm sorry you had to live with the lie."

"Mom. I know Sam isn't my father."

"And I'm so sorry I kept it from you!" Moon's hands plunged into her blonde hair and made fists; for a minute she looked like a seventies version of Mad Ophelia. "But there was a stigma, especially back then, and I couldn't go home and even though it was perfectly natural, even though it's what my body is for and it was beautiful and amazing, I was ashamed."

"A shamed hippie?" Fred wondered aloud.

"And then there was Sam—"

"So, even worse problems?" Fred guessed.

Her mother frowned and continued. "And I was so happy to see him again and he—"

"—had a thing for knocked-up blondes who puked in the morning?"

"Fred, I don't think you're—"

"Mom. I appreciate you getting this off your chest and all—" Fred tried not to stare at her mother's boobs. Fred wished the woman would get something *on* her chest, like a turtleneck. "But I had that one figured out by the time I was five. Not, by the way, that it makes it any easier to pretend his tongue wasn't where it was ten minutes ago. But yeah, I knew."

"You did?" Sam asked, shifting uneasily as pea water started to trickle down his butt crack.

"Dad. Sam. Whatever. Look at you. Look at me. I'm a mermaid and you couldn't get a membership at the Y."

Her mother threw up her hands. The blanket gaped. Fred stared at the ceiling. "And how such a wondrous creature can have such silly hang-ups is beyond—"

"Mom, ask anybody on the planet: would it weird you out to walk in the front door and see your mom on all fours? I guarantee—mermaid, human, blue whale, marmoset, pixie, leprechaun, zombie—they'll all say yes." She turned to her squirming father. "Remember that time you panicked in the tide pool and I had to get you out? I was seven, Dad, and the water was only up to my knees."

"There were *things* in there," Sam said, shuddering at the memory.

"Yeah, Sam. Minnows. It was the fourth or fifth time I'd had to save you, and I'd never had a swimming lesson in my life. Also, you have brown eyes and mine are the color of brussels sprouts. Also, you have—had—brown hair and mine's the color of the ocean.

Also, you never grow a tail and you're right-handed; while I'm—did you get this?—a *mermaid* and a *lefty*!"

"No need to scream," Mom sniffed.

"I hate it when you treat me like I'm freaking stupid."

"Nobody thinks you're freaking stupid," her mom soothed in her "I think my kid's freaking stupid" voice. "Everyone in this room is a living creature deserving of our love and respect."

"If you try to hold my hand and make a nurture circle," Fred warned, "I will kill you."

Three

Unfortunately for Fred and her sanity, the nightmare wasn't over yet. Her mother, gripped with the mania of truth-telling, coughed up the whole sordid story.

It seemed Moon Bimm (née Moon Westerberg) had been putzing around on Chapin Beach, Cape Cod, with a bunch of her idiot hippie friends, high on pot and *le Gallo Jug*, lonesome and wondering what it all meant, got separated from her pot-smoking, Gallo-swigging pals (which Fred would have thought a relief, but Moon didn't agree), and ran into a suave, green-eyed fellow and was *so fucking drunk she didn't notice he was half fish.*

"But if he was a merman, how did you—whoa. Whoa. Forget it. I can't believe, in light of recent hideous events, that I even asked you that. Do not answer. Do *not* answer. We are at DEFCON 3 and rising. We—"

"Oh, just stop it, you big baby." Her mother stretched her neck to squint at Fred's exasperated features. "Why you can't understand how beautiful and natural sex can be and why you have so many Puritan hang-ups about it—how a child of mine can be so—"

"Mom, now's not the time for the 'Peace and Lurrrv' lecture."

"He had legs like you do, of course," she said, completely ignoring Fred's emphatic backpedaling five seconds earlier. "I imagine he can grow a tail or not, as he likes. As you like." Moon frowned. "I guess any mer-person can. I thought you could do it or not because you were half human. But unless he was also half human—"

"That'd be super-duper for him. So he jumps your drunken bones, you have sand-pillow talk, then he leaps into the sea and disappears? So you're telling me . . . what? My real father's an asshole? And you're a slut? Because he owes you for years of child support payments, that's one. And two—"

"Must you always label people?"

"Must you shovel truth down my throat?"

"As I was saying," Moon went on with admirable dignity, considering recent events and what she was hardly wearing, "ten months later and there you were."

"*Ten* months?" How had she never done the math before? Easy. Her mom had never talked about her father—her real father—before. Just "oh and we met and got married because society will insist on that silly piece of paper and we've been a family ever since."

And Fred, knowing her mother would answer anything—*anything*—was the only kid on the block who never went through the "where did I come from?" phase. Moon not only would have answered the question in disgusting and embarrassing detail, she would have surfed pornography websites with her daughter to investigate different methods.

"It takes longer for mer-people to gestate." Sam was looking at Fred thoughtfully. He taught Natural Science at 4C (Cape Cod Community College). "Or hybrids. Or—"

"So why'd you marry her, Sam? It was all Free Love and all the

Mary Jane you could smoke and don't trust anyone over eighty back then."

"Thirty," her mother gurgled. "And marijuana? Wasn't on it. Poisons the body. Wine is bad enough." She winked at her daughter. "Look at the trouble three glasses of bad Chardonnay got me in!" Moon wouldn't take a Tylenol for a broken leg. Sadly, Fred knew this for a fact.

"Anyway—"

"No, no, that's enough," Fred broke in hastily. "I get it now. The gaping void inside me is complete, and filled with truth. No need to—"

"—your mother and I knew each other in high school, and went our separate ways after graduation. When I ran into her, she was just as radiant and glowing as I remembered her."

"Probably all the puking," Fred suggested.

"And we fell in love and Sam loved you long before you were born. We both did. We loved . . . the *idea* of you." Her mom closed her eyes and took on a dreamy expression Fred knew well. "And the first time I gave you a bath and your legs grew together and your scales came down and you splashed me and broke the baby tub, I was so amazed—and so thrilled—"

"Girl turns into fish, news at eight?" Fred suggested. "Come on, Mom. You weren't a little freaked out?"

"I thought you were a miracle," she replied, and the simple dignity in her voice wiped the smirk off Fred's face. "I still do." She turned to Sam. "Thank goodness I had a natural childbirth right here in this house! Think of the mess if all kinds of Western medicine had descended on poor Fred!" She turned back to her daughter. "I was scared to even bring you in for your vaccinations. And I quit once we realized you couldn't ever get sick."

"Well." Fred coughed. "That's—ah. That's nice, Mom. A miracle. That's—miraculous. So that's why you called me over? To tell me stuff I already knew?"

"We didn't *know* you knew," Sam pointed out. "And as your mother said, filling out all the paperwork, and all the meetings, got us thinking."

"Why are you adopting?"

Her parents gave her puzzled "why not?" looks.

Fred tried to explain. "Most people your age would be thrilled to have the place to themselves."

"Well, I don't know if thrilled is exactly the—"

"Sam, you don't even have to work—you still get checks from your dad's invention, right?"

"Right." Sam's father had thought up edible underwear. The family got a piece of every fruit panty or chocolate G-string ever sold. "But we have all this space . . ." He gestured vaguely to the kitchen. "And it's such a nice location."

Real nice. Right on the ocean—Fred knew that the four-bedroom, three-bathroom "shack" on the bay would sell for a cool two-point-two if her parents ever wanted to move. But her "earth mother" mother took to Sam's money like a—well, like a fish to water. And they would never sell.

And even with all the donations to the Audubon Society and the YMCA and the Cape Cod Literary Council and the Hospice of Cape Cod and the Hyannis Public Library, there was still plenty left every year. Every month.

"And you've got your own life now," Sam still droned. "We hardly ever see you."

"Work. Keeps me busy," she mumbled.

"Honey, it wasn't a reprimand!"

"Sounded like one."

"You're a grown woman, you have your own life."

Ha.

"And we have ours and we're just not—we're not ready for it just to be the two of us yet." Her mother reached out, and Sam, as he always did, took her hand. "It just feels wrong."

Ah, her life. Her wonderful life. She'd last been on a real date six years ago, her boss kept trying to fix her up, the fish at work were deep in rebellion mode, and whatever way you looked at it she was a freak.

Freak. Abnormality. Anomaly. Glitch. Genetic hiccup.

And this was why her folks wanted another kid? Because they thought they did such a hot job on the first one?

Well, maybe it'd be fun to raise one that didn't grow a tail and pick fights with tuna.

"Okay, well, good luck and all." Fred paused, waiting for a response. When none was forthcoming, she continued. "If you need a reference from, uh, someone you raised, I can write a letter. Or whatever."

"That'd be lovely, Fred." Her mother hugged her. Fred stood stiffly for it, then sneezed when the blanket fuzz tickled her nose.

"Mom. Kleenex."

"Never mind. Oh, I feel so much better now that the whole story is out! Don't you feel better, baby?"

"Ecstatic."

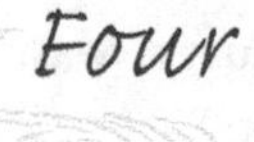

Four

Before leaving, Fred took a dip in the indoor saltwater pool. She could have jumped in the ocean just outside the back door, but didn't feel like worrying about tourists. And it comforted her parents when she used it. Finally, it felt better than the ocean—no seaweed ready to entwine in her hair, no nosy codfish following her around, and she knew damn well the mercury levels in her own pool were just fine.

Point of fact, she preferred pools to the open sea. The ocean was filled with horrors and fish shit. The pool was a controlled environment.

Now if she could just get a handle on those rotten angelfish at work—

That thought eventually propelled her back to her legs, and out of the pool, and into her clothes, and out the door. Her parents were nowhere to be found, meaning they had decamped to their bedroom and were finishing what Fred had interrupted.

Excellent. Well, not excellent, but she disliked good-byes, and her mom always acted like she was hitchhiking across Europe instead of driving to Boston.

With traffic, it was a ninety-minute drive to the Quincy T-stop, a twenty-minute ride to the Green Line, five minutes to the Blue, and then she popped out of the T at the New England Aquarium stop. It was late enough that she could hopefully slip in the employee entrance and get back to work without anybody—

"Dr. Bimm!"

Fuck.

She turned and beheld her boss, Dr. Barbara Robinson, a short woman with a blonde Valkyrie braid and almond-shaped brown eyes. Dr. Barb had her lab coat buttoned all the way to the top, as usual. Fred didn't even know where hers was.

Also as usual, Dr. Barb was trotting. Not walking fast, but almost running. She trotted everywhere: meetings, charity functions, feedings, seal shows. Fred couldn't imagine what the "kind of hurry" was. The fish weren't going anywhere. Neither were the tourists.

"Hi, Dr. Barb."

"Dr. Bimm, I'd like you to meet our new water fellow, Dr. Thomas Pearson. Dr. Pearson, this is Dr. Fredrika Bimm." She looked up at Pearson, blinking rapidly. "Dr. Bimm takes care of Main One for us."

"Fred," Fred said, sticking out her hand. "I keep the big fish from chomping on the little fish." She ignored Dr. Barb's wince. Dr. Barb liked full titles (yawn) and to make people's jobs sound more interesting than they were (double yawn). Fred's job was to jump into the four-story tank, toss dead smelt at the fish, and make sure the levels were good and the sea turtles didn't bully the sharks (sounded out of type, but it really happened on occasion). That was it. "Main One" indeed. The big freaking tank, that's what it was.

Dr. Pearson clasped her outstretched hand, winced at the chill (she didn't take it personally; everyone did), and shook it like a pepper shaker. "Hi there. Please call me Thomas."

"Muh," she replied. But then, he *was* gorgeous. Tall, really quite tall (she was lanky but he had a good three inches on her), with brown hair—except it wasn't just brown; even in the yucky fluorescent lighting she could see the gold and red highlights—cut short and neat. A lab coat, she noted disapprovingly; but then, he was new, and Dr. Barb probably wrestled him into it. Brown eyes—but again, not just brown. Brown with gold flecks. The flecks twinkled at her and sized her up at the same time. Strong nose. Swimmer's shoulders, long legs, and narrow hips. And . . . dimples?

"—new to the area so I hope you'll help the NEA family show him what a wonderful part of the country this is, particularly this time of year," Dr. Barb was yakking.

"Yeah," Fred said. *What was she talking about? What time of year is it?*

Dr. Barb must have interpreted the usual blank expression on Fred's face. "You know. New England in the fall, and all that."

"Um," she replied.

"Leaves changing? Autumn nip in the air? Kids going back to school, fresh beginnings?"

"Okay."

"Dr. Bimm. You had no idea it was September already, did you?"

"Not part of my job."

"Chatty, aren't you?" Thomas twinkled. There was no other word for it: he was grinning and his dimples were showing and his big dark eyes were shining and he was *twinkling* at her.

She shrugged.

"I love your hair," he said. "That's the most amazing green I've ever seen."

Dr. Barb frowned. "Dr. Bimm has blue hair."

Thomas shook his head. "No, it's the color of the grass on the first day of summer." He lowered his voice. "I write romance novels under the name Priscilla D'Jacqueline."

"You what?"

"But it's *blue*," Dr. Barb insisted.

"Um, shut up about my hair now?" Fred suggested.

"Right, right. Well, on with the tour." Dr. Barb started her hallway trot, dragging Thomas by the elbow. "Thank you for your time, Dr. Bimm. We'll leave you to your work."

"Okay."

"And don't forget to say hello to the new intern."

"I won't," she lied.

"It was nice to meet you, Fredrika!" he managed as he was dragged away.

"Not Fredrika. Fred. Not Dr. Bimm," she continued to the now-empty hallway. "Fred."

New water fellow. Yum.

After a moment's thought, she shoved Thomas out of her brain (he went fairly easily) and went back to work.

Tried to, anyway. On the way to her lab, she nearly collided with a creature of unspeakable evil and annoyance: an undergrad.

"Oh, hiiiiii!" the creature burbled, straightening her perfectly straight bangs and sticking out a small warm paw for Fred to shake. "Gosh, Dr. Bimm, right? Gosh! I'm super happy I have a chance to meet you! Yeah! Because I'm hoping to learn so much from you!" She laughed, as if the very idea was so exciting it could not be contained. "Yeah!"

Fred stared at the creature. She pegged the woman at about nineteen. Short—she came up to the middle of Fred's chest. Maybe—it was hard to tell from all the bouncing around she was doing. Elbow-length platinum blonde hair. No roots. A natural wave—almost a ripple—running through it, giving her hair bounce . . . unless it was the woman's actual bouncing that gave it bounce.

A flawless complexion, of course. Big, wide, blue eyes, of course, the color of the sky. A small, perfect nose. A small, pointed chin. Not a freckle or a pimple to be seen. A perfect little figure beneath the lab coat that (groan) Dr. Barb had no doubt made her wear.

Tiny (because, of course, her feet were small and comely), perfect high heels. Black, of course, because interning was a Serious Business.

"—and ohmigod I've wanted to work here since I—"

"Was a little girl."

"Ohmigod, yeah! Because I—"

"Loved dolphins."

"Yeah! Wow, they said you were, like, super smart or something but you're rilly rilly smart, like a genius! Yeah!"

"You're not," Fred asked with deep suspicion, "going to do a cheer or something, are you?"

"How did you know," Perfect Girl gasped, "that I was on the cheer team back home in Yarmouth?"

"I'm rilly rilly smart." Fred started backing away but Perfect Girl had taken that as an invitation to follow, and was stuck to Fred's side like a barnacle. "Why don't you, uh . . ."

"Dr. Barb said I should watch you and Dr. Pearson and Jamie and all the others on my first day to figure out where you need me."

"What if we don't need you?"

"Oh Dr. Bimm, you're rilly a riot! Ohmigod! Dr. Barb didn't tell me you were so funny!"

"Dr. Barb," Fred warned, "is in a world of trouble when I see her again."

"So ohmigod you're in charge of the big tank? You feed all the fish 'n' stuff?"

"Yes."

"But there's, like, gotta be more to it than that, right?" Perfect Girl tossed her hair. "Because just anybody could feed fish, right?"

"No, you pegged it. That's all there is to it. That's completely, totally all."

"Oh Dr. Bimm, you crack me up."

"I'd like to crack you up," she muttered.

"Ohmigod! I totally forgot." Again, she stuck out her hand. "I'm Madison Fehr."

"Fair?"

"No, F-E-H-R, but yeah, it's pronounced like that. And *Madison.* You know. *Madison.*"

Fred sighed. "As in the mermaid from *Splash?*"

"Exactly!" Madison squealed. "I mean is that, like, all serendipitous or what? It totally totally is."

Fred was fairly certain she was rocketing toward an insulin reaction of some sort. She had to get away from this gibbering teenager before something terrible happened. To both of them.

"Well, it was nice to meet you, Madison, but I have to get back to work."

"Oh, can I come with you? It'd be rilly rilly neat to see you work!"

"No," Fred said, recoiling. "You can't."

"Well, poop." Madison pouted, then instantly recovered. "I guess I'll go see if I can learn the register in the gift shop, then."

"Swell."

"But if you change your mind and I can, like, help you, just let me know. I've, like, got my Scoobie certification and everything!"

"Scuba."

"What?"

"Self-Contained Underwater Breathing Apparatus. Scuba. Not Scoobie."

"Right! Anyway, I can do that. I totally totally can. So if you want some help, just page me and I'll come right over."

"The inverse of that would be if I don't page you, you'll stay far far away?"

"Ohmigod, you are so funny! Okay, nice to meet you, Dr. Bimm!" She was already trip-trapping away on her little heels, and waving over one shoulder. "Bye!"

For a long, awful moment, Fred thought she might gag. She got control over herself and actually managed a halfhearted wave back.

Five

While she was struggling into her scuba suit, and trying to mentally scour Madison from her brain, it occurred to Fred that Thomas had actually noticed her real hair color.

Which wouldn't be so unusual, except nobody had ever, ever noticed her hair was green except her mother. In fact, when she complained about it, about the teasing and the crude jokes from strangers ("Do your cuffs and collar match?") her mother had told her something silly and hippieish, to wit: "Your true love will be the man who truly sees you as you are."

Uh-huh, yank the other one, Mom.

But Thomas had not only seen, he had commented. Repeatedly. Even after being corrected by his new boss. And no crass jokes, either.

Her ridiculous hair was like the ocean: although it looked blue to most people it was, in reality, green. And dry as straw and fraught with split ends due to all the time she spent being wet, but that was another issue. And really, more her friend Jonas's problem than hers. *(Note to Fred,* she thought: *L'Oreal just isn't doing the job; time to try the Philosophy line.)*

She was finally in her suit, a swollen sausage in its casing, everything where it belonged, all the dumb tubes in place (one or two tourists might notice that she wasn't using a mask or oxygen tank), her fins on, the whole outfit useless and silly beyond belief and a *lie*, and she sat on the edge of the top level of the tank, at the very top floor of the NEA, and fell backward into Main One.

And flailed around uselessly and fought the urge to grow a tail, to be real

(fake)

and staggered through a small school of angelfish and thrashed past a nurse shark and almost knocked a sea turtle sprawling and accidentally swam upside down for a few seconds until she got her bearings. Because she could not swim without her tail.

Just . . . couldn't. She had tried. She'd taken lessons for years. Moon had tried to teach her (what a disaster *that* had been).

It was no good. It was like her body knew she could grow a tail and fins and scales so what was the point of learning to swim with legs?

And so she couldn't.

She was a mermaid, employed as a marine biologist, who couldn't swim.

She was also a gainfully employed member of the New England Aquarium, charged with the care and feeding of the Main One inhabitants, who had forgotten the dead smelt.

Goddammit!

Well, the hell with it. She'd wait until everyone had gone home and then get the smelt. Nobody in the tank would starve to death if they had to wait another two or three hours. Instead she eyed the occupants of Main One and judged their health and overall appearance.

Everybody looked good. Unlike animals in zoos, fish tended to thrive in controlled environments. It was as though fish did well if they weren't constantly worrying about being chomped, and if the freedom of the open sea was what they gave up, it was a small price to pay.

Fred could relate.

A nurse shark swam lazily past her and she touched it with her mind. It wasn't any more difficult than adding double-digit numbers in her head.

You okay?

Hungry. Fish girl bring fish.

Yeah, well, so what else was new? Fish girl bring fish. Why not make it her new title, for the love of—

Something made her glance up and she looked through the windows of the tank and saw Thomas peering in at her, waving frantically.

Bemused, she waved a gloved hand back.

Six

"I know what you're thinking," Fred's best friend, Jonas Carrey, declared, sitting down opposite her. They were at their favorite window-side table at the Legal Sea Foods restaurant across from the NEA.

"I doubt that very much," she replied gloomily, stirring her strawberry margarita.

"You're thinking you're a freak, nobody understands you, you're a lone wolf in a pack of nutjobs, blah-blah." The waitress materialized and Jonas said, "An appletini, please."

"Oh, Jonas!" Fred practically yelled. "Those are so over."

"Hey. I'm secure enough in my sexuality to order any girlie drink in the world. Now tell me I'm right. Tell me I knew what you were thinking."

"I walked in on my folks doing it doggy-style less than four hours ago."

"Waitress!" Jonas screamed, clicking his fingers madly. "Bring two!" Then, more quietly, "You want a neck massage? A bedtime story? A bullet in the ear?"

"The latter," she sighed. "And on top of everything else, Mom would be super-pissed that I was seeing you and not trying to leap into your pants."

They both shuddered in unison. They had been friends since the second grade. To Fred, screwing Jonas would have been like screwing a brother. And Jonas liked blonde humans, not blue-haired mermaids.

"And I thought I had a bad day."

"You probably did." Jonas was a chemical engineer for the Aveda corporation. He was constantly struggling to invent a shampoo that didn't damage hair. Which was problematic, as by definition, all shampoos did.

"Speaking of work . . ." He set an Aveda bag positively bulging with, she knew, hair care products, on the table. "Honey, those split ends. I love you, but I can hardly bear to look at you. Seriously. Tend to them. Now."

"It's not my fault I'm wet more than I'm dry."

"Anything else go wrong today? Not that anything had to." The waitress set down two appletinis and he gulped at one thirstily. After a moment's thought, he slammed it down and began on the second one. "Actually, it's not picturing your mom, because she is an awesome-looking woman and I've had a crush on her since you brought me home after the fight . . ."

"Stop it," she said, but she was smiling. Jonas had proudly shown off his no-polish manicure on the first day of second grade, and two fourth graders had discovered rather large problems with their own sexual insecurity. Their solution was to take it out on Jonas. Fred, annoyed at being interrupted from her reading, had broken up the fight by tossing one kid into the monkey bars and dumping the other one, headfirst, into the sandbox.

Nobody had ever laid a finger on Jonas again through elementary, middle, and high school.

"—and there she was, a blonde angel of mercy, tending to my many wounds, and yelling at you because—"

"'Violence Isn't The Answer,'" they said in unison.

"Right-o. So I don't mind picturing your mom in the buff, but Sam . . . yech."

"Then they do this whole song and dance about how I'm not Sam's biological child."

Jonas slurped again. "Duh."

"What I said."

"I mean, you're a mermaid and Sam can't get himself out of the shallow end."

"I said that."

"Then what?"

"Then I got my ass back to work and met the new water fellow."

"What the hell is a water fellow? You scientists and your jargon."

"It's a marine biologist who travels around the world trying to explain to the bipeds that they're destroying the planet. He learns and teaches at every place and moves on after three months."

"Hey, hey," Jonas protested mildly. "I'm a biped."

A pretty cute one, too, and Fred was mystified that, at the ripe old age of twenty-nine, Jonas hadn't found someone to settle down with. He was tall, blond, lifted weights, had a black belt in aikido, was a brilliant engineer, was kind to children and small animals, and never judged Fred, not even when they'd gone swimming in the ocean a year after they'd met and he saw her tail.

Maybe it was because he was only eight at the time, and children were more open-minded about such things. Maybe it was because Jonas was generally open-minded about everything. Maybe it was because Jonas was—well, Jonas. Regardless, he had never judged her, he'd stuck staunchly by her, and she didn't have a finer, kinder friend on land or sea.

It made her sad that he was alone, and it drove her mother absolutely batshit. Because she couldn't understand why two people who had known each other forever couldn't settle down together. After all, she had married *her* school buddy.

"So, is he a nice guy? This water fellow?"

"He talked about my hair."

"Well, people usually notice that first."

"About how green it was."

"But it's blue."

She sighed and took a gulp of her margarita. "Never mind."

"So, did you order?"

"Yeah, I've got a salad coming."

"Waited for me like one pig waits for another, huh?" The waitress, as if sensing his need, again showed up out of nowhere. The two of them flirted outrageously while Jonas ordered the lobster and Fred tried not to yawn.

"So, what's next today? I mean, it could hardly get worse."

"New intern."

"Don't tell me: loved dolphins as a kid?"

"Still is a kid. Perky. Cheerful. Gorgeous. Enthusiastic."

"How awful for you." Jonas managed to say such a silly thing with convincing sincerity. "Well, cheer up. She'll only be around for the semester, right? That's how long any of the interns stay."

"Six months is a long goddamned time to put up with Madison Fehr."

"That's her name?"

"And she used to cheer."

"My God! I can't believe you didn't slit your wrists on the way over. What else?"

"I freaked out in the tank again."

"Swam upside down in your scuba suit?" he asked sympathetically.

"Yeah, among other things. And I forgot the fish food. So I'll wait until the place is empty and go back and feed the little buggers."

"Are they still on hunger strike? The fish?"

"I don't want to talk about it."

"I don't want to hear about it. I want to hear about how hot your mom still is."

"Nope."

"Uh . . . your love life?"

"What love life?"

"Right. I'm in the same boat myself. My trainer ran off with my nutritionist."

"Tessa and Mari were lesbians?"

"Apparently so. Leaving me high and dry. My one chance to have a threesome," he sighed, "and it blew right by me."

"Aw. Don't say blew." Fred's salad came, and she picked at it and tried not to flinch as Jonas tore through his lobster.

"I'm not eating one of your pals, am I?" he asked, butter dripping down his chin.

"No. It just makes me slightly ill to watch you devour—"

"A fellow sea citizen?"

"Something I'm allergic to."

Jonas snickered. "A mermaid allergic to shellfish."

"Shut up."

"Come on. It's kind of hilarious. I mean, if you lived in the sea, what the hell would you eat? Would you starve? Or would you slip onto shore, steal food, and race back to the water like the Loch Ness Monster, while people took fuzzy pictures of your bare ass? The only time you ever get sick—you have to admit it's funny."

"I'd like to get through the rest of this day without talking or thinking about bare asses, please."

"So this water fellow guy, what's his name?"

"Thomas Pearson."

"Well, other than needing to change his contact lenses, he seems okay. I mean, you've hardly bitched about him at all. And honey, you bitch about *everything*."

"He's all right. His hair is cute."

Jonas froze, his lobster fork halfway to his mouth. "Oh my God, you're in love."

"I'm not in love."

"'His hair is cute'? You never say anything nice about anyone. Coming from you, 'cute hair' is a mating call."

"I talked to the guy for thirty seconds. And then he waved at me while I was in the tank."

"Holy fuck, you're getting married, aren't you!"

"Will you simmer? I certainly am not."

Jonas tore through a claw, dunked the meat in butter, and slurped it like spaghetti. "You two were destined to be together. A marine biologist and a marine biologist. Meeting at an aquarium! What are the chances? It's, like, fate. God, what do they put in this butter—nectar?"

Fred pushed her salad away and pointed to his bread. "You going to eat that?"

"And fill up on empty carbs? Go on, take it. You'll swim it off anyway, you rotten bitch."

She grinned and grabbed the bread.

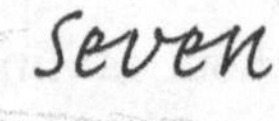

Seven

Fred crept back to the tank a little after midnight, let herself in by one of the employee entrances, climbed the stairs to the top level of Main One, stripped, grabbed a bundle of smelt, and dove in. She shifted from legs to tail without conscious thought; it was like breathing.

And in her mermaid form, it was a lot easier to hear the fish, demanding buggers that they were.

A barracuda passed by. *More fish more fish girl with fish more fish.*

I'm here, aren't I?

A sea turtle floated above. *Pounding more pounding outside pounding.*

Like hell. I'm not playing Pet Shop Boys for you guys anymore and that's it.

As happened with sea creatures confined to the same space for long enough, the fish and turtles and eels and everything else in the tank reverted to a group-mind.

It was nearly deafening.

Not eat not eat NOT EAT!

You'll eat.

NOT EAT NOT EAT NOT EAT!

Shut UP. You think I've got nothing better to do than come here at midnight and wave chum at you? You'll eat what I give you and never mind what I play on the speakers. You can barely hear it in here, anyway.

With the exception of the barracuda and a single shark, the rest of the occupants ignored her fish offerings. And the pair of hunger strike scabs were so loudly shouted down, they swam behind a boulder to sulk together.

Fred knew the hunger strike meant trouble. If they didn't eat, soon the larger fish wouldn't be able to help themselves: they'd prey on the angelfish and sunnies and other small fish stuck in the tank with them. Which would raise questions. Which would get Fred into a lot of trouble with Dr. Barb.

She had to admit she admired their principled stance—especially the smaller fish, who had the most to lose. But like hundreds of little finned "Ghandis" moving in glimmering schools, they valued their dignity (or at least their musical taste) more highly than their own lives.

Morons.

Not to mention the larger problem: she freaking hated the Pet Shop Boys. Any band who relied more on a mixing board than actual talent wasn't, in her mind, a real band. And who was in charge here, anyway?

A damselfish wiggled by. *Pounding more pounding outside pounding.*

Fine! Starve! She dumped the rest of the smelt into the water and lifted herself out of the tank, shaking out her tail and cursing under her breath.

Eight

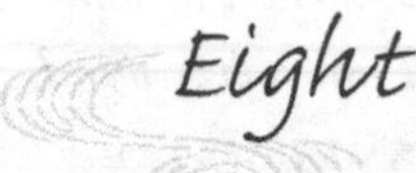

"You have a lot of food left this week," Dr. Barb told her.

"The fish don't seem to be hungry," Fred lied.

"Yeah, and like, that's not Dr. Bimm's problem, right?" Madison chirped, carefully applying lip gloss. "She can't, like, make them eat, right?"

"Umm. That's . . . hmm."

Fred almost grinned at Dr. Barb's discomfiture. She'd since heard through the office grapevine that Madison's parents were descendants of *Mayflower* embarkees (the original tourists and, later, the original illegal immigrants), owned half of the Boston waterfront, and thought their little girl should be able to intern wherever she wished, as long as she wished. And given how dependent the NEA was on private donations . . . "Thank you, Madison. Dr. Bimm, how are the levels?"

"They're perfect." Fred tried not to sound insulted.

"Maybe they don't like the new guy," Thomas joked. He glanced at Madison. "Or girl."

Dr. Barb looked at him over the tops of her reading glasses. "Very funny, Dr. Pearson. I don't like where this is going. If an aquarium guest sees a shark gobble a few angelfish—"

"Stampede?" Thomas guessed.

"And rilly rilly gross, too!"

"Visitors don't want to see blood," Fred said gloomily.

"None of that 'nature, red in tooth and claw' stuff for them, eh?"

"Quite right," Dr. Barb said, handing back Fred's clipboard. "Keep an eye on it, Dr. Bimm. Let me know if things don't change in the next few days."

"I'm off tomorrow," she reminded her boss.

"Right, right. Well, see how it goes Monday, then."

"Yeah."

"Dr. Pearson, you had something else for us?"

"Well. Yeah."

Fred waited. Dr. Barb waited. Madison blotted her lip gloss. Finally, with poorly concealed impatience, Fred said, "Well?"

"It's just, the levels in the harbor are really off. I mean, by about a thousand percent. And since we're right on the harbor . . ."

"Is that why you were sent here?"

"It's why I came here. I've been sort of following the toxic levels. The source is here, in Boston."

"Oh."

Fred thought for a moment. She hardly ever went into the ocean, vastly preferring Main One or her parents' pool. But she hadn't sensed anything off in the water the last few times she'd jumped in.

On the other hand, she had a ridiculous metabolism. She never got sick. Either mermaids could filter out toxins, or as a hybrid, she wasn't affected by poison in the water.

That's not to say the algae weren't, which would lead to the fish, which would lead to the bipeds.

Not that they cared, exactly.

"I could really use some help figuring this out," Thomas was saying.

"Well, we have several dozen—"

"I was thinking of Dr. Bimm."

"Me?" Fred nearly gasped, badly startled.

"Her?" Madison said, a little sharply. Obviously two coats of lip gloss and sparkly eye shadow had left Pearson unmoved. Certainly he hadn't done more than glance in her direction all morning. Fred wasn't sure why, but she thought that was just fine.

But this?

She was dealing with her parents adopting, a fish strike, trying to find the right woman for Jonas, and still, after twenty-six years, learning to swim. She had no time to play Nancy Drew. "Uh, that's not really my field, Dr. Pearson. I'm just in charge of the big fishie tank." At Dr. Barb's frown, she added, "Main One."

"I could help you, Dr. Pearson!"

Pearson ignored Madison, who had begun to bounce again.

"Oh, come on. I looked you up. You've got just as much book learning as me."

Fred gaped. "Book learning?"

"And I could really use the help," he coaxed, twinkling at her with those amazing dark eyes yet again.

"Yeah, but—"

"And we'd make a great team."

"But—"

"It's settled, then," Dr. Barb commanded.

"What is?" Fred felt like the planet had started spinning faster.

"I could help both of you," Madison announced. Just then, Fred's cell phone trilled the Harry Potter theme.

Saved by the bell. She flipped it open and practically barked, "Yes?"

"Fred, dear, it's Mom."

It was? Her mom sounded rattled. Really rattled. Missing her yoga class three times in a row rattled.

"What's wrong?"

"There's, uh, we have a visitor."

"Okay."

"And he wants to see you."

"Okay."

"Very badly."

"Okay."

"*Very* badly."

Fred puzzled it out. Her mom hadn't been this upset when Fred had caught her on all fours. Who could be visiting? A Republican?

After Sam had run the last one off with an empty shotgun, you'd think they would have—

"Well, I'm at work now, but—"

"Yes, I know, but I think you should come home *right now*."

Fred lowered her voice. "Mom, are you in danger?"

"I don't . . . think so."

"Is this stranger standing right there?"

"Yes."

"Put him on."

"I don't think—"

"Mom. Right now."

There was a short silence, and then a deep, gravelly voice said, "Yes?"

"Chum." It wasn't an affectionate nickname. She meant it literally: the fish guts and heads you feed sharks with. "You're scaring the shit out of my mom. Cut it out, unless you want to find out what your colon looks like."

"Fredrika, darling. So nice to hear from you after all this time. Your mother is a charming hostess, but I really insist on speaking with you."

"Oh, we'll speak, chum. You've got my word on that one. But if I get there and she's still freaking out—if she's got so much as a hair out of place—you and I will talk for about thirty days. And you won't like it. At all."

"Looking forward to it," the deep voice purred, and then there was a click.

"Gotta go," Fred said, dropping the clipboard on her desk with a clank and grabbing her purse.

"But—" Dr. Barb and Thomas butted at the same time.

"It's rilly rilly important," she said, and walked out.

Nine

She didn't bother with the front door. Went around the back, by the kitchen entrance (where her mother's phone was, and where she entertained, and where she was the most comfortable), and kicked in the glass door.

Everyone at the table—Sam, her mother, and the redheaded stranger—froze, then looked up at her. Fred brushed glass out of her hair and stepped into the room.

Dead silence.

"I'm here," she said unnecessarily. Damn. How had glass gotten into her jeans? She wriggled for a second and said, "On your feet, Red. Let's go outside and dance."

"Dance?" the redheaded stranger said blankly. He was looking at her with the oddest expression: admiration, and annoyance, and a little awe.

"Dance. Fight. Smackdown. I'll beat the shit out of you, and you'll go away. Then I'll go back to work before my parents—never mind. Step up. Right now."

"Fred, it's not exactly what you—" Sam began.

"I was a little startled at first," her mom added.

"I apologize if I upset your family," the stranger rumbled. "That was not my intent." He stood up. And up. And up. He towered over all of them, even Fred. *Towered.* He had shoulder-length hair the color of crushed rubies, and eyes that were—okay, were those contacts?—about two shades lighter than his hair. Cherry cough drop–colored eyes.

His shoulders were so broad, she wondered how he'd gotten

through the front door. He was dressed in a white shirt, open at the throat, and khaki shorts that showcased his powerfully muscled legs. No shoes, or socks. Big feet. A closely cropped beard the color of his hair. A broad forehead, a strong chin. And that voice! Deep, rumbling . . . like verbal velvet.

"But I think it's fine to step outside."

"What?"

"I think it's fine to step outside," the stranger repeated. "Or we could make use of your sire's pond."

"My what's what?"

"The pool." In a low voice, as if Fred couldn't hear perfectly well, he bent down (and down, and down) and murmured into her mom's ear, "Is something wrong with her mind?"

"No," her mom practically snapped. "She's a Ph.D., for crying out loud. Don't do that, it's freaky."

"Get away from her," Fred ordered, still edgy. Okay, she was usually edgy. But it had been a rough forty-eight hours.

"It's all right, Fred. I'm sorry I scared you. It's just—you're not the only one who makes dramatic entrances. This is—well—this is the High Prince Artur."

"Prince Artur," Fred repeated, like a parrot.

"Of the Black Sea," the stranger added helpfully.

"He says—he says you're one of his subjects," her mom continued.

"Oh, does he?"

"And that you owe him fealty and loyalty and such."

"Really."

The prince bowed. "It is always my great pleasure to meet a comely new subject."

"Really."

"And we, uh, we didn't really know what to think when he showed up and said all this and also said—uh—"

"Spit it, Mom."

"That your father is dead," her mom said, and burst into tears.

"Good lady," the prince said, looking distressed for the first time,

"I did not mean to upset you so. I had been told you but barely knew each other and that my subject had known your mate as her sire."

"We only spent an hour together but—but now Fred will never meet him. And I'll never get to thank him for giving her to me." Her mother covered her eyes like a child and sobbed.

"Okay, that's *it.* Get away from her right now."

The prince ignored her. "Our people will tell her all she wishes to know. And her sire was—he was not the type to appreciate his progeny," the prince said carefully.

"Bio father was kind of a dick, huh?" Fred guessed.

The prince patted her mother, almost sending her sprawling, then straightened. "Shall we adjourn?"

"Now? Right now?"

"Yes. Shall we?"

Fred noticed it was a command disguised as a question. But even though they seemed to be getting along, she was wild to get this huge redhead away from her folks. "Okay. Sorry about the door, Mom."

"It was one of your more dramatic entrances," her mom said, perking up right away. "I kind of liked it."

"Indeed," the stranger murmured, and led the way to the pool as if it were his house and not the place she'd grown up.

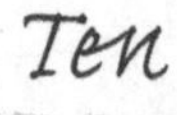

Ten

"So. High Prince Artur—can I call you Art?"

"You may not." The prince was—*eep*—stripping. The shirt went flying, followed by the pants. No underwear, she couldn't help but notice. Then he dove into the saltwater pool, giving her a glimpse of a muscular back and taut buttocks, and then he was under.

She squatted by the side of the pool. "Well, I'm sure as hell not calling you Your Highness," she yelled to the water. "I live on land. I'm not one of your damned subjects!"

He popped up, water glistening in his beard, and grinned at her, showing a great many teeth. Almost . . . pointy? How had she not noticed *that* before? "Oh yes you are, Little Rika."

"Fred."

"Ugh."

"Fred. Not Rika. Not Ugh. Fred. Not little anything. I'm five ten, for crying out loud."

"Little Rika," he said, and dove back down, splashing her with his tail.

His tail.

His *tail*?

Much longer than hers, wider at the hips, too. A much darker green than hers. The fins were wider at the base, and longer. She instantly deduced he was a faster, stronger swimmer—and she'd never met anyone or anything, land or sea, that could beat her in the water.

Well, shit.

"So why are you here?" she said to the water.

He popped up again and blew a stream of water at her. She ducked, cursing, and nearly fell in. "Come in and we will talk about it."

"I'm—" *Not getting naked in front of you*, was her first thought, which is when her mom spoke up in her head: *nudity is beautiful and natural*, blah-blah.

It wasn't getting naked. She didn't have much modesty. She always swam in the nude, unless she had to wiggle into that awful scuba suit. It was swimming with a merman. Someone like her. Except not like her: she hadn't inherited the strong, pointy teeth (doubtless for chomping through raw fish and bone), or the more powerful tail. Did she want to invite comparisons?

Fuck him and fuck what he thinks.

She stood, pulled off her shoes and socks, shucked off her jeans and panties, tossed her sweater over her head, unsnapped her bra, and dove over his head, straight down.

He came down at once, staring at her with unashamed curiosity.

You look . . . different.

Of course. Telepathy. How else would mer-people talk underwater?

Shut up. Why are you here?

I need you.

Do tell.

He swam closer and reached for her waist; she smacked his hand away, hard.

My subjects do not treat me thus.

Tell someone who gives a ripe shit.

They invite my caresses.

They need drugs. What do you want?

You, of course.

Yes, but for what?

He floated thoughtfully, then zipped past her with a powerful flex of his tail. She turned to watch him go by, and suddenly he was behind her, his arms wrapped around her waist where her scales met flesh. She felt a tingle that shot from her brain straight down her spinal cord and . . . lower.

She tossed an elbow back and caught him in the throat, which accomplished several things: he coughed explosively, sending out a stream of bubbles; let go; swam back and let her get some distance.

Hands off, chum.

You are unlike any of my people, Little Rika. I cannot resist you.

Try hard, chum. And it's Fred. Got it? F-R-E-D. She swam irritably past him, keeping an eye on his hands.

It is unfair that you have an affectionate nickname for me and I am not allowed one for you.

Affectionate . . . ? Oh, hell.

Last time: what do you want? Cough up or I'm back on tile before you can say "ow, my balls!"

My what?

Chum!

All right, Little Rika, do not distress yourself.

You haven't seen me distressed yet.

The bipeds are poisoning the harbor waters.

As far as thunderous announcements went, that one was weak.

She shrugged. *That's what bipeds do.*

My father, the High King, has charged me with finding you and enlisting your help to stop it.

Your father, the High King, can take a long walk off a short—

As one of our subjects, you are thus charged to aid us until our task is finished.

Well, lucky lucky me.

Wait. What had Pearson been babbling about? Toxins in the harbor?

Oh, hell.

Can you walk around on land for a few hours?

I do not like the surface, he admitted, swimming circles around her (literally), *but I can tolerate the environment as long as I must.*

Swell. Because I'm thinking there's someone you should meet.

She shot up to the surface, switched back to legs, and climbed out. She heard Artur come up behind her, but luckily for his continued good health, he didn't try to grab her again.

"Someone like you?" he asked, almost eagerly.

"No," she replied. "Not like me at all."

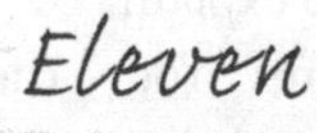

Eleven

Jonas stopped dead in his tracks when he saw Fred and who she was sitting with.

"Whoa," he said by way of greeting.

"Jonas, Prince Artur of the Black Sea. Art, Jonas."

"Prince what of the *what*? Oh my God! Your hair! Your eyes!" The prince courteously stood and Jonas wrung the man's hand like Fred would wring a wet washcloth, craning his neck to stare up at the man. "Have you thought about modeling?"

"I do not know what that is."

"Didn't you get my message?" Fred bitched. "I told you our dinner thing was cancelled."

"Oh, you always try to punk out on me. I didn't think you had, you know, an actual real reason. Like a date!"

"It's not a date," Fred began, but Jonas was already sliding into the seat beside Fred, forcing her to move over or be squashed.

"Hi, I'm Jonas, like the lady said. So, what's up with you, dude?"

"Bipeds are poisoning our waters."

Jonas arched a blond brow and turned to Fred. "So you were saying the other day. What's going on?"

Fred shrugged. "Nothing new."

"Nothing new? Have you *seen* this guy?" he cried as if Artur wasn't sitting three feet away. "Is he like you? He's a mer-dude, isnt' he?"

"Yeah," she sighed. "A mer-dude."

The waiter stopped by the table, set a tray of sushi in front of Artur and a bowl of miso soup in front of Fred, took Jonas's order and glided away.

"So again with this biped thing?" Jonas demanded. "What are you talking about?"

Artur quietly ate his sushi (with his fingers, she noticed; probably didn't get much practice with chopsticks at the bottom of the ocean) and said nothing. Fred assumed it was up to her to explain.

"Jonas, I *know* the bipeds are wrecking the planet. You—they—can't help it. As far as they're concerned, they don't feel the sea; it's just something else to claim and fish and gut and leave dead."

"Uh," Jonas said. He paused, then, again: "Uh."

"Quite right," Artur agreed with his mouth full.

"Come on," he protested. "We're not that bad."

Both Fred and Artur stared at him stonily.

Jonas, the chemical engineer, couldn't keep up the façade. "Okay, we're pretty bad. We wreck the planet and we're not potty trained. But I don't think anybody's dumping bad stuff in the water to—I mean, on pur—uh . . ." He trailed off, no doubt hearing the absurdity of his words.

Fred sucked down half her miso soup, waited to see if her tongue would blister, then said, "I still don't know why you want my help. I'll be frank—"

"Not Fred?" Artur teased, tossing a chunk of tuna sushi into his mouth.

"—and tell you I'm not real interested in solving your little mystery. I just wanna feed the fish and stay out of my mom's living room for the rest of my life. Like I said to Dr. Pearson—tried to say—it's not really my field."

"The sea belongs to you, as well."

"Oh, sure. All the mer-guys would welcome me with open arms."

"They would." In went some halibut. "And if they did not, they would answer to me. Would you like some? It's very fresh."

Fred shuddered and slurped more miso. "No."

"Fred's allergic to seafood," Jonas explained.

"You—you are?" Artur's jaw was sagging, which annoyed her to no end. "But—but what do you *eat*?"

"Everything else."

"So, your plan is . . . what?" Jonas was tapping his fingers on the table in an irritating rhythm. "You're gonna be the Dr. Watson to his Sherlock?"

Fred shuddered; she couldn't help it.

"You don't want to?"

"I don't care."

"So give him the old heave-ho."

"Apparently," she said dryly, "I'm one of his subjects and have to do whatever he wants."

"Since when has *authority* stopped you from being you?"

"Well. How weird is it that in forty-eight hours two guys show up both bitching about the same thing?"

"You're gonna team him up with the water fellow?"

"That's the plan."

"What is a water fellow?"

"Eat your dead fish," she told Artur. To Jonas: "Let them team up and solve the mystery. Let me get back to work. Everybody's happy."

Jonas was holding his head in his hands. Fred ignored it. Artur looked slightly alarmed. "Good sir, what ails you?"

"Artur, could you give us a minute, please?"

Without a word, Artur rose, crossed the room in four big strides, and started talking to their waitress, who was staring at him the way diabetics stared at sundaes.

"What?"

"Fred, what the hell is wrong with you?"

"What?"

"You've met two new guys and instead of, I dunno, trying to build a meaningful relationship or at least get laid by either or both of them, you're gonna match them up together and head back to the aquarium?"

"Yeah."

"Fred. You are dumber than an octopus."

"Octopi," she told him with raised eyebrows, "are among the smartest animals on earth."

"Why don't you guys work together? Huh? He came all the way from the Black Sea—where the hell *is* the Black Sea, anyway . . . well, it sounds far away—and you can't just dump him!"

"I can." She added, "Southeastern Europe. Oh, and Asia Minor."

"What?"

"The Black Sea. Connected to the Mediterranean by the Bosphorus and the Sea of Marmara, and to the Sea of Azov by the—"

"This is not the point—"

"—Strait of Kerch," she finished.

She ignored his moan of despair and fished the last piece of tofu out of her soup bowl. The fact was, both Thomas and Artur made her anxious. She wasn't used to attention from men. And she had no interest in being in a triangle. Not that *that* was likely to happen.

"When was the last time you went on a date?" Jonas was demanding. "And if you give me the patented Fred 'I don't give a shit' shrug, I'll beat you to death."

She laughed at him. Then thought about it. And thought. And thought some more. "Dr. Barb's ex-husband," she said at last.

"Oh, God, that's right. I totally forgot about him. You're lucky you didn't lose your job over that one."

"She's the one who set us up," Fred reminded him. What neither of them needed reminding of was that it was a complete disaster. Dr. Barb's ex, whose name Fred had by now forgotten, spent half the date making gross passes at Fred, and the other half pining for his ex-wife. They had ended the meeting with a handshake, and he'd gone home with a black eye when he'd tried too persistently for more.

"And ever since then, you've been stuck in the vortex of a—what? Six? Six-year dating dry spell?"

"Vortex?"

"And here's two hunky fellows climbing all over you—"

"They aren't—"

"—and all you can think of to do is stick them together and vamoose."

"I've got other stuff to worry about."

"That's why," he said kindly, "you're a moron. Just like an octopus. No, don't tell me, I don't care. They're stupid, too."

Twelve

Jonas cheerfully trailed behind his best bud and her massive, ridiculously good-looking new pal. He eyed the people milling around on the cobblestones and wondered if any of them had the faintest idea he was walking behind two mer-people. Hell, *he* had a hard time believing it, and he'd grown up with one of them.

Artur kept leaning over and trying to whisper in Fred's ear, and she kept batting him away like he was a persistently annoying fly. Jonas shook his head. It was so obvious that Artur—a prince! A freakin' prince!—had the hots for his pal. Did she notice? Nuh-uh. Would she have cared if she did notice? Probably not. Was she a nutjob of the highest order? Yup.

But then, if she didn't engage in that odd Freddish behavior, she wouldn't be Fred.

He still remembered the day they met. He'd been pretty shocked when the big kids had ganged up on him, and had barely noticed the small, stick-thin, blue-haired girl reading a book up against a tree.

Whether she didn't like the distraction from her book or couldn't stand to see the odds so badly out of whack (probably the former), it didn't matter. She'd gotten up and put her hands on the big kids and they'd gone flying, and then she went back to her book and ignored the stares and the whispers. Almost as if, at the ripe old age of seven, she didn't notice them anymore, or never had, or just didn't care.

He'd pestered her the rest of the day until she had sighed and agreed to bring him to her house. They'd been buds ever since.

He'd known. Not that she was a mermaid, but even as a child, Fred wasn't like anybody else. *Anybody* else. That was all right, though, because he wasn't a typical elementary school student, either, not when he knew how to do floral arrangements and had a collection of paint chips that he kept organized by tint and type (matte, gloss, et cetera).

And when she'd finally worked up the courage to show him her other form, he had been surprised, but not shocked. And not horrified, either. He'd thought her tail was pretty, and had told her so. She'd told him to shut up, and he'd ignored her.

Now he was tagging along, as he so often did, partly because he smelled excitement, and partly because he was hoping to get another glimpse of the delectable Dr. Barb. He'd been wondering for years what her hair would feel like in his hands—if it ever was out of that silly braid—if her eyes narrowed or widened or closed completely during orgasm. It was a full-on crush, the one secret he kept from Fred. Just the thought of her scorn (or indifference) made him cringe.

"It's pretty late," Fred said over her shoulder, leading them to a darkened employee entrance. "I doubt anybody's around. Which is good. Technically neither of you should be here."

"Technically, you're a frigid bitch," he reminded her.

"Shut up."

"*You* shut up."

Fred sighed. "Are you ever going to leave the second grade?"

"Are you ever going to do anything about those split ends?"

She ignored him, the way she ignored the stare Artur gave her. That was also business as usual. He'd long given up trying to point out the guys (and occasional gal) checking her out pretty much daily.

Fred wasn't gorgeous, but she had—something. The hair, of course. The long legs and waist. Skinny, so she could wear anything and look good. And the height. He had barely an inch on her. Altogether, she was a striking, if startling, woman.

And the smile. Fred had a perfectly beautiful smile, he happened to know from seeing it three, maybe four times in twenty years.

And a wonderful sense of humor. The trouble was . . .

He thought about it. The trouble was, she was also the loneliest person he knew. And it wasn't hard to figure why. She worked so hard shoving people away, nobody had a chance to dump her first. Psych 101, plain and simple.

"Yeah," he replied, "but Dr. Barb doesn't have a life any more than you do."

"Says the moron tagging along at ten thirty at night on a Friday." She turned, walked backward for a second, and narrowed her sea green eyes. "What do you care if Dr. Barb is here?"

"I'm just warning you," he covered.

"Muh," she replied, turning back around.

And lo and behold, the gods of frustrated sexual yearnings smiled on him as the employee door slammed open and out darted Dr. Barb! Who, he happened to know, trotted everywhere, like a little kid. She nearly slammed into Fred, checked herself, skidded to a halt, straightened, blew her bangs out of her eyes, and said, "Dr. Bimm! You're back. Everything all right at home, I trust?"

Instantly, Jonas seized Artur and dragged him away so Dr. Barb wouldn't realize Fred had been about to sneak two unauthorized persons into the NEA in the middle of the night. There was a convenient corner near the outdoor seal tank and he hissed, "Put your arms around me."

"Pardon?"

"Like we're boyfriends."

"No."

"Look," he snapped, "I don't like it any more than you do, but d'you want Fred to get into trouble?"

Stiffly, like a recently animated marble statue, Artur placed his arms around Jonas's waist.

"Not like *that*. You look like someone's sticking a gun in your ear."

"Someone will most likely have to very soon."

"Put some feeling in it," he commanded. "Love me tender!"

"No."

"Look, I'd much rather be snuggling with *her*." He jerked a thumb over his shoulder. "But we can't get caught, okay? And we can't get Fred into trouble. So snuggle. Now."

Instead of snuggling, Artur grabbed him by the shirtfront and hoisted him to eye level. This was the most alarming thing to happen since he had tried to invent chocolate shampoo and had blown up Lab Six.

"You do not touch her," Artur was telling him, while Jonas struggled and kicked, his feet a good foot off the ground. "Ever. Do you understand, biped?"

"Not—one of—your subjects," he coughed.

"Then I will simply have to beat you until you comply."

"This shirt—cost—one-fifty—at Macy's—" he gurgled.

Artur set him down (reluctantly, it seemed to Jonas).

"Good thing you did that," he said, straightening his clothing and blowing his hair out of his eyes, "because I was about to kick your fishy ass into the seal tank."

Artur laughed politely.

"Crushin' on Fred, eh?" It had to be Fred. It sure as shit better not be Dr. Barb or there'd be a beat-down, all right, and Mr. Hotshit Prince might get a surprise.

"I do not know what that—"

"Yes you do. Get in line, pal. But don't worry about me. Fred and I are nothing more than friends. Just realize there are other men out there. Even if . . ."

"Even if . . . ?"

"She's oblivious."

Artur nodded, stroking his too-cool red beard. Not too long, not absurdly short—like the little bear in Goldilocks, it was just right. "That is well," he said at last.

"Oh, right, real well. Listen—"

"Morons!" Fred's grating voice cut through their private chat. "Are you coming, or not?"

"Where's Dr. Barb?" he asked, peeking around the corner to make sure the coast was clear.

"She's outta here. Didn't even notice you."

"Oh," Jonas said. He faked enthusiasm. "That's good, then."

Fred gave him an odd look, and let them into the darkened halls of the NEA.

Thirteen

"It should be here somewhere."

"What exactly are we looking for, Nancy Drew?"

Fred gave Jonas a look. They'd both gone through an insane Drew phase in the fourth grade, read the entire Nancy Drew series, talked about her and her friends and her borderline-absentee dad, and at the end had both decided it was a miracle Ms. Drew lived through any of her wacky adventures.

"What. Are. We. Looking. For?"

"I heard you the first time, moron. Anything Dr. Pearson might have left. He's got to have notes, charts—something."

"I dislike this skulking about," the prince said, looking around the small, cluttered lab with distaste. "It ill becomes royalty. I prefer action."

"Indulge the commoners, will ya?"

"Yeah, do that." Fred picked up a clipboard and instantly became absorbed. Much more interesting than listening to the men in her life bitch and moan. How did wives and moms stand it?

"I don't know why I'm here," Jonas was saying, looking absently around the lab. "It's not really my field. Now, if you want to talk about a hand cream that doubles as perfume . . ."

"I don't know why you're here, either." Jonas, she had decided three years ago, had an odd affection for the NEA. He'd been in it about a thousand times, and was always chatting up her boss and colleagues . . . even the volunteers who worked the gift shop. She happened to know he didn't give a tin shit about oceans, sea life, stuffed seals or penguins, so it was a bit of a mystery. "So go."

"Yeah, maybe I will." In another of his odd mood swings, Jonas had gone from keen interest to yawning boredom in less than thirty.

"Then be off," the prince commanded, sitting on a lab stool and nearly toppling off when he realized the chair didn't have a back.

Fred swallowed a laugh and kept her gaze glued to the clipboard. Pearson had the handwriting of a serial killer, and she was having a tough time deciphering if this was a toxin sheet or his grocery list.

"You're pretty strong," she heard Jonas say to Artur, obviously ignoring the prince's command to "be off." "Fred is, too. I once saw her pick up her mom's fridge to get one of my Hot Wheels."

"That is interesting about Fred. It is also an accurate observation."

"I'm guessing it's the whole mer-angle, right? I mean, you can't swim around on the bottom of the ocean day and night—all that pressure—and not build some upper body strength. I mean, you guys are under *literal* pressure, not the usual 'the HR rep hates me, I can't stand office politics' pressure."

"Do not feel shame. An air breather is by nature much weaker."

"Uh—okay, yeah, I'm not really a shame-feelin' kinda guy, but thanks anyway. I'm betting you can see in the dark like a cat, too, huh?"

"What is a cat?"

"Because I bet it gets pretty dark down there, too, right?"

"It is dark in many places," the prince said, sounding slightly confused. She couldn't blame him. Jonas had all the tact of a pit bull once his mind starting chewing on a problem.

"So all mer-people—"

"Undersea Folk," the prince corrected.

Fred resisted the urge to roll her eyes. Well, he could have picked a worse one, like Ben-Varry or Caesg or Meerfrau. Seemed like all of her research on mer-folk came up with stuff that was ninety percent outright wrong, and silly-sounding names.

"Right, right, that's what I meant. All Undersea Folk are super strong, and can see in the dark, and can breathe air and water—how *do* you breathe air and water?"

"We just—do." Artur looked from Fred to Jonas, puzzled. "Are you not comrades? How do you not know these things about a friend?"

"Because *Fred* doesn't know a lot of these things. She was raised by humans. Heck, I didn't even know she was a fellow mammal at first, because she's so clammy all the time. You think her mom ever let her near a doctor?"

"I'm never sick," Fred said absently.

"Anyway, back to what we were talking about. Fred doesn't have gills. Not even when she has a tail."

"Never mind her tail," the prince ordered. "And why would she? She is not part fish. She is one of the Undersea Folk. She is one of *my* people."

"Oh, take a pill, handsome. I'm just making observations, here, and you're getting all touchy." He added, oddly, "Resist the urge to pick me up and shake me like a juice box."

Artur sighed, the quiet groan of a man picking up a heavy, chattering burden. "We pull air into our bodies when we are on land, and when we are underwater we pull air from the water."

"Okay, that was super helpful. Lemme just grab some clarification, 'kay? So—like, you get oxygen from the water, how? The cells of your body somehow open up and grab the oxygen and bring it into your system? You're, what, like starfish?"

Close, Fred thought. It really was difficult to explain. Just as people didn't think about breathing, she didn't think about water-breathing.

No, she didn't have gills, and she wasn't half girl, half fish, but a mammal that simply resembled such a creature. A large, hostile mammal whose baseline temp was eighty-eight degrees and whose resting heart rate was thirty.

She just—just never needed to come up for air when she was swimming. Interesting that even though she had a doctorate in marine biology she never gave much thought to her *own* biology. (Though it had been amusing, picturing her professors' reactions if she had shown off her tail during a wet lab.) Very likely the pores in her skin were able to extract oxygen from the—

"This is useless," she said, bored with the "how do you not drown" talk, and annoyed with Pearson's notes. "A bad idea. We should have come during business hours."

"Oh, sure," Jonas said snarkily. "*That* would have been easy to explain. 'Hi, Dr. Barb, this is the Prince of the—'"

Fred gave him a look. "Don't you have somewhere to be?"

"Sobbingly, no."

"Well, let's think about this. I'd like to try feeding the fish again, anyway, so I might as well do it while we're here. You—what's your plan?"

"For what?" Artur replied, looking startled when she pointed at him.

"For—you know. Waiting until tomorrow to meet the *other* guy who's bugging me about your little problem."

"I will return with you to your dwelling, of course."

"What?" she cried. "I don't have the room or the temperament for a royal roommate. And don't wait for an invitation or anything."

"You are my subject," he said, looking even more wide-eyed. "Of course you will open your home to me."

Jonas snickered. "Fred, meet Artur. Artur, meet Fred."

"I do not know what you—"

"Fred doesn't 'of course' do anything."

"There's a Marriott right next door," she forced through a tense jaw. "We'll get you a room. You might be in town for a while."

"The Prince of the Black Sea has an American Express?" Jonas asked gleefully, being more annoying than usual. Then, before Artur could ask what he was talking about: "You got any money on you? Dough? Moolah? Treasure?"

Artur's red eyes actually glowed with comprehension. "Ah! Treasure. Yes, of course. The sea is generous. But I—"

"No pockets, huh? Left all your doubloons at home?"

"Yes."

"I'll put the room on my Visa," Fred gritted.

"You refuse your home to me?"

"Yes."

"You may not."

"It's a one-bedroom apartment. Just watch me."

Artur glared at her. She glared back. Jonas watched, enjoying himself far too much. Then they both glared at him.

"Well, I'm sure you two will work it out." He coughed. "I'll just, you know, hit the trail. Call me tomorrow," he said to Fred.

"Nuh," she said, fumbling through the papers on Pearson's desk. The guy had been in town less than three days and his lab looked like a tsunami had hit it. How he could find anything, much less research his little problem, was beyond her. "This is hopeless. My dumb idea of the year. I'd better see to the fish." She thought of something and looked up at Artur, who was still looking at her with narrowed eyes. "You any good with fish? I mean, do they listen to you?"

"Of course."

She sighed. "Of course."

"Of course," Jonas called over his shoulder as he left.

"Well, suit up. Or whatever you do."

"Summon an underling to tend to your chore," he said, waving her responsibilities away with a hand the size of a baseball glove. "Greater problems require your attention."

"Around here, *I'm* the underling," she snapped. "Some of us work for a living, Prince Artur."

He blinked, his eyes like banked coals in the poor light of the lab. Creepy eyes. But kind of interesting. Hard to look away from, really. "I can assure you, setting out from the Black Sea to find you was considerable work."

"Good for you. Let's go."

"Where?"

"More subjects for you to meet."

Fourteen

"Those tiny creatures are not my subjects," the prince observed, staring down into Main One. They were at the top level of the aquarium, the observation deck, looking down into the main tank. The prince, on the way up, pronounced the NEA "acceptable," deciding it was "a miniature kingdom." She had bitten back an acid remark; maybe he'd decide to take the place over and give her a new problem to worry about.

"But they'll listen to you, right?"

"Some will. The predators will."

"And the others?"

He smiled at her with his very sharp teeth. "The others will see me as the predator, and flee."

Briefly, she imagined herself explaining the mass carnage to Dr. Barb. "Ohhh . . . kay. New plan. How about you stay here, then? I'll do this myself."

He eyed the smelt bucket with distaste. "These menial tasks are beneath you."

She cursed herself for not having Jonas take Artur with him when he left. Jonas could have checked him into the Marriott, gotten the guy all settled, fluffed his pillows, told him all about the good bars, whatever. Now *she* was stuck with him. "Why?"

"Because—" He groped. Not literally, thank God. "Because you are above such things."

She prayed the Marriott still had rooms at this hour. "Why?"

"Because you should be tended to and coddled and pleasured and teased."

She gaped at him. He was staring down at her, his big hands in his pockets, his eyes thoughtful and almost—dreamy? "Why?"

"Would you like to be a princess, Little Rika? I think that would suit you. I think that would suit you very well."

"Artur, do you have to take any medications if you're out of the water for a while?" She racked her brain, trying to figure out the poor guy's damage. "Do you need to lie down, maybe? Do you feel dehydrated? Do you have a headache? I don't think you're getting enough air. Or probably too much air. Yeah, that's it!" In her excitement, she reached out and grabbed his arm. He felt just right; not feverish, like Jonas felt on the few occasions she'd touched him. "Do you feel light-headed? Dizzy?"

Somehow, he had edged closer without her noticing. Now he was *very* close. Almost kissing close. "Yes," he murmured.

"You do? You feel dizzy?"

"Yes."

"When your king father sent you, he didn't warn you? That you might not be able to take it?"

"As a matter of fact, he did not."

"Well," she fretted, "you'd better lie down."

"Yes indeed." His hand was on the back of her neck. He probably didn't want to fall down. Which was too bad, because if he went, they both would. She doubted she could keep him from—

His lips covered hers and pressed, hard. No tentative brushing of lips for *this* guy. No, his mouth was all over hers, almost hard enough to bruise, and his fingers were like iron on her neck, it was overwhelming, it was the hardest, most possessive kiss of her life and she brought her hands up in outraged surprise, tried to shove him away except, weirdly, she wasn't shoving him. She was touching, feeling . . . stroking?

Was *she* getting too little air?

She managed to tear free and leaned on Pearson's desk, gasping. "That's—don't do that."

"Oh, I think I will, Little Rika. It was far better than I imagined, and I have a *large* . . . imagination."

She stared at him, her mouth hanging open, and her brain once again erroneously reported that the planet's spin had sped up. It was all—it was just too much.

It was *too much*, really! For anyone to deal with. Her mom on all fours. Her dad not being her dad. Her dad being *dead*. Pearson showing up. This one showing up. Somebody poisoning the harbor. This one sticking around. Pearson waving at her—following her all the way down the tank to wave at her. This one all grabby. Pearson all chatty about her hair. This one—

"Are you well, Little Rika?"

"No."

"I did not think so. You look odd."

"I have to go to work," she said, feeling stupid. That wasn't what she had meant to say. At all. Why couldn't she think of what she meant?

He shrugged, turned his back, dismissed her, started heading down the stairs. "Then work. I will view the displays, like a good biped termist."

"Tourist."

"That, yes."

"Don't eat any of the exhibits," she couldn't help adding, then fled.

Fifteen

She hopped on one foot, struggling out of her stubborn shoe, and it seemed as if everything was fighting her: items of clothing, the doorknob, the packets of smelt. Breathless, she hit the water and grew a tail.

Fish girl bring fish.

And realized she was still gasping from the kiss. Jonas's inquisitive comments about how mermaids breathed without gills—

Fish girl bang bang fish girl bang.

—flitted past her brain and she realized her mouth was closed. So she was gasping in her brain.

Fish girl bring bang bang thud thud.

Or thought she was gasping.

Fish girl bring bang bang thud thud.

Or—

Fish girl bring BANG BANG THUD THUD.

EVERYBODY SHUT THE HELL UP!

Startled, an angelfish swam into a chunk of coral reef, reeled dizzily for a foot, then straightened and darted away.

She took a deep breath. Or thought she did. And tried to think. Yes, get Artur into the Marriott Long Wharf tonight, *tonight*, then get

(sneak)

the hell back to her apartment on Commonwealth Avenue. Tomorrow was another day, and all that. Yes.

How she would keep a strong-willed, large, immensely powerful man at arm's length was tomorrow's problem. She just—didn't he understand? This wasn't how things were supposed to be.

She offered fish to fish, and some of them, cowed from her mental screeching, actually fed. Distractedly, she fed several reef fish and a couple of the turtles. The sharks grinned as they swam by, and ignored her offerings. That was all right, though. She had plenty of other problems right now. So many that she couldn't be elated that some of the fish had given in without her having to blast "West End Girls" over the PA system.

For example, the tourists and what they'd think if the sharks turned on, say, the eels at exactly the wrong moment. Like the guy she could see through the window. He'd probably freak out at a feeding frenzy. Or maybe he'd get off on it; you never could tell. A bigger problem was that the guy was here wicked late—the place had closed a couple hours ago. Did they even *have* security guards in this place anymore?

And what *was* he doing? Leaning on one of the fifty-two windows and staring at her. Like there weren't 650 other fish in the tank to glare at. No, he had to gawk at her. When were the tourists going back to wherever the hell they spawned? Wasn't it autumn already?

Well? *Wasn't it?*

She irritably tossed another smelt and glowered at the dark-haired gawker, then realized with something like relief that it wasn't a tourist, it was Thomas Pearson. Hmm, another geek with no life; he'd fit right in at NEA. Why else would he come back to the aquarium in the wee hours of a Friday night?

And he was looking right at her. Guess he was giving the toxins a rest. Was that flattering or annoying?

You have a tail right now.

She had a tail right now. She'd been so distracted from Artur's top tank pawing that she'd completely—

Their eyes met across a crowded tank of fish. Thomas's face was actually squashed up against the glass, "the better to see you with, my dear." His hands were plastered flat. His breath fogged the pane.

Then he vanished.

She dropped the smelt, put her arms over her head, and with a powerful flick of her tail shot to the top of the tank. She thought, *Right this minute he's sprinting up the stairs. That's three flights he's got to go up. I can—*

What? Haul her big white butt out of the tank, dry off, get into her clothes, and pretend it was some *other* green-haired mermaid in the NEA tank?

She grabbed the edge of the tank and flicked her tail, just as Thomas galloped into the observation room. He was breathing hard and his dark hair had tumbled into his eyes. He jerked his bangs back and clutched his collar, actually yanked at it until the top button flew off and exposed his throat. He gulped air and she thought, *Good thing he wasn't wearing a tie or he might have been strangled.*

He pointed at her, his big dark eyes practically bulging from his head. "I knew it!" he practically screamed. "I knew you weren't like all the others!"

"Dr. Pearson," she began, but trailed off in mystification as he ran to her, lost his balance, actually slid on his knees until he was leaning against the top of the tank, and then leaned over and kissed her spang on the mouth.

Okay. I guess it's just going to be that kind of a day. The kind where men I've just met have this odd illness where they can't keep their hands off me.

"Dr. Pearson," she tried again, but "ffgggrrrll" is what came out, since he was still kissing her. And she was kissing him back, holding on to his shirt so she wouldn't drop the rest of the way back into the tank. His lips were warm, almost hot; they were burning her, he was *scorching* her with his kisses, and she wasn't minding. No, she wasn't minding at all.

His hands on her shoulders were equally hot, making her think about rolling around under the sheets with him on a cold winter day, when the only way to stay warm was to snuggle with the guy in the bed with—

Weirdly, he was gone. Like he had teleported. Or been grabbed from behind and hauled away from her. But Pearson was a big guy. Who'd be strong enough to—

"Artur, don't!"

She almost covered her eyes; it was going to be too awful. Pearson, looking astonished. Artur, red eyes slits of rage. Pearson, looking not exactly happy himself. She opened her mouth to yell—what? She had no idea.

Then Thomas whipped an elbow back, catching Artur in the throat. This loosened the giant redhead's grip long enough for Fred to realize that Pearson was going to—yep, she knew that move from watching Jonas's self-defense tournaments. Thomas grabbed Artur's left arm and threw the guy over his shoulder, right into Main One.

Artur hit with a spectacular splash, wriggled around beneath the surface for a moment, and then popped up beside Fred, his shorts whirling toward the bottom of the tank, momentarily covering a sea turtle. Artur's tail was easily seen in the water—more easily, in fact, than Fred's had been.

Thomas gaped down at them. They stared up.

"Okay," Thomas said after a long moment. "I'm gonna need a minute here." And he sat down on the deck, propped his exhausted chin in his hands, and just gawked at them both.

Sixteen

"Until you came along, nobody but Jonas knew my secret," Fred bitched.

"Do not keep your rightful self hidden."

"Who's to say legs aren't my rightful self? I'm just as much a human as I am a mermaid."

"Undersea Folk."

"Don't correct me! If I want to call myself a Havmand there's not a damned thing you can do about it."

"Havmand?"

"Scandinavian mermaid," Thomas called, still staring at them like a kid getting his Saturday morning cartoon fix.

"Right. Or a—wait." She focused on Thomas who, she was relieved to see, no longer looked like he was going to stroke out. "Oh, don't tell me."

He shrugged. "I'm afraid so."

"What?" Artur asked sharply.

"Mermaid geek," Fred sighed. There were, she had noticed as a grad student, three types who went for the doctorate in marine biology: women who *lurrrved* dolphins as little girls (see: Madison, the annoying); men and women who wanted to come up with the newest bioactive drug and make big bucks working at a pharmaceutical company (see: the greedy); and men who fantasized about mermaids. Thomas, it appeared, had no interest in pharmacology or dolphins.

"I am not surprised at all," Thomas was saying. "That's what's so surprising."

"Sure. You staggered around looking like an M.I. about to happen because you were unsurprised."

"M.I.?" Artur asked.

"Heart attack."

"Okay, I was taken off guard for a few moments. But I've since recovered," he insisted, still pale. "Because I've had this theory since I was eight—"

"Yeah. Well. Theory realized."

He crept closer. "So, obviously you're more the Daryl Hannah–type mermaid than the Hans Christian Andersen–type—"

"That's enough of that," she said, nicely enough.

"Is this the biped you wished me to meet?"

"Huh? Oh. Prince Artur, this is Dr. Thomas Pearson. Thomas, this is Artur, High Prince of the Black Sea."

Thomas had scooted all the way up to the edge of the tank as she talked, and now stuck his arm out. Artur leaned up, balancing on his tail like a dolphin, and they shook hands. Thomas nearly fell in while trying not to make it obvious he was still staring at them. "Nice to meet you. Sorry about kicking your ass right into the tank like that. You sort of surprised me."

"Indeed," Artur said dryly. "I, also, was surprised to see your mouth on one of my subjects."

"I'm not one of your subjects. I mean it, Artur, cut that shit out right now. I was born in Quincy, for God's sake. I have American citizenship, okay?"

"Dual citizenship, it looks to me," Thomas said, ogling her tail.

"You are *not* helping."

"You may not put your mouth on her without my—ow."

"I'm trying not to stare but you guys keep giving me new things to look at. That punch, for example. Didn't it hurt like hell?"

"It did," Artur said, gingerly pressing the flesh below his eye.

"We have enough shit to worry about without this weird possessive streak of yours. If I want all twelve Boston Celtics to put their mouths on me, that's my business and not yours."

"Yeah," Thomas added.

"And *you*."

He leaned away from the tank. "If my theories on differences in strength evolution between bipeds and mermaids are true, I really don't want you to slug me."

"You're not helping, either. Both of you, quit with the groping and the kissing." She had never, in her life, had to say such a thing. And she never, in her life, could have imagined the circumstances in which she was saying it.

"Then there is little for me to do," Artur teased.

"No, there's a lot. Artur noticed your little toxin problem," she said to Thomas. "I thought you guys could work together."

"Ummmm," Thomas said, eyeing Artur. "That's pretty interesting. I s'pose you guys would notice that stuff way before we did. What, you live around here?"

"No, I live on the other side of the planet. Some of our folk were in the area and reported what they sensed. When word reached my father, the High King, he set me this task."

"So the royal palace or coral reef or whatever is in the Black Sea?"

"Yes."

"I wonder why word took so long to—"

"There are only a million of us on the planet."

"Oh. Ah. Hmm. And with the planet being mostly water—"

"Exactly."

Exactly indeed. It explained why Fred had never bumped into another of her kind, though at one point she'd swum along the entire eastern seashore. Telepathy, she supposed, could only reach so far.

"Then how—"

"You know, I just did this with Jonas not half an hour ago," Fred broke in. "You two run along and get acquainted."

They both frowned at her. "What are you talking about?"

"The question of my lodging has not yet been settled."

"Yeah, but now you have someone new to settle it with."

They frowned at each other, then turned their sour expressions back on her. She elaborated. "Uh . . . you guys team up, like Nick Nolte and Eddie Murphy. Or Owen Wilson and everybody. Solve the case. And I'll—" *Get back to my life,* was her thought. Her nice, boring, controlled, uncomplicated life.

Why didn't it feel as appealing as it had this morning?

"But you have to help us," Thomas said at the exact same moment Artur commanded, "It ill becomes you to set aside your duty."

"Aw, no . . . not both of you at once . . ."

Thus followed a lecture, from both of them at once, about the sanctity of the seas and her duty as a scientist as well as a mermaid and how three heads were better than two and how her duty was to her prince and her career, yak-yak, until finally she was almost shouting, "All right, all *right*, I'll help, just cut it out!"

Thomas sat back and smiled. "Alrighty then."

Artur was also smiling, which wiped Thomas's smile away. "Yes, well said."

"So it's settled."

"Indeed; and well said."

Fred briefly toyed with the idea of leaping into the harbor, striking out for the horizon, and never looking back, not once.

Seventeen

"So here it is," Thomas announced, zipping his key card through the slot and throwing open the door to the Presidential Suite. "It's not home, but it's much. I stole that," he added cheerfully, "from Olivia Goldsmith, God rest her lipo'd soul."

Fred, raised by far-from-poor parents, and Artur, son of royalty, were both impressed, and said so.

Thomas shrugged. "Well, like I said my first day . . . You remember," he said to Fred. "I write romance novels."

"Of course I remember. It was—" She looked at her watch. "The day before yesterday."

"Right. Has it really only been two days?"

"Tell me about it," she muttered.

"Well, when I'm running around doing this stuff, I try to pay for my own lodging. It's not much to me, but sometimes it helps them. You know how the water programs . . ."

Fred nodded. At Artur's puzzled look, she elaborated. "A lot of the programs for water fellows got their government funding slashed. Or don't have much to begin with. Not just the water fellow programs, either. Just about every aquarium in the country depends on private contributions."

Artur's mouth thinned. "I was not aware, but I am not surprised." In unison, they said, "Bipeds."

"Now cut that out," Thomas said, tossing his key card on the eight-foot-long mahogany dining room table. "We're not all like that. I'm the one who came out here to try to fix the toxin problem, remember?"

"Congratulations," Artur said silkily, wandering around the suite. "One out of a thousand bipeds maintains awareness that the planet is not yours to ruin."

Fred snorted and Thomas said, "Now you're just being mean. Uh, the other bedroom is back there, on your left. There's another bathroom back there, too." As Artur disappeared from sight, Thomas beckoned.

Curious, Fred walked over to him. He put his warm hands on her shoulders, leaned down, and whispered, "There's plenty of room for you, too."

She grabbed his hands, ignored his yelp of pain, and wrenched them off of her body. "Tempting, but no."

"Ow ow *ow*. I meant the couches are all fold outs."

"Oh, that's even more tempting. Sleeping on a bar while you two save the world, refreshed from sleeping on queen mattresses."

"King. And hey, I didn't want to team up with Aquaman," he growled. "That was your idea." Then he added hastily, "Not that I mind. I've got about a thousand questions for him. Think he'd let me run an MRI on him?"

"I doubt it. But go ahead and ask." Out of sorts, and not really sure if she should stay or leave (and even more out of sorts that she was wondering . . . usually if she had to leave, she left, and didn't waste a second wondering about it, either), Fred wandered around the suite.

Gold brocade couches, ankle-deep carpet, dark wood everywhere, three phones that she could see, a bar, a plasma screen, four tables, and a fireplace . . . and that was just the sitting room! She could just imagine the master bedroom.

"Little Rika," Artur called. "Come!"

Thomas sniggered. "You know, I just have to wait him out a day or two and—"

"And what?"

"Never mind."

With a warning glare over her shoulder, Fred stomped into the back. *The only reason I'm going is to show the other one that—what? I better think about this for a minute . . .*

"Do not call me like a dog," she began, pushing open the bathroom door. "And . . ." She fell silent. Artur, spectacularly nude (maybe there was something to her mom's "nudity is natural and beautiful" mantra), was standing, hands on his hips, in front of a double-head shower in a bathroom that looked slightly more complicated than the cockpit of Air Force One.

She prayed he knew how the toilet worked.

"I see the problem. Okay, you just turn this one here, and turn this one here . . ." She leaned in, felt his arms slip around her waist, sighed, adjusted the water level, grabbed the shower head, and squirted it at *his* head.

"Aaggghhkk! Very well, Little Rika, I will desist." He groped blindly and she handed him a towel. While he blotted, he added, "For now."

"Right. Well, you're all set up for a while. In fact, it was awfully nice of Thomas to let you stay in his suite—"

"I am aware of my responsibility to my host," he sulked. "I cannot help it if I preferred a different host."

"Great. Work on helping it. I'm going."

"Going?" Artur looked (and sounded) alarmed. "But there is sufficient room for you to stay."

"Yeah, finding a place to sleep isn't the problem."

"Then what is?"

She gave him a look.

He smiled. "Ah. That."

"Yeah. That. And so I bid you fond farewell, sweet prince."

"The words seem correct," he said suspiciously, "but the tone—"

"Can't put one over on you, handsome."

She turned and walked out, ignoring his hollered, "So you do find me pleasing to the eye?"

Meanwhile, Thomas had emptied his pockets. She suppressed a smile; he carried around more junk than a little kid. Cell phone, spare change (from several countries), money clip, string *(string?)*, earring (?), broken pencil, and T-pass. The debris was scattered all along a table she suspected was brought over on the *Niña*. He was jabbing at his cell phone but looked up when she walked in.

"Taking off?"

"Yes."

"Already?"

"Finally."

"I'll walk you to the door."

"The door's six feet away. I can find it."

"Now, what kind of a host would I be?" He hurried to her side. "Uh-oh."

"Name of all the gods, now what?"

"Check it out." He held something yellow over her head. "Mistletoe!" he said brightly, leaning in for a kiss. He caught her on the bottom of her chin, since she was looking up.

"That," she informed him, "is a leaf from a maple tree."

"It is?" the scientist asked. He yelped and leapt out of the way as she jerked the door open. "Aw, don't leave already. It's early. Hey, Artur! She's jamming!"

"I am aware," the prince's voice drifted out.

"See you tomorrow," Fred said and thought, to her credit, that she deserved full points for saying it without groaning.

Eighteen

Jonas got to the NEA just in time to hear Artur's roar.

"I detest this puttering about! I insist on action at once!"

Whoa. Jonas practically scampered over to the jellies exhibit, where Fred had promised the three of them would be when the NEA opened the next morning. He waved his pass at the elderly woman staffing the cash register and ran past the penguins, his nostrils flaring at the fish-poop smell he knew he wouldn't even notice five minutes from now.

Before he could triangulate their position from Artur's scream, he was waylaid by a little blonde cutie waving a schedule of events at him.

"Hi! Welcome to the NEA! Would you like a schedule for the seal shows?"

He slowed down for a look. What the hell; she *was* awfully pretty. A little shrill, and disturbingly bouncy, but mighty pleasant to look at.

"I've been here lots of times," he told her, noting the I Heart Dolphins pin over her left breast. Ah-ha! The annoying new intern Fred had bitched about. "I've pretty much got all the schedules memorized."

"It doesn't hurt to keep a reminder," she giggled, waving the paper at him.

"You must be one of the new interns."

"You bet! My name's Madison. Say, if you're so familiar with the place, maybe you could give me a tour." She giggled again, hiding her mouth with perfectly manicured fingers.

"Nice offer, but I'm supposed to meet a friend."

"Oh." She pouted. She was a good pouter, and he suspected she knew it. "Maybe next time."

"Yeah, maybe. Nice to meet you, Madison." He wondered how much time would pass before Fred strangled the poor girl, and gave her about seventy-two hours.

Hurrying away from the delectable intern, Jonas saw Fred, Artur, and Thomas, and approached the group from behind. They were in a tight little huddle, Fred's hair shining like blue cotton candy under the ultraviolet lights, Artur and some other guy sort of blocking her—kind of protectively?

Jonas skidded to a halt and took another look. Hard to miss Artur with the height and the shoulders and the hair looking like it was on fire, especially now, with all the yelling. And hard to miss Fred, trying (unsuccessfully) to shush him, bony arms like windshield wipers as she held up her hands in a soothing, un-Fredlike way.

But the third guy filled up space just the same way those two did; almost as tall as Artur, almost as broad, dark instead of fiery but more intense, waving his arms around and trying to be heard over Artur's roars.

The new water fellow! So Fred had hooked them up, as she had planned. But was still stuck with them, which he knew was decidedly not in the plan.

Jonas stifled the urge to cackle. *Oh boy, oh boy! I didn't miss anything!* He raced up to the group, nearly trampling a busload of Girl Scouts.

"Hey," he panted. "What'd I miss?"

The small circle froze in midargument and turned to him.

"Well, the Prince of the Black Sea isn't a big believer in the scientific method," Fred began, blowing a lock of hair out of her eyes with an irritated puff. "Wanting instead to just jump in the harbor and start kicking ass. Because it's just that easy, don't you know."

"That is not what I—"

"And Thomas, here, thinks we need to do a tad bit more research first before we get an injunction, and when Artur found out an injunction was essentially a strongly worded piece of paper—"

He waved the rest of her explanation away. "Never mind. I get the gist." He stuck out a hand and the water fellow, looking bemused, shook it. "Hi. Jonas Carrey. Fred's best friend. Her oldest, best, dearest friend. The one from whom," he added, testing New Guy, "she has no secrets."

"I know they're Seafolk, if that's what you're getting at."

"Oh, good. Everyone's on the same page."

"I don't think everyone is," Fred grumbled. She was looking rumpled and out of sorts in a "Nantucket" T-shirt, cutoffs (the legs of which did not match in length, he noticed with an internal groan), and sandals. He shuddered at the state of her sandals, but as usual, Fred made it work. Or, rather, nobody looked at her clothes when they looked at her.

Certainly *these* two gents didn't give a crumbly crap that Fred was disheveled and hadn't had a pedicure since the first *Pirates of the Caribbean* hit DVD. In fact, they were looking at her the way Jonas looked at a plate of freshly steamed *edumame* sprinkled with sea salt.

He tried to intervene. "C'mon, Artur, you gotta give it more than half a day. The whole reason Dr. Pearson—"

"Thomas."

"—Tom—"

"Thomas."

"God, you've been around Fred a day and look what's happened to you! Okay, okay. Artur, the whole reason Thomas is on the team is so he can do all the grunt paperwork."

"Hey, thanks. You really know how to make a guy feel welcome. Why are *you* on the team?"

"Because we'd have to kill him to get him off," Fred muttered. She looked awful, even for Fred; now that he was closer he noticed the enomous dark circles, almost like bruises, under her eyes. He had a pretty good idea what had kept her up all night. "Don't knock it, Thomas. He can go out for sandwiches and stuff. He knows every waitress between here and Comm. Ave."

"That's true," he said modestly, inwardly bristling at being reduced to Sandwich Boy.

"This endless rambling grates on me unendurably."

"I gathered from the whining."

"Royal sons do not whine."

Thomas and Fred snorted in unison.

"Look, Artur, just give us another couple of days. We—" Fred looked around, motioned Jonas closer, and they all bent together in some sort of geeky, multispecies football huddle. "Thomas already has a bunch of the info compiled. We need to pinpoint the source; we can't just wade into the harbor and start kicking random ass."

"That's true," Jonas said. "Random ass is never a good thing. Though there was this girl from Revere once, who—"

"Then what am I to do in the meantime?" Artur had looked momentarily startled when Jonas and Fred each slung an arm around his shoulders and urged him to bend forward, but now his frustration was evident—more than evident, in his odd football huddle position. Jonas felt a stab of sympathy for the guy, who was probably used to wrestling great white sharks in his spare time. And he probably didn't like anything that would give Thomas an edge—even if it helped his cause. "This frittering is—"

"Yeah, we got that," Fred interrupted. "Look, this is all quite weird already, thank you. Don't do anything to make it—"

"Dr. Bimm?"

Fred audibly groaned, and Jonas inwardly cheered. An exciting morning, made even better by the appearance of the yummilicious . . .

He turned. "Dr. Barb!"

Dr. Barb looked startled at the volume of his greeting, and Jonas cursed himself. "Uh, hello, Jonas. Dr. Bimm. Dr. Pearson. Ah—" She tipped her head *way* back to look at Artur. "Sir, I couldn't help but notice your voice is scaring the—"

"That's why we came over to talk to him," Fred said.

"What?" Thomas asked. Then, "Right! Dr. Bimm and I, having no lives, came to work bright and early on a Saturday, but on the way to the labs, via the jellyfish exhibit on the other end of the building, we saw this guy making a ruckus, and came over to see if he needed to be escorted out." Then, lower, "Wouldn't bother me at all to kick his ass again."

"Oh." Dr. Barb looked slightly bewildered at both the glib response and the idea of Fred a) noticing a tourist, b) caring about a ruckus and c) then deciding to tend to the problem. "Ah. Good work, Dr. Pearson and, uh, Dr. Bimm, but we have, uh, security for that sort of thing."

Fred made a noise that sounded an awful lot like "ha."

An awkward silence fell. Around them, visitors were chatting and the din was pretty good, but the five of them were just looking at each other without a word. Even the glowing jellyfish bobbed around silently. In one of the curious silences that sometimes falls over a large crowd, Madison could be clearly heard to say, "Yes, I'm doing my paper on the dolphins in Boston Harbor."

Freshly distracted, Fred practically spat. "Good God!"

"Dr. Bimm."

"There *are* no dolphins in Boston Harbor!"

Dr. Barb sighed. "Dr. Bimm."

"How did that half-wit get in to Northeastern? And why the hell are we stuck with her?"

"Dr. Bimm. Remember, the NEA is heavily dependent on charitable donations."

Dr. Barb was practically dancing from one small black flat–clad foot to the other; he imagined she'd rather go for a quick jog around the lobster tank.

Then: "Why *are* you here this morning? Neither of you is on the schedule."

"Uh," Fred began, then looked at Jonas. It must have been a long night for all three of them, because they all looked a little helpless. "We—"

Jonas coughed. "Hey, Dr. Barb, you had breakfast yet?"

"I—what?"

"The first meal of the day? Start you off right? Give you sprinting energy through the lunch hour? Eggs? Bacon? Pancakes with real Vermont maple syrup?" As if there were any acceptable substitute in New England.

"I had a cup of yogurt," she replied, blinking up at him with her exotic, almond-shaped eyes. Oooooh, he was getting that trembly/firm feeling he got whenever he talked to Dr. Barb. And not just because he knew he could give her a kick-ass makeover. "Nonfat."

"You call that breakfast?" he cried.

"Well. Yes."

"Ham and eggs, that's breakfast. Grits and anything, that's breakfast," he added, taking her by the elbow and trying not to be obvious about dragging her away from the group. "Eating nonfat yogurt is punishment for jaywalking, right? Come on, I know a great place right across the street."

"Well," she began, and it must have sounded so good she said it again. "Well . . . I couldn't be gone for long."

"Aw, who are you kidding? You probably weren't on the schedule for this morning, either."

"Well . . . I'm the one who draws up the schedule . . ."

"So cross yourself off it long enough to have a bagel with yours truly." He noticed her toes were practically skimming the tile and eased up, but didn't let go of her arm.

"Well . . . as I said, I couldn't be gone very long . . ."

"Right, right, place'd probably implode if you left for more than ninety minutes. We'll have you back in eighty-nine." *After Fred and the guys get lost.* "But you can't expect to go charging all over the NEA on yogurt. I thought you were smarter than that, Dr. Barb."

"I had no idea you were so worried about my welfare. Thank you, Jonas."

Jonas felt a thrill inside. Was it possible that Fred—dour, sour Fred—was shooting him the most grateful, sweetest smile of her life? *And* he was about to take his longtime crush on their first date?

This is the greatest day of my life! he thought, exalted, as he steered Dr. Barb past the throngs of tourists and students. He saw Madison's stare turn into a glare, but managed to give her a cheery wave. *And it's not even ten fifteen in the morning!*

Nineteen

Barb Robinson was having a puzzling morning.

First, her dry cleaner hadn't had her eight lab coats ready, so she was down to three, low starch. Having so few symbols of her authority available to her made Barb extremely nervous. How was she expected to keep order at the NEA when everyone else there was so much smarter, younger

(better-looking)

and better educated? Answer: a crisp, blinding white lab coat with her name (Dr. Barbara Robinson, Ph.D.) in red script over the left breast. She could feel her authority shoring up whenever her coat settled over her shoulders, when she buttoned it all the way to the top. She kept her long hair in a braid so everyone could see her name. So the volunteers and fellows could easily spot her.

You could, Barb had thought more than once, talk people into almost anything if you were wearing one of these things. It reeked of authority. The lab coat whispered to their subconscious, *trust me, do your work as diligently as I do, tell me your troubles, promise to work late on Friday.*

It was less effective, she thought wryly, in an Au Bon Pain.

"You want to take that off?" Dr. Bimm's nice gay friend said to her. He'd insisted on paying, almost like it was a real date, and had bought her a bagel with lox and cream cheese, and two milks. ("Dairy is dandy," Barb's nutritionist mother had been fond of saying.) "So you don't spill on it?"

"Oh, no. I'm fine. Thank you for breakfast."

Jonas gave her an odd look. "No big, Dr. Barb. You looked a little hassled."

"Oh. Well, you know. Saturday morning at the aquarium. Always a bit of a madhouse."

"Yeah, but it doesn't all need to be on your shoulders. I mean, you've got ticket takers and volunteers and stuff to worry about all that, right?"

"Well, I—yes. But the NEA is my responsibility."

"Boy, you and Fred," he muttered, working on his second chocolate croissant.

"Dr. Bimm is very dedicated to her work," Barb said proudly, for she had handpicked Dr. Bimm from a pool of several dozen highly qualified candidates, and had been justified in her decision many times over.

Of course, the odd punk hair made some of the fellows nervous, and Dr. Bimm wasn't the cheeriest employee she'd ever had, but her work was top quality and her devotion to duty was unwavering. She could think of no greater compliment to bestow upon anyone. "She is a credit to the NEA."

"Yeah, and two guesses when she had her last date." Jonas colored and Barb watched, puzzled, then realized Dr. Bimm's last date—oh, no. It couldn't have been—

"Not . . . Phillip?"

"Phillip," Jonas confirmed with his mouth full, lightly spraying her with crumbs.

"That was most likely a mistake," she admitted, taking another bite of her bagel. "But she seemed so—and we parted amicably enough—at least I did."

"If you don't mind me asking, what happened? Who'd be crazy enough to drop-kick somebody like you out of their marriage?"

Barb smiled, feeling a warm glow of pleasure. It was nice that Dr. Bimm's best

(only)

friend was so nice. It was a pure crying shame he was off the heterosexual market, with that blond hair and the incredible body which, she happened to know, he honed weekly in the dojo.

She had seen Madison flirting with him and felt sorry for the girl; she probably should have taken her aside and warned her, but Jonas's orientation was nobody's business. Certainly Madison's flirting was nobody's business also.

She realized he was waiting for an answer.

"I dumped him, actually."

"Oh."

"It was my fault, really. I just couldn't overlook all the sleeping around."

"Oh." Jonas grinned. "Don't stop now. Dish!"

She found herself telling him. How they'd met at a fund-raiser for the NEA. Both in their late thirties, both ready to settle, both wanting to get married.

But *getting* married wasn't the same as *staying* married. Phillip had really wanted someone to go to events with, someone to be on his arm. A name on a mortgage application. The ability to check the "married" box on any form. Not a living, breathing, loving wife who expected him to stay out of other beds.

"The nerve!" Jonas mock-gasped. "You and your incredibly unrealistic expectations."

"Right," she said dryly, sipping her milk.

"What a dumbass! Man, if I'd known *that*, I never would have let Fred go out with him. No offense."

"None taken. But could you have prevented Dr. Bimm?"

"Well . . . she only went because—I mean, she didn't want you to—I dunno. It was, what? Six years ago?"

"About that, yes. Who is Dr. Bimm's new friend? The large man with the red hair?"

"Oh." Jonas's blue-eyed gaze went vague, and he waved off something invisible. "Just some guy from out of town. Let's get back to the dumbass you married. I mean, he's got you and he's out cheating?"

"Uh, yes. But I—" She looked down at her lap. She'd never see forty again, she didn't get much exercise, she was devoted to her work, and she had worn her hair the same way since ninth grade. Why *wouldn't* Phillip look for something a little

(younger)

fresher? Somebody like

(Madison)

a college student?

"I guess the thought of a long-term marriage just made him feel blue," she said, her smile fading. Blue made her think of Dr. Bimm's hair, and Dr. Bimm made her think of . . . "This man, he's from out of town, you say? How does he know Dr. Pearson? And why were they all—"

"Shit!" Jonas leapt out of his chair, and she saw the dark stain spreading across his shirt.

She jumped, too, grabbed her napkins and dabbed at him frantically. "Are you all right? Are you burned? Get that shirt off," she ordered. Coffee burns could be nasty, even after all the silliness with the suit against McDonald's. If she could get the hot cloth away from his skin in time, he might not be—

In response to her command, Jonas instantly stripped off his polo shirt, revealing a lightly furred chest, gorgeous pecs, nicely defined shoulders, and a by God six-pack set of abs.

She stared.

"I don't think I'm burned."

She stared.

"Dr. Barb? Am I burned?"

She stared some more.

He clicked his fingers in her face. "Dr. Barb? Come back now."

"My God," she said at last, almost shaking herself like a dog out of a pond. "I could grate cheese on your stomach."

"Uh—maybe later."

She inspected his skin closely and after a minute actually remembered why she was staring at his taut, muscular flesh.

"You're not burned," she assured him. *She* was feeling rather warm, but that was just too bad. Jonas was always nice, always seemed pleased to see her, was always hanging around Fred, was always lugging around Aveda bags and—

"Look, let's go up the street and hit Filene's. I need a new shirt, and you've got to let me do something about those lab coats."

—loved to shop.

It just wasn't fair.

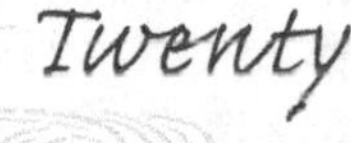

Twenty

"Ah, Little Rika. At last I have you alone."

"Sshhhh!"

Fred had Artur by the hand and was leading him to the waterline. That was tricky at the NEA on Saturday mornings, as the place was jammed. She and Artur couldn't just strip in public and leap in.

"I do not understand why we do not merely leap in."

She rolled her eyes and they crept closer. They were beneath one of the observation decks, a glorified cement dock that, luckily, led straight to the water. With luck, they'd be twenty feet in and way deep and no one would see them.

"Look, Artur, you might not care if the entire world knows what you are, but I do. I managed to keep my secret from everybody until you got to town. I don't want anybody else finding out."

"You should not feel shame for—"

She swung around and let him feel the full force of her glare. "It's not about being ashamed!"

"It is."

"Like hell! It's about not wanting to spend the rest of my life as a zoo exhibit! Do you know what the bipeds would do to me?"

"No."

"You didn't see *Splash*, did you?" Of course he hadn't. Dumb question. Next! "You've seen what they do to the planet. You've seen the NEA. It's a nice cage for the fish, but it's still a cage. I like my freedom."

"If you were to come to my home, you would know nothing but freedom."

Now, why was that idea as exciting as it was terrifying? Just being able to swim around and do whatever, with her own personal tour guide none other than the High Prince.

"I like it here," she said shortly. Which was the truth. Right?

"You like hiding? You like being a commoner?"

"I come from a long line of commoners. Strip."

"Ah, you see, Little Rika? I am yours to command."

She smiled at him (she couldn't help it; he *was* kind of funny sometimes), kicked off her shoes, and started to take off her clothes. Above her, out of sight, she could hear the excited murmuring of NEA visitors looking at the outdoor exhibits.

Artur had been about to spontaneously combust, so she figured he was due for a break. And Thomas wanted more time to number crunch. She could have stayed to help Thomas, in fact had been sorely tempted, but in the end she decided to try the harbor herself. (Not to mention, there was no telling what mischief Artur might make if left alone.) Maybe she could smell or taste something in the water that would help. Artur's senses were no doubt much better instruments than hers, but she had the scientific background he lacked.

In fact, what was his background? Did they have colleges under water?

"What are you grinning about?"

"I cannot help feeling joy that you have chosen my company over his."

"Uh, it's not about that, Artur. It's just that the last time I was in the harbor I didn't notice anything was wrong, so this time—"

"Yes, yes." He waved her perfectly logical explanation away. "Whatever your rationale, you will be with me for the rest of the morning, while the biped pushes his papers around and makes numbers."

"Careful, pal. I was almost pushing papers and making numbers with him."

His smile widened. "My point. You are not."

"This isn't a contest, you know."

His smile slipped away and all at once he looked like the predator he was. "Everything is a contest."

"Hmmph. I am going to swim now. Try to resist the urge to take a chomp out of my butt."

"I shall try, but I make no promises."

She grinned; she couldn't help it. "Okay, that came out wrong." She dipped a toe into the water, then walked in a couple of feet, enjoying the breeze. She knew she felt chilly to other people, but one of the nice things about being a hybrid was that she didn't feel much cold. Which made sense, because there were plenty of places in the ocean that were *quite* cold. It was also the reason Jonas constantly gave her shit when she wore tank tops in November.

"Wasn't it great of Jonas to get my boss out of our way?" she said suddenly. "He really helped us out there."

"You choose your allies well."

"He's not an ally, he's my . . . you know. Jonas."

"As I said."

"He really took one for the team, taking Dr. Barb out for breakfast. I've worked for the woman for six years, and I've never seen her eat. It must be like taking your speech teacher out for drinks. Weird."

"That is for Jonas to fret about," Artur pointed out, slipping into the water beside her and easing out of sight. In her mind, he finished the thought: *Not you or I.*

"That's the team spirit," she muttered, and ducked under the water. It took a few seconds for her eyes to adjust—Boston Harbor wasn't exactly the clear azure of Cabo San Lucas. She kept a wary eye out for large clumps of seaweed—just the feel of the stuff on her skin made her . . . well, it made her skin crawl! And when it got in her *hair* . . . nightmare.

Maybe that's why she considered the sea a living thing, an entity all on its own. Because so much of it was so alive. Just swimming through it, she could feel how alive it was. It wasn't just the smell or the taste or the texture . . . or, rather, it was, but it was all of that and more.

She understood intellectually how the bipeds could use the ocean as a garbage dump, but could never get it emotionally. But then, they used the atmosphere as a garbage dump, too. You just couldn't count on any of them to—

She felt something clammy on her tail and shrieked. Uh, mentally. Artur let go of her and swam up beside her.

What ails you, Little Rika?

How did you get behind me? Oh, forget it. This. THIS ails me. She clawed at her hair. *Yeeesh!*

Our mother, our home? How can you be more comfortable in a sterile inland pool?

Two words: no seaweed.

Little Rika, you never cease to amaze. Or amuse. Ah! Nice to have room to breathe again.

Yeah, it's swell.

They swam together close to the bottom, avoiding the thousands of boats and ships that had turned the harbor into a saltwater highway.

I do not deny I have often wondered what it would be like to dance in the waves with you.

Was that—? It was! She snatched the clot of seaweed out of her way and threw it as hard as she could, which, fifteen feet underwater, wasn't very.

Ick! Ick!

I admit, this is different from what I imagined.

Shut up. How could you "often wonder" anything? You haven't even been here three days yet.

My father knew his queen at once.

Bully for him. That doesn't have anything to do with me.

It could.

She chose to ignore that absurd statement and they swam in silence for a while. She swam ahead in a quick circle, then came back.

I don't smell anything so far. I mean, it's busy, you can tell it's the harbor and not the middle of the Caspian Sea; it's not exactly pure, but I'm not getting anything unusual.

The water here is not as fresh as I would like, but you are correct; neither is it poisoned. It may take us time to find the source. However will we pass the time?

Don't get any nutty ideas, Prince Grabby.

I cannot help it, Little Rika. Seeing you in your true element, your true form, with no interference from arrogant bipeds . . .

You've got nerve, calling anybody arrogant. She stopped swimming and he nearly banged into her. They bobbed together for a moment and she told him, *When I have legs, that's my true form, too, Artur. Half 'n' half, except not as creamy. Er, that could have sounded sexier.*

He put his arms around her and kissed her gently, nothing at all like the bruising, possessive kiss from earlier. Perhaps because he didn't feel he had anything to prove in the water? Away from Thomas?

She let him. What the hell. She deserved a treat after the stressful week she'd had. And kissing Artur, no doubt about it, was a treat. She felt positively tiny in his arms, cradled, protected. She had the feeling that he could handle whatever problem came up: a great white, a sarcastic barracuda.

Ah, Rika, my Rika.

Shut up. More kissing.

He chuckled and obeyed, snuggling her into his embrace. At least he didn't point out that, this way at least, they could chat about current events the entire time they were making out and never miss a smooch.

She realized they were actually bobbing upside down, but was too giddy from the kissing to care much. She felt the vibrations as one of the party yachts sped by above them, doubtless dragging more drunken tourists through the shit and—

No, she meant dragging them through the shitty harbor—shit! What was wrong with her?

Artur abruptly stopped kissing her. *Do you smell that?*

Smell it, of course I can smell it! She tried to spit. It didn't work. *I can taste it. Oh my God, I'm tasting shit!*

Artur grabbed her arm and flexed his tail, and they rocketed away from that particular spot. Despite his speed, despite his quick action, for a long, awful moment Fred was sure she was going to vomit. She struggled with the urge, thinking she must not, must not, must *not* barf in front of royalty. Not to mention, she hadn't barfed since the time she got drunk on Pepsi (a case) and vermouth (four bottles), and that had been over ten years ago. She had no plans to break her non-vomit streak.

And it was better now. She could still faintly smell it, but suspected it was more imagination than fact. The way you could still smell dog shit once you've stepped in it, no matter how often you scrubbed your shoes.

Artur had gotten them away from the stream, or the bad spot, or whatever you wanted to call it, and he had done it with speedy efficiency . . . she wouldn't have been able to swim that fast with a speargun in her ear.

Thanks, Artur. That was pretty bad for a second.

I, too, had momentary discomfort.

Oh, thought Fred. Is that what they call it?

I can't ever come swimming here again . . . I'll always think I'm smelling shit even if I'm not. We gotta fix this.

Artur nodded. He didn't try to touch her, which she figured showed as well as anything how grossed out he was, too. *Thus my father's concern when he heard the news. I, too, feel the morning has been tainted.*

That was shit. I don't mean toxins. I don't mean poisons. She was swimming for the shore as quickly as she could, Artur keeping pace with no trouble. *I mean shit. Somebody's gonna pay. And I don't mean EPA fines, either. I mean pay through the NOSE.*

I quite agree, Little Rika . . . and it is a pleasant change to see your anger directed at a head other than my own.

It was shallow enough for her to stand, and she did, her legs as always forming without conscious thought. She shook her wet hair and managed to smile at him as he emerged beside her. "Some romantic swim, huh?"

He spat. "As I said. Not quite what I had envisioned."

Twenty-one

Thomas nearly jumped out of his skin when the door to his lab was thrown open and Fred, the mermaid of his dreams, snarled, "Some tin prick is throwing his shit into the harbor."

He turned away from the slides and microscope. Fred was splendidly drippy, her green hair plastered to her head, her T-shirt almost transparent in a couple of interesting places, her feet bare and pink and comely. She carried her shoes in one hand. The pretentious lug from the Black Sea, Artur, was looming behind her like a mugger, carrying his own shoes.

Where does he get clothing? Thomas wondered.

"Are you paying attention?" she demanded.

"Yeah, Fred, I know. It's why I'm here, remember?"

Fred stomped toward him. He wasn't sure whether to back up or try for a kiss. Since her hands were both in fists, he decided to compromise and stay where he was. He could hold his own in a fight, but he imagined Fred could rip him in half without much trouble.

And that redheaded bum, Artur, would be happy to help.

"You're not listening," she said, jabbing a bony finger at his chest. "Somebody is dumping his *shit* in the harbor. *Literal* shit."

"Oh, great," he groaned. "That's really nice. How lovely. Right into the harbor. Did you get a noseful?"

Her lips made an odd twisting motion, like she wanted to spit but was stopping herself. "I got a *mouthful*, feels like. It still feels like."

"All right. Well. I'm sorry to hear that, but it's actually helpful."

"How could you not know, with all your papers, what it was?" Artur demanded.

Thomas gave the lug a look. "It's a big ocean, Artur. And shit, for want of a better term, is all natural. It can be mixed up with a few things, I'm sorry to say." He took a breath and turned back to Fred. "Anyway, thanks for telling me this. I'm sorry you had to get a snootful, but at least it narrows down—"

"I figured. That's why we came to tell you."

"I was just over at City Hall and got copies of all building permits granted to anyone in a three-square-mile radius—" He gestured at the new pile of paper. "That, coupled with the fact that none of the Undersea Folk noticed the, uh, shit until recently, and *you* didn't notice, and the fact that it's, you know, *shit*, makes me think it's a new building."

"Duh." Fred, his darling, looked annoyed she hadn't thought of it herself. "It's a hotel."

"Why do you think this?" the big red lug asked.

"New building by the harbor? That amount of shit? It's a new hotel. They probably played fast and loose with the city council and now there's a pipe in the wrong place, dumping the crap of tourists into our harbor."

"A hotel like the building in which Thomas and I reside? A place strangers call home for a short period of time?"

"Yeah. And every room has a bathroom. And all that water—and what it takes away—has to go somewhere. It should go to a treatment plant first. Unless someone cut corners."

"Contrary to what they taught us in *Finding Nemo*, all pipes do not lead to the ocean. Unless you design them that way."

Artur looked revolted. "You bipeds never fail to astonish. Do you not realize—"

Thomas swallowed his annoyance, figuring that if the two of them had had to choke down shit earlier, he could hold his temper. "Stop lumping us into one category. I'd no sooner dump my own waste into a body of water than I'd run over a cat. *I'm* the one who showed up and told Fred the problem. *I'm* the one who's done all the research. *I'm* the one who spent the morning in City Hall. And *I'm* the one who's been at work while you two went off for a romantic swim."

"Poor you," Fred sneered. "I guarantee your morning wasn't as miserable as ours."

Artur looked wry. "I had thought it would be romantic, and it was. Until . . ."

Thomas almost smiled. He had not been happy, at all, when Fred had taken off with the big red lug, but at least the guy hadn't gotten very far during his alone time. Bad news: the guy was a prince. Good news: Fred didn't care. Bad news: the guy was huge and great looking and could show her a world the average person would never know. Good news: Fred didn't care.

Besides, Thomas figured, *I can show her a thing or two right here on dry land, I bet. And I won't give her crap for being half-and-half, like some of Artur's people would.*

Fred was picking through the plans piled on his desk, looking intrigued. Artur watched her, shifting his weight impatiently.

Ha! Got her. He knew the scientist in her couldn't stay away from the lab for long. Sure, Artur was a fellow Undersea Folk, but eight years of formal schooling left its mark, no matter if you grew a tail to swim or just put on swimming trunks from Target.

He watched her open up a plan and read it. Even from the back, she was breathtaking. Long, graceful limbs, and that hair . . . and that gorgeous, pretty tail. Green in some lights and blue in others, it was like a peacock tail, except a million times sexier.

He was aware that he had built Fred up in his mind because of what she was and not who she was. His mother had told him so many stories of mermaids that by the time he was ten, he was hopelessly besotted with the idea of jumping into the ocean and finding a friend who could follow his family all over the world.

Whereas his mother entertained him for hours with her wonderful stories (*The Little Mermaid*, *The Mermaid Wife*, *The Sea Morgan's Baby*), his father was simply not around much—he went where the navy sent him. And when you were the new kid and knew you'd be moving in another eight or ten or twelve months, there really wasn't much point in making friends.

So he read. And dreamed. And listened to stories. And *dreamed* . . .

Even before he knew Fred's secret, he was taken with her. She was the first woman scientist he'd ever met who wasn't, on a subconscious level at least, interested in male feedback. Or even aware the person she was interacting with *was* male. She was also the first woman—person—who wasn't paralyzed by conventional mores and standards of behavior. What she thought, she thought, and if people didn't like it, she didn't care. Or notice.

He blessed the impulse that had brought him back to work the night before, figuring he'd fight insomnia with toxin tables. And then he'd seen her, lazily swimming back and forth in Main One, her gorgeous blue-green tail shimmering, her long arms making graceful sweeping motions as she fed the fish, her green hair floating around her face in a gorgeous cloud that looked like liquid emeralds.

He had honestly thought, for a long moment, that his heart was going to stop. It just didn't seem possible. It was a hallucination brought on by fatigue and bad pizza. He had snapped under the pressure of not getting laid for seven months.

And then he'd stared some more. She didn't notice him right away, so he could look his fill. And he finally convinced himself: Fred, the cool, distant woman he'd met earlier, was a mermaid. An honest to God mermaid!

He couldn't help it: he'd raced to the top of the stairs and, once there, had to touch her. *Had* to. And once his hands were on her, his lips soon followed. Because here was the living embodiment of all his childhood fantasies, and he had no plans to let her go.

Ever.

And if a certain big red lug got in his way . . . well. He had a few ideas about how to stop a member of the Undersea Folk. And not just with aikido.

"Why don't you have a seat?" he said with forced politeness to Artur. "It looks like Fred and I will be here for a while. You know, frittering with paperwork and other things you're bad at."

Artur gave him a black look, but said nothing.

"Careful," Fred warned. "That's your new roommate you're irritating. It'll make your nightcap together awkward."

He grimaced. He was already regretting the mad impulse that had prompted him to offer up his suite to Artur. Still, in his own way, he was fascinating, and Thomas had plenty of questions for the man.

Too bad they were rivals. He knew it. Artur knew it. Jonas even appeared to get it.

Everybody but the object of their adoration, who was even now bitching, "Thomas, is English your fourth language? I can barely read your writing."

"Shut up," he said warmly. "You've got bigger problems than my writing."

"Impossible," she said, looking alarmed.

"If it's a new hotel—let's see, who do we know who just popped up at the NEA whose parents are rich and own half the waterfont?"

Now she was looking positively revolted. "No."

"There is a suspect?" Artur asked.

"No," Fred snapped.

"I'm just saying," Thomas added.

"No."

"It wouldn't hurt to talk to her."

Fred grimaced. "Obviously you haven't talked to her."

"Oh, I have, honey, believe me. She threw a pass at me that nearly knocked me unconscious with its subtlety."

"How awful for you," Fred sneered.

He ignored the sarcasm. "That whole 'look at me, I'm a sub-human twit' thing could be a front."

"Olivier wasn't that good an actor."

"Have it your way. But you have to admit, it's an interesting coincidence. And talking to Madison Fehr can't be worse than sucking down shit." Her glare was so sizzling, he nearly flinched, and changed the subject. "I'm getting pretty hungry. Are you guys?"

Both Undersea Folk looked positively ill.

"Oh. Sorry. Yeah, that'd put me off my feed for a while, too. But I can't help being hungry. It's lunchtime."

"Well, Jonas can run out and get you something . . ." Fred suddenly looked around, then looked at her watch. "Where the hell *is* Jonas? Not still with Dr. Barb, I hope. Poor guy."

Thomas thought of the way Jonas had run off with Dr. Barb, who was in awfully good shape and pretty young to be running the NEA, and didn't think the guy had it so bad at all.

"Hey, Artur. Maybe you could get me a sandwich." He couldn't resist.

He chuckled at the prince's expression, deciding it was worth Fred's sigh of exasperation. Yes, the day was definitely looking up.

Twenty-two

"Okay, come out."

"Jonas, I can't."

"Will you come out already? How can I tell you how it looks if you won't let me see?"

"I'll tell you how it looks. It looks silly."

"I'll be the judge of that, Dr. Lab Coat. Out."

Blushing to her eyebrows, Dr. Barb pushed open the dressing room door and stepped into the tiny hallway. She was wearing one of the four outfits Jonas had bullied her into trying on and, in his opinion, the most flattering.

It was a navy two-piece suit, the skirt falling softly just above the knee, the jacket double-breasted and held together in the middle by one big button. And it was a Givenchy. *On sale!*

Jonas stared at the button. "We have to pick out a bra in the same color as the jacket."

"No we do *not*. Jonas, I feel half naked in this thing! You can see my brassiere, for heaven's sake."

"News flash, Dr. Barb: people stopped saying brassiere forty years ago."

"I'm trying to be an authority figure not a—a Playmate of the Month."

"Barb, bras are trendy right now. Women are buying strappy tees and then buying bras so they can coordinate. And don't forget the whale-tail trend—you know, when you can see a woman's thong above the waistline of her jeans?"

"That," she said firmly, "was a trend for the young."

"Well, the young can't afford this suit. Showing an inch of the front of your bra is hardly the same as forgetting to wear shorts and bending over a tractor to be Miss February."

Her face went, if possible, even redder, and without a word she turned around to duck back inside the changing room, but he caught her by the elbow and gently pulled her back. "Come on, let me get a good look," he coaxed. "I think it's fabulous. Let me tell you why."

He led her to the three mirrors at the end of the room. "See, the skirt is long enough so you don't look like an escapee from the *Ally McBeal* set, but short enough to show off your legs. You have really terrific legs. And the color is awesome. Brings out your eyes, puts some color in your cheeks, even brightens up your hair. Which we'll get to in a minute. Now, the jacket . . . wrist-length sleeves, but not too much padding in the shoulders, so you don't look like you've OD'd on *I Love the 80s.* The cut in the front really doesn't show much skin. See, you could wear this under an open—*open*—lab coat and look like a million bucks, and still be the boss, and show everybody how gorgeous you are at the same time."

She tried to pull away. "Oh, Jonas, you're sweet, but I'm not—"

"That is a gorgeous forty-year-old woman in there," he said, not letting go of her arm, and pointing to the mirror with his other hand. "Sexy and smart and The Boss. I mean, what could possibly be hotter than that?"

"Forty-five. As my ex never failed to remind me," she added, a little bitterly, "I'm never going to see thirty again."

"Fuck your ex. I think this is the one. We should get this one. And a matching bra."

Dr. Barb stared at herself for a long minute. "Well. The color *is* nice."

"The color is fucking phenomenal, I'm telling you, it brings out all your natural color, brightens up your—oh, right. Your hair."

She clutched her braid and tried to back away. "Never mind my hair."

"Come on, Dr. Barb. All I'm asking is that you cut two feet off of it."

"No!"

"But it would look *so* much better if it wasn't dragging your whole face down. I'm thinking layers around your face, and shoulder length. And," he added slyly, "everybody could still read your name on the coat."

"No, Jonas. No. Not the hair."

"Yes, the hair, listen, trust me. I'm an impartial observer. Besides, you think I do this for every woman?"

"Certainly you've never done it for Dr. Bimm," she said slyly, and he laughed. She looked at the mirror, and it was almost like his laughing reflection helped her make up her mind. "All right. I'll take it. But when the board fires me for dressing like a slut, I'm moving in with you."

"Done," he said fervently. "Okay, hurry up. We've got time to hit the lingerie counter and then it'll be lunchtime."

"*Lunch*time?" Dr. Barb practically shrieked, looking at her watch. "Oh, Lord! I should have been back—"

"Dr. Barb, what in the world is the use of being The Boss if you can't fuck off for a Saturday? I mean, a *Saturday*. Come on."

"You are very bad for me, Jonas," she scolded, stepping into the dressing room and (rats!) closing the door. "You are a bad, bad boy."

He leaned against the wall so he wouldn't fall down. God, he loved the older teacher type thing she had going, but when she *scolded* him! He hoped to God she didn't notice the raging boner lurking in his boxers.

"I never even let Phillip pick out my clothes," she said from the other side of the door, and laughed. "I can't imagine what he'd think of this."

"He'd think 'when did I turn into the world's biggest dumb shit?' is what he'd think."

She laughed and he heard the sound of rustling clothing. He squashed the urge to mash his ear against the door and imagine what she was putting on. Or taking off. "Considering the fact that you never had the pleasure of meeting him, you certainly have strong opinions about him!"

"He's a dumbass. Anybody who'd let you go isn't worth a nanosecond of my time. Or yours."

"Oh, Jonas," she sighed. There was more of that tantalizing rustling. "You're so very good for my ego!"

Twenty-three

"Dr. Bimm is lucky to have a friend like you," Dr. Barb was saying over arctic char half an hour later. They were at the Legal's right by the NEA, within sight of the building in her charge. As long as she was sitting where she could see tourists weren't stampeding out, or the building wasn't collapsing in flames, she was almost relaxed. "It was so sweet of you to take me shopping. Especially when you were the one who needed a new shirt."

Note to self: Fred owes me a new shirt. I ruined a Ralph Lauren polo for that ungrateful harpy! "Yeah, well, I was free. And it was fun. I love to shop. And I got three new shirts out of it, too." Dr. Barb had insisted on paying for his clothes, even though he'd dumped his coffee on himself on purpose. And Fred *still* owed him a new shirt. He could have been scalded to death!

"I don't understand how it's possible for a man like you to have a free Saturday. Why haven't you ever settled down, Jonas? Too young?"

He laughed. "You're talking like you're ready for a nursing home. You've only got about fifteen years on me."

Dr. Barb looked away. "Ah—don't remind me. But let's get back to you. Why hasn't someone snapped you up?"

"Well. I've been—I mean, you know, I see people. I get out. A helluva lot more than you NEA geeks, that's for sure."

She raised an eyebrow at him. "I think you should set your goals a bit higher."

He laughed again. "Right, right." The waitress brought him his appletini and a ginger ale for Dr. Barb. They clinked glasses. "To the new, sexy, awesomely gorgeous you, who really isn't new, but now other people will figure it out, too."

She blushed—God, he didn't know women still *did* that!—and they clinked glasses again. Then he resumed the chatter that either irritated Fred or bored the hell out of her, but which the luscious Dr. Barb appeared to find fascinating.

"Anyway, I see people and go out and there's always a party going on and stuff like that, but I just, you know, haven't found that special someone."

"That's amazing to me. You must have people lining up."

"Well . . . I don't know about that . . . but I've kind of got a crush on someone. So it makes it hard to want to get to know someone *else*, get it?"

Dr. Barb nodded. "Of course, I understand perfectly. What is that you're drinking? It's the color of lamb jelly."

"Appletini. Try."

She picked up his glass and took a sip, raised her eyebrows, and took another one. "Oh. That's wonderful! I'll have one when I'm not working."

"You're *not* working today, Dr. Barb."

She giggled. *Giggled.* He thought it was adorable. He wanted her to do it again. *Maybe if I juggled?* "Oh yes I am. I'm going back after lunch."

"You can't. After lunch we're going to Sergei's."

"Who?"

"Only the hottest stylist in town right now, booked for months, but he owes me a favor—I introduced him to his husband—so he'll see you. And he'll give you a discount on the cut."

She shook her head and set his glass down. "No, Jonas. No haircut. No Sergei."

"But you're so close to goddess-hood!" he wailed.

"Goddess-hood? Oh, Jonas. We have to stop. You're going to give me a swelled head. Soon I'll forget I'm a middle-aged frump and then where would we be?"

He stared at her. "Frump? *Frump?*" he repeated, incredulous. Okay, maybe that last one was a little loud; the table in front of them turned to look. "Dr. Barb, when we were in that department store with all the mirrors, did you bother to look in any of them? You're as far from a frump as—as—" He groped for a simile. Or was it a metaphor? "As Fred is from Miss Congeniality."

She reached across the table and took his hand. Took. His. *Hand!* "Jonas, you're so sweet. You've given my ego such a boost, I can't thank you enough. And I'm thrilled that you see me that way, really I am, even if I can't quite make that leap myself. Now, you've done so much for me, I'd like to do something for you. Tell me about this crush you have. Maybe we can get you hooked up, as the kids say."

Oh. Gulp. "Well . . . I've known this person for years but haven't really screwed up the courage to get to know them very well. I can hardly even be in the same room—you know how it is."

Dr. Barb nodded. "Now, Jonas, you listen to me."

"Sterner."

She looked puzzled, but raised and hardened her voice. "Now, Jonas, you listen to me." He got all tingly when she used her schoolteacher voice. "You are a wonderful guy: handsome, funny, smart, sweet. You're going to make some man very happy. The trick is finding Mr. Right, as they say."

"What?"

"You've got a lot to offer some lucky fellow, and I'm sure the gentleman you've got a crush on will see that if you can just get to know him a little better."

"But—" In his surprise, he blurted out the truth. "But *you're* the gentleman I've got a crush on!"

They stared at each other. Dr. Barb froze with her ginger ale halfway to her mouth. And Jonas cursed himself. This wasn't the first time a woman had assumed he was gay, but he never dreamed that Dr. Barb would think—Couldn't she tell he could hardly keep his hands—Couldn't she *tell*?

"But—you're gay. You're Dr. Bimm's gay best friend."

"I'm not gay."

"But you are."

"Dr. Barb," he snapped, "I think I would know, okay? Trust me, I'm not even bi. I'm just very very very secure in my masculinity, okay?"

Color began to climb in her face. "But—you like to—"

"Metrosexual."

"But you also like—"

"Secure in my masculinity."

Now she was red-faced and stammering. "But I—I never s-see you w-with any girls—women, I mean—"

"You've never seen me with anybody."

She closed her mouth so quickly, he heard the click of her teeth coming together. When she spoke, her voice was very small and she sort of breathed the whole thing out, really fast.

"YoumeanI'mtheoneyou'vehadacrushonallthistime?"

"Sure. I liked you the first time I saw you, even though you were wearing that awful green pantsuit under your lab coat."

"But Jonas—I'm so much older than—"

He snorted. "Fifteen years—"

"Sixteen, I believe."

"Big deal, that hardly makes you Methuselah. And I *love* older women. Love. Them. Especially really smart ones. Especially authority figures. Especially—never mind, I think you've had enough shocks for one day."

"It's just that I never—I mean, Fred never—and I never had—I mean you never said—I mean—" She was looking around wildly, possibly for the fire exit.

"Believe it or not, I know what you're thinking. You thought you were having a totally platonic sexual tension–free morning with a gay guy who would never ever have sex with you, and now that you're replaying the morning, you've realized we were actually on a date and I saw your bra in the dressing room."

She was spry, that Dr. Barb. She was on her feet and he hadn't seen her move. "No, I'm—it's impossible. It's just not possible." She threw her napkin down on the table.

"Which part? The part where I've been crushing on you for six years, or the fact that you've been the object of my fantasies? Or the part where I think you're hot and gorgeous? Or the part where I'm not crushing on Colin Farrell instead of you?"

But he was talking to nobody. She had turned and run out of the restaurant.

"Waitress! Three more, please."

He laid his head on the table, pulled out his cell, and stabbed Fred's number.

"What?"

"Dr. Barb's on her way back."

"Okay. We've done about all we can here, anyway. Everybody wants to break for something to eat. Wanna come?"

"Frankly, no."

"Oh. Are you all right? You sound kind of . . . hollow."

"My heart has been stomped on."

"So no lunch then?"

"No."

"Okay, well, bye."

Fred hung up. He didn't hold it against her. It just wasn't in her nature, when she was working on a thorny problem, to notice anything else. Or anyone else.

Besides, for once in his life, he had no urge to tell Fred anything. At all.

Twenty-four

Fred hung up. "He sounded weird."

"I've just met him, but are you surprised?"

"No, really, even for Jonas." She shrugged. She had enough problems right now. "I'll talk to him later. He'll magically show up and find me, probably when I least expect it. That's his superpower."

"Ah. I wondered if bipeds had any abilities beyond destruction."

"Well," Thomas said cheerfully, opening the door for Fred, "some of us can toss princes ass over teakettle into fish tanks."

Fred snickered; she couldn't help it—it *had* been funny. Thomas stepped in behind her, neatly cutting Artur off so that he nearly walked into the door frame. Artur in turn gave Thomas a "friendly" shove—and he nearly went sprawling into the wall.

She turned and frowned. "Play nice, you two."

"What?" Thomas said innocently.

"Little Rika, you have a suspicious mind."

"I have a headache from the trouble you two are causing, not to mention all the shit that's probably still in my lungs." That was a small lie; she didn't have a headache. She never got sick. But still. They were driving her to one, and that was bad enough.

"Legal's okay?" Thomas was asking, shouldering into a leather jacket. "Or do you want to go back to that sushi place? Art? You need raw fish?"

"No. I can eat many of your foods."

"Uh, you guys—aren't you going to be cold? I mean, it's probably only sixty degrees outside today." He gestured to their T-shirts and shorts.

Fred and Artur looked at each other, then at Thomas. "No."

"Oh. Right. Well then. Fancy? Or fast? Raw or cooked? Or Souper Salad? Subway? Clam Shack?"

"Let's go to Faneuil Hall," Fred suggested. "Artur can get a look at all kinds of stuff. And there's bound to be something there for all three of us." Also: she loved Faneuil Hall. Well. The food. Not the crowds.

It was only a few blocks from the NEA, and they were there after five minutes of brisk walking. Brisk walking in silence, Fred was relieved to see. She felt exhausted: not just physically—in fact, not physically at all—her brain was tired. Being around Artur and Thomas was like walking a tightrope. Made of glass. In bare feet.

And their little shit problem—when she got hold of the nasty fuck who was dumping his crap into the ocean, they were going to have a long talk. Possibly in the ICU.

The sights and smells of Faneuil Hall lifted her spirits, and she quickened her step so that she was almost running to the food stalls. Even better, at this time of day, it was hardly even that crowded.

"Is this a gathering place for your people?"

"Only the hungry ones."

Artur sniffed appreciatively. "I smell . . ."

"Everything."

"Everything?"

"Pretzels, steamed clams, clam chowder, hamburgers, turkey legs, ice cream, sushi, gelato, bagels, doughnuts, pizza, chocolate chip cookies, milk." Fred took a breath. "Smoothies, rice, curry, noodles, frozen yogurt, lemonade, enchiladas, milkshakes."

The marketplace was brilliantly lit, and they went into the main building, which, from one end to the other, was stall after stall of food.

"Great oceans," Artur gasped. "I have never seen so much food in one place!"

"Do you guys even cook your food?" Thomas asked. He tried to sound idly curious, but Fred wasn't fooled; there was barely contained eagerness there for anyone who cared to see it.

"At times we collect on land and have feasts, yes. The ones who can build and control fire are revered in our culture."

"I'll bet."

"But never in all my years—"

"How old are you, anyway?"

"I have forty-nine years," Artur answered absently, his gaze shifting from Steve's Greek Cuisine to La Pastaria.

"For . . . forty-*nine*? As in, almost fifty?" Fred was shocked. If asked, she would have put Artur at early thirties. "Wow! You're way older than I am."

"That makes sense, though." Thomas put his big warm hand on her face. "Cool to the touch. I bet your BP's in the basement, too. Sluggish heartbeat. And all that time in the water, of course. Keeps you looking young. Because you don't look twenty-nine, gorgeous. Not even close."

"How'd you know how old I was?"

"Took the time to find out," he said carelessly, like it was no big deal. Like it wasn't borderline stalking.

She took his hand away and gave him a look. "Well. It's true, I get carded everywhere I go. But—"

"You know, Fred, I think it's great that you don't look your age. I mean, I don't care how old you are. I wouldn't care if you were an ancient, drooling, doddering old man like Artur is."

She grinned. "Watch it, pal. You may have flipped him once; but I get the idea you might have gotten lucky that first time."

"Not lucky enough. You were naked, as I recall."

"Thomas. I didn't have legs. And, by necessity, the place between them."

"A guy can dream, can't he?"

She laughed. "I can't tell if you're open-minded or just a pervert."

He edged closer. "Find out," he said, his breath warm on her lips. She couldn't help it; she closed her eyes and moved closer to his warmth, and—

"You two! Come at once! I require a King Corn Dog!"

Thomas groaned and backed off. "Honey, I thought we were going to get a sitter for the baby."

She snorted and trotted after Artur. He was standing in the middle of the walkway (bad Faneuil etiquette, but she'd tell him later) staring wildly all around. It almost looked like he wanted to try everything at—

"I also require a bread bowl of clam chowder and a fruit cup and a Frappuccino and an éclair."

"Jeez, Artur, I didn't win the lottery on the way over here. Hey, rich romance novelist! Get over here!"

"Oh, bad enough he's living with me? I have to pay to feed him, too?"

"Produce the money items from your clothing," Artur commanded. "I shall start with the éclair."

It was great fun watching Artur sample everything from coffee-flavored gelato to a chicken sandwich. He had a stomach of iron and was inexhaustible. He even wore Thomas out; the guy finally just handed Artur a bunch of twenties and sat back to watch.

"You don't have any allergies that I as your roommate should know about, do you?" Thomas asked, nervously watching Artur slurp down another Frappuccino.

"By my father's name, this food is fit for a king! I ought to know. What is this?"

"Lo mein."

"And this?"

"A sugar cookie."

"And this?"

"A lobster roll."

"And this?"

"A slice of pepperoni pizza."

"Mmmph," Artur said. He had pretty good table manners for a man mastering eight cuisines at once.

"I have to admit," Thomas said, grinning, "this is a shitload more fun than I thought it was going to be. Wait 'til he discovers room service."

"Don't say 'shit,'" Fred groaned. She picked at her salad. "My appetite was almost coming back."

Artur shoved a lobster roll under her nose and she recoiled. "Artur, I'm allergic! I'll puke for half an hour if I eat that thing."

"Little Rika, you do not know what riches you deny yourself." A small bit of lobster roll hit Fred on the left cheek; she brushed it away. "I wish the High King were here. He loves a fine feast."

"Maybe you should go home," Thomas suggested with all the subtlety of a sledgehammer. "I mean, to bring him back for a visit. Someday."

"Someday, perhaps." Artur was in too good a mood to be baited. "Again my thanks, good host."

Thomas waved it away. "Glad you're enjoying it. They open in the morning, in case you want to come back for breakfast."

"Ah. Breakfast!"

Fred smirked and forked a cherry tomato into her mouth.

Twenty-five

The next morning, Fred grimly followed the sound of the singing. It was (ugh!) "Part of Your World" from the Disney (ugh!) soundtrack. The voice was a perfectly on-key soprano, pleasant and carrying, and Fred followed it all the way up the stairs to the top level of Main One. It was after hours, and, thank heavens—no crowds. But it also meant that she had Madison (bleah) to herself.

At the top of the tank she found Madison, leaning over the edge and crooning to the fish.

"Stop that immediately," she ordered, resisting the urge to clock the woman on the side of the head with the bucket of fish.

Madison jumped. "Oh! Hi, Dr. Bimm! I didn't hear you come up. You're rilly rilly quiet."

"How could you hear anything over all that yowling? What are you doing?"

"Oh, it's one of my theories, like," the girl explained helpfully, dressed in a pink shell top and a miniskirt so brief it looked like linen panties. *Real* appropriate for the workplace. "I think the fish do better if they can hear pleasant things like music 'n' stuff."

Know any Pet Shop Boys? "Yeah, that's . . . yeah." She peered into Main One and dropped a smelt, which was quickly scooped up by a passing barracuda. Excellent. The strike, brief as it was, appeared to be over. She'd pop into her scuba suit after she finished interrogating the idiot and feed them properly.

The idiot was talking; better pay attention.

"You're the marine biologist, Dr. Bimm. What do you think?" She blinked her big blue eyes at Fred and twisted a blonde curl around one finger.

"About what?"

"About singing to the fish. Do you think it helps them?"

You don't want to know what I think. "So, your parents are rich, huh?" She cursed herself; Thomas would be better at this. And Jonas would be masterful at it. But the crumb had disappeared and Thomas was ass-deep in lab work. And Artur would probably scare the hell out of this twit. "Old Boston family and all that?"

"Umm-hmm."

"So what brings you here?"

Her big blue eyes got, if possible, bigger. "Oh, Dr. Bimm, I've just wanted to work with dolphins since I was just a kid."

"Since the Dark Ages, huh?" Fred watched the younger woman dabble her long pink fingers in the water. *Hope one of the turtles mistakes those for shrimp,* she thought viciously. "You're aware there are no dolphins at the NEA?"

"Huh?"

"There. Are. No. Dolphins. At the NEA." *You. Fucking. Idiot.*

Madison smirked. "Not yet."

"Oh." Fred thought that one over. "Your folks are buying you dolphins and plunking them into a new tank in the NEA?"

"After they fund the new habitat."

That made sense. It was stupid, but it made sense. "So that's why you're here?"

"Of course!"

"But what if it takes longer than the length of your internship?"

"Oh, Dr. Barb said I could, like, volunteer here as a long as I wanted."

"Of course she did. Your folks haven't, uh, built a new hotel and designed the bathroom pipelines to empty into the bay, have they?"

"Ewwwwwwwwwwww!"

"Interview over," Fred said, bored, and left. The strains of "Part of Your World" followed her all the way down the stairs, out the door, and onto the cobblestones.

Twenty-six

She pounded on Jonas's door for the third time, pressed her ear to the wood, and—yep, she was positive. Someone was rustling around inside.

"Jonas, open the damned door! It's been three days! If I find you dead in there it's going to be a *huge* inconvenience for me!"

More sinister rustling.

"Jonas! You have until I count to one. Then I'm kicking your door in and you'll lose your security deposit. Ready? One—"

She raised a foot just as the door swung wide. Jonas stood there, wrapped in the goose down quilt from his bed. His blond hair stood up in clumps, not the carefully moussed waves he usually spent hours coaxing to life. His eyes were bloodshot. And for the first time in recorded history, he wasn't wearing Aramis cologne.

"My God. You look like the run half of a hit-and-run. Where the hell have you been?"

"Dying," he said hollowly.

"Well, it's going around because Dr. Barb's got it, too."

She'd been following him past piles of takeout boxes and nearly walked into him when he stopped short. "She has? I mean, she hasn't been coming to work?"

"Yeah. Which makes it easier to sneak the guys in, but it's seriously weird not having her there. Nobody can remember her ever being sick. I mean, it's gotta be a plague of some sort."

"Of some sort," he mumbled.

"God, it reeks in here. You've got some explaining to do, chum. How could you disappear for three whole days like that? Artur and Thomas have been driving me up a goddamned tree."

"Leave me alone," he moaned, plopping facedown onto his couch. "Can't you see I'm dying?"

"You're not dying. You're sulking. What's wrong, did Sergei pack up his salon and leave town? Did Ralph Lauren stop making shirts?"

"Worse," he said hollowly.

Fred was stymied. Jonas didn't have problems. Ever. She was the one who was often plunged into despair.

She played the guilt card. "You haven't called, you haven't come around—I was half afraid you had left town without saying anything to me."

"Sorry."

Time for the sympathy card. "Uh—cheer up?"

"I appreciate the effort, Fred. Go away now."

She prowled around the living room, racking her brain. "Uh—want some breakfast?"

"No."

"Come on. Pull yourself together. Whatever it is, it's not any worse than my problems. It can't be."

He sighed and rolled over to face her. "Fred, just because they're not your problems doesn't mean they're not problems."

"Oh yeah? Try this on for size. If Thomas isn't trying to steal kisses, Artur is. And Artur is going to blow pretty soon; we've been spending a lot of time in the lab because I have zero interest in jumping into the shithole that is Boston Harbor."

"What?"

"See? If you'd been hanging around you'd know. The mysterious toxins? It's shit."

"You mean—literally?"

"Oh yeah. Gah, I can still smell it. So we've been going through permit paperwork and toxin reports and all that happy crappy—literal happy crappy, I guess—and we finally narrowed it down to a couple of suspects, one of which I was able to eliminate, but not until I'd heard way too much singing, and now, I'm sorry to say, we're taking the *Lollipop* out today."

He looked alarmed. "Fred, you can't get on a boat."

"I know."

"You're terrible on boats!"

"I tried to tell them. But the alternative is letting them go alone, and they'll probably beat each other to death."

"Your love life is twice as exciting as mine."

"This kind of excitement I can do without. And they're not in love with me. It's just an infatuation."

"Sure it is."

"Don't start that whole 'Fred dismisses love because she has a fear of abandonment' bull again."

"But you do. And you do." Jonas stared at the ceiling. "I'm in love. I finally told her."

"And?" Fred assumed it was going to be awkward.

"She ran out. *Ran.*"

"Oh, ouch. Who is this bim? Just point her out. See how well she can run when I break both her legs."

He sighed. "Tempting, for all sorts of reasons, but never mind."

"Well, forget the loser. Whoever she is, you can do better."

"She's not a loser," he snapped, showing signs of life. "Don't call her that again."

"Jonas, if she couldn't see how wonderful you are, she's a big fat stupid giant loser and I never plan to call her anything else."

"I've been in love with her for six years."

"Uh—time heals all wounds?"

"Nice try."

"Look, clean yourself up and come down to the NEA with me. It'll do you good to get out. And I could really use your help. You're so good at distracting the guys from hurting each other."

He sighed again. "I can't."

"How come?"

"I don't have any underwear."

"Since when," she demanded, "do you feel the need to wear underwear every day?"

He thought about that for a moment. Then: "Point." And went to take a shower.

Twenty-seven

The *Lollipop* was moored at the NEA dock beside the *Voyager III*, which tourists used for whale watches. Much smaller, the *Lollipop*—

"As in, 'the good ship'?" Jonas asked. "Get it? No? Never mind."

—was for the aquarium's scientific expeditions and research. As a water fellow, Thomas could sign it out and commandeer the crew whenever he wished; so could Fred.

With Dr. Barb's permission, of course. But she wasn't around, so they dodged that bureaucratic bullet nicely.

"See?" she said, forcing cheer that sounded unnatural. "Isn't it nice to be out on this beautiful, um, autumn day?"

"It's raining." Jonas turned up his coat collar.

"Oh, a little water won't hurt you. Take it from me. At least you're getting some fresh air. Want to come on the boat?"

"With you?" He shuddered, the insensitive creep. "Absolutely not. No way. No. I'm only here because you bullied me out of my safe cocoon. Once I bid you toodle-loo, I'm sinking back into despair."

"I promise I'll sit in one spot and not move."

"Fred. No."

"Okay, okay. It's probably all for the best."

They heard clomping noises at the far end of the dock and turned to see Artur and Thomas heading toward them.

"Oh, like Undersea Folk never take a shit in the ocean!"

"Our shit, as you put it, breaks down when exposed to seawater.

Certainly we do not pump concentrated loads of it into our living room."

"I've had about enough of the smug routine, Artur. Show me the living breathing person who never screws up and I'll show you nobody alive on the planet."

"But surely you agree that your kind 'screws up' at a level unsurpassed by any other species. And many who 'screw up' aren't in fact making a mistake at all. They do it purposefully, and generally for the sake of conquest."

"Profit, really."

"Same thing."

"A million Undersea Folk running around the oceans eating all the raw fish they can get their hands on, and you guys aren't causing *any* damage?"

"You did not know of our existence until this week."

"Yeah, but every culture has mermaid legends. They sprang from somewhere, pal. People didn't just pull the stories out of their asses. And you guys probably control those krakens that yanked all those seventeeth-century European ships into the water, killing—"

"I tire of this topic."

"Tough nuts. We—"

"Ah, my boys," Fred said with mock fondness. "What would I do without them? They've quit with testing each other physically, so now it's debate, debate, debate. Kill me now."

"You don't get off that lucky," Jonas muttered.

Fred was about to retort when her cell rang. Irritably, she plucked it off her hip and flipped it open. "Yeah?"

"Dr. Bimm?" It was Dr. Barb. "I see by the sheet that you and Thomas are signing out the *Lollipop* today."

Oops. "Yeah."

"I think, in light of what happened last time, I feel strongly that—wait. I'll come out."

"But—" Fred was talking to a dead line. "Dammit. Good thing you're here, Jonas. I'm going to need you to distract—"

"Good morning, Little Rika."

"Hey, Fred."

"Howdy, fellas." She pulled Jonas to the side so the men could board the ship. "I'll be right there." She turned to Jonas. "Okay, now it's really good that you're not coming."

Jonas shrugged. "Who cares?"

"Jonas, whoever the bimbo is, forget about her! She's obviously a moron of the highest order and you're way too good for her. So put the bitch out of your mind and focus on me now, please."

"Oh, it's Fred time. Must be Tuesday. Or one of the other six days of the week."

"Sarcasm does not become you," she said stiffly. "And furthermore—"

"Hi, Dr. Bimm!"

They looked. Madison was scampering up the ramp, waving. She wore a peach-colored shell (did she have a closet full of them, in all different colors?) and khaki pants that showed her pubic bone.

"My God," Jonas muttered. "I can see her five o'clock shadow."

Madison screeched to a halt in front of them. "Hi, you guys! Are you going out in the ship?"

"Yes."

"Can I come with? I can look for dolphins."

"No."

"Besides," Jonas said kindly, "there aren't any dolphins in—"

"Oh please please? I won't be any trouble, I swear. You won't even know I'm there!"

"That," Fred said, "is a lie."

Madison looked crushed. "Well . . . maybe your friend can keep me company." She batted her long lashes at Jonas. Actually batted her lashes! Fred didn't think women did that anymore.

"Thanks anyway, honey," Jonas said, "but I'm in mourning for my sex life."

"You—oh. *Oh*." Fred watched while Madison jumped to the conclusion that Jonas was gay. Normally she'd be irritated for her friend and wouldn't hesitate to correct the mistake, but in this case, Madison was doing Jonas a huge favor.

Furthermore, Dr. Barb was here, approaching them rapidly. Jonas had his back to her, but from where she was standing Fred had a perfect view of—a navy blue suit?

She stared. And stared more when Dr. Barb saw them and dramatically slowed her trot. In fact, she stopped altogether. And if Fred didn't know better, she'd think Dr. Barb was standing like that to . . . pose?

"Holy cow!" Madison peeped. "Dr. Barb got a haircut! And new clothes!"

Jonas's eyes bulged and he whipped around like it was the boogeyman coming up behind him instead of good old Dr. Barb.

"Jeez," Fred said, impressed. "She looks really good. I had no idea she had such a cute figure under those lab coats."

He whipped back around and now he was glaring at her. "Well, if *you've* noticed, it must be a bona fide transformation."

"Easy there, Bitchy McGee. Don't take your bad week out on me. I'm in charge of taking my bad weeks out on you."

Dr. Barb was slowly (?) making her way up the ramp leading to the loading dock. The clipboard she was holding was forgotten, hanging from one hand down by her side. Jonas turned back around to watch her walk up to them.

"Hi . . . Jonas."

"Hi, Barb."

"I, uh, it's nice to see you again."

"You, too. You look beautiful."

Dr. Barb—eh?—blushed.

Blushed?

"It was, um, a little scary to come in today. I'm afraid I've been avoiding you."

"That's okay. I've been avoiding you, too."

Fred turned to Madison. "Go clean out the lobster tanks."

"But this is much more—"

She gave the younger woman a helpful shove, almost knocking her into the bay. "Bye, now."

Meanwhile, Dr. Barb and Jonas were staring into each other's eyes, oblivious of the nauseating picture they presented.

"I'm so sorry I ran out like that. It was all just such a—"

"That's okay," Jonas said, coming to life for the first time all day. "I kind of sprung it on you."

"Oh, no! I shouldn't have reacted the way I did. I was too silly to realize the enormous compliment you were paying me. I'd—I'd really like to go somewhere *private* and talk about it."

"You—you would?"

Fred, who had been staring back and forth like she was watching a tennis match, broke in. "You would?"

Jonas reached out. Dr. Barb put her small, chubby hand in his. They started walking down the ramp together. Suddenly Dr. Barb turned, waved the clipboard, and said, "Have a nice ride, Dr. Bimm!"

"Have a nice ride? Don't you remember what happened last time? Don't you care about my welfare? And why are you holding hands with my best friend?"

Jonas waved without even turning around. "Bye, Fred."

"Stop that! Stop that immediately! I don't have time for more complications right now! Jonas! Get your hands off my boss! Jonas! Joooonaaaassss!" Then, in a near whimper, "Dr. Barb?"

Luckily, Jonas obeyed, dropped Dr. Barb's hand, and raced back to her. Now that was more like it! He sure had gone above and beyond in this whole "distract my boss" thing, but now—

"Give me the key card," he hissed.

"What?"

"Thomas's key card! I know he gave you a spare. Hand it over. You guys aren't going to be back for a while, right?"

"I'm not giving you the key card to a hotel room that isn't mine so you can bang my boss!"

"Yes you are," Jonas said. "Or I'll kick your fishy ass right into this harbor. With all the shit."

"Fine, take it." Fred sulkily handed it over. "Unnecessarily complicate my life, see if I care."

"Okay. Bye!" He scampered back down the ramp, toward the woman he'd had a crush on for six years.

"I didn't mean any of it!" Fred shouted, but the lovebirds ignored her.

Stifling the urge to kick something, she stomped the rest of the way up the ramp.

Twenty-eight

Captain O'Donnell was not at all happy to see her.

"Get this nautical menace off my ship," he said by way of greeting to Thomas.

"Calm down, O'Donnell. This is official NEA business."

"And my father's," Artur piped up, interrupting his conversation with a dazed-looking first mate.

"Low profile, dumbass," Thomas snarked.

"That goes for you, too, dumbass," Fred said. She turned back to the captain and gave him her nicest smile. He recoiled. "Now, Captain, all that stuff is behind us, right? I was a completely different person back then . . . ignorant, willful—"

"It was two months ago, Dr. Bimm."

"But we've both aged decades since then in wisdom, haven't we." At his look of disbelief, she added crossly, "Well, *I* have!"

O'Donnell turned to his first mate. "When was the last time we had a VSC?"

Artur sidled over to her. "The king of the ship seems agitated."

"It's a long story, Artur."

"What is a VSC?"

"Vessel Safety Check."

The first mate checked a chart and said helpfully, "Two weeks ago yesterday, Cap'n."

"Hmm. I *guess* that might be all right." He shot Fred a distrustful look. "Possibly."

Now Thomas was on her left. "Why is the crew treating you like you've brought the plague on board?"

Fred waved away his concern. "A silly misunderstanding that led to, uh, the sinking of his last boat." At Thomas's incredulous stare, she added, "But this one is much nicer than the *Fiona*. Bigger, prettier. Insurance paid for the whole thing, too."

"Dr. Bimm." O'Donnell had approached her carefully, like she was a rattlesnake. "Please go over there. Sit in that chair. Do not move from that chair until you need to throw up. Those are the circumstances that will allow me to overlook the fact that your name was nowhere on my paperwork for today's runs."

"No problem at all, Captain!" she said with a heartiness she didn't feel. She was getting off lightly, and she knew it. He had the power to order anyone—even Dr. Barb—off his ship.

"Little Rika, what did you do?"

"A trifle. I swear!" She started to head to the chair, tripped over a coil of rope, and went sprawling. She would have skinned her nose on the deck if Artur hadn't moved like lightning and caught her. "Uh, I hate to trouble you, but if you could carry me over to my assigned chair?"

"It would be my pleasure, Rika." He set her down in the chair from which she wouldn't move until the puking started. "There you are."

"Thanks." To Thomas: "Stop staring and close your mouth."

"But—you're a marine biologist."

"I'm aware, Thomas."

• • •

"But we're only in the harbor."

"I'm *aware*, Thomas!" She leaned over the railing and tossed the rest of her breakfast into the waves.

"Little Rika, how is it that you're ill?"

"Seasick," she groaned, and threw up again. Oh, this was just lovely. Just perfect. Two guys had weird crushes on her and she was sexily throwing up.

"But," Thomas was hissing in her ear, "you're a mermaid!"

"I. Am. Aware. Now get away from me unless you want some on your shoes."

Thomas didn't back away. Instead he leaned on the rail beside her and rubbed her back. "Why didn't you take any Dramamine?"

"Because I metabolize it too quickly. I'd have to take forty for it to work and even then I don't know if—urrgghh."

"Fascinating. And disgusting," he added.

Now there were two hands rubbing her back. "Little Rika, perhaps we should go back and do this tomorrow when you are not ill."

"She's not coming back tomorrow!" Captain O'Donnell yelled from his cabin, where he and the first mate were frantically counting life jackets, flame arresters, and visual distress signals.

"Not even if you paid me a million bucks," she snapped back. Then, quietly, "It's no good, Artur. The same thing would happen tomorrow."

"Uh—how are you two going to get in with me without these guys seeing it?" Thomas said.

"Trust me, O'Donnell will be thrilled to see me dive off his ship. As long as I stay out of his way, he could care less what Artur and I are doing."

"You're kidding. He's a maniac about boat safety, but he won't care if you—"

"He's a maniac about boat safety. Not passenger safety. Trust me."

Thomas shook his head and went to put on his scuba suit.

Twenty-nine

They had narrowed down the suspects to the new seafood restaurant (Cap'n Clammys!), the new Sleepytime Hotel, and the old (but recently massively renovated) World Trade Center. The plan was for the three of them to dive in, check out the underwater sites, pipes, and other detritus of construction, and see if they could pinpoint the bad guy. What they would do then, even if they could find a pipe pouring shit from one building, Fred wasn't sure.

Artur favored strangling the owner until his neck cracked. Thomas leaned toward ratting them out to the EPA. Fred was torn. Surely the culprit, whoever it was, knew what he (or she) was doing. So there should be a greater consequence than a fine. But neither did she favor murder (though Artur claimed it would be a simple case of self-defense).

Talk about putting the cart before the horse, she thought, diving in beside Artur as Thomas went, in the scuba-approved fashion, over backward. *First we gotta find the guy. (Or gal.) Right now, I'd settle for that.*

Instantly her uneasy stomach settled and she felt loads better. She playfully gave Thomas a pinch (which he probably couldn't feel through all the rubber) and darted past both men.

Feeling better, Little Rika?

Thomas was giving her a cautious thumbs-up.

Loads. Don't use your telepathy to exclude Thomas. She gave him the thumbs-up back.

Do not use my what to do what?

Never mind. Keep your eyes open. And your nose.

I confess I do not know how to feel. I have no urge to taste that particular taste again.

Right there with you, Artur. Oh, look at this.

Thomas was gesturing them over, shining his undersea light at what she assumed was Cap'n Clammy's from below.

Let's get to it.

Ah, Little Rika, your devotion to duty is commendable.

Yeah, that's what they keep telling me.

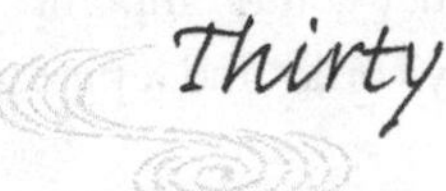

Thirty

It was difficult to work the key card when Barb had already yanked his pants halfway down to his knees, but Jonas managed. They staggered into the Presidential Suite, struggling with each other's clothes, kissing, panting, groaning, gasping. Jonas tripped over a divan and down they went.

"Ooof!"

"I'm so sorry!" Barb cried, leaning over him. "Are you all right? Am I too heavy? I'll get off."

"Not until I do," he growled, and yanked her down for another scorching kiss. He heard the thud as one of her pumps hit the carpet (the other one, he was pretty sure, had been abandoned by the door). He undid the one button on her Givenchy jacket and saw the Victoria's Secret matching navy bra beneath.

"Don't you think—" Gasp, moan. "—that this is—" Groan, kiss. "—much better than—" Slobber, sigh. "—lab coats?"

"I'm not giving them up. I just might stop buttoning them all the way." She was straddling him, tugging at his belt, when suddenly she went over as well. Now she was the one groaning, "Ooof!" and he was on top.

Not that he minded being on top.

"Fuck this," he laughed. "Let's go to the bedroom."

"A place this big must have one," she agreed, and he stood and pulled her to her feet.

In the ridiculously opulent bedroom, he carefully pulled off every item of clothing that he had so carefully picked out. She was considerably less careful; at least two of his shirt buttons were gone and he was afraid she had thrown his belt in the garbage.

"I've been thinking about what you said." Tug, tear. "For three days, I've been kicking myself for being such a fool." Yank, pull. "I had a perfect opportunity and I ran away like a ninny." Jerk, rip.

"I've been hiding in my apartment for three days," he said, pushing her back on the bed. "That's not much better. I just wasn't up to facing you after what happened."

"Yes, but that's my fault."

"Well, like I said, I kind of sprung it on you."

"Yes, but like I said, I—"

"Barb?"

"Yes?"

"I'm about to live the six-year fantasy. Can we stop talking for, um, ten minutes?"

She grinned up at him. "Ten? Oh, dear."

"Look, it's been a while."

"I'll try to stifle my humiliating laughter."

"That'd be great." He kissed her mouth, her lush, ripe mouth, savoring it so he could replay the moment over and over later, in his lonely bachelor's bed. He kissed her neck as her fingers ran through his hair (thank God Fred had bullied him into a shower!), as she caressed and stroked.

He tugged the cups of her bra down, exposing large creamy breasts and pink nipples that hardened when he stroked them gently. She gasped when he leaned down and sucked one into his mouth.

"Oh my God—Jonas—it's been years since—don't stop."

"Like I could if I wanted to." He kissed her cleavage, stroked one breast while he lavished attention on the other one, and while he was doing that she was yanking at her bra and wriggling out of her underwear.

She rolled over until she was on top, and jerked and pulled at his shorts until they were on the floor. She looked over her shoulder and stared with some satisfaction at his hard-on.

"This is no time for a cutting remark," he warned her.

"In no way was I thinking of one. I was thinking about how men can be beautiful, too."

If possible, he got harder. Definitely the boner of a lifetime. A one-of-a-kind boner, never to be repeated. Yep, there was no topping *this* bone, no way in hell.

"Now fuck me," Barb growled in her schoolteacher voice. "Right *now*."

He was wrong! And never so thankful for it. He watched in admiration and lust as she straddled his hips with hers, as she seized him firmly in her hot little hand and guided him inside her. She was more than ready for him and he slid all the way in without the smallest bit of resistance.

"That's better," she said cheerfully, and began riding him like a cowgirl. All she needed was the twirling rope.

He grabbed her hips and surged against her on the downstroke, thinking *I'm going to die I'm going to die she's killing me and thank God thank God . . .*

"Oh, Jonas, that's *wonderful*! Don't stop!" Bounce, bounce.

"I thought you weren't going to talk for ten minutes." He groaned while she slid up and down with exquisite strokes, while her breasts bobbed before him, begging to be kissed, while her mouth curved into a smile and her eyes sparkled.

"I never agreed to that," she said primly, which was a riot given what they were doing.

"I s'pose that's fair." He felt the familiar rumbling in his balls that meant the festivities would soon be over—he hadn't gotten off so quickly with a woman since college. He reached and found Barb's clit and stroked it gently, barely touching it, then more firmly on the downstroke, until she was riding his fingers as she was riding his cock, and then she shivered all over, leaned back, and shrieked at the ceiling.

His fingers whitened on her hips as he felt the rumbling start in his balls and race through his body until he thought the top of his head was going to come off. The room actually tilted one way and then the other as he desperately tried to focus, as Barb collapsed over him with a groan, as the greatest orgasm of his life tore through him like a—those things Fred talked about—

Don't think about Fred, idiot.

Tsunami. Like a tsunami, that was it.

"Oh my," Barb gasped in his ear.

"You're my tsunami."

She sat up and stared down at him thoughtfully, face and breasts flushed from their exertion. "We'll work on the pet names," she said at last, and he tickled her until she begged for mercy.

Thirty-one

"Well, that was a huge waste of time," Fred grumbled, tripping over an ice chest but righting herself in time. The captain helped her onto the ramp and she stomped down it. "Not to mention breakfast."

"We'll keep trying," Thomas said, white-faced with exhaustion. They had been in the water for hours. Fred was sort of ready for a nap herself.

"Perhaps I will go back later, now that I know the locations under suspicion." Artur, annoyingly, looked like he'd just jumped out of bed after fourteen hours of sleep. Stupid full-blooded mermen.

Fred yawned. "Now who's got a commendable devotion to duty?"

"I do not wish to cause you more distress—which the trip on the boat seemed to. And although he annoys me sometimes—I do not wish to see harm come to this one." He pointed to Thomas. "It would not be honorable."

"Yeah, okay, whatever."

"Whatever is right," said Thomas. "I'm going back to the room so I can fall on my face and die for a few hours."

"The room?" Fred halted midway down the ramp. Behind her, the first mate groaned. She flapped a hand at him in a "don't worry" motion and reached for her cell phone. "The room. Right. Let me just see if Jonas wants to come. I mean join us."

"Join us taking a nap?"

"Just let me call him. Right now."

Barb was cuddling into his side and all was right with the world. "I swear," she murmured, "I haven't had that much fun since my divorce. Actually, since about a year before my divorce."

Jonas yawned. "Right . . . didn't you say he was cheating on you the whole last year?"

"Mm-hmm."

"Dumbass."

"Mm-hmm."

"Not that I'm complaining, but I can't believe someone didn't swoop down on you after you got rid of the idiot."

She giggled. "Someone did. It just took them a few years to get their act together."

"Off my case. Keeping Fred out of trouble is a full-time job, and I already *have* one of those."

She was tracing circles around his left nipple, which his entire body thought was fine. "That's my ex, too. He's always taking on new projects, extra jobs. He built a hotel just a couple blocks away from here—would you believe he had the nerve to send me an invitation to the grand opening last month?"

"Should have told him to stick it where the sun never ever shines." He ruffled her newly short hair—shoulder length, layered around the face. Just as he had suggested. "I love your hair like this. God, it's like silk, it's—your husband did what?"

Barb's eyes were closed as she luxuriated in his touch, but now they popped open. "I didn't quite catch that."

He could hardly hear her. He was trying hard to remember what Fred had said about their little harbor problem. Literal shit into the water. Likely from a new building. One built in the last year. And then there was the personal angle, something he bet neither Thomas nor the prince had considered.

What if someone was fucking up Boston Harbor to wreck things for the NEA? Tough to get tourists down to Shitville. Tough to do much of anything when the entire harbor smelled like a Porta Potti.

"Your ex. What's his name?"

"Phillip King."

"So you've always had your own name."

"Jonas, what's the matter?"

He ignored the question. "Think this one over before you answer, Barb. Did you guys really part amicably?"

"Yes. Although—it's quite funny you should bring this up, because a year ago he started trying to, I guess woo me would be the word. But I wasn't going down that road again, and I told him so. There were some pretty hard feelings that time, and he left a few nasty messages on my machine, but I had my lawyer tell him to cease and desist and that was really the end of—Jonas, what's the matter? You look like you're going to faint."

He could hear his cell phone ringing from somewhere and sat up, gently pushing Barb away. "Help me find my pants," he said urgently.

"But what's the—"

"My pants, woman!"

She hopped off the bed and they both looked in the bedroom and the sitting area. On the third ring he found them hanging from the front doorknob. He lunged for them, found his phone, fumbled with it, dropped it, bent, picked it up, clawed it open.

"Fred, don't hang up!"

"That's not your midorgasm voice, is it?"

He slid to the floor, relieved. "No, but I did just give your boss the banging of a lifetime."

"Oh, Jonas!" she shrieked. "Stop that! I have to work with the woman, you know."

"Ow!"

"What? Did you bruise a testicle?"

"No, she pinched me. Guess she didn't care for my confession, either." She went in for another pinch and he batted her away. "Listen, you guys have any luck?"

"No we did not, dammit, and everybody is pooped—except the King of the Ocean, here, who looks ready to take on the Chicago Bulls—so we're all coming back to the room for a nap and you'd by God better be finished and *fully* dressed when we get there, because one more shock my heart *cannot* take and if you had any sensitivity at all you wouldn't have had sex with my boss in the water fellow's—"

"Fred, *shut the hell up and listen, goddammit*!"

Barb, bending over to shake out her skirt, froze.

"Did you have an aneurysm for lunch?" Fred demanded. "Because—"

"Barb's ex-husband is really pissed at her. And he just built a new hotel. Guess where?"

"Oh, no."

"Right on the harbor."

"Oh, fuck."

"Yup."

"Oh, jeez."

"Yeah. Sic 'em."

"You mean we've been up to our eyeballs in paperwork and Artur and I have been breathing shit—literally breathing shit—and all that we needed to do to crack the case was stand back and let you bone my boss?"

He took the skirt from Barb and tossed it on the dining room table. Then he lifted Barb to the same table. "Looks like. Listen, take your time coming back, will you?"

"Oh, that is just disgus—"

He hung up on her.

"What's this about my ex?" Barb asked, leaning back and stretching out on the table, which was plenty big enough for four more Barbs.

"Oh. That. He's the bad guy."

"Oh. I'll likely be much more concerned about this . . ." Jonas began to nibble her cleavage. "Later," she sighed.

"Ummmm," he agreed.

Then, after a long moment: "Is Dr. Bimm angry?"

"Only because she didn't get laid. And that's her own damn fault, believe me."

She arched beneath his hands and wrapped her legs around his waist. "That's nice," she sighed, kissing him back.

He came up for air. "Wait, wait! I've always wanted to try this." He went to the small credenza at the other end of the dining room table, opened it, and withdrew a pack of cards.

"Oh, oh," Barb said, but she was smiling.

Jonas shuffled the cards. "Okay, check this. We'll play poker to get our fantasy."

"We'll do what?"

"We're going to role play. If I win, you're a damsel in distress and I have to save you, blah-blah. If you win, you're a Catholic schoolteacher and I've just been caught putting a smoke bomb in the boys' room."

Dr. Barb started to laugh, then choked it off and looked grave. "You feel the need to play cards to bring this about?"

"Hey, I'm a traditionalist." He did a fast box shuffle, then dealt them each five cards. He picked up his hand and observed the three aces. "Okay, whatcha got?"

"I have two twos," she said triumphantly.

He tossed his hand down and grabbed her. "You win, teacher."

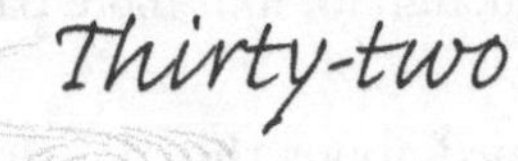

Thirty-two

"Are you sure you're not too tired?" Fred asked as the three of them charged into the Sleepytime Hotel. It was a twelve-story building built right up to the harbor. From the outside it looked like a perfectly respectable, almost luxury hotel. Not at all the den of evil they now knew it to be.

"Now? No way. As soon as you told me, I got a massive adrenaline surge. Let's kick some ass and then turn him over to the EPA."

"After we snap his spine," Artur added.

"You just keep your hands to yourself, buster, until we figure out what we're going to—Phillip King, please," she told the receptionist. In a moment that would haunt her nightmares for eternity, she'd blanked out and had to call Jonas back to get the guy's name. And her friend was so out of breath he could hardly spit it out. And there was an odd thumping noise in the background—not like they were on a bed, but maybe—

"Remind me not to eat anywhere in your suite until I figure this out," she muttered, shrugging when Thomas gave her a mystified look.

"I'm sorry," the receptionist said, "but Mr. King is in a meeting right now and can't be—"

"Tell him," she said, "it's about his ex-wife. I bet he'll see us."

"I bet he will, too," the receptionist muttered. Then she pushed a couple of buttons on her console, gestured to the elevator, and said, more graciously, "Top floor."

"Remember," Fred said as they marched into the elevator, "nobody use the bathrooms while we're here."

"Oh, Fred, that's gross!"

"Just sayin'. Artur, what the hell's the matter with you?" For he had suddenly thrown himself against her and was clutching her hard enough to hurt.

"This little metal box—moving—up?"

"Yeah, it's an elevator, it's perfectly normal, now leggo." She tried to pry his fingers off her arm. "Artur, calm down."

"But what is to prevent the box from shooting right out of the top of the building?"

"Nothing," Thomas said cheerfully. "Happens at least once a week in this city."

"Owwwww," Fred bitched. "Artur, you're cutting off the *circulation.* Thomas, cut the shit."

"I just think he should prepare himself."

"Owwwww!"

There was a *ding* and then the elevator slowed to a stop and the doors hummed open. Artur lost no time in getting out. Thomas went sailing after him, thanks to Fred's helpful shove. He stumbled into Artur, sending them both sprawling in the hallway.

"I swear, the trouble you two cause me on a minute-by-minute basis . . ." She stomped past them and resisted the urge to kick Thomas in the ribs. At least they were helping each other up like gentlemen.

"You have to admit, I gotcha good," Thomas said.

"Indeed you did. I shall remember your deviousness and address it another time."

"Bring it, you redheaded overgrown—"

"Dr. Bimm, Dr. Pearson, and Prince Artur of the Black Sea," Fred announced, walking into the conference room the receptionist had directed them to. Artur had made it clear he wanted his true name and affiliation known when they finally confronted the bad guy.

Bad *guys.*

Fourteen men were staring back at her, and they were all shifty-eyed and shiny-suited, and wore suspicious bulges under their armpits—even the guy at the head of the table, a balding, cadaverously thin man with eyes the color of dust and the longest fingers she'd ever seen. And her mom taught piano.

Of course, on their date, he hadn't been packing. But otherwise she recognized him immediately.

"You said this was about my ex?" Phillip King asked, standing at the head of the table.

"No, it's about what you're *doing* to your ex. Specifically, pumping all the shit from your hotel into her harbor. Well, Boston Harbor. But we know why you're doing it."

That ought to fix him, she thought, folding her bony arms across her chest. And right in front of his partners, too!

One of the shiny-suited men looked at King and said, "I thought you said there was no way to get caught."

"Uh," Fred said. "What?"

"There wasn't," King said, looking startled.

"I thought you said it'd be cheaper to just dump the stuff straight to the harbor—"

"It *is.*"

"—and nobody'd be able to tell it was us."

"They can't!"

That's true, Fred thought. They didn't have any hard evidence yet. Which might be problematic.

"Before you get any wise ideas," she added, suddenly *very* glad there were two men on her side, and they were Thomas and Artur, "we told at least a dozen people about this today before we came over here."

"Your hair is still wet," King observed.

"Yeah, but—" She cast about for a convincing lie.

"Miscreant! You admit your wrongdoing? Then be prepared to pay the penalty!"

Which Artur completely ruined.

"You guys are way too mob chic," Thomas said, staring at the men. "Don't even tell me you got laundered crime money to help you build the hotel."

"Of course I did," King snapped. "Where else would I have been able to raise the money so fast? Get the building up so quickly? Get around certain pesky rules and regulations on waste treatment?"

"He's only telling us this," Fred explained to Artur, "because he's going to try to kill us. Just so you know."

"Is that a custom in your world? Talking, then killing?"

"Yeah, I'd say so—Thomas?"

Thomas nodded. "That's the way we bipeds do it."

"You three, go wait in my office. I want to hear more about my ex. And you guys—wait!" For all the other men were standing, getting coats, grabbing suitcases, and generally making the noise of men about to leave. "There's no need to cut the meeting short. I've got charts that show just how profitable a whole Sleepytime chain could be and there's no reason why we can't—"

"A chain?" Fred gasped, horrified.

"We'll see how you handle this problem first," one of the shiny-suited men told him. "Then we'll be back. Maybe."

Fred watched with relief as the mobsters left. She had no desire to explain to Artur about gunfights. Or organized crime.

Phillip King opened the door connecting one room to the other and disappeared.

"I guess he's going to his office," Thomas said.

"Then let us meet him on his own territory," Artur announced, striding after him.

"Oh, yeah, I'm sure he just wants to chat," Fred muttered, following the men. Still, King was just one guy—a biped, as Artur would say—and there were three of them. She wasn't especially worried now.

She walked into a brightly lit office with blueprints plastered on every wall (no doubt plans for the mighty Sleepytime empire) and looked at King just in time to see him point something shiny at them.

"Down!" Thomas shouted, and batted her sideways so hard, she flew back into the conference room. At the same instant, or so it felt to her, there was a loud *bang* and a chunk of wood where her head had just been leapt from the wall and fell on the carpet.

Thomas shoved her under the table, yanked Artur down, and in a few seconds all three of them were crouched beneath the conference room table while King screamed things like, "I'm turning that whore's water zoo into a shit hole!" and "It's her fault I'm in debt up to my eyeballs!" and "Why couldn't she just look the other way like a normal wife?" Each rant, of course, punctuated with a gunshot.

"Uh . . ."

"He's nuts," Thomas said, squinting up from beneath the table. "And that is my professional opinion as a water fellow."

Her phone rang and, out of pure dumb habit, she flipped it open. "Yeah?"

"Call the cops on that thing!" Thomas hissed.

"You bipeds and your odd loud weapons."

"It's possible," came Jonas's pant, sounding like he'd just run the two hundred, "that her ex is emotionally disturbed."

"*Now* you tell me. Say, could you send the police to his hotel, if it's not too much trouble?"

"Why? What'd you do to him?"

"Nothing! Except possibly disrupt his illegal funding. But seeing as how he's *shooting* at us, *maybe* you could finish *boinking* my *boss* and *call* some *authorities*." She slapped the phone shut. "Jonas is calling the cavalry. I think. Now what?"

"Well. It looked like a revolver to me. Six shots. I've counted four so far."

"Super. A water fellow who knows about guns." To Artur, "That means he has two left."

"Two what?"

"Two small pieces of metal which his weapon will hurl at us so fast, if it hits a vital organ it will kill us."

Artur made a face. "A distasteful way to fight."

"Hey, let's talk him into stopping, I'm all for it. Any actual ideas?"

"We hope he fires off two more shots in his hysteria, which, if they're anything like the last four, won't come near us. We wait for the police and let them deal with it." Thomas was ticking their options off on his fingers. "Or we goad him into using his last shots. Or we try to take the gun away from him."

"Cowering in terror while we hope he wastes his last two sounds good to me," Fred said.

"Or you could goad him while Artur and I try to sneak in through the other door and jump him."

"Naw."

"Yes," Artur said. "You excel at goading. And hiding does not befit royalty. Come, Thomas."

"Wait a minute!" Fred hissed. But they were already crawling to the other end of the table and slipping out the door. "Dammit!"

She thought for a second. Then took a breath and yelled, "Hey, King! Did I mention your ex is fucking my best friend?"

Long silence, followed by, "That's a lie. Barb's frigid. She hates sex."

"Sex with *you*, maybe. Either that or my friend cured her because brother, she's already done it twice today. And it's not even . . ." She looked at her watch. "Three o'clock! Guess she's not missing you too much, huh?"

"Who's your friend?"

Fred wasn't sure which was scarier: when he was out of control and firing a gun at random people he'd just met, or when he was scarily calm and trying to think his way out of a hole.

"Put the gun down and maybe I'll tell you. Heck, put the gun down and I'll bring you to him. Them. Did I mention my friend—his dick is about a foot long, according to legend—gave Dr. Barb a make-over? She looks awesome. Did you know that dark blue is her color?"

"White is her color! She buttons her lab coats all the way to the top!"

"Not today, pal. Today I bet she doesn't even know where her lab coat *is.* You know how it is, young love and all that . . ."

King snorted. "My ex is a lot of things, but young isn't one of them."

Gotcha. "Well, maybe, but that doesn't bother my friend. He loves older women. Literally! As in, I'm pretty sure he's loving one right now. She's got to have fifteen years on him."

"She's fucking . . . a younger guy?"

"Multiple times," Fred assured him, no longer having to fake cheerfulness. *This is kind of fun. The guys were right: goading is my gift.* "I hope they're using birth control, because Dr. Barb's not exactly ready for the nursing home yet."

"She's on 'the pill' for her cramps," King replied absently.

"Oh, well, no bouncing babies for her right now. That's okay; with her career, and my friend's career, and all the hot monkey sex they're having, they prob'ly aren't ready for kids."

Silence.

And more silence.

Fred cautiously looked up and saw King framed in the doorway between his office and the conference room. He was pointing the gun straight at her. The barrel, from her standpoint, looked awfully big. She raised her hands and slowly climbed to her feet, thinking, *Damned if I'm going to die on my knees.*

"I'm a big fan of shooting the messenger," he said. "And you're another frigid bitch, if memory serves."

"Why does that not surprise me in the least?" *Come on, guys, what are you waiting for?*

As if in answer to her prayers, the other office door splintered down the middle. But King didn't look around. He didn't even jump. Instead, he shot Fred with his last two bullets.

Thirty-three

There were three things Fred would never forget from that afternoon.

Number one: when you're shot, you don't stagger dramatically backward or plunge out the eleventh-story window. You just stand there.

Number two: Artur can break a man's neck with one effortless twist, and it sounds like the sound ice makes when you crunch it between your teeth.

And number three: Thomas carried a switchblade.

"Uh," Fred began, as King's body was falling, as Artur went red with rage, as Thomas was trying to get her to lie down. "I think I'm—uh—shot."

"You are shot, Fred. Twice."

"Why are you pushing me?"

"Because I want you on your back while I'm getting the bullets out."

She removed his hands. "I really don't like the sound of that." She felt she was being calm and reasonable, and didn't understand why Thomas was as pale as Artur was purple. It didn't hurt at all. And the bad guy was dead.

"Artur! That cabinet over there. Bring me one of the bottles with either white or brown liquid in it." Thomas swept his foot beneath hers and knocked her off balance, then knelt on her chest to keep her on the floor.

There was the sound of glass breaking, and then Artur was kneeling beside her. "Will these assist you, Dr. Pearson?"

That's the first time Artur's called him Doctor. "Hey, wait a minute!"

Fred yelled, wriggling beneath his knee. "He's not a *real* doctor! I mean, he is, but he's not a medical doctor. He's a water fellow."

"I got my M.D. before I went back for my Ph.D. I just found out I had zero interest in triple shifts and other benefits of residency. I don't like working *too* hard to save people's lives."

"You sound like a real winner, Doc."

"Fred, you're never sick. And you said you have an incredibly fast metabolism. So I'm betting your bullet wounds will be all healed over tomorrow." He wiped his blade on the carpet, and then on his pants.

Artur was kneeling beside them and, at some odd prearranged signal she must have missed, suddenly tore her shirt straight down the middle.

"Hey!"

Thomas ignored her. "So we can leave the bullets in you, which would be bad, or we can take you to a hospital for removal, where they'll do all sorts of tests, which would be bad. Or I can take them out right here before they heal over." He unscrewed a bottle of Jack Daniels, thumbed the button on his switchblade, and poured booze all over the knife and his hands.

"But—"

"Hold her down," Thomas said shortly, and went to work.

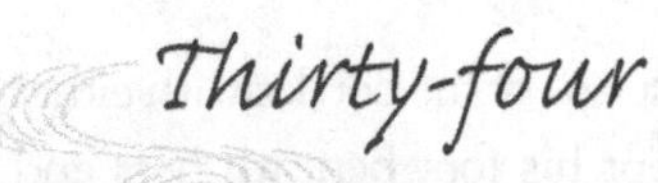

Thirty-four

Jonas and Barb were sitting at the bar in the Presidential Suite, drinking wine (eh, Thomas was rich, he could afford a bottle of Chardonnay), and having a perfectly nice chat about how they planned to spend the rest of their lives together, when the front door rattled.

"Fortunately we're fully clothed," Barb teased. "Finally."

"I still say we should have gone over to your ex's hotel and caught the ruckus. I mean, there were a million sirens a while ago. I bet it was cool."

Barb shook her head. "If the police require a statement of course I'll cooperate. But best to leave things to the professionals."

Fred stomped in, looking like somebody had worked her over pretty good. Jonas was off the stool and on his feet before he was aware he'd moved. She'd been his sparring partner more than once, and taken full kicks in the face without so much as a bruise. But now Fred was wearing a blood-stained bra and her favorite (and now also bloody) pair of track shorts. And how many times did he have to beg her not to wear tennis shoes without socks? Yech.

Thomas and Artur came in behind her and they looked almost as bad: both of them spattered with blood

(whose blood?????)

and Thomas sporting what was going to be one hell of a black eye, and Artur with a split lip.

"Little Rika, surely you could see Dr. Pearson knew what he was—"

"Fred, come on, don't be mad. I did it to save you from—"

"I said *no* talking to me *ever*!" Fred whirled on Barb. "And you! Your crazy ex husband *shot* me. Twice! Also, he's dead."

Barb's mouth hung ajar. "What? Phillip is dead?"

"And he *shot* me."

"But you never get hurt," Jonas managed.

"Well, if someone points a big gun at me and pulls the fucking trigger, I can get hurt, okay, genius? Luckily, Dr. Demento and his faithful lab wretch, Artur the Psycho, were there to save the day. And by save the day, I mean commit federal fucking assault!" Fred kicked the leg of the eight-foot dining room table. Said leg collapsed like it was a toothpick, and there was a tremendous *whud* as the thing crashed to the floor.

"And you two! Boning the afternoon away while we're cleaning up the shit your ex left behind! Him and the *Mafia*. Thanks for nothing!"

"Phillip has ties to the *Mafia*?" Barb gasped.

"Had, Dr. Barb. He's dead."

"We did call the police and send them over," Jonas said weakly. "How could we have known a matter for the EPA was going to turn into a Mafia-laden bloodbath?"

"On the same day both of you get laid for the first time in years? You didn't think that was a sign of the Apocalypse? Because I sure as shit did! You two can't have sex again, ever."

Jonas and Barb looked at each other, then at Fred. "You mean ever ever? Or just with each other?"

"I think, to be on the safe side—" Fred stopped in midrant and put a shaking hand to her forehead. Artur and Thomas quietly walked up until they were each standing just behind her. "I think—I think you better not—ever—"

Then the oddest thing of the entire afternoon (and it had been a doozy) happened: Fred's eyes rolled up until Jonas could only see the whites, and she pitched backward.

Thomas and Artur caught her, neat as you please, and Artur lifted her up and laid her on the couch.

"Is there any more of that wine left?" Thomas asked, once he had made sure Fred would be fine. He touched his swelling eye and winced. "It's been a helluva day."

"If that is a drink like ale or grog, I also would like some." Artur's split lip was also swelling nicely.

Barb poured. They clinked. They drank. Fred snored.

Thirty-five

Fred rolled over, felt a stabbing pain in her shoulder, grabbed it and groaned. Grabbing it made it worse, so she opened her eyes.

She was on the couch in the living room of the Presidential Suite. And it was dark out.

"Wakey wakey," Thomas said. He was holding her wrist in one hand and looking at his watch.

She yanked her arm out of his grasp and fought the urge to blacken his other eye. The holding-down bullet-removing game had not been fun. For any of them.

"What's going on? Where is everybody?"

"Barb and Jonas are down at the police station giving their statements. Artur is conked out in the bedroom."

"I'm not speaking to you," she said coldly, "but if I was, I would wonder how you explained King's neck being broken by a merman."

"We don't know anything about that. We didn't see what happened. Maybe he slipped. Maybe one of his mob buddies came back and paid a visit. All we know is that he tried to kill a couple of people, we ran away, and he violated about a thousand EPA regs. He's dead, so I don't give a shit. Let the cops and the bureaucrats sort it out."

Thomas sounded pretty cold during his little speech, and Fred suppressed a shiver. "What are you so mad about? Which is what I would ask if I were speaking to you. Which I am not."

He had leaned in to look at her pupils, but suddenly his gaze shifted and he was seeing her, not her eyes. "Fred, he shot you! If Artur hadn't broken his neck, I would have stuck my knife into more than his kidney. He just stood there and shot you. And then I had to dig my knife into your shoulder while Artur held you down and you screamed the place down and cried and begged me—God!" He ran shaking hands through his dark hair, making it stand up in wild clumps. "For putting all of us through that, I could kill him right now all over again."

"Well, all right, calm down. It's no big deal. It's all over. Bad guy's dead. We win. Drinks all around." She started to sit up, grimacing. "I'd kill for an aspirin to work, there's no doubt about—oof!"

Thomas had put a hand on her chest and slammed her back down. "You *stay down*," he said.

"Don't push your luck," she warned him.

"Stay," he said again. "Do not make me get Artur in here to make you lie down, Fred. You won't like it and neither will I." He got up and started to pace, looking like he was going to leap out of his skin.

She watched him, amazed. "Thomas, what in the world's gotten into you?"

He whirled on her, dark eyes flashing. "What's gotten *into* me?"

"Well, yeah, that's kind of where I was going with my whole 'what's gotten into you' question."

"How about this? I love you, you silly bitch, and thanks to that fucker King I had to hurt you. Not exactly all part of my plan for a romantic goddamned evening!"

"But—you—but you don't even—we haven't even known each other a week!"

He plunked down in the chair opposite her and waved away her objection. "Oh, hell with that. I knew the minute I saw you in the tank. Of course I love you. How could I love anybody but you?"

"But you're only going to be here for a couple of weeks! Then it's off to Millport!" Millport was the University Marine Biology Station in Scotland.

He smiled at her, but oh, such a tired, bitter grin. She almost wished he hadn't smiled at all. "Been checking on my schedule, huh? And it's sooner than that, babe. My project here is finished."

"Well. I wasn't sure how long our shit project was going to take, that's why I checked your schedule."

He propped his hand on his chin and looked at her for a long moment. Finally, he said, "Go back to sleep. I'm sorry I dumped all that on you. I should have waited until you were feeling better."

"You shouldn't have dumped it on me at all."

Thomas shrugged. "Better get used to hearing it. If I have to think it, you have to hear it."

Fred, having never been in love before, said crossly, "I don't think that's how it goes."

"Go back to sleep."

"I'm not tired."

"Yes you are. You lost a ton of blood in the conference room. You almost ended up in the hospital despite my best efforts."

"Well. Thanks for that."

"Finally, a glimmer of gratitude. I may faint."

"Shut up, I'm still not speaking to you."

"I know."

"And I'm not tired," she said, and while they were arguing about it, she fell asleep.

Thirty-six

"Rika?"

A hand on her, shaking her. Time for school already? Wasn't it Saturday?

"Rika?"

"Five more minutes," she groaned.

"Little Rika, I will be gone in three."

That was not Moon Bimm. That was—

She opened her eyes. Artur was on his knees beside the couch. He was so close that strands of his red hair were tickling her face.

"Gone in three?" Why did her brain feel like it had turned to oatmeal? Why was she so tired? Where was everybody? "Why? Where is everybody?"

"Your supervisor and your friend went back to your friend's domicile many hours ago. Thomas is resting. And I must leave. The king requires a full report."

"*Leaving* leaving? Leaving right now?"

"The king calls and I must answer. But I could not leave without seeing how you are. I do profoundly apologize for violating your boundaries—"

"What?"

"Holding you down," he translated. "But I felt Thomas was right. It was best to remove the metal things from your body. Metal does not belong in bodies. However, doing so against your will was—" He looked away. "Difficult."

"Oh, yeah. I can see how that must have been so difficult. For *you two.*" She rubbed her shoulder, which still ached. "Lucky for me I'm not prone to infections."

"Rika, when you are strong once again, I will return."

"Why?"

"Because you are my princess meant," he replied simply.

"What?"

"My—fiancée? Except you have not given me your hand so we are only promised to be promised."

"Artur—*what?*"

"You will be the Princess of the Black Sea," he told her, completely ignoring her shushing motions, "and one day you and I will be the High King and Queen after my dear father is gone."

"No. We. Won't!"

He smiled at her. "Ah, yes. Biped wooing. Thomas warned me."

"*Thomas* warned you?"

"Yes, it is an odd thing, being fond of my greatest rival, but I cannot help it. He is decisive, clever, duplicitous, and violent. All the things that make the bipeds formidable. He informed me that you will be his and not mine, but we have agreed to woo you in our own ways and ultimately let you make the choice when you are ready."

"But—but—but—"

"He will lose, of course. And now, I go."

Artur got to his feet without using his hands, which looked impressive, and strode to the door. She sat up, swung her legs off the couch, ignored the shooting pains, and raced after him.

"You can't just leave!"

"But I must."

"But you can't just say all that—that *stuff* and then just march out the door!" *Not both of them,* she thought frantically. *Not* both *of them!*

"But I will come back." He cupped the back of her neck, kissed her sweetly, then opened the door. "I will always come back."

He closed the door with a soft click.

"But I don't want to be the High Queen of the Black Sea!" she shouted at the closed door.

"What are you doing out of bed?" Thomas asked sleepily, standing in the bedroom doorway.

"It's not a bed, it's a couch. And who could go to sleep right now?"

He yawned. "Did Artur leave? God, finally. He's not bad, for an arrogant, entitled, overbearing, nonintellecutal, pompous . . ." There was more in this vein, but Fred didn't catch it, as Thomas had turned around and gone back to bed.

The doorknob rattled and she stared at it fearfully. What was that line from Dorothy Parker? Or was it Shakespeare? "What fresh hell is this?" From Hamlet or some damned thing, and that's just how she felt, too, like some fresh hell was lurking around the—

She yanked the door open. Barb and Jonas were in a clinch, from which they separated with difficulty.

"You two," she said bitterly, and went back inside. She fished a bottle of water from the wet bar (what the hell, Thomas could afford it) and ignored the cooing, cuddling couple behind her.

"Feeling better?" Jonas asked with grating cheer. "Because, girlfriend, you look like shit on a plate."

"Thank you so much," she replied, taking a deep swig. "Not all of us could spend the afternoon mating like rabbits. And what are you doing here, anyway?"

"It's seven a.m.," Jonas pointed out. "Barb wanted to get an early start at the NEA since she played hooky yesterday, and I figured I'd check on you and give you a ride home if you wanted. Oh, and give you a shirt. Seeing as how your last one—"

"Don't remind me. Artur left."

"Yeah, we saw him in the hall, but he's coming back pretty soon."

"And Thomas has to go to Scotland."

"Yes, I imagine now that he's solved his toxin problem, he'll be leaving sooner rather than later," Dr. Barb said. "I'd better get started on the paperwork."

"They're both in love with me. I mean, they said they were."

"Well, duh," Jonas snarked.

"Of course they are," Dr. Barb said. "Didn't you know?"

Fred glared at her boss and her best friend. "What am I going to *do*?"

"Heal up," Jonas suggested.

"Yes, get well soon," Dr. Barb replied. Two peas in a pod, these two. That wasn't going to get old fast, oh heavens no. "I suspect you will need all of your strength in the coming weeks."

Jonas winked at her when Barb couldn't see. Well. At least she had *some* secrets left. And Dr. Barb was sure right about needing her strength. Because if this is the stuff that happened to her when men were in love, she shuddered to think of the engagement.

Not that she was going to get engaged. To either of those yo-yos. But if she were, she would definitely pick . . .

Er . . .

Well, for *sure* she'd pick . . . ah . . .

Oh dear, she thought glumly, and downed the rest of the water in three gulps.

Swimming Without a Net

This book is for everyone who was ever irritated by a Disney heroine. Detox with Fred, and rejoice!

It's also for my dear friend Cathie Carr, who had a crummy year, was lied to (repeatedly) by loved ones, deceived by friends (who had good intentions, but still), did everything she could to save her marriage only to be rewarded with a boot in the face (repeatedly), and managed to pick up the pieces anyway. I'm thirty-eight now, and I never thought I'd meet someone with a bigger pair of plums than mine. Cathie's plums make mine look like raisins. Or is that an overshare?

ACKNOWLEDGMENTS

I could never write a book without adding an acknowledgments page (or two, or six). Some readers find this puzzling (and often annoying, but hey, nobody's sticking a gun to your head, right?), but for me it's always been simple.

All writers know they didn't create the book/story/play/commercial jingle/tampon ad on their own. Just having a partner to keep the kids out of your hair is worth a mention on the acknowledgments page. And I've been lucky enough to have far more than that.

My friends are quite jaded by now; when I told my buddy Todd he was getting a mention on the acknowledgments page, he said, "Can't you send me cash instead?" Yeah, well, drop dead twice, O'Halloran.

So! Thanks, in no particular order, are due to: my husband and coauthor (we write the Jennifer Scales series together), my children, my sister, my parents. My agent, my editor, the copy editors, the line editors. The marketing reps, the catalog designers, the cover designers, the flap copy writers.

See, I just put a bunch of gibberish out and it happens to land on a page. The people mentioned above are the ones who take a messy, 300-plus page rough draft and turn it into a book. Maybe even a great book.

For this book in particular, I ended the first draft on page 200. Even for me, notorious for my tight (read: short) single titles, 200 pages is BAD. Even 300 is skating on the edge. As I explained to my editor, "I got nothin'." I got to the end, it was done, the story was told, and I was on page 200.

So Cindy, bless her heart, read the manuscript and sent me a page of suggestions. Pointed out where I broke Awful Writing Rule #1: I told, not showed. Suggested scenes I skipped altogether (it's because of Cindy that we saw Moon Bimm again, and speculation about Fred's mysterious merman father started up so quickly). Because of Cindy, we saw Dr. Barb in the Caymans and the disaster (and Jonas pummeling) that nearly followed.

(Also, for those of you who haven't read the preceding book, *Sleeping with the Fishes*, fear not: I think I did a pretty good job explaining the events in that book. You shouldn't be too lost. But hey, if you are, just buy the first book!)

(Go ahead. We'll wait.)

(We're still waiting, here. You think we've got nothing better to—)

(Ah. Very good. Thanks. Great cover, huh?)

I must warn you, dear readers, that there is an act of somewhat annoying violence in this book, an act I pretty much glossed over. Cindy coaxed a truer scene out of me, one more suited to the situation and the story and the characters.

The end result, I think, was not only a longer book (my true goal) but, thanks to Cindy Hwang, a better book.

The latter, of course, is up to you, dear reader. And so, finally, thanks for picking up the book and giving it a try. If the cover caught your eye, hooray! If it was the flap copy, even better. If it was name recognition, that's swell. But as every reader knows, there are all kinds of reasons to pluck a book off the shelf . . . or not.

So thanks for the pluck. I'll try not to let you down.

MaryJanice Davidson
www.maryjanicedavidson.net

AUTHOR'S NOTE

Note from the author (that's me!): The actions of Fred's third blind date were inspired by the fabulous movie *Better Off Dead*, starring John Cusack. I must have watched that movie a thousand times as a teenager. I saw a chance to pay homage to one of my all-time favorites, and jumped at it.

Not everything is a mermaid that dives into the water.

—RUSSIAN PROVERB

I declare that civil war is inevitable and is near at hand.

—SAM HOUSTON, AMERICAN GENERAL

I started early, took my dog,
And visited the sea;
The mermaids in the basement
Came out to look at me.
And frigates in the upper floor
Extended hempen hands,
Presuming me to be a mouse,
Aground, upon the sands.

—EMILY DICKINSON, *Part II, Nature*

To Jove, and all the other Deities,
Thou must exhibit solemn sacrifice;
And then the black sea for thee shall be clear.

—*The Odysseys of Homer*

The greatest trick the devil ever pulled was convincing the world he didn't exist.

—BAUDELAIRE, *Le Joueur généreux*

One

Fredrika Bimm trudged down Comm. Ave. (known to tourists and other mysterious creatures as Commonwealth Avenue, Boston, Massachusetts) and tried not to think about the Prince of the Black Sea, or famed romance novelist Priscilla D'Jacqueline.

She had, in fact, spent the better part of the last twelve months determinedly *not* thinking about them.

And why should she? She had a fulfilling job. Okay, an irritating job. She had her own home, which she never had to herself anymore. She had a best friend who was infatuated with a new girlfriend and never had time for her anymore.

A pity party already. And not even two o'clock! A new record!

It was a typically lovely autumn afternoon—yawn—and her Wordsworth book bag bulged with D'Jacqueline's last two novels, *Passion's Searing Flames* and *The Rake and the Raconteur.* This did not count as thinking about Thomas Pearson, a fellow marine biologist who made big bucks writing under the D'Jacqueline pen name. This was supporting a colleague. That was all.

A colleague with brown hair and lush red highlights, broad shoulders, long legs, and dimples. A colleague who carried a switchblade among other various illegal weapons. A colleague who told her he loved her and then left for eleven months and fourteen days.

"Stop it!" she yowled aloud, ignoring the startled looks of passersby. "He had his fellowship to finish and he only knew you a week so just cut it out! What are *you* looking at?" she added fiercely, and the kindergarten-age child scuttled behind her mother's legs.

No, Thomas was gone and that was all. So was Artur, for that matter, the *other* man she determinedly did not think about. A full-blooded member of the Undersea Folk—a merman, in other words. Not a half-and-half hybrid like herself.

More than that: a prince, the eldest son of the High King of the Black Sea. A prince with hair the color of rubies and eyes the color of cherry cough drops; a prince with big hands he couldn't keep to himself. And a red beard that tickled whenever he *did things she would not think about.*

She stopped at her brownstone, practically ran up the stairs, jammed her key in the lock, and rushed into the foyer. Too keyed up for the elevator, she walked the three flights to her apartment and almost knocked the door down instead of fumbling with her key.

She kicked the door shut behind her and snarled, "What are you two doing here?"

"Waiting for you," her best friend, Jonas Carrey, chirped. He was a tall blond, a couple of inches taller than she, who held several black belts and loved appletinis. Oh, and her boss, Dr. Barb, who was currently sitting on his lap.

"Dr. Barb," Fred sighed, tossing her book bag onto the nearest counter.

"Dr. Bimm." Her boss was a stickler for titles under all circumstances, even if Jonas's hand was trying to undo her bra clasp.

"Dr. Barb, you've been dating my friend for a year. Don't you think it's time you called me Fred?"

"No, Dr. Bimm."

Fred sighed again. She liked her boss, under normal circumstances, but since the woman had started banging her best friend, it was harder and harder to be around the two of them.

For one thing, they were still in the "oooh goo oooh" stage of courtship, when anything either of them did was greeted with cries of delight. Jonas could find a worm in his oatmeal and Dr. Barb would find it charming.

For another thing, like most couples, they felt all Fred's problems would be solved if only she could Find Someone. To that end . . .

"Sam's going to be here any minute," Jonas informed her, like she could forget. "Is that, um, what you're wearing?"

"Yes." She almost snapped. For the hundredth time, she wished she hadn't given Jonas a set of her keys. She never knew when she'd find him (them) lurking in her apartment. "Why, what's the matter?"

"Besides the fact that it's sixty degrees out and you're wearing cutoffs and a T-shirt? And would it kill you to wear a bra?"

Fred barely restrained a sniff. As a mermaid, she didn't much notice the cold—Jonas ought to try the Arctic sometime if he thought Massachusetts autumns were chilly. And, frankly, she didn't need a bra. Never had. Either gravity was being kind, or it was another benefit of her half-and-half heritage.

"At least a pedicure," Jonas was begging. "And brush your hair. You'd be so gorgeous if you—"

"That's not nice," Dr. Barb said reproachfully. Jonas had performed one of his miraculous makeovers on her just before they'd started going out, and it had gone straight to his head.

Normally tightly bound in a braid, Dr. Barb's beautiful dark blonde hair now tumbled halfway down her back. Her almond-shaped eyes were carefully made-up, and she was wearing a tailored red suit. Her tiny, red pump–shod feet dangled several inches above the floor and she snuggled farther into Jonas's lap.

"Fred doesn't need any help to look good," her besotted boss was saying. Fred, meanwhile, had opened her fridge and was desperately hunting for a beer. Or Drano. "You leave her be."

"Sorry, baby."

"You're forgiven, for a kiss."

"Two kisses!"

Fred kept hunting. Could she get drunk off of two measly wine coolers? Maybe if she spiked them with the spoiled milk . . .

"Done!" Jonas cried, and then various smacking noises cut off the annoying conversation. Of course, now she was dealing with a whole new set of annoying, but—

"Success!" She snatched the Miller Lite left over from some party. Let's see, the last party Jonas had made her host had been in the twentieth century . . . Did beer go bad? Oh, who cared?

"Your hair is so soft," Dr. Barb sighed, running her fingers through Jonas's carefully coiffed locks.

"So is yours, baby, but you should use more of that deep conditioner I left at your place." Jonas was a chemical scientist who worked for Aveda, and was always dropping off free product. Fred ignored it, but Dr. Barb took it to heart. "Just wrap your hair in a towel and leave it in for half an hour or so, then rinse."

"I will . . ." Fred looked around for a bottle opener, then gave up and wrenched the cap off with her bare hand. "For a kiss."

Fred guzzled.

"Done!" More smacking sounds.

Fred finished the beer and noted, with despair, that her damned superior metabolism had taken care of any meager alcohol offered by the good people at Miller, Inc. She should have known. But desperate times called for desperate—

"I love your eyes," Dr. Barb sighed, coming up for air.

"I love yours," Jonas said, caressing Barb's long strands of hair.

"I could look into yours all day and never get tired of the view," Dr. Barb said, stroking Jonas's shoulder.

Jonas nibbled on her ear in response. Fred coldly watched the primates groom each other and actually wished her blind date—the third in two weeks—would show up already.

In answer to her prayer, there was a sharp rap at her door.

"Oh thank God," she mumbled. Then, louder, "Get out, you two. I've got to go. Uh . . . what's this one's name again?"

"Sam Fisher," Dr. Barb said patiently.

Fred shot Jonas a look. Dr. Barb didn't know Fred was a mermaid . . . yet. "Is that supposed to be a joke?"

"We had the same advisor in graduate school. It's not his fault he ended up in marine biology."

"Out!"

"We're going, we're going," Jonas said.

"I'm sure you'll just love him," Dr. Barb said doubtfully, climbing out of Jonas's lap. "You'll have lots to talk about."

"And brush your hair before you take off," Jonas added, following his ladylove to the door. Jonas yanked it open, nearly got a fist in the face (Sam liked to knock, lots, and *loud*), and said, "Nice to meet you, good-bye."

The door shut behind them and Fred sized up her latest blind date. To her amusement, he was frowning at her. Tall and whip thin, with wire-rimmed glasses and a shaved head, he had the most amazing green eyes she'd ever seen, the color of moss on a rainy day.

"Hi," she said. "I'm Fred Bimm."

"Sam Fisher. Look, the only reason I'm here is because Barb has been on my ass to hook up ever since she started getting laid regularly."

Fred swallowed a cough of surprise. "It's, ah, nice to meet you, too."

He raised an eyebrow at her. "And I bet *you're* only here—besides the fact that you live here—because *your* friend wants you to hook up, too."

"It's not the only reason."

He frowned at her.

"It's the only reason," she admitted.

"I'm perfectly happy with my life right now, not to mention you're too young for me."

"I'm thirty," she protested.

"A mere infant. Also, my TiVo is on the fritz and if I take you to dinner, I'm going to miss *Lost*."

"You're trying to get out of a date to watch TV?"

"It's the season opener!"

Fred shrugged. "They're not going to really tell you anything. You know that, right? Every week is just another hand-job, courtesy of ABC."

Sam's frown deepened. "If the subtle clues fly over your head, that's not ABC's fault."

"Hey!"

"But as I was saying. Assuming we went on this travesty of a date—"

"Hey!" Fred was used to being the most irritating person in the room. Sam's attitude was startling, to put it mildly.

"—we'd take the T to Le Meridien—I'd treat for the subway tokens."

"I have a T card," Fred volunteered.

"Fine. We'd have drinks and dinner and, since I'm a generous tipper . . ." He tipped his head back and stared at the ceiling. "Call it a hundred fifty bucks."

"No dessert?"

He ignored her. "Then we might decide to take in a late show. Call it another twenty bucks. Plus popcorn and drinks. Another twenty-five."

"I'd still be full from dinner. No popcorn for me."

"Nothing must be left to chance. So that brings us to one hundred ninety-five dollars. But since you're a modern woman, you'll insist on paying for half."

"Also, I don't want to feel obligated to put out."

"Too right. Which makes your share ninety-seven dollars and fifty cents."

Sam waited expectantly. Fred swallowed a grin and said, "Will you take a check?"

Two

"So that's what you do? All day? You feed fish?" Blind Date Number Four (she could not remember the man's name for her life) asked, forking more linguine with clams into his maw, which was always open—either for food or inane chatter.

"That's all," Fred replied, repressing a shudder and attacking her salad like a moray eel going after an angelfish. She was allergic to shellfish and watching Number Four shovel it in was fairly nauseating. "I feed the fish, make sure the little ones aren't getting chomped, like that."

"I think I've see you in the tank!" Number Four exclaimed, and a tiny piece of masticated clam hit Fred's left cheek. "You're one of the guys in the scuba suits who hang out in that big tank."

"Main One," she corrected him, concealing a shudder as she wiped her cheek with a napkin. It was telling how much this one was irritating her; she never called it Main One. That was strictly a Dr. Barb rule. "And I doubt you've seen me."

If he'd seen her flailing around in her wet suit, he certainly would have remembered. She couldn't swim with legs; only with her tail. It made her job trickier than it had to be, for sure. For one thing, she always ended up upside down in Main One, and her scuba gear always tried its best to get tangled, despite her years of certification.

"I monitor the water levels and pull out any sick fish and stuff like that."

"Cool! So what's that pay?"

She gave him an odd look. Number Four had managed to work money into the conversation a record seven times. She already knew what his house cost, what his annual salary was, what his tax bite was, and what a flight to Tokyo cost these days.

"Enough to keep a roof over my head."

"I'm gonna say fifty," he guessed. He looked like an accountant—brown suit, brown hair, mud-colored eyes, stubby fingers. Not unattractive, just . . . blah. "Fifty K. You've got an advanced degree, that's gotta be worth some bucks."

Fred laughed. "Shows what you know about advanced degrees . . . and private nonprofits."

"So quit and work in the public sector."

"I like my job."

"I bet you could make six figures in the public sector."

"Sure, thinking up new and improved crap to dump in the ocean. No thanks."

"Six figures!" Number Four repeated, spraying more clam sauce.

"Don't care. Don't need it. Getting bored."

"Want dessert?"

"Hell, no."

For the third time, Fred explained to Number Four that he didn't need to drive her to her apartment in his new Lexus hybrid ($75,000, after rebate).

"It's just twenty minutes by subway. I'll be fine."

"Oh, come on. Leather seats!"

"I'm all atingle," she replied. They were walking past the restaurant toward the Park Street T stop. "Really."

"Then how about something for my trouble?"

"Nope."

"Leather seats!"

"Go away," she told Number Four.

"Aw, come on! I took the whole afternoon off for you."

It was true; it hadn't been dinner, it had been lunch. Dr. Barb had given her the day off, which should have instantly roused her suspicions.

"And I'm pathetically grateful. Good bye."

He reached out and seized her arm. "Just one kiss," he said, breathing clams and garlic in her face. "And maybe a hand-job."

Fred blinked. It wasn't that she was inexperienced, or a prude. She just hadn't met an asshole of this magnitude since she, Thomas, and Artur had killed Dr. Barb's ex-husband last fall.

She smiled at him. She wished, in that moment, she'd inherited the sharp teeth of her father's people instead of the flat grinders of Homo sapiens. "I'll be happy to give you a hand-job," she said.

"Great!" He yanked her by the elbow toward the cemetery outside the T stop. "C'mere, we can have some privacy."

"No need for that," she said, effortlessly extricating herself from his grip, seizing each of his thumbs, and popping them out of their sockets.

He didn't scream so much as whinny, and bent forward to cradle his odd-looking thumbs between his thighs.

"Thanks for lunch," she said, stepping around him and already fishing for her T card.

Three

Fred saw the lights on in her apartment and stomped up the stairs. This time she'd give Jonas a piece of her mind, as well as Dr. Barb, never mind that the woman was her boss. Enough was enough! Clam globs in her face, garlic breath, sexual harassment. And it wasn't even Wednesday!

She unlocked her door and shoved it open, and was momentarily startled to see the happy couple sitting stiffly on her couch as opposed to grooming each other or, worse, getting to third base.

Standing just inside her doorway were two strangers. One was a young man—early twenties?—with startling orange hair (jack-o'-lantern orange) and matching eyes. Beside him was a petite young woman of about the same age, with dark blue hair and eyes that were even darker, the way small sapphires almost looked black in the right light.

She knew at once they were Undersea Folk, and mentally she groaned. Apparently the high point of her day was going to be dislocating Number Four's thumbs.

Before either stranger could speak, Jonas leapt up from the couch, said (too heartily), "Good, great, you're here, we told your friends we'd wait with them, but now you're here so we'll be going, see you, good-bye."

"Good-bye," Dr. Barb managed as Jonas dragged her out the door. "Young lady, whoever does your hair is doing a magnificent—"

Jonas slammed the door.

Fred surveyed the mermaid and merman. "Hit me," she said at last.

The two exchanged puzzled glances. "Those are not our instructions," the man said. "I am Kertal. This is Tennian. We were sent by the High King."

"Well, I didn't think you were here to take a survey. Something to drink? Some chips?"

"No, thank you," the woman—Tennian—said in a soft, lovely alto. "You are Fredrika Bimm, of Kortrim's line."

"If Kortrim is my bio-dad, you're right. But I prefer to think of myself as being of Moon Bimm's line. That's my mother," she added helpfully.

"Yes, His Highness has told us of your lady mother," Kertal said.

He towered over her and had the ropy muscles of a long-distance swimmer. Which, of course, he was. She was having a terrible time not staring at him. Both of them. Their coloring was so extraordinary! It was odd to be in a room and not feel like she had the freakiest hair there. "We were instructed to try you at your home if we did not find you at the aquarium."

"You went to where I *work*?"

"Yes."

"Oh my God," Fred said, and collapsed on her couch.

"We asked of you, and spoke of you to your friends. They brought us to your"—Kertal looked around the tiny apartment with an unreadable expression on his face—"home."

"You didn't tell them who you were, did you?"

"Our business is with you, not them."

"I'm going to take that as a no." She rolled over and stared at the ceiling. "Thank God. My boss doesn't know I'm a mermaid and I'd like to keep it that way."

Again, the two strangers exchanged glances, and again, it was Kertal who spoke. "We are charged by the High King to summon you to the Pelagic."

"The Pelagic?" Fred could almost feel her mind buckle under the strain and she giggled until she lost her breath. "I don't know what you guys think it is, but here a pelagic is an open zone in the ocean that's not near a coast or even a sea floor. How can you bring me to *a* pelagic? And will you sit down? You look like a couple of Army recruiters. Unclench."

Neither of them moved. "A Pelagic is a meeting that can only be called by a majority of the Undersea Folk."

"I thought you guys were a monarchy."

"Our good king has acceded to the request of his people," Tennian almost whispered.

"Can you speak up, please? It's hard to hear you over the roaring in my ears."

"Will you come?" Tennian asked, slightly louder.

"To this Pelagic thing? Sorry, I'll need a little more info before I go gallivanting off with you two. Like, what exactly is it? Where is it? And why am I invited? And will you two *sit down*? I'm freaked out enough."

The two Undersea Folk gingerly sat on her kitchen chairs. Fred's apartment was an open design. The kitchen, the dining room, and the living room were all one big space. The small bedroom was off to the left, the bathroom off to the right.

Fred had fooled the eye into thinking the place was large and airy by painting all the walls white. The place was stark enough to belong to a monk, which suited her fine. She hated clutter.

She spotted the brand-new Aveda bag beside the kitchen chair, and nudged it beneath the table with a toe. "So. You were saying?"

"As you know, Fredrika, the royal family makes its home in the Black Sea. It is also the seat of our government."

"Right, the king and Artur. Got it."

"And His Highness Rankon, and Her Highness Jeredna."

"He's got sibs? He never said. And would it kill you guys to have a Jenny or a Peter?"

"It is not for us to know the workings of the royal mind," Tennian murmured.

"Ha! I know all about the workings of Artur's mind, and he's only got one thing on it. That's—Never mind. You were saying?"

"May I have a glass of water?" Kertal asked.

"Sure." Fred jumped up, glad to have something to do. She guessed what Kertal's problem was—simple dehydration—and filled two glasses, one for each of them, to the top. As Artur had told her last year, Undersea Folk could walk around on land, but not for long, and they weakened quickly.

Tiny Tennian drained hers in three gulps and politely asked for a refill. And another. Thus, it was a good five minutes before either of them got back to the subject at hand.

"I assume you guys hang out in the Black Sea because it's enclosed? Easier to stay hidden? I mean, up here, you're—we're—myths. No one's been able to prove the Undersea Folk exist."

"You are correct, Fredrika," Kertal said, setting his empty glass down on the kitchen table. "Your studies of the sea have served you well."

"Yes, I have my name on all sorts of pretty papers."

"Many centuries ago the royal family chose the Black Sea for precisely that reason. That is not to say we all live there; the Undersea Folk are scattered all over the world."

"I live in Chesapeake Bay," Tennian whispered.

"But the seat of power has always been in the Black Sea. However, there are so many of us, and it can be a difficult place to get to in a short time without rousing suspicion. So the Pelagic will be held in the waters of the Cayman Islands."

"Ah, the glorious Caymans. What are you, repping the chamber of commerce?"

"No," Kertal the Humorless replied. "We will wait while you collect your things."

"Hold up, hold up. So this Pelagic, the purpose of which neither of you have bothered to explain, won't be where the royal family hangs out, and we won't be going to Turkey. But we'll have a fine time hanging out in the Caymans."

"I do not know how fine a time it will be," Kertal said soberly.

"Oh, here we go."

"Many of our people do not wish to remain myths."

"Oh, ho."

"This goes directly against the wishes of the royal family."

"Fascinating."

"Thus, the Pelagic: a meeting of all Folk, to decide a common action. They are quite rare; the last one was held—ah—" He glanced at Tennian and the small woman shook her head. "—was a while ago. Decades."

Fred smelled a rat. Or a fish. But there was time to get to the bottom of that later. "So you guys are getting together to figure out whether to go public or not?"

"Not 'you guys.' All of us. You, too, Fredrika."

She raised an eyebrow. "Is that a fact?"

"The High King insists."

"So? I'm not one of his subjects."

"Excuse me," Tennian murmured, "but you are."

"Want to arm wrestle for it?"

"The king requires your presence," Kertal droned on. "As does His Highness, Prince Artur."

"And I'm *definitely* not at *his* beck and call. Sorry you came all this way for nothing, help yourselves to more water, good-bye."

"The prince suspected you would be . . . intractable."

She folded her arms across her chest. "Try unbudgeable."

"He asked us to remind you that he saved your life."

"He didn't stop me from getting shot!" And why was the thought of seeing the redheaded bum again so thrilling? Not to mention the idea of meeting other Undersea Folk. Of course, if they were all as stodgy as these two, it'd be a long time in the Caymans. Which reminded her . . . "How long is this Pelagic supposed to last?"

"Until the majority comes to an agreement, approved by His Majesty."

"But that could take—I have no idea how long that could take. How many mer-dudes will show up?"

"Thousands."

"Thousands?"

"Perhaps. There is no way to tell."

"Is there anything you *can* commit to?"

"We cannot leave without your agreement and attendance."

"Oh, friggin' swell." Fred rested her chin on her fist and thought. The other two watched her do it, and said nothing. Finally she said, "Is Artur sending duos of ambassadors to *all* the Undersea Folk?"

Again, they exchanged a look. But this time Tennian spoke up. Barely. "No. You are considered a special case, and essential to this gathering."

"According to whom?"

"The entire royal family."

Fred gave thanks she was sitting down, because otherwise she was fairly certain she would have fallen on her ass.

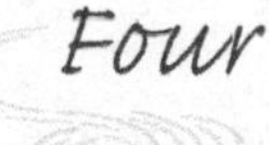

Four

"But why?" she managed after gasping like a landed trout.

"It is not for us to know."

"Just 'go fetch Fred,' is that it?"

"Yes," Kertal replied.

"And I'm supposed to pack a bag and follow you guys to the Caymans?"

"Yes."

"And if I don't?"

"You owe a debt to the royal family," Kertal reminded her.

"And you're a subject," Tennian added unhelpfully.

"I am not! And I do not." Still. Talk about a once in a lifetime opportunity. The marine biologist in her was itching to get a look at a meeting populated with thousands of mermaids. But it chafed, being ordered to go like that. Shit, her mom had quit trying to give her orders by the fourth grade.

She wondered how the other Folk knew to come to the Caymans, then remembered how her father's people communicated: by telepathy. Duh. How *else* did you talk underwater?

Fred opened her mouth to argue more when she heard the rattle of keys and her front door burst open. Jonas was framed in the doorway, panting, clutching her doorknob so hard his knuckles were white. "What'd I miss?"

"Apparently I'm going to the Caymans."

"How come?"

"Super secret mermaid business."

Her friend beamed. "Great! I'll go pack your things. Good thing you've got tons of vacation time coming. Don't worry, I'll fix it with Barb."

Fred covered her face with her hands. "Shit."

"Will I need a passport?"

"You're not coming," she tried, already knowing the outcome.

"Ha! Think I'll miss out on a chance to stock up on some of that yummy rum? And do you know how long it's been since I've had a vacation? Never mind how long it's been since *you've* had one." To Tennian and Kertal: "Classic workaholic, you guys. No hope at all." To Fred: "Besides, you'll just get into trouble by yourself."

"Sir, you are not invited," Kertal said.

"Sir, I'd like to see you stop me. I would also like to find out who does your hair."

"Bipeds are not welcome," Tennian mumbled.

"And *your* hair."

Fred saw her chance, and jumped at it. "I'm only going if he goes." Had she really just said that? She mentally replayed the last five seconds. Yes, she had. "That's the deal. Take it or leave it."

This time, the Grim Duo didn't bother exchanging glances. They just nodded in perfect weird unison.

"Woo-hoo!" Jonas yowled. "I'll go pack my swim trunks."

Five

"I don't know why you're so excited," Fred grumbled as Jonas stomped on the accelerator. As it was fall, and midweek, traffic to Cape Cod was light. And Jonas was enjoying his new toy, a gray Ford hybrid. "I haven't even decided to go."

"Yuh-huh!" He beeped the horn at a dawdling tourist—they both hated it when morons went fifty miles an hour in the passing zone—and whipped past the small blue Volkswagen.

Fred slammed her finger down on the window button and yowled into the wind, "Passing zone is for passing, shithead!"

"Don't make me put the child locks on the windows again," Jonas warned. "And you did so say you were going. You told what's-their-names you'd go if I could go."

"Yeah, well, I lost my temper there for a second. Frankly, I can't figure out why we're even going to my mom's."

"Because *nice* and *loving* daughters *tell* their hot moms when they're *leaving* the *country*."

"That's enough about my hot mom," Fred warned, knowing it was no use. The former hippie, Moon Bimm, was in ridiculously good shape for a woman in her early fifties. To Fred's eternal despair, she had personal knowledge that Moon still had the sex drive of an eighteen-year-old.

"Say," Jonas said cheerfully, reading her mind as usual, "remember last year when you walked in on her and Sam doing the wild thing on the—"

Fred jabbed the volume button.

"Didn't your stepfather have to go see a chiropractor after you threw him off your mom?" Jonas screamed over the music.

Fred rolled the window back down and stuck her head out, doglike, for the next half hour.

"Come on, show me," Jonas begged.

So she took her friend around the side of the cream-colored Cape Cod house with the hunter green shutters, and showed him the now-fixed sliding glass kitchen door. The one she'd broken through last fall when she thought her mother was in danger at the hands of a merman. The first one she'd ever met.

"Jeez," Jonas said, impressed. He rapped his knuckles on the glass. "This shit is *thick*. And you just walked through it?"

"Kicked it in. Then walked."

"The extreme always makes an impression," Jonas said, quoting a line from his all-time favorite movie, *Heathers*. He'd had an absurd crush on Winona Ryder since *Mermaids*.

"Then what?"

"Then I met Artur, High Prince of the Undersea Folk, whom I had assumed was committing felony assault on my folks."

"Not knowing," Jonas added, having begged to hear the story about a thousand times, "that Moon had already charmed him with her extreme hotness and everything was fine."

"Anyway," she continued with a glare, "Sam got the door fixed the next day, end of story."

"Ah, Sam. Ridiculously fortunate (wealthy) hubby to the delicious Moon, trodden stepfather to the grumpiest mermaid on the planet. Agh!"

Fred flinched, then looked. The man in question, her stepfather, was blinking at them through the glass (and his bifocals). Sam was a few inches shorter than Fred, with graying brown hair pulled back in his usual ponytail, which only highlighted his bald spot.

He hit the latch and slid the door open. "Hello, Fred. Jonas. We have a guest." Code for: ix-nay on the ermaid-may uff-stay.

"We won't stay long," Fred promised, stepping past her stepfather.

"Maybe only for dessert. Did Moon make ice cream again?" Jonas asked.

"Are you kidding?" Sam smiled and opened the freezer. "What's your favorite flavor?"

"Wh-who's that?" a trembling voice asked.

Sam stretched out one of his rough amateur carpenter's hands and, after a long moment, a little girl (Fred put her age at about five, unless she was malnourished, which was certainly likely given her bone structure and large, almost bulging brown eyes) reached out and grasped one of Sam's fingers. "Ellie, this is my daughter, Fred, and her best friend, Jonas."

Ellie was now standing almost behind Sam, and Fred could only see one big brown eye. Jonas, busily building himself a six-scoop sundae, looked up from licking a spoon and waved.

"Who's he?" Ellie whispered.

Sam knelt, very slowly, and took Ellie by the shoulders, very gently. "That is my daughter's very best friend in the world. He was picked on all the time in school and Fred had to watch out for him. She protected him. He would never, ever hurt you."

"But you don't know." Ellie's expression had the faraway look of a child in a nightmare she would never wake from. "Only God knows everything."

Fred coughed, which caused Sam and Ellie to look over at her. "Hey, Ellie. Watch this."

Mentally apologizing to her oldest friend, Fred seized Jonas by the shirt collar and heaved him out of his chair and through the (fortunately open) sliding door.

Six

Jonas was densely built ("Deliciously so," Dr. Barb might have said over the sound of Fred's retching), but no match for Fred's hybrid strength, and the air velocity he achieved was really quite something.

Fred ignored his wail ("My sundaeeee!"), which became easier to do the fainter it got. "See that, Ellie? Like Sam said, my friend would never hurt you. But if he did, if he contracted rabies and went crazy and actually tried to put his hands on you in a way you didn't like, I'd kick his balls up so high, he'd choke on them. 'Kay?"

Ellie edged around Sam and peered up at Fred. "Do you work out?"

"No, I hate gyms. And I hate tracks. I never work out if I can help it. Well, I swim." She thought, something so fun and necessary wasn't really *working out*, was it? "A lot."

Fred, of course, had known about the foster children her mother and Sam had been taking in. Some only stayed a week or two while various paperwork plodded through the system. Some only stayed a few hours. And some, like Ellie, had been around for months, because Sam was the only adult male she would tolerate. Ellie had been known to set fires around males who frightened her. Burning to death, she had explained to an ER attending (as well as several social workers), was preferable to Being Touched Like That Again.

The girl, as terrifying as she was vulnerable, was looking up at her. "I like your hair," she almost whispered.

"Thanks." Fred self-consciously fingered her greenish strands. "Can Jonas come back in?"

"It's your house," Ellie pointed out, holding out her hands in a gesture of helplessness, which showed Fred the severe scars crawling up and down the girl's forearms.

"Actually, it's Sam's house," Fred corrected her mildly, gnawing on the inside of her lower lip so she wouldn't shake the biological father's address out of the kid. "And my mom's. But if you don't want him to come back in, he can have his ice cream on the lawn."

"I hate youuuuuu," Jonas's voice floated in.

To Fred's amazement, the solemn, damaged child smiled. "He can come in. As long as you're here."

"As you wish, Ellie." Sam knelt and gently pulled the little girl around until she was standing in front of him. "But even if Fred wasn't here, I would protect you. You know that, don't you?"

"Yes, Sam. I have to go. Commercial's over." She walked out of the kitchen without another word.

"What the hell?" Jonas bitched, walking back in while brushing leaves out of his not-so-perfectly coiffed hair. "Do you ever ask yourself why you don't have a large social circle, Fred? Do you?"

"Sorry." She wasn't. "Had to make a point for the foster kid du jour."

"Oh, right. I forgot. But jeez! A little warning next time! Thanks for aiming me at the big pile of leaves."

"Welcome," she said, pretending she had done so on purpose. "Finish your sundae, you slob."

"Hey, I'm crawling with leaves and dead bugs and I *still* look better than you do."

This was true, so Fred dismissed the argument and turned to Sam, seeing him with new eyes. Oh, he *looked* the same. Myopic brown peepers blinking almost constantly, slim build, small potbelly, the perpetual ponytail.

He'd been there from her earliest memory, and she'd always known he hadn't been her *real* father, even though her mother hadn't told her so until Fred was nearly thirty. For heaven's sake, Sam panicked in a tide pool, whereas Fred had been breaststroking alongside wild dolphins since she was seven.

No, Sam was Sam, and for once she was grateful, for she realized how much this gentle man had to offer a child, any child. Certainly he treated her mother like a queen. And not out of fear of what Fred would do to him, either.

In fact, she was forced to admit to herself, it couldn't be easy having a mermaid for a stepdaughter, especially one as, uh, passionate as she was.

"What kind of marks are on her arm?" she asked abruptly, because the last thing she was going to do was go all mushy on *Sam* of all people. "Kitchen knife?"

"You should see her back," Sam said quietly, taking off his glasses and wiping them furiously on his faded Rolling Stones T-shirt. "Box cutter. Her dad works in a liquor warehouse. Likes to keep one on him for emergencies."

"File."

He blinked at her with watery brown eyes and put the glasses back on. "Sorry?"

"Her file. Gimme."

Sam actually smiled. "I was hoping you'd drop by, Fred, and her file is in my office, in your drawer."

Your drawer. A Sam-ism for a large file cabinet in the west corner of his office. Three feet deep, four drawers high. Never locked. Meticulously organized. Every drawing, every clay pot, every useless ashtray, every book report, every term paper Fred had come up with, from kindergarten to her doctoral thesis, was in that file cabinet. Sam had always left notes, books for her to read, information he wanted her to have, in the top drawer in the file marked "Fredly Fire." That's where Ellie's file would be. No doubt along with a copy of *Seven Highly Effective Habits for Undersea Folk.*

Sam usually put up a bit more of a fuss when it came to violence, or proposed violence, so Fred narrowed her eyes at him and asked, "Isn't this the part where you preach peace and love?"

"I'll leave that, in this case, to your mother. Who is watching cartoons in the living room with Ellie. I'll go get her."

"Hey, Sam."

He turned and arched his graying brows.

"Thanks." And not just for Ellie. But she wouldn't—well, couldn't—get into that now.

Her stepfather nodded and padded out of the kitchen.

"Foster parents get files?" Jonas asked, scraping his bowl. "You'll be able to track down Daddy-o? Maybe pitch him headfirst into an industrial dryer and push Spin? Don't even think about going without me."

"Of course I'm thinking about going without you. Given Ellie's phobia around grown men, it's not hard to figure out who the bad guy is. And as a matter of fact, they *don't* give very detailed files. You know the term hacker, of course."

"Enlighten me, o brilliant fish tail," Jonas said with a mouthful of strawberry ice cream. "Pretend I'm an ignorant slob just like you."

"The term was *created* for Sam." Fred was smirking in spite of herself. She'd figured *that* out on her own by age ten. "He could use a computer as a spyglass before anyone knew it was possible. And he doesn't take a kid into his house until he knows *everything*."

"Not very hippielike," Jonas said, trying (and failing) to sound disapproving.

"Everybody's got bad habits."

"Fred! Sweetie!" Her mother, Moon, a short, good-looking blonde with silver streaks and shoulder-length hair, hurried into the kitchen and squeezed Fred so hard she nearly gasped. She was dressed in a faded pink T-shirt (one that had been red when Fred was a fourth grader) and jeans that clung to her chubby thighs. "What earthshaking revelation brings you back home this time?"

"Earthshaking," Jonas said with a mouthful of chocolate. "Ha!"

"Oh!" Moon jumped, then beamed. "Jonas, sweetie, I didn't see you there."

"That's because Fred's all hulking 'n stuff in the doorway. Great ice cream."

"I was not *hulking*."

"Did you find the banana?"

Jonas nodded. "It's beside the blueberry sorbet."

"How do you stay so slim?" her mother wondered, eyeing the remnants of the heroic sundae Jonas had nearly demolished.

"Clean living," he replied with his mouth full.

"And that cute new girlfriend, I bet." Moon winked.

"That cute new girlfriend is my boss, and let's change the subject," Fred interrupted, because Jonas and Moon could banter for hours. "I gotta leave town for a while."

"Business trip?"

"Yes," Fred said at the exact moment Jonas said, "No."

They glared at each other.

"Uh-oh," her mother said, blue eyes twinkling. "And to think, it's been so dull around here the last few months. Except when Ellie forgot to put the top on the blender," she added thoughtfully, "and pushed Puree."

"It's no big deal, Mom."

"It's a *huge* deal, Moon," Jonas said. "You look great, by the way."

"I would find that flattering yet creepy," her mother said with a smile, "if I didn't know about your girlfriend. And as for you, Fredrika Bimm." The smile vanished. "I wouldn't stand a lie from you when you were three. What makes you think anything's changed?"

"It's a Pelagic."

"Nor will I stand for your marine biologist geek-speak, which you so often use to avoid a direct answer. You can't hide behind language, young lady, so out with it."

Fred cursed the rotten luck of having a smart mother. "It's a meeting, okay? A meeting of all the Undersea Folk. You know, the name they use for themselves."

"It'll be Mermaid Central," Jonas added, "and Fred's ringside."

"Really?" Moon pulled up a chair and sat, leaning her elbows on the table. She was thinking so hard, her laugh lines were going the wrong way. "They're having a meeting and they invited you?"

"Yeah."

"Boggles the mind," Jonas added, "don't it?"

The laugh lines reversed and Moon's face lit up. "But that's wonderful!"

"Why," Fred asked suspiciously, "is it wonderful?"

"It means they're accepting you as one of them! And—and—"

Fred let her mother grope for words, not having the heart to say that Jonas, too, had an invitation to the Pelagic and certainly was *not* accepted by them. One didn't ensure the other. And Tennian and Kertal had been creepily vague.

She didn't like it. At all. She was only going because they'd gotten stubborn about Jonas and she couldn't resist jerking their chains. It had nothing to do with the possibility of seeing Artur again.

Nothing.

At all.

Shit, the guy was probably married with a wife who'd already popped out a litter of guppies. No, she had enough on her plate without worrying about Artur and who he'd been banging and what he'd been up to. Like . . . like . . .

Thomas! Thomas, for instance. She wondered what Thomas would think of the Pelagic. Shit, that was a lie. She knew exactly what he'd think. He was a marine biologist; he'd be wild to go.

Firmly, she shoved Artur and Thomas out of her mind and focused on what her mother was saying.

"—maybe even see your father again!"

Fred's jaw sagged and she clutched the back of the empty chair so hard she heard it crack. Here was a nightmare she had never even considered.

"You'd better sit down," Jonas worried. "You look really white. Even for you."

"I'm not going to the Caymans for a fucking family reunion!" she yowled.

"Oh, this Pelagic thing is in the Cayman Islands? Lovely this time of the year." Moon frowned. "I think. It's not hurricane season, is it?"

"Mom, I don't even know if my father will be there."

"It's a big meeting? Important? Obviously someone tracked you down and presented an invitation. That's a lot of trouble for, say, a slumber party."

"Yeah," Fred said grudgingly.

"So it's obviously a very important thing, this Paregoric, if they're tracking everybody down for it."

"Pelagic. A paregoric makes you pass out. On second thought," Fred admitted, "that might be the right name after all."

"Then he might be there! In fact, he's *sure* to be there!"

"Wait, wait, wait." Jonas held up a strawberry-stained hand like a traffic cop gone off his diet. "I thought Artur said your dad was dead. Remember, last fall? Just before Fred broke down the kitchen door?"

"He said he *thought* Fred's dad was dead. That he hadn't been seen for many years. But the ocean is a big place." To Fred's dismay, Moon had that "everything will work out" expression on her face. "He could be alive! Sure he could! And Fred could meet him."

"Mom, I wouldn't know my bio-dad if he swam up to me and hooked me in the gut. And he wouldn't know me."

"Then I'll describe him," she said, and the horror continued. "He was built like a swimmer—"

"Ha, ha."

"—with the broad shoulders, you know, and the narrow waist? Oh, the body on your father! It was too dark to see his hair color, and besides, his hair was wet, but I imagine it's a darker shade of yours."

"Mom, I'm going to break Jonas's ice cream bowl and eat the pieces if you don't stop."

"His eyes were the purest green I'd ever seen, even darker than yours, sweetie. He was . . ." She looked over her shoulder, satisfying herself that Ellie and Sam were engrossed in *SpongeBob.* "He was the most mesmerizing creature I'd ever met."

"Vomit, vomit, vomit."

"I hardly noticed when he was inside me because I was just so enthralled by his eyes, his hair, his shoulders . . . and then it was done—"

"Mesmerizing," Jonas noted, "but fast."

"—and then he rolled off me and dove back into the ocean and I watched for him until dawn, but he never came back. I watched for him at that spot every night for three months." Moon sighed and looked out the kitchen window. "But he never came back."

"You want me to track that shitheel down? Fuck that!"

"Fredrika," her mom warned.

"Mom, he banged you and then he forgot about you. If I *do* find him, I plan on kicking the fins out of him. Nobody treats my mother like that!"

"Fredrika, Sam and I will not be here forever."

"Not the 'you gotta find a man' speech again, for crying out loud."

"I'm not implying you need a man to be happy. I'm saying your blood relatives are rare and wonderful things. Yours in particular," she added, unconsciously eyeing Fred's hair. "If you could find your biological father . . . Even if it's true, even if he's dead, maybe you have . . . I don't know . . . aunts? Cousins?"

"Forget it, Mom. It's a Pelagic, not a family reunion." Whatever that meant. "I'm going to this meeting and that's it. Jonas thought we ought to stop by and let you know we'll be out of town for a while." And it was for just this sort of reason that she tended to avoid trips to the Cape. "Oh, and I gotta get something out of Sam's office. And then we're out of here."

"Will Prince Artur be there?"

Fred groaned. "Yes."

"It's a regular Hottie Convention," Jonas said. "It's just stupid how all the Undersea Folk are gorgeous."

"Hmmm," her mother said.

"What, 'hmmm'?"

"It's amazing how a person such as myself, generally open and friendly, could have raised such a suspicious creature."

"Well, so what if you did?" Fred snapped. "Who cares if Artur's there? Not me! I haven't even thought about the guy since he said he wanted me to be a princess and then swam out of town. And I don't *want* to think about him, and I'll thank you two to stop cramming him down my throat!"

Jonas and Moon blinked at her.

Fred coughed and lowered her voice. "Also, I'd like to use Sam's office for a minute. And also the bathroom. And then we're out of here."

"Well, that's fine, sweetie. Have fun at your Pelican."

"Oh, sure," Fred muttered. "Tons of fun at the Pelican. Pelican, here I come."

"Here *we* come," Jonas corrected her, cheerfully.

Fred bit back several retorts, contented herself with a final baleful glare, and exited the kitchen.

Seven

The van pulled up to the Pirate's Cove Resort on Little Cayman Island with its engine laboring. It was painted serial-killer green, and smelled like feet.

"Finally!" Jonas said, peering out a dirty window. "I thought we'd never get here."

"And I thought you'd never shut up." It had been an excruciating twelve hours, made more difficult by the fact that Fred was not a fan of flying. But she only had herself to blame for the long day. She had declined the Grim Duo's offers to lead her to the meeting place via the ocean. She didn't think she could swim all the way to the Caymans in less than four days. In fact, she'd never been farther south than Florida. And she sure as hell couldn't keep up with a couple of full-blooded Undersea Folk. She'd pass on the humiliation, thanks.

As he had promised, Jonas had fixed her time off with Dr. Barb. He'd even packed their bags and cleaned out their fridges. Fred just sat back and let him organize her life. It made things easier on her, and seemed to calm him down.

She and Jonas climbed out of the van, fetched their luggage, then coughed as the driver roared off in a spume of dust.

"Real friendly around here, aren't they?" Jonas gasped, waving the cloud of dust away from his face.

"Well, we were promised privacy. Can't have mermaids beaching themselves on public property."

Jonas snickered and slung his bag over one shoulder. He was bizarrely attired in a yellow Hawaiian shirt, buttercup yellow shorts, and penny loafers without socks. He had forgotten his sunglasses, and so he squinted. His hair, as always, looked perfect.

Fred, by contrast, felt as wrung out as an old washcloth. Her green hair was matted to her head, she needed a shower, and her shorts kept trying to climb into her ass. If she actually cared about her appearance, this could be—

"Hey! You're here!"

And before she could say anything, or step out of reach, Dr. Thomas Pearson ran up to her and planted a kiss on her mouth.

Eight

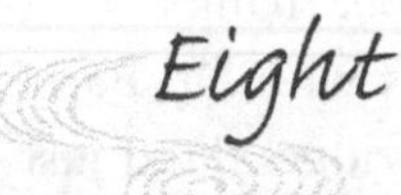

"Wh-what?" She dropped her bag. On her foot, unfortunately, but she was too amazed to reach for her throbbing toes. "What are you doing here?"

"You kidding? Who do you think is paying for the resort?" Thomas spread his arms, indicating the deserted buildings and empty beach. "I promised Artur I'd clear out the resort so you guys could have your big meeting. Booked the whole place for a month and gave the staff paid time off. Bad news is, we have to do our own cooking."

"You *know* about the Pelagic?"

Her fellow marine biologist laughed hard. "Yeah, is that a great name, or what?"

"I don't get it," Jonas complained. "Stop talking in your secret marine biologist language, you geeks. But it's nice to see you again, Dr. Moneybags."

"You, too, Jonas." The two men shook hands. "You still seeing Barb?"

"Ohhhh, yes!"

"Don't get him started," Fred begged.

She made a mighty effort to recover from her shock. As if the upcoming Pelagic wasn't unnerving enough, as if the Grim Duo hadn't been annoying, now here was Thomas, friendly as a puppy and ten times as cute. Her mouth actually burned from his kiss.

She tried again. "What are you doing here?"

He slung an arm around her and she shook him off. "You've only got yourself to blame," he said cheerfully. "Artur tracked me down in England and invited me to the meeting. Apparently it's bad form among mer-people to pursue a lady while fixing it so your rival *can't.*"

"What?" Fred was having a terrible time tracking the conversation.

"Oh ho!" Jonas cried, and she was annoyed to see that her friend was having zero trouble tracking the conversation. "Artur won't try to get Fred into bed unless you're also trying?"

"Basically."

"What?"

Jonas cringed away from her, but Thomas, to his credit, stood his ground. "Who am I to argue with Undersea Folk tradition?"

"I think I could take a crack at it," Fred retorted.

"Hey, it's actually pretty civilized when you think about it."

"Too bad," she grated, "no one ran it by me."

"Besides, you think I'd miss this chance? No way in hell!"

"The chance to try to bone Fred?" Jonas asked, wiggling his blond brows. "Or to see a thousand topless mermaids?"

"Whatever." Thomas beamed. "It's all good."

"I'm getting a migraine," Fred muttered. "Which hut is mine?"

"The one I'm sleeping in," Thomas said hopefully.

"Nice try. I'll take that one." And she marched toward number six.

Nine

The insistent banging on her hut door woke Fred from an uneasy nap. In fact, at first the pounding incorporated itself into her dream.

It was thirty years ago and she was trying to break into her mother's house to warn her not not *not* to have sex with the merman she found on the beach. But no matter how hard she pounded, her mother didn't heed, or even turn her head. Fred pounded harder—

—and woke up.

Her door was actually rattling on the hinges; whoever was outside was in a hell of a hurry to talk to her (or possibly to use her bathroom). She rolled off the bed and staggered to the door.

"All right, hold your pee!" She yanked the door open and felt herself seized, lifted off her feet, and squeezed in a mighty bear hug.

She punched the Prince of the Undersea Folk in his left eye, and he set her down. "Ah, my Rika. How nice to see you again." He touched his eye, which was starting to swell. "As gracious as ever."

"That's what you get, Grabby Pants." She tried to sound grudging, but was quite pleased to see him again. And he looked wonderful, as always. Big. Vibrant. Hair and beard those unbelievable shades of red. Like King Neptune in the flesh. And speaking of flesh, he was clothed (barely) in a pair of tattered khaki shorts and that was it. He wiggled his sand-covered toes in her direction. "What's the big rush?"

"Only to see you, Little Rika. I am pleased you accepted our invitation."

"The Grim Duo didn't make it sound like I had much choice."

"Grim?" Artur's kingly brow furrowed, then smoothed. "Ah, Tennian and that other fellow, what's-his-name."

"Comforting that you can't remember them all, either. Anyway, they sort of goose-stepped me until I showed up."

Artur threw his head back and laughed. "As if anyone could force your hand, Fredrika Bimm!"

"I think that was a compliment."

He beamed at her. "And how is your lady mother?"

"She's great. She and my stepdad have started taking in foster kids."

Artur's brow wrinkled. "Foster . . . ?"

"Kids whose parents beat on them or are orphans or whatever."

"Your people . . . *beat* children? *Your own children?*"

"Well." She coughed. "Yeah. Some of them. Us."

Artur made a mighty effort and managed to clear the look of horror from his face. "Well, that is a fine thing your mother does. A great lady."

"Thanks. You're looking good." Mild understatement.

"And you, Little Rika, *you* look good enough to gobble up raw."

"How sweet. You want to explain what Thomas is doing here?"

Artur scowled, and Fred barely swallowed the giggle that tried to escape. "He is my chief rival for your affections."

"Yeah, okay, keep going."

"It would be unseemly to whisk you away somewhere he could not access. I must show every courtesy to my rival. Also," Artur added thoughtfully, "I wish for my father to meet him. He is a formidable warrior. For a biped."

"So you said last year."

"Ah, your wound." He poked her shoulder, and she restrained the urge to punch him in the other eye. These people had no sense of personal space. "You have healed well?"

"Sure. No thanks to you two psychos."

"You cannot fault our concern."

There was plenty she could fault them with. But now wasn't the time. "Well, brace yourself. Not only is Thomas here, but you're stuck with Jonas, too. He sort of came with the package."

Artur didn't smile, but he didn't freak out, either. "Your friend has behaved honorably in the past, and has kept your secret for . . . what?"

"Going on twenty-five years."

"I do not fear Jonas; he is discreet."

"Discreet? You must be thinking of another Jonas."

"It was good that Thomas accepted my invitation," Artur continued. "He and Jonas will be the first surface dwellers in the history of our kind to come to a Pelagic."

"Yeah, and it's all gone straight to his head."

"That would be because of your presence, Little Rika, not mine."

"Ha," she said sourly. "And speaking of my presence, you want to explain why it was so hot-damn important for me to come to your meeting?"

"Ah . . . yes. But later. Have you dined?"

"I had some Pringles on one of the planes."

"I do not know what a Pringle is, but it sounds vile. Come." He held out a large hand, and she took it. Her own paw was swallowed in an instant. She sensed rather than felt the crushing power held in check. She was strong, but Artur was a redheaded Superman. "We will eat."

"Don't think I don't know I'm getting the runaround on this Pelagic thing," she warned him as he practically dragged her out the door. "I keep asking and people keep blowing me off."

Artur beamed at her. "We have grouper."

Ten

Artur led her past the swimming pool to the main hut—the lodge, in other words—which had the largest bar she'd ever seen. The thing was the size of her living room, and at least twenty of the bottles were rum. And, like her home, it was set up as one big room . . . the bar led into the cocktail lounge, which led into the dining room, which led into the kitchen. All tastefully decorated with plastic dolls strung up in fishnets. Sort of an *Alice in Wonderland* meets *CSI* crime scene look.

Supper had been set up buffet-style and Fred didn't hesitate to dig in. Thomas had warned there wasn't a cook, but someone was sure doing a great job with the kitchen. She had been so hungry she'd forgotten she was hungry—funny how that happened sometimes—but the minute she had smelled the savory grilled vegetables she'd started drooling like a hyena.

As she dished up salad and vegetables, the only other diners—Jonas and Thomas—raised hands in greeting. Jonas quit eating his grouper long enough to lope over to the bar, fix her a vodka sour, and lope back. He plunked the glass down in front of her and went back to shoveling in fish.

"Thanks. Where is everybody?" she asked as she and Artur sat across from them. She glanced out the large windows and saw what she had seen when the van dropped them off: absolutely nothing and no one.

"Mmmph," Jonas replied.

"Oh, they're around here somewhere," Thomas said with a calculated vagueness that didn't fool Fred. No way would a mermaid geek *not* know where at least a few of the Undersea Folk were.

"Eat your salad," was Artur's answer.

If she hadn't been so hungry, she'd have firmly plonked her fork on the table as a dramatic attention-getting device and refused to pick it up again until she had answers. As it was, she barely had enough time between forkfuls to mumble, "What's going on? What are you guys hiding? Badly?"

"Eat your asparagus," Jonas replied.

"Who's hiding?" Thomas asked, looking guilty.

Artur loudly cleared his throat, a noise that sounded like a cement truck going up a gravelly hill in low gear. "What do you bipeds call this?"

"We call it strawberry pie," Fred answered. "And seriously, this changing the subject thing . . . You guys are terrible at this."

"So, my new book debuted at number twenty-six on the *USA Today* list," Thomas remarked, scraping his plate.

"I assume you bring up such a thing to garner praise?" Artur asked.

"Yeah, he's garnering," Jonas said, draining his rum and Coke. "That means a bunch of bipeds bought his tree-murdering book."

"Well, jeez, when you put it that way," Thomas mumbled, crestfallen, and Fred snorted into her drink.

"It's a good thing," Jonas finished, quoting one of his idols, Martha Stewart. He still maintained she'd been framed by the bigwigs at Enron to take the heat off themselves. "That's part of the reason he was able to fix it so we'd have this whole resort to ourselves."

"Yes, and although my lord father gave thanks, I myself have not done so yet," Artur pointed out. "We are not without funds, and if you do not mind being compensated in gold, we can—"

Thomas started to demur, when Fred interrupted. "You've met the king?" she gasped. "*I* haven't even met the king!"

"Well, you should," Thomas said, trying (and failing) not to sound smug. "He's a great guy. Managed not to vomit at the thought of a disgusting surface dweller muddying up his Pelagic."

"What's he look like?" Jonas asked.

Thomas pointed his fork at the prince. "Picture Artur here in another thirty years."

"I do not think we count time the same way," Artur said, pausing before demolishing his third piece of pie. "My lord father had sixty-two years when I was born."

Fred and the bipeds—err, her friends—gaped at the prince. "You—what? Seriously?" she asked.

"We have discussed this before," Artur said mildly, his princely aura dimmed by the glob of strawberry preserves on his upper lip. "Undersea Folk live longer and age slower."

"And are super strong and have gorgeous coloring and gravity is kind to them because they don't need bras," Jonas said in one breath. "At least, the two mer*maids* I've seen—Fred and Tennian—sure don't."

"Gosh, I'm all atwitter." She chewed furiously on a broccoli head. "And speaking for Tennian, mutter, mumble, mumble."

"Hey, they can't all be as charming and warmhearted as you," Jonas said, leaning forward and spearing a baby carrot off her plate.

"Are you talking about that gorgeous blue-haired girl?" Thomas asked, visibly surprised. "Don't knock her, you horrible woman. She's sweet."

"How can you tell? She never raises her voice. I don't even think she has teeth. You know those people who are so quiet they make me nervous? I was actually wishing one of *those* was in my apartment at the time. She doesn't talk!"

"As opposed to some of my folk, who continually speak," Artur teased. "And of course she has teeth. You should see her in a school of shrimp."

"Is today 'shit on Fred and steal her food' day?" she demanded. "Because nobody told me."

"My lord father is coming a-land tonight and would like to see you then," Artur explained. "Right now he is dining with some council members."

"Hey, you got out of a state dinner," Jonas pointed out.

"Yes, and I have my biped friends and Little Rika to thank for it."

"Gee," Thomas said, coughing into his napkin. "That gets me right here."

"I'm thinking about getting you right there," Fred warned, waving her fork threateningly. "So where is everybody?"

All three spoke in unison:

"Eating."

"Sleeping."

"Exploring."

Fred sighed into the embarrassed silence. "Well? Which is it?"

"Well, first they ate, and then they took naps . . ." Jonas was clearly making it up as he went along. "Then they, um, explored. Because there's all kinds of stuff to explore here. In the Caymans."

"Undersea trenches and such," Thomas added, trying to help Jonas.

"You guys. It's just so sad. I'm embarrassed for you, I really am." She savagely chewed a final asparagus tip, swallowed, and added, "Fine, don't tell me. But I'm gonna find out." She shook her head and got up to get a slice of pie.

Eleven

After dinner, Artur and Jonas disappeared somewhere—it was still light, and Jonas wanted to get in some snorkeling while he could. So he took off in the direction of the equipment shed, while Artur went to check on his dad. Which left Thomas and Fred walking on the beach.

"I've got to give this place credit," Fred said, peering at the horizon. "Being here is like being trapped in the Discovery Channel."

"I assume you meant that in a nice way."

"Of course. What other way would I mean it?"

"Hard to tell with you."

They walked in silence for a few seconds, until Fred couldn't bear the quiet another moment and blurted, "I was really surprised to see you today."

His teeth were a white flash in the near dark. "Excellent."

"Well, I was."

"Yeah, well. Think I was going to miss this? The Pelagic? *And* the chance to see you again?"

She stopped walking and, after a moment, he noticed and came back to stand beside her. "You had a year to see me again," she pointed out. "And you didn't."

He shifted his feet in the sand, but didn't break her gaze. "I had projects. Work to finish. I couldn't just show up on your doorstep playing a guitar and serenading you until you agreed to go out with me."

Why not? She shook the odd and unworthy thought aside. "Yeah, but an e-mail? A postcard?"

"We're here now, Fred. Together."

She barked laughter. "Oh, sure. You, me, Jonas, Artur, and ten thousand mermaids. Not that any of them have bothered to come ashore. And don't think I didn't notice."

"It's . . . complicated, Fred. It's—"

"Never mind. I just—"

"What?"

Missed you. Thought about you all the time. Wished you would have come sooner. But she could say none of those things to Thomas without also saying them to Artur. And that was the worst kind of unfair. "I just think it's weird, how we're all together again for this meeting," she improvised.

"Tell me about it. But I've been prepping for the meeting, and I've got something to show you. See that?" Thomas pointed to what appeared to be a float anchored several yards out. "You up for swimming out there?"

"Up for it? I haven't been wet in two days." The double entendre made the color rush to her face and she ignored Thomas's grin. "Not to mention, I'll get out there five times faster than you will."

"Great." Thomas was pulling his shirt over his head and kicking off his shoes. "Then I'll see you out there."

"And we're swimming out there *why*?" she called after him as he scampered into the surf.

"Like I said, I've got something to show you!" he shouted over his shoulder, and then dived in.

"Yeah, well. I'm a scientist. Chances are I've seen it already," she muttered, but waded in after him, stripping off her clothes as she went and tossing them back toward the beach.

Twelve

She floundered clumsily in the surf for a few seconds until it was deep enough for her to shift to her tail-form. Then she was able to go from fighting the water to being part of it.

At first she just stretched her muscles and gloried in being able to get some decent exercise for the first time in too long. Then, as the sand floor dropped away from her, she was able to take a good look around and really appreciate her surroundings.

In just the short distance to the float, she saw at least forty different species of fish. It was astonishing. She was very much afraid she was swimming around like a tourist, with her eyes bulging and her mouth hanging open.

And the water was delightful—warm and clear. She almost didn't mind swimming in the ocean if it was like this. (Almost.) As opposed to back home, where the Atlantic was chilly and murky, and hid unpleasant surprises.

Here she could see everything coming—sea turtles, manta rays, sharks, angelfish. She could hear their fish-chatter whispering in the back of her brain, a far cry from the hectoring nagging of the fish at the New England Aquarium, who often went on strike to get what they wanted.

And the sand! It looked like sugar, pure and perfect and gorgeous. It was almost possible to believe they hadn't wrecked the planet if there were still places like this left.

She had passed Thomas almost at once and now circled the float, waiting for him. She stroked a sea turtle as it paddled past her. It snootily ignored her and paddled away.

She laughed, causing a stream of bubbles, and nearly crashed into the underwater ladder when she saw the surprise.

It was a small submarine, but unlike any sub she had ever seen. It was sleek and shiny, and had more windows per square foot than metal, or so it seemed at first glance.

It was obviously brand-new; no barnacles, no clinging seaweed. So the bobbing rectangle above wasn't a float; it was a marker for this little sub, and a way for people to climb down and—

Thomas had finally reached her, gone up for a big breath, then swam back down. He motioned to her (she assumed . . . who else would he be gesturing to?), opened the air lock, and swam in. She was right behind him, consumed with curiosity and delight.

He shut the air-lock door, drained the water, and grinned at her. "Ready for the nickel tour?" he said, raising his voice to be heard over the pumps.

"You've been busy the last few months," she commented, trying to hide how impressed she was.

"Well, duh. I don't spend all my money on bookmarks and renting resorts, y'know. Come on."

She followed him in.

Thirteen

It wasn't so much a submarine, Thomas explained, as an underwater RV, complete with tiny kitchen, shower, and bedroom. And it was far more comfortable than any submarine she'd ever seen. And . . .

She took a deep, appreciative whiff. "Ah, that new car smell!" She covered her nudity with a towel and rubbed her hair with another one. "Just like you drove it off the lot!"

"Yup." It hadn't taken him long to show her around the underwater RV, or URV (pronounced "Irv"), as he called it. Everything was miniaturized (even the bed . . . bigger than a twin, not quite as big as a double) and brand-spanking-new. And everything was state of the art. "I brought along a bunch of DVDs, the galley's stocked, and as long as you don't mind saltwater showers, the bathroom's all yours."

"Thanks."

He shuffled his feet awkwardly, looking more like a sixteen-year-old than the formidable (and full-grown) Dr. Thomas Pearson. "I mean, I know you've got your hut on the beach, and you've got the run of the ocean, but if you ever want to, you know, get some space or retreat from a couple hundred Undersea Folk, you're always welcome in the URV."

"Well. Thanks." Fred wasn't quite sure how to respond to that. It was a generous offer . . . unless it was all part of his plan to get into her pants, in which case it was vile and underhanded. So she should either give him a sisterly hug, or punch him in the face. What to do, what to do . . .

She coughed. "How long did this take to make?"

"Well, I had the plans for a few months—I designed them after I went to Scotland last year."

She remembered; it had been the last stop on his fellowship. They'd defeated the bad guy, both he and Artur had declared their love, and then both of them had *left*—Artur to go back to the Black Sea and do whatever it was princes did; Thomas to finish his fellowship.

"When Artur got in touch, I had the URV built." He lowered his voice, although the two of them were the only ones in the URV. "I was just waiting for an excuse, you know? I've been fantasizing about the URV since I was a kid."

Uh-huh. Not *too* disturbing. "He's a marine biologist, he's an M.D., he writes books, he's rich, and he designs underwater love nests. Is there anything he can't do?"

"Well, I can't talk about myself in the third person without creeping myself out, so knock it off."

"Wait a minute, wait a minute." Fred frowned, thinking about it. "So this Pelagic . . . The Folk have known about it for at least a few months?"

"Yeah, I guess. Well. The royal family did, anyway. Who knows when Artur and his dad told everybody else."

"Hmm."

"I'm just jazzed they even invited me, y'know?"

"Yes. Can't blame you for that one at all. I'm kind of jazzed myself."

"Like you wouldn't be invited."

"Some half-breed loser who was raised by vicious, bloodthirsty bipeds?" She smiled grimly at his stricken expression. "Right, you and I know that's not the case, but they don't, and like I said, I'm glad to be invited. I s'pose." She sought to change the subject, and so looked the URV up and down and all around. "I'll bet you've got cameras set up all over the—"

"Well, sure. Among other things, the URV is a portable television studio. Lights, sound, picture—it's got—"

"But you know Artur and his dad—not to mention the other eighty thousand Undersea Folk—aren't going to let you put this footage on CNN."

"No," Thomas admitted, "but I couldn't pass up the chance to film, even if it just stays in my own library. Besides, it's going to be helpful for my next book."

"The Mermaid and the Milkman?"

"The Anatomy and Physiology of Homo Nautilus," he retorted stiffly. "You gotta admit, with my background, I'm in a pretty good position to write that book." It was true; Thomas was not only a Ph.D., he was an M.D. "And if they 'come out' to the world, so to speak, we're going to have to know how to take care of them. My book could be in every hospital, every med school, every medical library in the world."

She didn't even try to hold back her laughter. "*Homo Nautilus*?"

"Also known as the Undersea Folk, and stop laughing, you rotten bitch."

With a mighty effort, she got herself under control. "Yeah, but what if they decide to stay put?"

Thomas shrugged. "Then the manuscript stays on the shelf and my tapes stay in the URV and nobody has to know. I'll respect their decision."

"You will unless you want Artur kicking your balls up into your throat."

"Like I'm scared of *him*," he sneered. Fred had to admit he was entitled to his fearlessness; there had been a throw-down between the two of them last fall, and Thomas had held his own. A good trick, given that Artur was bigger, heavier, and probably three times as strong.

Then he shrugged. "I'm looking on the bright side. If they do decide to come forward, I'm perfectly positioned. If they don't, it was still a once-in-a-lifetime experience. Well worth the time." He leered at her. "On several levels."

"Pig. And Artur and his dad know all about this. The taping you're doing for the Discovery Channel, I mean."

Thomas coughed. "No. They don't. And I'd appreciate it if you kept it to yourself for now, Fred. If it comes to it, of course I'll let them in on my project, but for now there's no point in saying anything."

"Knock yourself out, Mermaid Geek. Just keep me out of it."

Thomas slowly shook his head. "Not this time, Fred. This time, like it or not, you're *in* it. In fact, you're practically the guest of honor."

"Sure," she snapped. "That explains why none of the purebloods want to be around me except Artur, and he's got brain damage."

Thomas flushed, but didn't look away.

"So what's going on?" she demanded. "Why are they keeping their distance?"

"Well." Thomas cleared his throat. "I'm not sure it's for me to say."

"You'd *better* say."

"It's kind of private Undersea Folk business."

"But *you* know it? Forget it, Thomas. Cough up, or cough up blood."

"Okay, okay, I'm not up to taking a punch, so just relax. Here, have a seat."

She let him steer her to one of the narrow bar stools in the galley. "Okay. So what's going on?"

"Well, I can't just blurt it out."

"You'd better!"

"I'm just saying, there's background, there's stuff to cover. Okay. So, it's like this. See, your fath—"

There was a click, and the intercom system came to life. "Ho inside, Thomas!" Artur's booming voice. "My father and I require entrance!"

"Hit the red button and come on in," Thomas called. He shrugged apologetically at Fred. "I guess we'll talk about that later. But now you get to meet the king."

"Oh, goody."

Fourteen

Artur and an older, craggier version of Artur stepped out of the air lock and into the URV. "Ah, Thomas," Older, Craggier Artur boomed, not noticing (or not caring) that he and Artur were dripping water all over the galley. "Do you have more movie-shows of the great warrior Al Swearengen for me to view?"

"Sure, King Mekkam. Season two is all set to go."

Al Swearengen? Now why did that sound so—

"And this must be Fredrika, the spirited beauty who has my good son twisted so far around he can see the back of his own tail." The king pulled Fred into a rib-shattering hug and she groaned. He pushed her back, beaming. Clearly his father had no more clue about personal space than Artur did. Very grabby, the Undersea Folk. "It is a great delight to meet you at last, Fredrika. And how is your lady mother?"

"Mom's fine," she gasped. Awfully worried about blood relatives, these guys. Artur *always* asked about her mom, though he'd only met her the one time. And the king, she was certain, had never met Moon. "I'm fine." This was a rather large lie. "We're all fine. Nice to meet you, too. Thanks for inviting me to your Pelagic."

"Oh, no. Indeed, no." King Mekkam frowned, and Fred realized that Thomas had described him perfectly. He really did look like an older, grayer version of Artur. They were even the same height.

They were also naked, but Fred was trying not to let that bother her. After all, they couldn't teleport to the URV, now could they? No.

They had to swim, and the best way for a merman to swim was *not* layered down with Lands' End apparel.

And she had to face facts. Despite the efforts of her hippie mother, Fred was uncomfortable because of the repressed sexual mores of a society that had been heavily influenced by the Victorian Age. Her father's people, of course, had no idea who Queen Victoria even was, much less why they should be embarrassed to walk around with their dicks swinging—

"No, it is I who must thank you," the king was saying. "It was kind of you to join us on such short notice. I am not unaware that you had to disrupt your life and your plans to come to our meeting. And for your friend to come as well! You do my people such an honor as they have never been done before. And that is excellent," he added, almost muttered.

"Yeah, King Mekkam, that's great, listen—maybe you can explain how—"

"*Deadwood*, season two," Thomas announced, waving the box at the king, who nearly swooned like a girl with a crush.

"Excellent! Oh, that is excellent, Thomas, thank you! Do you know of this movie-show?" the king demanded, snatching the season two DVD set out of Thomas's hand.

"Uh . . . yeah, I heard about it. Mostly the uproar when HBO decided to cancel—"

Mekkam steamrolled right over her. "The hero is a treacherous, aging warrior named Al Swearengen. He is as perfidious a biped as I have ever seen, and he is the king of Deadwood. He has many enemies and triumphs with a combination of violence and deception." The king said this with total admiration.

"You've got him watching *Deadwood*?" Fred hissed, twisting Thomas's ear until he yelped. "*That's* the part of human culture you decided to expose him to?"

"It wasn't my fault! I had it on when I was giving these guys the tour."

"Now, unless you motherfuckers are going to join me," King

Mekkam continued, "I insist you sons of bastards all be quiet so I may view more of King Al."

Fred groaned.

"Uh, King Mekkam, about the swearing," Thomas said, clearing his throat and rubbing his ear. "I'm not quite sure you've got the hang of it just yet, and—"

"In our culture, it is polite to speak to others in their dialect," the king said firmly. "So all you motherfuckers shut the fuck up. Now, Thomas. Where is your son of a bitching DVD machine?"

"Oh man, oh man, oh man."

"You're going to hell for this one," Fred told him. "If nothing else."

"And do you have any motherfucking potato chips?"

Fifteen

The next day, Fred found out why her father's people were going out of their way to avoid her, no thanks to Thomas, Jonas, or Artur. Naturally.

On the whole, she would have preferred to remain in ignorance. Not that the Terrible Trio had any right to keep it from her. But she sort of understood their reasoning. Sort of.

She had gotten up early, had oatmeal with milk and cane sugar, then gone for an early morning swim. The sun had just started peeking over the horizon and no one else was stirring. Fred was not normally an early riser, but the night before she hadn't slept for shit.

Stress, she decided. Nerves. Because God knew she'd been exhausted after all the traveling and should have slept like a dead thing. Still, she figured she clocked in maybe two, three hours, max. Depending on when the Pelagic started, hopefully she could sneak in a nap.

Anyway, come sunrise she'd been wide awake. Some kind person had laid out oatmeal, cold cereals, bacon, a variety of juices, and ice-cold milk. She'd bolted a quick breakfast alone, and then headed out.

She swam past the URV into deeper water, curious to see what other varieties of marine life were out and about at this ungodly hour, and had stroked a manta ray. (They were so silky she was always amazed . . . They were like giant mushrooms with eyes.) That was when she saw him.

He was lean, as most of her father's people seemed to be, almost too thin. She could count his ribs, even twenty feet away as she was. Due to the glorious clarity of the water she could see him perfectly, even through schools of darting fish.

His hair was the same startling blue as Tennian's; his eyes the same shade of dark blue—almost black. His long, broad tail was a thousand shades of green, the colors so vivid they were almost hypnotic, rather like a peacock's tail.

Her tail, in contrast, was shorter and narrower. And it had as much blue as green in it. Full-blooded Undersea Folk were superior swimmers, of course, and stronger than she was. That had been difficult to get used to. Before meeting Artur, she had prided herself on being one of the fastest things in the ocean.

Ha! Not anymore. Not hardly.

I'm staring, she thought, embarrassed. Too late to cover it now. Better say something.

Morning, she thought at him.

Without a word, he turned around and began swimming away.

Hey. HEY! I'm talking to you! Thinking at you, anyway. She darted after him with a flex of her tail. *What, did I get the super secret mermaid handshake wrong?*

I do not wish to be seen with traitor's kin, he replied, not even turning around. In fact, he was rapidly putting distance between them.

Traitor's what? Hey! Get your fishy ass back here!

Please forgive my brother, a new voice thought. *He frets about his reputation so.*

Startled, she whipped around to see Tennian swimming up on her blind side. *You!*

Me, she agreed. *Good morning.*

Morning. He didn't even like me! Don't misunderstand; I'm used to it. She folded her fist under her chin, thinking. *But he didn't even* know *me. Usually people have to be around me for at least half an hour before they decide I'm a jerk.*

Sometimes, Tennian added without cracking a smile, *much less than half an hour.*

You're way more talkative underwater, anybody ever tell you?

No. Tennian was now swimming in slow, lazy circles around Fred. *I am not comfortable with outlander styles of speech. It hurts my throat, though courtesy dictates we try. But I do not have to vocalize now.*

Uh-huh, great, good, fine, and while we're chatting here, what the hell was your brother bitching about? And is he your twin or something? He looks just like you, although he could use a protein shake.

We were born of the same mother at the same time, yes.

Fred was beginning to have a sinking idea what Tennian's stiff-ass brother had been complaining about. God knew nobody ever talked about her father.

Her mother never talked about him, of course, because they'd only been together the one night. Fred had known by the time she was five that her mother didn't know a damned thing about her dad . . . not even that he'd been a merman. Moon Bimm only put two and two together when she was bathing the newborn Fred at home . . . and her green-haired baby had popped a tail, right there in the baby tub.

But the other Undersea Folk Fred had met? They hadn't talked about him, either. Which was weird, if you thought about it. *None* of them thought she might want to know about her birth dad? Or if they did, felt they couldn't discuss him? But why?

It could only be because he'd done something fairly horrid. And what had stiff-ass said? Or thought?

I do not wish to be seen with traitor's kin. Yeah. That was it.

Fred sighed internally, then braced herself. *All right. Hit me.*

She could feel Tennian's surprise, and hastily added, *Tell me what he did. Better yet, tell me about the last time a Pelagic was held. You and Kertal got a little squirrelly in my apartment when I was asking questions about it, so cough up.*

She sensed Tennian trying to decipher Fred's slang, and realized one advantage telepathy had over verbal communication was that even if you didn't understand the other person's exact words, you at least got their meaning.

Tennian blew out a breath, making a stream of bubbles that startled a wrasse into darting away, and seemed to be thinking hard about how to begin.

Finally: *Your father, Kortrim, felt that good King Mekkam's family had been in power quite long enough. Six generations . . . and seven, once Mekkam is no more and Artur is king. And Kortrim was able to talk many of the young ones into assisting him, ones bored with our hidden life and hungry for more power.*

Palace coup, eh? Fucking great.

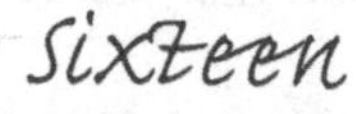

Sixteen

Fred was still trying to grasp the idea that her father, whom she'd never much thought about, had been a traitor. Someone who had tried to overthrow Mekkam and his whole family. Someone who likely would have *killed* Mekkam, Artur, and the rest of the royals.

The thought made her heart want to stop, but she forced herself to follow it to its logical conclusion.

Yes, of course her dad would have executed Artur and the others. He would have had to. Rule number one after a hostile takeover: get rid of the old guard.

I cannot believe, she thought, and hoped the thought was private, *that I'm descended from a murderous betraying asshole.* The asshole part? Not such a surprise. The betraying murdering part? Ugh. She tried to imagine the circumstances that would lead her to try to get Dr. Barb fired behind her back (or even to her face) . . . and hit a blank wall.

She and Tennian were floating rather than swimming, letting the current take them back to shore. Fred impatiently batted a grouper aside. *So in your tactful way, you're telling me that Dear Old Dad tried to overthrow the monarchy.*

Yes.

What was his beef with Artur's dad?

She could sense Tennian's hesitation and added, *Well, fer Crissakes, don't stop now!*

Your sire felt that the accident of birth enjoyed by the king's line was no reason to keep a crown.

Huh?

His mind-touch.

Whose? Fred was utterly mystified. *Mekkam's? Or Artur's?*

Both. All.

Mind-touch? All right, this is clearly a cultural thing, so Fred would decipher that later. *Never mind. Obviously Dear Old Dad failed, otherwise he'd be King Dear Old Dad and I'd be Princess Fred.* Now that was a laugh!

And may be still.

What?

Yes. He failed. In fact, many of those he thought he had brought to his side were only pretending so they could report his duplicity to the king.

So the betrayer got betrayed. Okay, that's interesting. I guess. Actually, there's a kind of elegant irony to it. So, what? They killed him?

Oh, no! Fred felt real shock behind Tennian's horrified thought. *We never. We NEVER. We are not like surface dwellers, to take life so lightly!*

All right, all right, calm down. Fred decided it wasn't a good time to remind the younger woman that she was half–surface dweller. *So if they didn't kill him, and if he isn't here, then where . . . ?*

Banishment. The thought was as flat as a sugar cookie, but not nearly as sweet. *It is our most severe punishment.*

I bet.

The ocean is vast. And I do not have to tell you how dangerous it can be. It is . . . a difficult place to face alone. It is one thing to go off by yourself for a day or two, but for the rest of your life? And our kind are much, much longer lived than your mother's.

Fred was feeling pretty horrified herself, and tried to keep it from Tennian. No sense in scaring the girl into clamming up again.

She tried to imagine living in the sea her whole life, only to be cast out by everyone she had ever known. Water covered three-fourths of the planet; it would be beyond awful to face all that alone.

Not for a year or two. Not for a decade or two. But for decade after decade after decade, leading into centuries, until . . . How long *was* the life span for an Undersea Folk, anyway?

Not to mention . . .

That's a good way to get killed, isn't it? Without the group to protect you, to look after you . . . I mean, he must *have died. Artur was sure of it, or he wouldn't have told my mom he was prob'ly dead.*

We think . . . but we do not know. No one ever saw him again, and no one speaks of him. It was assumed, once King Mekkam discovered your existence, that your sire perhaps came ashore that very night and lay with your lady mother. It was the last documented sighting of him, at any rate.

Fred made a mental note to never, ever tell this to her mother. Moon Bimm still had the hippie's romanticized view of life, and The Night Fred Was Conceived was one of her more cherished stories.

The mysterious stranger showing up on the beach. Moon, tipsy on cheap wine, and lonely. The drunken fuck (or, as Moon called it, "the tender, life-making lovemaking"). Followed by five months of morning sickness and, eventually, a mer-baby.

No, she'd never tell Moon that the only reason her dad had come ashore was because his people had thrown his ass out.

She also made a mental note to find out how, exactly, Mekkam had learned of her existence. Because Artur had alluded to that last fall, hadn't he? He'd told her, while they were in her mother's kitchen at the Cape Cod house, that his father had sent him to seek her out.

I'm getting it now! That's why no one spoke of it to me. Why everybody keeps dancing around my questions. Do they blame me for what my dad did? They must. But that doesn't make any sense . . . Anybody who knows I'm his kid also knows I never met the guy. So are they really that dumb?

She'd been deliberately provocative (she didn't know any other way to be), but Tennian didn't rise to the bait.

Not . . . dumb, Fredrika. But family is all, to the Undersea Folk. Responsible for everything, the author of everything. We believe personality traits are passed down as easily as hair color and tail length. Some of us . . .

Reluctance now, extreme reluctance, and Tennian looked away from Fred, snatched a damselfish from the middle of its school, and disposed of it in four chomps. All this with the absent air of someone biting their fingernails. Fred struggled mightily not to barf. The blood didn't bother her; the casual carnivorousness did, not to mention the sight of Tennian's needle-sharp teeth. *Some of us believe that if your sire could act in such a treacherous way, so might you. But for the prince . . .*

What about Artur?

He is most fond of you. Surely, she added, waving away the blood and scales, *this is nothing new.*

Oh, he's babbled something along those lines. I wasn't paying much attention.

You may wish to. Fred could sense Tennian's dry amusement. *He has made no secret of the fact that he wishes to make you his princess. And but for that . . .*

Are you telling me if Artur wasn't sweet on me, nobody'd want me around?

I cannot tell you what might be, or might have been, Tennian said tactfully. *Only what is. Or was, if I have that knowledge.*

Fred floated for a few seconds, thinking. Then: *So your twin gave me the cold shoulder, but not you? How come? Not that I'm complaining. But nobody's come ashore since I got here. Except for Artur and the king and you, nobody's talked to me. I'm apparently the guest of honor, but nobody's even tried to look me up. So why are you being so friendly? Relatively speaking.*

I like your friend, Tennian said shyly. *The blond one. I never knew a surface dweller could be so loyal.*

The blond . . . Oh, Jonas! For God's sake. *Jonas* was why Tennian was breaking The Mermaid Code of Silence? He'd laugh his ass off when she told him. Assuming she decided his ego wouldn't go all Fourth of July from the stimulation.

His Highness says your friend has kept your secret for many years. For a surface dweller that would be accomplishment enough, but your friend is different.

You don't know HOW different.

As a man of science he could have gotten a great deal of gold if he had whispered the right thing into the right ear.

Jonas isn't a big fan of gold. He likes to play the stock market, when he's not raiding the racks at Nordstrom's.

Whatever he likes to play with, Tennian thought at her seriously, without the slightest flicker of a smile, *he does not do so with your reputation, or your life. I was . . . unaware of that quality in bipeds. It has made me wish to speak with them, when I never wanted to before.*

That's why you're talking to me? Because I've got good taste in friends?

Well, as they say, you cannot choose kin, only allies. And you chose well. It made me think you would be wise in other things as well. Oh, I am *sorry! That was rude of me.* Tennian used a tiny bone to pick her sharp, sharp teeth. *Did you want me to catch something for you?*

Good God no! Fred calmed herself as Tennian's eyes went wide in surprise at the vehemence of her tone. Thought. Whatever. *I mean, no thanks. I'm allergic.*

Allergic?

Fish makes me sick.

Fish . . . makes you ill?

Yeah, but don't worry. I eat plenty of vegetables, protein, stuff like that. Really, Tennian, don't worry.

It makes you ILL?

Well, remember, I'm only half Undersea Folk. Luckily, Mom and Sam were vegetarians, so it was never really a . . . Are you all right?

Then Tennian did something that amazed Fred: she laughed so hard she ended up upside down, her long blue hair actually dragging in the sand as she clutched her stomach and rolled back and forth in the current.

Ho ho ho, Tennian thought, rolling, rolling.

Fred watched her for a long moment, unamused. Finally: *You're an odd duck, Tennian.*

ILL? It makes you ILL? Ha! Ha! HA!

I could really, Fred added, *get to dislike you.*

Oh, I hope not, Tennian said, shaking sand out of her hair. *Because I think I will like you.*

You think you will like me? Fred was amused in spite of herself. Or, maybe, because of Tennian.

Oh yes! You and I will be great friends, I think. You will pretend I annoy you, while you secretly become more and more fond of me.

Think so?

Tennian put a small white hand out to Fred who, surprised, took it. *Of course. Because you are lonely, as am I. And lonely people have to stay close to one another. Do you not find that is so?*

And Fred, who disliked being cornered on any subject, couldn't help a nod of agreement.

Seventeen

I appreciate your laying all this out for me, Fred said. *God knows nobody else has said shit.*

You asked, Tennian replied simply. *How could I not answer?*

You'd be surprised how easily people haven't answered. Fred fumed and snorted to herself for a moment. *Not answering is not a problem at all for most people, seems like. So thanks.*

Courtesy to a guest is—What is THAT?

Fred looked. There, floating forty yards away, was Thomas's pet project. *That's the URV. My—uh, my other biped friend, Thomas, he built it.*

It is so shiny! Like a shot, Tennian had crossed the forty yards and was swimming around and around the small silver URV. *So this is where the king keeps disappearing! We have been wondering and wondering, and to think, I, Tennian, have discovered the secret!*

Yeah. Good work.

Then this is Artur's rival for your affections, this Thomas.

Yeah.

Tennian stroked the shiny silver hull and looked up at Fred, dark blue eyes gleaming. *My people were positively humming at the thought of a half-bree—um, of a stranger attending the Pelagic. You can imagine our reaction when King Mekkam granted permission for a surface dweller to attend!*

Total freak-out, huh?

To put it mildly! But there was some concern as to how he was going to join us. Some thought he would have to bring air tanks and fins.

Right, a scuba suit.

Skooba?

Self-contained underwater breathing apparatus. Air tanks and fins. You've never heard that bef—Never mind. When would you have? Anyway, yeah, that was one option. But not very practical if you guys are going to be meeting for more than a couple of hours, which it sounds like you are.

Tennian had gone back to swimming in admiring circles. *He has built a little house for himself under the waves! How very, very clever!*

Why did Tennian's honest admiration make her uncomfortable? *Yeah, he's a clever guy.*

I knew of that quality in bipeds. But I did not know one could build something so aesthetically pleasing. It is not at all like those horrid clunky things that search for other war makers.

And, clear as thought, the image of a nuclear submarine left Tennian's mind and popped into Fred's. *That's a submarine, although war maker is as good a name as any. And you should see the inside of a Burger King if you think this is cool.*

Tennian was now pressing her face against one of the windows and tapping her long fingers on the glass. Except it probably wasn't glass; it was probably some kind of durable—

He sees me! He is waving!

Of course, Fred thought sourly. *Why am I not surprised he's in there?* He's probably finding some other inappropriate HBO series for Mekkam to practice his vocabulary on. *The Sopranos*, maybe? *Entourage?* Oh, the horror.

Yeah, he's spending a lot of time in the URV.

He is beckoning for me to come in! May I?

What do I care?

It is allowed?

Fred nearly swam into the URV's smooth, curved corner. *You're asking* me?

Well. Tennian looked up at her. *He is unmated and you are unmated. So that is acceptable. But His Highness the prince has explained that this biped also wishes to make you his, so I—*

Tennian. We're just friends. He wants more, and I'm dealing with that.

This felt like "not quite the truth," and Fred tried to shrug off her unease.

Not very well, as it clearly communicated to Tennian, who was frowning and keeping her distance. *But—*

Go.

Are you sure I will cause no offense?

My God, Fred thought. *I'm going to have to physically shove her into the URV or she'll think I'm in love with Thomas.*

I'm sure! Go!

Still, Tennian hesitated. *I think that you are being kind.*

Then you haven't been paying attention AT ALL.

I think that if I go in I will cause offense. I will stay out here, with you.

Tennian! I think it's physically impossible for you to cause offense. Come on, I'll introduce you.

You will? There will be a formal introduction?

Well, I don't know about formal—

I may go inside? It's permitted?

For God's sake. Come on.

Much later, Fred would come to bitterly regret that impulse. But for now, she was relieved (she was pretty sure) to see Tennian dart toward the air lock.

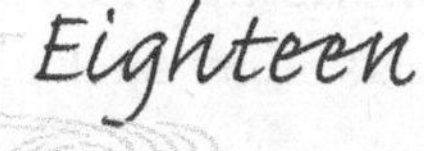

Eighteen

"Thomas, this is Tennian. Tennian, this is Dr. Thomas Pearson."

"It is good to meet you, Thomas."

"You, too, Tennian."

"That reminds me . . . I noticed you guys don't use last names. Do you even have them?"

"Last . . ." Tennian had been looking eagerly around the URV, but managed to wrench her attention back to Fred. "Oh, you mean family names! We have them—I am Tennian of the Meerklet line; and Artur, like his siblings and his father, are of the Zennor line—but we do not use them."

"Why not?" Thomas asked.

"Because . . . because we do not. It is not necessary. Normally," Tennian added, staring with big adoring eyes at the coffeemaker in the galley.

"Oh. Thanks for clearing that up." Fred cleared her throat. "Usually among bipeds, you don't call someone by their first name unless they ask you to, or you've known them for a while."

Tennian actually gasped in horror. "Then I have given offense!"

"No," Thomas breathed. "Not at all."

"Yeah," Fred said sourly. "Not at all."

"It is good of you to overlook my lapse."

"No problem," Thomas murmured.

"Yeah, don't even worry about it."

Thomas was trying not to gape, or leer, and Fred actually had a bit of sympathy for the guy. He'd been minding his own business in his underwater dorm room, and suddenly two naked women were dripping all over his tile.

In fact, Thomas was so determinedly making eye contact and avoiding looking elsewhere, his own eyes were almost watering. Given that Tennian was lithe, exotic, and pretty, and had the nicest set of knockers Fred had ever seen outside of a Victoria's Secret catalog, that was quite an accomplishment.

"I saw you outside," he said, then coughed to clear his throat. When he continued, he sounded more like a man and less like a Ford 4X4. "You were like—like a daydream I had once."

Tennian smiled shyly, and Fred was startled—and annoyed—to

feel a stab of jealousy. And not a little poke, either, but a vicious stab. It felt like someone had slammed an icicle through her chest. Her face was probably as green as her hair right now.

Jealousy?

Not only was it stupid, it was pointless. She had absolutely no right to that emotion at all. She'd spent an awful lot of time shoving Thomas *and* Artur away. And had been devastated when they'd both actually up and left. Now here they were, the three of them, together again. And she was still pushing them away.

Make up your damned mind, she told herself savagely, *very* glad she wasn't underwater where just anyone could pick up her thoughts.

Pick one, or pick neither, or become a Mormon and pick both, but stop all this wishy-washy *bullshit*.

"—known Fredrika for long?"

"We met a year ago. Your king sent Artur to Boston—that's a city on the coast—"

"She lives in Chesapeake Bay, Thomas," Fred said, exasperated.

"Oh. Then you know where Boston is. Anyway, King Mekkam sent Artur to find Fred and help figure out who was dumping poison into the bay."

"Yes, yes!" Tennian actually jumped up and down. This did excellent things to her cleavage. Thomas's eyes watered even more. "His Highness Prince Artur had many exciting tales when he returned! We were shocked that he took life, but it seems as though the villain left him no choice."

"Not hardly. He was shooting up the place. He shot Fred, too."

"Yes! It was so exciting!" Tennian glanced at Fred. "Ah, although it was regrettable that you were injured."

"Oh, she was totally fine," Thomas said, waving away Fred's gunshot wound to the chest. She glared at him so hard she thought her skull was going to crack, but he was oblivious. "But anyway, here you are, so let me show you around. This is the galley—are you hungry? Do you want a snack?"

"She had one outside," Fred said, still shuddering at the memory.

She wondered if Thomas would still be so infatuated once he saw gentle, shy Tennian chow her way through the belly of a nurse shark. "She's probably still got fish scales in her teeth."

"Great, that's great. Something to drink?"

"Your tiny house makes drinks?"

"Sure!" Thomas opened the small, silver fridge. "Here, have a Coke. Do you like Coke?"

Tennian found she did. In fact, the caffeine and sugar from the three Cokes made her as talkative as she ever got out of water. In fact, for Tennian, she was practically gushing.

"—so shiny and beautiful from the outside! I was drawn to it like—like—"

"A crow is drawn to tinfoil?" Fred suggested.

Thomas gave her a look. "Never mind Dr. Sourpuss over there; she's always grouchy. And here's where I sleep."

Fred had been following them through the small ship, feeling out of place but also strangely reluctant to leave the two of them alone. Thomas was a mermaid geek; when he was a little boy his mom had read him all kinds of mermaid stories and the lonely little boy (his dad was always off on some mystery job or other) often fantasized about finding a friend in the sea. He'd become a marine biologist as a direct result of those stories, and that childhood.

And maybe . . . maybe he only liked Fred *because* she was a mermaid. To posit that further, maybe he'd like *any* mermaid.

Well, sure he would. And why not? God knew Fred was no Miss Congeniality. She wasn't even a Miss October. And this month Thomas was going to meet scads of mermaids. Hundreds. Maybe even thousands.

Her rotten luck that he ran into Tennian, who was apparently pretty open-minded for her people. Any other mermaid probably would have been scared shitless of him (treacherous bipeds, don't you know). Or disdainful. But not this mermaid. Of all the rotten! Damned! Luck!

Tennian was patting the bed, then sitting on it, then bouncing on it. "If you can't sleep underwater and let the current rock you, this is likely the next best thing," she said, her blue hair flying all over the place as she bounced, bounced, bounced. Thomas lost the battle and stared at her breasts, which were also bouncing.

"So. I. Uh." Thomas cleared his throat. "I noticed you're a natural—I mean, that's your natural hair color. I mean, obviously it's your natural hair color. A very, um, striking and vivid blue. Is that, um, common in your family? Ow!"

"I'm sorry," Fred said sweetly. "Was that your kneecap?"

"Right, thanks," he muttered. Then, louder, "Sorry, Tennian, those were pretty rude questions. It's not every day I have a naked, gorgeous mermaid in my—ow, goddammit!"

"I'm sorry. Was that your other kneecap?"

Thomas hobbled over to the chair in the corner and sat down, groaning softly.

"Are you well, Thomas?" Tennian asked, stopping in mid-bounce.

"As well as can be expected," he said through gritted teeth, rubbing his knees. "Anyway, that's all of the URV."

"It is wonderful!"

"Thank you. I worked hard on it."

"What, work?" Fred scoffed. "You drew up the plans and then hired a bunch of people to build it for you."

"You know how many sex scenes I had to write to afford this thing?" Thomas griped. "Let's just say all my characters aren't going to be doing anything below the shoulders for a while. I'm so burned out it's not even funny."

"Burned out? Sex scenes?"

"Biped talk," Thomas said hastily.

"Don't you want to tell Tennian about your girlie books?"

"Maybe later. Say, Tennian, do you know when the Pelagic is supposed to start?"

"Tomorrow morning. His Majesty wanted to give you and Fredrika plenty of time to rest from your travels."

"Well, that was thoughtful. Oh, that reminds me, Mekkam's coming back tonight for season three. I don't know when the guy sleeps."

"Season three?" Fred yelped. "You couldn't have tried him out on the Discovery Channel? Let him watch *Meerkat Manor* or a show about grubs? Jeez, anything but HBO, even *Dirty Jobs*, fer Crissakes."

"Look, he saw me watching *Deadwood*, he wanted to watch *Deadwood*. I'm supposed to tell a king what to do? Back off, Fred, or I'll put the bullet I pulled out of you right back in."

"I'd like to see you try, Romance Boy. I can't believe that out of all the people the king could be hanging out with, he picked you."

"That will be very helpful for you," Tennian said, shaking the last can of Coke in a vain attempt to get three or four more drops out. "Do you know why?"

"Uh . . ."

Fred made an impatient sound. "Because when the rest of her people find out Mekkam likes you enough to hang out in the URV and watch HBO reruns, they'll warm up to you a lot quicker than they normally would have."

"Oh." Thomas looked surprised, then pleased. "I didn't think of it like that. You don't suppose Mekkam's faking the interest, is he?"

"Our king does not *fake*," Tennian said, all trace of mirth gone from her face. She had been rolling around in the blankets but now abruptly sat up.

"Okay, sorry. I didn't mean to offend, or imply that King Mekkam lied. It's just hard for Fred and me to accept all this in such a short time. She's a half-and-half, and I'm a surface dweller, but the royal family is welcoming us with open arms. You can't blame us for wondering."

"I can, but I shall not." Tennian shook her head and looked wry. "Only bipeds would view the gift of friendship with suspicion."

"Yeah, sneaky rotten bipeds like Thomas, here," Fred said helpfully. "Disgusting! Two hairy legs, no tail, no stamina in the open water . . . It's enough to make you barf, when you think about it!"

"It's probably just the novelty. Which in Fred's case, at least, wears off," Thomas joked.

At least, she was pretty sure he was joking.

Fred resisted the urge to kick him in the knee again. One to grow on, as her stepfather might have said.

Nineteen

"And then . . . then! He was practically slobbering all over her. Granted, she was a gorgeous naked woman with striking blue hair—and blue pubic hair—but still."

"Fred."

"Slobbering! Like a summer hound." Fred was pacing back and forth beside the pool. "And she was all, 'Oh, Thomas, you're so clever. Oh, Thomas, you built such a pretty underwater dorm room. Oh, Thomas, can I have a tenth Coke?' Sickening."

"Fred."

She stopped pacing and stood over him. "And why do I even care, anyway? Don't I have enough to worry about without giving a crap if Thomas likes a mermaid who isn't me?"

"Fred!"

"What?" she snapped.

"Move." Jonas, clad in crimson swim trunks patterned with green sea horses, and sunglasses (which he'd picked up at the small gift shop off the kitchen), and nothing else, shaded his eyes with a forearm and squinted up at her. "You're standing in my light. Then I'll have a Fred-shaped shadow across my rock-hard abs, and Barb will laugh at me so much I'll lose my hard-on."

"Gross!" she squealed.

"Hey, it's reality, baby. Deal. And speaking of reality, were you planning on hiding Thomas from all the other mermaids?"

"No."

"And you're not in love with him, or Artur. In fact, it sort of pisses you off when they start—how'd you put it? Slobbering? It's no secret that you get mad when they slobber all over you."

"I know, I know! I'm aware of how stupid and junior high all of this is."

"Well, get your shit together," her alleged best friend said heartlessly. "Either you want Thomas (or Artur), or you don't want Thomas (or Artur). Pick one. Or don't. But shouldn't you be worrying more about the Pelagic than about the sad, pathetic state of your love life? Your love life is always pathetic, but Pelagics only come along once every three or four decades."

Fred plunked down on the concrete beside her best friend. Funny how Jonas's sensible advice often sounded like the advice she gave herself. In fact, sometimes the advice she gave herself actually sounded like Jonas.

"Yeah, everything you're saying is a hundred percent right. But I'm not a computer, Jonas. I can't turn it off like a switch."

"At last, she admits she has feelings!" He adjusted his sunglasses. "A breakthrough."

"Shut up."

"So what'd you end up doing?"

"Oh, Tennian offered to show him the Cayman Trench."

Jonas snickered.

"Don't be such a pig. It's not a sexual euphemism."

"Are you sure?"

She ignored that. "He'll need scuba gear, but she'll give him an all-expense-paid mermaid tour."

"And of course he took her up on it."

"Of course!" Fred had to admit, even to herself, that Thomas could not be faulted for that, no matter how hard she tried. "He's a mermaid geek, remember. He would have taken Artur or Kertal up on it, too. Not that Kertal would have asked. But—Oh, shit! That reminds me. My dad was a traitor."

"Yeah, I heard."

She nearly fell into the pool. "What?"

Jonas adjusted his sunglasses. "Artur told me. He was worried some of the other mer-dudes might give you shit. I said you wouldn't give a shit if they gave you shit. He seemed relieved about you not giving a shit about getting shit, and then he dropped the whole thing."

"Swell. Why didn't you tell me?"

"He asked me not to. He was trying to figure out how to break it to you."

"And you agreed to this?"

Jonas yawned, unmoved by her wrath. "Hey, calm down. I gave him until the end of the week. If he hadn't spilled it to you by then, I would have."

"Neither of you did. Tennian gave me the whole story. And after Daddy-o's little takeover failed, they kicked him out."

"Huh." Jonas sat up, examined his (not very tan) stomach, then lay back down. "I didn't get that part of the story."

"And then he washed up onshore and knocked up my mom."

"What a lovely ending to a depressing story."

"Which reminds me—"

"—we aren't telling Moon that your dad was the bad guy a generation ago. Got it."

Fred almost smiled. It was so comforting, being around someone who knew her so well.

"Maybe you should go tell Thomas you want to fuck."

"What?"

"Date! I meant date."

"Yeah, but . . ." She had tried to picture herself doing just that. And had frozen like a Mrs. Paul's fish stick every time. Nor could she picture herself telling Artur the same thing.

She wasn't afraid of them. Not afraid they'd hurt her, at least. She wasn't afraid of any man. And she liked sex (if memory served). But the thought of essentially telling one person, *one* man, "I'm going to make myself vulnerable to you, so hurt at will!" was terrifying. Her throat actually went dry when she contemplated it.

"You're such a chickenshit," Jonas said kindly, accurately reading her expression. "Would it kill you to *try* being in a relationship?"

"Says the guy who got dumped about a thousand times before hooking up with my boss."

"Yeah, and it was all worth it to find Barb, ya idjit!"

Fred said nothing. It would be too cruel (even for her) to remind Jonas of all the times he'd sobbed into his couch. The times he'd ignored his personal grooming for as long as a week when he'd been dumped. The way he'd eat trans fats to get over a breakup. Or wear socks that didn't match his tie.

She shuddered, recalling the horror.

Oh, sure, Dr. Barb was in his life now and everything was rosy. Oh, yes, everything was swell, including his view of all past breakups.

No, she wouldn't remind him of the pain he so conveniently glossed over. Nor was she in a hurry to go through anything like that on her own.

She had the nagging thought that she was being a coward, and shoved it right back out of her brain.

"Meanwhile," her friend was nagging, "you've got two awesome guys who would chew off their own arms—or each other's—for the chance to make you happy, and all you can do is freak out."

"Yup." Fred glumly rested her chin in her hand. "Freaking out. That's all I can do. It's all I've *been* doing ever since I got here. And the damn Pelagic hasn't even started yet!"

"Well, worry about that, then. And if Tennian gets fresh with Thomas, sock her."

She grinned down at her friend. "Now *that's* advice I can use."

Twenty

To her extreme annoyance, Jonas's mouth fell open and he stared past her as she bitched about the URV, Thomas, Tennian, the Pelagic, her mom, and her period, which was due within the week.

"Oh my God, help me remember my hot girlfriend," her friend murmured, and Fred knew without turning around that it was—

"Good evening, Fredrika. Sir. I thought I might—if you did not mind, I thought I might . . . dine . . . with you?"

"Tennian, Jonas. Jonas, you remember Tennian." *Tennian the hottie, who has apparently started following me around.* "Sure. We'd love it if you had supper with us."

Jonas had bounded to his feet and was shaking hands with the nudely gleaming Tennian. "Hi there! Niceta see you again! Chilly this time of night, eh?"

"It is good to see you, sir. I have heard many nice things about you."

"You have?" Jonas was frankly staring. "About me? Not from her, anyway." Jerking a thumb in Fred's direction.

"You'd better drop it while you can still count to five on that hand," she muttered. Then, louder: "Nice to see you again."

"Indeed!" Tennian glanced down at herself, then back up. "Fredrika, may I impose upon you? I require clothing."

"Sure, sure, there's plenty in my hut."

"Nonsense!" boomed her friend (who, laughably, was thought to be gay by the casual bystander). "It's a come-as-you-are dinner! No need for shorts. Or a shirt!"

Tennian smiled at him. "You are kind, but I will abide by your customs."

"Nuts."

Without another word, Fred led Tennian toward her hut.

Tennian was devouring meat loaf (What, Fred wondered, could it be made of? Were there cows on the island?) and listening to the others chatter. Even Fred, slightly begrudging the lovely girl's company, couldn't deny that Tennian was fascinated and thrilled to be taking a meal with them. It was kind of fun to be ringside.

"—of course I came down like a shot. The prince was really great to invite me," Thomas was saying, his plate untouched in front of him.

Fred rudely stuck her finger in his mashed potatoes, then sucked on her finger. He noticed, but didn't care . . . just pushed his plate closer to her.

She hated mashed potatoes.

"You give me too much honor," Artur replied amiably, gulping down a fourth helping of conch chowder. "My good father invited you. I only extended the invitation on his behalf."

"Aw, come on, you're being too modest."

"Not very damn likely," Fred muttered to her corn chowder.

"We're breaking ground, right here." Thomas gestured to the room, still creepily decorated with nets and baby dolls. And to the diners: himself, Artur, Jonas, Fred, Tennian. "Surface dwellers and Undersea Folk getting along fine. Shit, Fred and Jonas are best friends! I think this is really promising for how the Pelagic will turn out. And for future relations with our people, of course."

"Apples and oranges," Fred muttered.

"And Fred is a hybrid," Artur said, nicely but with no doubt about his meaning. "Who did not know her people until recently. Who else did she have to befriend but Jonas? No offense, good sir," he added hastily.

"Hey, none taken," Jonas said, working on his third Bloody Mary. "It was either me or Sandy Caturia, and Sandy was a nose picker."

Fred was startled into a snicker; she hadn't thought of their nose-mining fellow student in many years. "Don't sell yourself short, jerk. You've been a good friend."

"Yeah, but that's not the issue, is it?" Thomas asked intently. "It's not who Fred picked to be her friend, it's who decided to befriend her. And even if she was buds with the president of the United States, the fact that she's a hybrid would always bring doubt on that friendship, right?"

Artur looked uncomfortable, but could not lie. Not that Fred gave a shit, but it was interesting to watch him wiggle. "You speak the truth, Thomas; it is one of your finest qualities, and also the most exasperating. Although I daresay Fred could befriend anyone she wished."

"Sure, she's a regular Miss Congeniality," Jonas snickered.

"I have heard horror stories about surface dwellers for nearly all my fifty years," Tennian commented, pausing for a minute to suck the meat out of a tiny lobster leg, then chew up said tiny leg, "but I had never known one well enough to talk to. You do not seem like barbarians to me."

Fred jabbed an elbow into Thomas's side. "Fifty. Didja hear that? *Fifty!* Hope you packed the URV with Depends."

"I think it's like anything else," Jonas said, getting up to fix himself another Bloody Mary. "With every species. Some of 'em are assholes, some of 'em are saints, but most fall somewhere in between."

"O my Tennian," Artur said, smiling, "you will have your nose everywhere, will you not? So it has been," he told the others, "since we were children together."

"Your Highness implies equality among our families when there is none. You lead, we follow. That is the way of it."

Hmm, Fred hmm'd. Tennian was being too modest. She came from important people; that was obvious. Maybe the Undersea Folk equivalent of aristocrats?

"In this, you are leading, and it pleases me greatly," Artur said.

Tennian didn't blush, but she stared into her glass and said nothing.

Fred figured Artur meant the huge step of walking out of the ocean and taking a meal with Traitor Bait.

"His Highness knows of my stubborn streak."

"His Highness," Artur said, creepily referring to himself in the third person, "has had cause to be grateful for it more than once."

The two Undersea Folk shared a warm look, which Fred, later by her own admission, would admit she completely misread.

So she slid over until she and Artur were hip to hip, climbed onto his lap, and planted a kiss on his mouth (which was hanging open with surprise).

Twenty-one

"Whuf?" Artur managed, or something close to it. But Fred was lost in the sea of sensation she had brought upon herself. She could feel her thighs warming against Artur's (darned cutoffs); could feel his warm mouth recover from the surprise and begin actively kissing her back; could feel his ridiculously strong arms wrap around her.

She kissed him, she kissed him, she kissed him and forgot about the Pelagic, and her father, and the way Tennian had apparently bewitched both of the men Fred refused to date. She even, for a brief glorious moment, forgot about Moon, Jonas, and Dr. Barb.

"Say, is that the time?" Jonas exclaimed, speak of the devil. "It's so late, it's, uh, way past my bedtime. Way way way past."

"It's seven twenty-five," Thomas said, sounding (hooray! Wait, what?) disgruntled.

"Right, that's what I meant. Time to call Fred's boss and get me some phone sex."

"Is this, ah, I don't mean to intrude on a cultural taboo," Tennian said, "but is this normal for—"

"Fred? No. Ordinary people surrounded by hotties? Yes. Come on, gorgeous. I'm dying to fix your hair."

"It does not need fixing," Tennian commented, and, thank goodness, her voice was getting fainter.

"Oh, honey! The things you don't know, living like a slug on the bottom of the sea. First we'll do a protein pack. Then a trim, I think. How about a crew cut? Your bone structure would be killer with that look."

The door shut and, with sweet suddenness, Fred and Artur were alone.

She stopped kissing him at once.

"Ah, my Rika, I think you have left this tiny portion of my mouth unexplored." Her legs dangled as he pointed to a minuscule spot on his lower lip. "Perhaps you should see to it at once."

"Don't get any funny ideas," she warned him, looking around. Yep, Jonas and Tennian were gone. So was Thomas, although she hadn't heard him leave. The guy could move like a cat when he wanted. "I was just—just—"

"Marking your territory, as do your dogs?" the prince teased, shifting her weight on his lap so she rested easier. "I have no objection to being marked, Little Rika. Not by one such as you."

"She has a lot of nerve, don't you think?" Fred cried, beating her fists on Artur's chest. "First she bewitches Thomas, then she throws herself at you. There's only so much a girl can take, even one with a (sometimes) tail."

Artur stared at her for a moment, then threw back his head and did the kingly booming laugh thing. "Tennian! And I! Oh no, oh no, oh no-no-no."

He tapered off into snorts and giggles, but when she tried to climb out of his lap he tightened his grip and she stopped. "Don't even say it."

"I do not have to, Little Rika, you have deduced it on your own."

"Tennian wasn't making a play for you."

"We are cousins," he explained gently, but his red eyes gleamed and gleamed until they looked like lamps. "We played together as babies."

"Oh, friggin' great!" Fred threw up her hands and nearly dislodged herself from Artur's lap. "Cousins! Which nobody bothered to tell me! Doesn't that make her an earl or a duchess or something?"

"Tennian's family has always eschewed titles," he explained, stroking her waist with both hands. "She did not knowingly deceive you."

"She doesn't knowingly irritate the shit out of me, either, but guess what?"

"That is not what I would deem an exclusive club, Little Rika."

"Hmph." Fred slumped, sulked, crossed her arms over her chest, kicked her feet. "I guess it's not such a big deal, then."

"Ah, but it is, Little Rika. I like your jealousy. In fact, I adore it greatly."

"I wasn't jealous," she lied. "Just showing her she's not the only hottie at the table."

"Very wise," he said gravely, "but even now I am having inappropriate thoughts about my father's brother's daughter. Perhaps you should remind me of your hottie status."

"You wish," she began, but his lips covered hers and that was as far as she got.

Twenty-two

Fred spent another sleepless night fantasizing about surgically removing Tennian's ears and then stuffing them in her mouth.

And wondering if she had "bad" blood . . . traitor's blood.

And wishing King Mekkam wasn't quite so infatuated with the *Deadwood* prostitutes. (Apparently the queen, Artur's mother, was long dead.)

And wondering if she shied away from committing to either of the men in her life because of honest disinterest, or fear.

It hadn't been easy, extricating herself from Artur's lap and grasp. Not least because she had been *way* too tempted to remain. But after a few well-placed kicks she'd been free to go . . . though if she'd known she was going to be in for a night of staring at the ceiling, she might have lingered.

The alarm went off—not that it woke her—and she was glad. Anything was better than lying in bed fretting.

And it was all so stupid! It's not like she'd been hurt in other relationships, she thought, throwing the blankets back and beginning to get dressed. In fact, far from it.

Her adult life had been a series of one or two dates, blind dates, and occasional work dates. She hadn't been interested in boys as a high school student, and then she'd been so busy at UMass there hadn't been time for a steady relationship. And then she'd been concentrating on getting her Ph.D., and then her work at the aquarium had pretty much consumed her time.

She'd just never had *time* for a serious relationship. It had nothing at all to do with keeping men at a distance so they couldn't reject her as a freak of nature.

Wait. Where had *that* come from?

Then she realized what she was doing, cursed, and pulled off all the clothes she'd just carefully put on. She couldn't wear *clothes* to the Pelagic, for God's sake! Nobody else would, that was for sure. She'd stand out enough without showing up in shorts and a shirt.

Naked, she walked out the door and nearly ran Jonas over.

"Whoa! Where's the fire? My goodness, you're looking . . . perky."

"Shut up," she growled.

Jonas fell into step beside her as she walked toward the surf. "Don't take this the wrong way, but you look hideous. You're hardly even pretty this morning."

"Didn't sleep."

"Who could, with all that pressure you're under? Look, don't worry about it, they'll love you."

Fred snorted.

"Right, okay, well, they'll think you're interesting at the very least."

"Do I keep men at a distance because I'm afraid they'll reject me once they know I can grow scales?"

"Yes. Now just remember to be yourself. And—"

She skidded to a halt in the sand. "Wait. Yes?"

"Sure. Don't you remember Jeff Dawson asking you out in our sophomore year? And Mark Dalton our junior year? And—"

"Those were all varsity morons."

"Yeah, but you could have gone out if you'd wanted. You just didn't want to." She'd started walking again, and he was hurrying to keep pace. "Now don't let the other mermaids intimidate you. And play nice with the other kids. And—"

"Be myself? That's your advice? Be grouchy and antisocial and foulmouthed?"

"And it wouldn't hurt you to say please and thank you once in a while."

"Thanks for all the swell advice, Jonas." She plowed into the surf, thankful once again that the water was so pleasant. "Don't wait up."

"And try not to pick any fights! It's bad for your complexion!" he yelled after her, and then she was diving beneath the waves into that other world, her father's world, and, mercifully, Jonas was very effectively cut off.

Twenty-three

She forgot all of Jonas's advice the minute she saw Tennian's twin.

Good morning, she thought at him.

He was talking to two mermaids and a merman—the merman was Kertal, but she didn't recognize the women—and didn't turn.

GOOD MORNING, JACKASS! Then she swam right up behind him and poked him rudely between the shoulder blades.

She thought she saw Kertal grin, but couldn't be sure. Tennian's brother slowly turned around and said, with great reluctance, *Good morning.*

I'm Fred. And you are . . . ?

Rennan.

Hello again, Fredrika, Kertal said politely. He gestured to the women, one a tiny creature with true black hair—not dark brown, *black*—and matching eyes, the other long and slender, with grenadine-colored hair and eyes. *This is Meerna, and Bettan.*

Hi, ladies.

It was kind of you to join us, Kertal added.

Oh, heck, I wouldn't have missed it. So! Isn't it so incredibly awkward that my father tried to overthrow the monarchy three decades ago?

Again, she thought she saw a smile on Kertal's face, but it vanished too quickly for her to be sure.

The small, black-haired mermaid blinked and finally replied, *Yes. I suppose that is awkward.*

Is it true you've lived nearly all your life on the surface? the tall redhead asked. She was pale, like every Undersea Folk Fred had ever met, but so pale her skin was almost translucent. She'd probably burst into flames if she ever set foot on land.

Yeah, that's true. I never knew my father, so I never knew about you guys.

Then it is well that King Mekkam found you.

Fred wasn't sure about that at all, but now wasn't the time. *I s'pose.*

I need to see to my sister, Rennan said stiffly. *Excuse me.*

Super great to see you again! Fred thought after him. *Let's have lunch!*

I do not think he will dine with you, Kertal said soberly.

No shit. I was just yanking his chain. I can handle anything but being ignored.

And in that, Bettan said coolly, *you are much like your sire.*

Without another word, she swam off.

Oh, Jonas, Fred thought, suddenly terribly lonesome for her friend, for land, for the sky, for *air. What good is being myself if they've already made up their minds about me?*

Well. We had better go take our places, Kertal said. *It was—it was nice to see you again.*

Good-bye, Meerna added, not looking Fred in the eye. And off they swam.

Fred slowly swam after them, taking her time so they could pull as far ahead of her as they liked. She could see several clusters of Undersea Folk, and simply followed them.

A few miles out from shore, they were plenty deep but it was difficult to swim anywhere without bumping into a mermaid. She caught herself looking for spotlights or bleachers and reminded herself that this was not going to be like any other meeting she had attended. Why in the world was she picturing an underwater pep rally?

For one thing, even if a boom mike could somehow work down here, it wouldn't be needed in a group of telepaths. Which reminded her, Thomas was going to have no idea what they were talking about.

Hmm. Perhaps the king wasn't being quite as open-minded as they were giving him credit for. What did he care if a surface dweller who already knew about mermaids saw a bunch of them getting together? Especially when the only way he'd know what they were discussing would be if someone told him?

And, speak of the devil, here came the URV, gliding almost silently toward her. She could see Thomas behind one of the windows, at the controls, and he waved madly at her before settling down to navigate. The URV glided past her and then settled into what appeared to be a stationary orbit, giving Thomas several angles to shoot from.

And, as with any school of fish, there were a lot more Undersea Folk than appeared at first glance. She tried to estimate and thought there were at least five hundred that she could see. And the meeting would be "projected" telepathically to the Undersea Folk who wished to participate but couldn't make it to the Caymans in time.

Unbelievable.

Most of them were slender, with the typically longer tail that was broader at the hips. The tails were all in shades of blue or green (or both), while hair and eye color tended to match, or only be off by a shade. Attending the Pelagic was like looking at a fabulous living rainbow, because there were no brunettes or blonds or strawberry blonds. No, there were blue-haired folk, orange-haired, forest green, cotton candy pink, buttercup yellow . . .

Unbelievable.

And there was apparently some sort of statute that all Undersea Folk had to be attractive, because they all *were*. It was ridiculous.

(It did not occur to Fred that she wasn't exactly hard to look at, either.)

She was staring, and knew it, and was helpless to stop. But that was all right, because she caught quite a few people looking at her as well.

Looking at her, and then looking at each other. Talking to each other. Gossiping, to be perfectly blunt. But Fred couldn't hear them. So perhaps Undersea Folk telepathy was a little more complicated than she had first imagined. You couldn't "overhear" something you weren't meant to; the thought had to be projected at you, into your mind.

She thought, *Too bad about all those great whites headed this way.* But it was just a stray thought; she wasn't trying to "talk" to anyone, or be overheard.

Nobody looked toward her; nobody reacted.

Hmmm.

Let the Pelagic come to order, Mekkam's voice boomed in her head, and just like that, it had begun.

Twenty-four

Fred paid careful attention, but found she was able to eyeball the other Undersea Folk while following the events of the Pelagic, and that was fine by her.

And she was beginning to get an idea why her father had wanted to overthrow King Mekkam. How had Tennian explained it? An accident of birth? Mekkam's mind-touch?

Well, that was for sure; Mekkam controlled the meeting and kept everyone on track, *and* made sure Undersea Folk halfway around the world could "hear" what was going on as well. No friggin' wonder he was the king! And if Artur had that kind of telepathy, it was no shock that he'd be the king after Mekkam bit the big one.

How, Fred wondered, *could my dad have ever thought he could overthrow this guy?* For one thing, Mekkam could *read everybody's mind.* Even if, as she suspected, an Undersea Folk had to make an effort, put a specific thought into somebody's mind, Mekkam could still probably head off any plot he wanted.

She shook off thoughts of her traitorous (and apparently idiotic) father and focused on the Pelagic.

The way Mekkam explained it to everyone (though she imagined most of the people at the Pelagic knew the scoop), there were two basic factions among the Undersea Folk.

The Air Breathers, mostly younger Folk who didn't necessarily think the king was the be-all and end-all, felt that hiding from the surface dwellers was something out of the twentieth century (and the nineteenth, and the eighteenth . . .).

The Air Breathers felt they had just as much right to walk around on land as any surface dweller and they didn't want to spend even one more generation in hiding.

The Traditionals, those who follow the dictates of the royal family without question, felt that the royal family has had it right for the past six generations: there is far, far more ocean than land, and there was more than enough to hide from bipeds while at the same time living a comfortable life.

Thus, the Pelagic: a meeting to decide whether the Undersea Folk were going to stay hidden . . . or show themselves to CNN, among others.

Once Fred realized exactly what was at stake, she began to get a niggling feeling about the reason why she had been urged to attend. Because she, unlike anyone else here, was a child of both worlds. She imagined it was only a matter of time before Mekkam called for her testimony.

And what in the world would she say?

Twenty-five

"Then what happened?"

Fred accepted a Coke—she was amazed Tennian had left any in the URV's galley—and cracked the can open, then slurped up the foam before any could hit her shirt. Well, Thomas's shirt. He had offered her a clean pair of boxers and one of his T-shirts, and her hair was bound up in a towel. At least she wasn't parading around naked in front of him. Anymore. For today.

It was different when she was in her tail form, that was all. It could be argued she was just as naked then, but it sure felt different.

"Fred? Then what happened?"

"Oh. Sorry." She forced herself to quit contemplating Thomas's boxer shorts and answered him. "Then a bunch of my dad's people got up and reminded everyone—like we needed it—that you horrible surface dwellers are treacherous, disgusting, rotten sonsabitches who shit where you eat."

Thomas raised an eyebrow at her, and she shrugged in return. "Don't forget, you were the only biped Artur had ever met who *didn't* shit where he ate."

"Yeah, yeah, don't remind me. So that's really what all this is about? It's just that some of the mermaids really want to come out of the closet?"

"Yep, some of them do. They just have to talk all the others into it. And don't belittle it; it's a huge deal."

"So they're going to, what? Debate back and forth?"

"Until Mekkam figures out a majority are ready to vote. Then they'll—we'll—vote."

Thomas perched on the tiny galley counter. "I guess it has to be all or nothing, doesn't it? If fifty of them want to walk up on a beach, they can't unless the entire—what? Race? Species? Anyway, they all have to be on the same side, don't they?"

"Yeah, they—"

"So how are you going to vote?"

"Me?" she gasped. "I'm still freaking out over being invited; I have no idea how I'll vote."

"Vote yes!" Thomas begged. He leapt off the counter, seized her by the hands, and began to waltz her around the tiny galley. "Then we won't have to hide your tail from all my cousins. We can get married at the New England Aquarium and go swimming in Main One."

"Let me go!" she protested, trying not to giggle at the thought of her in the main tank, clad in her tail and a bridal veil. "Stop acting like such a numskull."

He dipped her. "Marry me, vote yes, come out of the water closet—get it?—and we'll see the world in the URV."

"Will you stop goofing around?" She struggled out of the dip and (gently) removed his hands from her. He was just clowning around; Jonas did the same thing every damned day.

Except her heart didn't pound when Jonas did it. She didn't feel faint when Jonas did it. She—

The intercom buzzed and Thomas hopped down from the counter. "That's Jonas."

"Agh!"

He raised an eyebrow at her. "Uh, sorry, I didn't think it would, y'know, terrify you. Having him here and all. I called him when it looked like you guys were breaking it off for the day. Hit the red button and then come on in!" he called.

Fred swallowed her disappointment. She had hoped to have a bit more alone time with Thomas. After spending the day surrounded by her father's kind, and with various people in her head of all places, she was hoping to wind down with one, count 'em, *one* fella. And not Jonas, though she loved him to death.

"My Christ, that's a long swim!" Jonas gasped. "I felt like Flipper's stunt double!" He was dripping wet (naturally), his snorkel and mask dangling from one hand. Unlike most of the people who walked through the air lock, he was wearing shorts and fins. He stood on one foot to yank each flipper off. "You'll be sorry if I drown on the way out here."

"I'm moored not even fifty yards offshore," Thomas protested mildly. "There's almost no tidal activity to swim against and the water's crystal clear all the way out. Admit it: you're only on the Islands to work on your tan."

"I'd never deny that," Jonas said, tossing the fins in a corner and then hopping up and down on one foot, shaking his head. "I swear to God, I've got half a gallon of water in each ear."

"Is that why you swam out here?" Fred asked, taking another gulp of Coke. "To bitch?"

"Naw. So tell me about the big meeting."

Briefly, Fred filled him in on day one of the Pelagic.

"Huh. Well, that explains why they were so hot to get you down here," Jonas said.

"It's a really good thing," Thomas commented, "that you're smarter than you look."

"Fuck off, Pearson, or I'll never buy another one of your sleazy books ever again. So how are you going to plead?"

"What?" Fred asked.

"For or against humanity?"

"I don't know," she admitted. "I haven't had a lot of time to think about it."

"I think you should tell 'em to go for it. I think the Air Breather contingent has a point: Why *should* they hide from most of the planet? It's just as much theirs as it is ours."

"I don't know," Thomas said quietly. "As a species, we've got a long history of intolerance and genocide. Maybe they're better off staying hidden. The oceans are gigantic. We'd never have to know. Hell, they managed to convince all of *us* that they're myths. That's quite a trick, when you think of it. A shame to undo it."

"See, that's where I run into problems." Fred finished her Coke. "I can see both sides of the issue. There're plenty of reasons to do it. There're plenty not to, also."

"Is that what you're going to get up there and say? 'Hi, my name is Fred, my dad tried to kill the royal family and I'm not sure if you should speak up or stay hidden.' Hmm, that actually might make Artur fall out of love with you." Jonas began excitedly jumping around the URV. "That could do the trick!"

"Shut up, Jonas. You're supposed to be helping."

"I am helping," he said, hurt.

"You want to make Artur fall out of love with you?" Thomas asked, leaning forward.

"I'm just—we're just joking around."

"Because," he added, giving her a slow grin, "I know a perfect way to do that. Or, if not make him fall out of love, at least really make him mad."

"Down, boy." But Fred couldn't help it; she grinned back.

Twenty-six

The intercom beeped again. They could hear the air lock re-cycling, and then the king of the Undersea Folk stepped inside. "Hello, my motherfuckers," he said cheerfully.

Fred smacked her forehead and simultaneously glared at Thomas, who was laughing like a hyena.

"Sorry, *what* did you say?" Jonas gasped.

"Are you letting these other motherfuckers know what went on in the Pelagic?"

"Yeah, and after that we're going to hunt up some whores and pan for gold." She whirled on Thomas. "You couldn't have shown him an Animal Planet DVD, ohhh, noooo."

Thomas shrugged. "What can I say? King Mekkam likes what he likes."

"I did not mean to interrupt your motherfucking meeting," Mekkam went on, far too perkily given the long day they'd all had.

He was in pretty good shape for someone who was close to a hundred years old. His chest was broad, and grizzled with graying red hair. His shoulder-length hair was also streaked with gray, but he wasn't "in good shape for his age." He was in good shape, period.

"But I wanted to warn you, you little motherfucker, that I will be calling on your testimony first thing tomorrow. Also, my motherfucking son is on the way to your hut to ask you to dine."

"Great," Thomas muttered. "Uh, guys, the URV wasn't exactly built to hold all of us at once."

"I can take a motherfucking hint, Thomas."

"So can I," Jonas said, still giving Mekkam incredulous glances.

"I thought you were trying to make Artur fall out of love with you," Thomas added, and was he—was that a sulk?

"The last thing I should be worrying about right now is my love life," she informed him, but why was his unhappiness making her so darned happy? It was sick, that was all, sick, *sick*!

"I don't suppose . . ." Mekkam began hopefully.

"Sir, that's it. There aren't any more. They cancelled the series," Thomas explained.

"Cold-blooded bastard motherfuckers."

"Yes, that's exactly what the Bring Back *Deadwood* chat rooms were buzzing about. Too bad. Well, good-bye."

"You have no more cultural documents I can view?"

"No!" Fred and Jonas shouted in unison.

Thomas folded like origami. "Well . . . I could probably find something . . ."

"I'm outta here," Fred muttered. "Where's Artur?"

Mekkam's gaze went faraway and after a long moment he said, "He is coming ashore now, intent on knocking on the door of your hut."

"You—you know that? You can find him with your mind?" Thomas asked, fascinated.

"Of course." Mekkam actually shrugged. "That is what it means to be king."

"Any of them?" Thomas was nearly stammering in his excitement. "You can find any of the Undersea Folk? Anytime you like?"

"Of course."

"Is that how you found me?" Fred asked quietly.

"Yes, Fredrika. But I felt it prudent to leave you with your mother until—"

"Until you needed me," she finished bitterly.

"Until you were ready to meet your father's people," he said, correcting her with firm gentleness.

"Oh." She swallowed. "Uh. Sorry."

"Quite all right, my little motherfucker."

"That's *it.*" Fred's hand slammed down on the air lock release. "I'm outta here."

"Wait, wait!" Jonas cried. "Uh, Mekkam—king, sir, whatever—one thing I don't get. About Fred's dad, I mean."

Mekkam's red eyes went narrow, but his friendly expression didn't change. "He is one we do not speak of, Jonas. I do not expect you to understand all of our cultural—"

"Excuse me, sir," Fred interrupted, "but seeing as how it's *my* dad, I should have a say in what happens next, don't you think?"

A short, difficult silence followed her statement. Given how anxious she'd been to leave the closing walls of the URV just a few seconds ago, she couldn't believe she was finding an excuse to linger.

"Jonas can ask whatever he wants about my family," she finished, wondering if Mekkam could throw her into the clink, or whatever the Undersea Folk equivalent was.

"Uh, thanks, Fred. Anyway, King Mekkam, the thing is—how could Fred's dad hope to be king? If you have all your special king powers?"

Thomas's eyes were wide but he said nothing; Fred imagined he was going to suck all the information he could out of whatever Mekkam's response was. Not that she could blame him; she planned to do the same thing.

Mekkam was frowning, but it was thoughtful, not angry. "We know now that he could not have succeeded," he said carefully. "And not just because many of his 'followers' were still loyal to my family. Yes, I can find an individual subject if I focus on that person. Yes, I can direct the thoughts of the Pelagic and project them into other minds. But none of it is unconscious. I must focus. I don't—I can't—"

"Eavesdrop?" Thomas suggested.

"Exactly, yes! Eavesdrop! I cannot do that."

"So, does being the king give you extra special cool powers, or do your extra special cool powers make you the king?"

"All of my line can do as I do," Mekkam replied, still being careful. Fred had the sense that the king did not want a misunderstanding to spring up. "Because of that, we are the royal family. Fredrika's father felt our time was done."

"Was he a really strong telepath, too?"

"Indeed, yes," Mekkam replied simply. "He *could* eavesdrop. But he did not have the control my line has built over generations. He was all raw power and ambition. And that is why we are here, and he is not."

A slightly longer silence fell, broken by Jonas's, "Okeydokey. Thanks for clearing that up, sir."

"You are a curious species," the older man said, kindly enough. "You have done great things as a result."

"Well." Jonas puffed up a little. "What can I say? We've been kicking ass and taking names since—"

"Third grade," Fred interrupted. "I'm outta here, Artur's waiting for me."

"God fucking forbid His Royal Majesty be kept waiting," Thomas muttered.

"Play nice," Fred scolded, inwardly smirking. "You guys are staying here to plunder your DVD collection?"

"Indeed, yes!" Mekkam boomed.

"Oh, I am *so* out of here."

"Me, too," Jonas said. "Can I borrow a scuba tank to get me all the way back?"

"For God's sake. It's not *that* long a swim."

"Says Fishgirl!"

"Do not . . ." she said through gritted teeth, stripping out of the clothes Thomas had lent her—Jonas didn't care, Mekkam didn't notice, and Thomas was too busy grilling the king on his telepathy to pay attention to her now-nude state—"call me that. Ever again."

"You won't even care if I drown," Jonas said mournfully. "You'll just swim off and go have dinner with your handsome prince."

"He's not 'my' anything." She paused, and grinned evilly. "And yes, I'd leave you and go have dinner."

Twenty-seven

Cruelly outpacing Jonas, Fred was shaking the water out of her hair and walking up the beach less than five minutes later. To her surprise, Tennian and Rennan, the evil blue-headed Undersea Folk twins, were sitting on the beach (nude, but then, that was normal for her father's people), watching the horizon.

"Good evening, Fredrika," Tennian said to the sand.

"Hi, Tennian. Rennan."

He didn't answer, just kept squinting at the horizon. Fred was about to verbally humiliate him when Tennian's left elbow slammed into his side so hard, Fred actually heard a crack.

"Good evening," her brother managed, then slowly flopped over on his side and moaned into the sand.

"We look forward to hearing your testimony tomorrow," Tennian added, looking up and smiling shyly.

"Do you?"

"Also, His Highness, *our prince* . . ." This was followed by a glare at her writhing twin. ". . . is looking for you."

"Yeah, Mekkam—*your king*—already told me. Thanks. Nice to see you guys again."

"Do you—" Tennian cleared her throat and tried again. "Do you know where Thomas is?"

"The URV. He's picking out movies for the king to watch."

"Oh."

Fred knew it was a perfect time to leave. Rennan had shattered ribs and would think twice before snubbing her again. Artur was waiting. The king was out of her hair. Thomas was out of her hair. Tennian didn't have the courage to interrupt her king, so she didn't have to worry about what Tennian and Thomas were up to.

Perfect.

There would never be a better time to leave.

Never.

So: time to leave.

"Thomas wouldn't mind if you swam over," Fred said to Tennian, surrendering. "In fact, he'd be delighted to see you again."

"Oh, but he is meeting with the king. I couldn't—"

"What meeting? He's lending the king DVDs. Never mind what they are," she added as Tennian opened her mouth. "The point is, it's not official business. Go ahead."

Tennian had already leapt to her feet, showering her moaning twin with more sand. "Well. Perhaps I will. In the interest of—of—"

"Interspecies communication," Fred suggested, cursing herself for having a conscience.

"Exactly!" Tennian cried, then scampered toward the surf. At once she stopped and turned. "Oh. Rennan. Good-bye."

"Yeah, toodles," Fred told Rennan, who had slumped over like a beached manatee and just lay there, breathing hard.

And off Tennian went, to slobber all over Fred's boyfriend. Well. One of her boyfriends. Not that they'd decided on anything official, because they certainly—

"Little Rika?"

"Coming!" she called, and stepped over Rennan's body to run up the beach.

Twenty-eight

"I have something to show you."

That was all Artur had told her. Then he'd led her to the shore and they'd waded in until the water was up to their hips. Then they dove, shifting to their tail-form.

I've spent enough time in the water today, don't you think?

I think you complain to hear the sound of your own voice, Little Rika.

And I think you should blow your—

Here!

She looked . . . and nearly gasped. Artur had led her to what appeared to be a good half an acre of seaweed. The dark green contrasted beautifully with the bone-colored sand, and the vegetation went on and on and on.

He caught her by the hand and led her to it, and she picked a large leaf off a plant and cautiously nibbled it. Then, growing bolder, she stuffed the waxy, plump leaf in her mouth and chewed.

It tasted salty and green, like the seaweed that came wrapped around maki rolls in a Japanese restaurant. It was delicious!

She grazed contentedly for a good twenty minutes, hoping Artur wouldn't make any cruel observations as to her manatee-like behavior.

See? I knew you would like this. Even those of us who eat fish like this.

It's delicious. I could make a salad out of this stuff. A little olive oil, a little rice vinegar, some sesame seeds . . .

Only I could show you this.

You, or any marine botanist.

She heard him snort in her head, and she stuffed a last leaf in her maw. *Yum! Better than spending your evenings cracking open clams like a damn otter or something.*

Little Rika, when the Pelagic is over, I wish you to come home with me.

Whoa! That had come out of nowhere. She thought they were having salad, not discussing living arrangements. *Home, the Black Sea home? That home?*

Yes.

She thought about it and he let her; they both floated just above the seaweed spread. Finally: *I think that might cause you some problems, Artur.*

Ha! My people are slow to change, but they do *change. Why do you think it has taken us so long to even meet on this subject, much less make a decision?*

Tennian laid it all out for me. That if it wasn't for you, everybody'd be dissing me all the time.

But I am here, and I want you to be my princess. If you are my princess, no one would dare be "dissing" you.

That's a pretty poor reason to marry into the family. To get people to like me.

I do not presume to know your reasons, Little Rika. I only know my own.

The entire twelve months I had to stay away, there was not a day I did not think of you and wish I could be with you. Did you not think of me?

He had swum up behind her and was holding her around the waist, where her belly met her scales. His big hands were stroking, stroking.

Yeah, I—I thought of you. And one other.

You do not need to answer me this moment. Or even this week. But I do not wish to return home without you, Little Rika. I understand it is much to ask. But I can give you much in return.

And my job . . . ?

You can apply your training for the betterment of our people. Yours and mine. And one day you will be their queen.

Eeeesh. I dunno, Artur. It's a lot—

Yes. He nuzzled the slope of her neck and she was having a hard time concentrating on what he was saying. Thinking. *And I offer a lot in return. Only say you will ponder my offer, Little Rika. That is all I require of you this night.*

Okay. I'll think about it. I promise I will.

Then all is well. Abruptly he released her, and she was actually disappointed. Usually he got gropey and then she punched him. That was their thing.

Maybe Artur was trying a different approach.

Scratch *maybe*, she thought, swimming after him. Definitely. Question was, what was she going to do?

She thought about it all the way back to shore.

Twenty-nine

She and Artur were still shaking the seawater out of their hair, ankle-deep in the surf, when she heard the resort van wheeze into the driveway.

Okay, that was weird. Everybody was here already. The staff had been dismissed. Thomas had promised them privacy. It was probably just a grocery drop-off . . . but at this time of night?

She turned to Artur. "Get lost. I'm not sure who's here."

"As you like, Little Rika. I already have what *I* want." And with a devilish grin, he waded back into the surf, dived in, and vanished.

Fred trotted up to the pool, where any number of towels were still scattered. She started frantically grabbing and discarding towels.

Jonas, still dripping and panting from his swim back from the URV, was sprawled on a lounge chair. "What?" he groaned as Fred hurriedly started wrapping towels around her waist, chest, and hair. "I almost *died*, you know. I almost died!"

"Shut up, you didn't almost die. Help me."

"Help you with what?"

"We've got company, but I don't—"

"Jonas? Honey?"

Fred knew that voice. She *knew* that voice! She'd been hearing it for years and, these days, had been hearing it far more than she ever had before. Not just at work, but at dinners, in her apartment . . . and now here.

Oh, God, please not here.

"Jonas?"

Horrified, Fred and Jonas stared at each other, then in the direction of the voice.

And—yep, there she was. Staggering down the path with a suitcase the size of a hope chest. And it was probably stuffed with lab coats.

"Dr. Barb!" Fred nearly screamed.

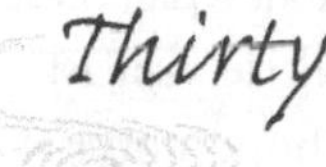

Thirty

"What the hell is she doing here?" Fred hissed.

"Don't hit me!" Jonas shrieked, cowering away from her. "Or at least, not the face! I just had a cucumber mask treatment." He threw his arms across his face and staggered up from the lounge chair in one oddly graceful movement. Fred resisted the urge to hook her feet between his ankles and knock him over. "I didn't invite her, I swear! I only—"

"Told her where she could find you. Left detailed instructions 'in case of emergency.' This is obviously some sort of repellent romantic surprise!"

"You don't have to make it sound like she brought the plague," he snapped back, cautiously lowering his arms. Dr. Barb was about ten yards away and gaining; Fred could hear the shorter woman puffing as she lugged the suitcase. They didn't have much time to finish their fight. "In fact, it's kind of sweet, her flying all the way out here to surprise me."

"Oh, it's very fucking sweet, it's fabulous, it's wonderful!"

"Just because you're threatened by the appearance of anyone's romantic commitment—"

"Oh, like I give a shit about that right now, and you know it!"

"Wait. What? I know you don't give a shit, or—"

She roared right over him. "Now not only do I have to watch my ass, all the Undersea Folk in the area have to be careful, too! And guess who's going to get the blame for this? God *damn* it!" She kicked a lawn chair into the pool.

"Stop your whining for two seconds and try to remember that everything isn't about *you.* The person who'll get blamed for this is me, which is fine, because I'm the one who's got it coming. Now quit with the temper tantrum, force a smile onto your stupid craggy gargoyle head, and make nice with my girlfriend and your boss!" Jonas forced the entire diatribe out in one hissed breath, then his face broke into a beatific smile, and he turned and spread his arms. "Honey pie! Sweetie! Oh my God, you have *no* idea what a surprise your little visit is!"

"Really?" Dr. Barb chirruped, dropping her hope chest—uh, luggage—and rushing into Jonas's embrace. "Really, you're not mad? I just got so lonely, and the NEA can take care of itself for a few days, and I thought it'd be fun to fly down and surprise you." Dr. Barb looked at Fred with anxious dark eyes. "I know your family reunion is private; Jonas and I will of course stay out of your way."

"Fam—uh, right, right. Yep. My family is . . . well, they're just insane about their privacy. Almost pathological. You probably won't see any of them the whole time you're here." *God willing.* "And how long *are* you here?"

"Only 'til the end of the week."

"Come on, I'll show you my hut. I'll help you unpack. Could take hours," he added over his shoulder, imparting a final "behave!" glare to Fred before they left.

Fred jumped into the pool to retrieve the lawn chair, then gave in to her tantrum and crumpled it up into a rough ball. She watched it sink into the deep end and only wished Jonas's mangled body was sinking beside it.

Thirty-one

"Artur, Artur!" She realized what she was doing, cursed her stupidity, waded in, ducked her head under, and called, *Artur!*

She listened hard, and heard nothing.

Artur! Hello? It's an emergency! Artur!

Still nothing. Well, shit. She wondered what her range was. King Mekkam's appeared to be limitless; obviously run-of-the-mill Undersea Folk had to be content with the equivalent of shouting in an empty room. Or maybe that was a hybrid thing. Maybe—

—ttle Rika.

What? Artur? Are you coming?

Yes, Little Rika. And she could feel him getting closer, coming into her range. Damn. She was almost getting the hang of this mermaid thing. *What ails you? Have you hurt yourself?*

No such luck. My boss is here!

Your . . . from the aquarium on land? The woman Jonas has taken to mate?

Yes! She saw him and realized she'd floated out over her head; he was swimming toward her with powerful strokes, strokes that gobbled the distance between them and made it look easy. *She flew out to surprise Jonas! So you've got to tell your dad, so he can warn everybody. Jonas will do his best to hole up with her in his hut, but she's got to eat, and I imagine she'll want to swim and sunbathe and, I don't know, work on my annual review.*

As you wish, Little Rika. He reached for her and she let him, actually submitted to a hug, to being held. *Why are you so distressed, dear one? My people are well used to hiding; your Dr. Barb will not know we are there, even if we swim right beside her. This is nothing new.*

It's just . . . this is private. The Pelagic is private. I made them accept Jonas, and your honor made you accept Thomas. Now Dr. Barb's here. It's turning into a mess, and it's all because of me.

My Rika, you are too strict with yourself, surely.

It's just hard enough to get people to talk to me after what my dad did; now everybody's going to know there's another biped at the Pelagic. Good old Fred: totally dependable for traitorous behavior.

Fredrika, that is not so. He hugged her again and stroked her back. *You are tired, I think.*

And you're condescending.

But you are tired, he teased. *Only exhaustion would lead you to own problems that are not of your own making. You fret over things you cannot control, or change.*

I've got a lot to fret over!

So you do. And now you must rest; tomorrow you have much to do. He clasped her hand and started swimming for shore. *Come. I will take you back.*

Be careful of your tail!

He actually rolled his eyes at her.

Fine, next time another stupid biped shows up at your super secret meeting, I'm not saying a damned thing!

Oh, Little Rika. Do not tease.

One disadvantage swimming in fins had: she couldn't kick him with her tail.

Thirty-two

She'd actually fallen asleep. The last few days with no sleep—followed by the stress of the Pelagic, not to mention Artur's proposal, then the arrival of Dr. Barb, and her fight with Jonas—had fixed it so she was snoring by 9:30 p.m.

Which made it all the more annoying when someone started pounding on her door.

"G'way," she moaned into the pillow.

Whoever it was took that as an invitation, because her door opened and she remembered . . .

"Why did I give you a key to my room?"

"Because you've been in love with me since the third grade," Jonas promptly answered. "What? You were asleep? It's not even ten o'clock!"

"Shut up. Go away." Her air conditioner was clanking and wheezing in the corner, and she finally took pity on it and got up to shut it off. "Never mind; make yourself useful and open the windows." She yanked one open herself. "What are you doing in here, anyway? Shouldn't you be having sex?"

"Oh, please, I did it twice already. And may I add, each time with me is more fantastic than the last."

"I actually threw up a little bit in my mouth just now," Fred informed him.

"You don't fool me. You're just mad because you never got to try a slice of Jonas."

"There it goes again! At what point does 'throwing up in your mouth' become just 'throwing up'?" She crossed the room and spat in the bathroom sink.

"Anyway," Jonas sighed. "Barb's wiped from the trip, among other things." He wiggled his eyebrows. "She's taking a nap; we probably won't see her again until breakfast."

Fred realized: "Hey! I'm not speaking to you. We're in a fight, remember?"

"Sure, I remember, but the good news is, I've forgiven you."

"You've—!"

"I thought I'd dig you up and we'd go grab a few drinks at the bar. But you're being your usual antisocial self, I see."

"Mumph."

"Man, that Tennian gal—blue hair? Blue eyes? She is a *key*-uutie!"

Fred rubbed her eyes. Tennian. Right. Between Artur asking her to live with him in the Black Sea, and Dr. Barb showing up, she'd forgotten all about the blue-haired troublemaker. "Don't remind me."

"She and Thomas swam out of the surf a while ago and walked down the beach looking like something out of a travel poster, except she was naked."

"Shut up."

"And where'd you disappear to before supper, anyway?"

"You mean before my boss showed up at a secret mermaid meeting? Artur took me out." Literally.

"Oh ho! So you've finally picked!"

"I haven't picked anything. He took me out and Thomas likes anything with a tail."

Jonas flopped onto the end of her bed. "Me-ow! If you're jealous—"

"I'm not jealous! Just disgusted. I could be anybody, you know. Anybody at all. It's not me Thomas likes. It's mermaids."

"Right, that's why he saved your life last year."

"He did not! I would have healed up on my own."

Jonas let that pass; they both knew there was more to it than that. "Well, did you like your dinner with Artur?"

"Yeah, actually. He showed me—he reminded me that there are things on the planet that only he could show me. Or, only one of my father's people. As much as I may like Thomas—and I absolutely don't—if I stayed with a biped, I'd be closing down an entire part of my life."

"Nothing you're not used to," Jonas pointed out. "I don't mean to belittle the sacrifice, but if you stayed with, ahem, a biped, it's what you're used to, comfortable with."

"Yeah, but with Artur, I can have it all. Also, he asked me to marry him and be the princess of the Undersea Folk and, later, the queen."

Jonas actually froze in ecstasy; she knew that look. He was having a "tilt! overload!" moment, imagining himself in charge of a royal wedding.

"Princess Fred!"

"Shut up, I haven't said yes."

"Which means you haven't said no!" He jumped off her bed and bowed low. "Your Highness, is it your plan to make it a policy that all the women have to look as bedraggled as possible?"

She snorted, and threw a pillow at him. "Nothing official."

"Oh my God! Princess Fred! I can't stand it, I absolutely can't stand it." He was actually spinning in a circle, clutching his elbows and whinnying in ecstasy.

"You know, there's a reason most people think you're gay on casual acquaintance."

"Stop it. You'll have to get married on land, of course—no way am I going to a royal wedding in fins, or that tin can Thomas built. Plus, there's your mom to think of."

"Will you calm down? I haven't said yes. I've got other things to worry about—like avoiding your girlfriend. And what I'll say to the Pelagic tomorrow."

"Yeah, yeah." He waved her citizen's responsibilities away. "Who'd pick Thomas over a prince? No offense. He's a nice guy and all. And rich; that helps. And you guys have the same educational background, the same training. But he writes romance novels. Artur's the prince of the Black Sea!"

"I'm aware," she said dryly, "of what they both do."

"So hurry up and tell him yes, before he changes his mind and decides to pick another mermaid. There's (literally) plenty of them in the sea, you know. Frankly, I'm amazed he didn't come to his senses all last year . . ."

"Will you get out of here? I'd actually like to get some sleep before I try to convince five hundred people who hate me that I know what's best for them."

"Hey, Princess Di didn't have it easy, either," he said, backing out her door. "But she became an icon! Fred the icon! I can see it now."

"Great, Jonas."

Thirty-three

You all know our next speaker . . . or know of her. *Her father was Kortrim, of whom many of us no longer speak. Her mother is the Lady Moon, who loved her and raised her as her own, even though she was a surface dweller.*

What a nice backhanded compliment, Fred thought, the snarkiness helping soothe her jangled nerves. I'll be sure to let my mom know that she managed to not chop me up into sushi despite being a drooling psychopathic biped.

She is a child of both worlds . . . She has lived among the surface dwellers all her life, but is also of our people.

In other words, neither fish nor fowl.

She has kindly agreed to join us and bring her unique perspective to our Pelagic. Fredrika, if you will come . . . ?

Fred slowly swam toward Mekkam. Unlike a courtroom, there wasn't a specific place to sit (float?) and give testimony. Instead, she approached Mekkam, knowing he would pick up her thoughts and share them with people all over the world.

She thought, not for the first time, that it was no fucking wonder he was king.

Hello. And thank you for that nice welcome, King Mekkam. Yes, my name is Fred. Dr. Fredrika Bimm, that is, which means I studied marine biology for many years. I . . . have an affinity for it, you might say.

No one actually laughed out loud, but she could sense an amused rustling. She saw Tennian sitting very close and nodded at her; the young mermaid nodded back and smiled. She probably meant it to be encouraging, and it would have been except for all those scary sharp teeth . . .

I've been thinking a lot about your decision. Our decision, I guess. And I can honestly say I can see both sides of the issue.

That must be why an outlander has been given a chance to speak today, on such an august occasion.

A merman she didn't know, one about her size, was floating about ten yards to her left. He had hair the color of snow. His eyes were the same color; it was such a startling contrast to his pupils that he looked blind.

You do not wish to hear what she has to say, Dessican? Artur asked, seeming amiably interested.

It is not a question of what I wish. It is a question of what is right. Her line has not been welcome here for longer than I have been alive.

Must be why you're so freaking threatened by me, then, Fred thought to herself, amused. Dessican had a look she well recognized: young punk, biting off more than he knew. And unwilling to back down in front of everyone.

Do you think we are not aware of her line? Artur asked, still sounding almost bored. *That my father did not know, and take it into account?*

If all can be heard at a Pelagic, I can be, too. And I do not think the king—

What? Now Artur's tone was almost a lazy purr. *You do not think the king . . . what?*

Dessican seemed to realize that, though others might object to Fred's presence, none of *them* were speaking up. And it was because all could be heard at a Pelagic that Fred had been invited to speak at all.

Invited by the king.

I am not the only one who thinks this, Dessican began lamely, looking around the large group.

Indeed. Just the only one ill-mannered enough to question the king's logic, not to mention his personally invited guest. Are you quite through, Dessican?

There was a long silence, odd in a group of telepaths, and then Dessican lifted his proud white head. *I am finished.*

Fredrika, Artur said, courteously gesturing her forward.

Ah . . . right. Okay. Glad we got that out of the way. Actually, glad somebody brought it up. I mean, Dessican was right about one thing. It's on everybody's mind. What my father did.

She swam in a small circle, thinking. She could feel all the eyes on her and, even more, could feel the *minds* on her, bending in her direction, trying to pick up every word.

So let's talk about it. Me, I didn't know a thing about it until I got here. After the king invited me. But no need to belabor that point. *And I'll have to admit, I was really, really shocked. Not just because I couldn't believe somebody who supposedly gave me my smarts would do something so dumb . . .*

An amused rustling; Dessican actually laughed out loud, and Fred watched the stream of bubbles for a moment.

Not just that, but because I know Artur. I had met the king by then, too. I couldn't believe somebody who knew them would want to hurt them. Kill them.

And I couldn't believe my own father *would try to do that. And for what? To try to take over. Try to be the boss of all the Undersea Folk.*

We don't have kings where I come from; everybody votes for the person they want to be the leader. And some people, they'll run for the job of leader just for the thrill of the title. Just to be called *the leader, not to be actually doing the job.*

I think that's what my dad wanted. To be called king. To be bowed to and respected, but not to actually look out for you guys.

And what I think about that is, I think he must have been an ungrateful, treacherous bastard. I think if he was here right now I'd gouge out his eyes and show them to him for daring to try to put hands on the king.

So that's where I stand on the whole "Fred's dad tried to take over the world" thing.

I just thought we might want to get that cleared up before we went any further.

There was another one of those rustling silences, and a lot of people looked at each other, then at her, then at each other. Finally, someone Fred couldn't see spoke up.

Fredrika, would you continue your testimony, please?

Someone else: *The question before the Pelagic: should the Undersea Folk claim this planet along with the bipeds, or not?*

Fred tried to gather her thoughts. She'd expected the crap about her dad to take up half the day. Boy, once these people made up their minds, that was it. Something to remember.

Right. To come out of the water closet, or not. Okay.

Okay. Well, as I was saying before, there are two sides to this question, and I—due to being raised by a surface dweller—I can see both of them.

On the one hand, why shouldn't all of us—all of you*—have the run of the planet? Why should you hide? I can say that as someone who can breathe underwater, I'd sure like to be myself all the time, not just when I'm with a couple of trusted friends, or my mother.*

Several of the Air Breather contingent murmured approvingly; she saw at once that many more people were looking at her than had before. Despite Mekkam's warm welcome, despite Artur's stated intent, despite Dessican's scene, many of her father's people had seemed set on ignoring her.

Not anymore.

But on the other hand, bipeds are treacherous. There's an excellent chance a lot of you could end up in an aquarium. Or a research lab. Bipeds have a way of thinking anybody different isn't human, isn't real, *and therefore they can do whatever they like. And if you don't believe me, try to find a Sioux or a Cherokee Indian and ask them. Those are the guys who* used *to think the planet was just as much theirs. As a scientist, I've seen firsthand what the bipeds can do to the planet.*

So what to do?

I don't know. I wish I could tell you that if you all chose to show yourselves to the rest of the world, things would work out fine and you'd be able to go wherever you like, unmolested. But I've seen too much of the human condition to be dumb enough to make guarantees.

On the other hand, if you stay hidden, you've lost nothing.

Of course, you won't gain anything, either.

I guess I'm saying it's up to you. All of you. I'll help you if you decide to show yourselves to my mother's people. I'll do whatever I can, even if that means "coming out" myself. Because I can hardly stay in hiding if all of you are brave enough to show yourselves to the world.

I guess . . . I guess that's all I have to say.

Fred "stepped down," or whatever the Pelagic equivalent was. She simply backed off and took her place in the crowd. Mekkam stood stock-still in the currents, his eyes closed, and after a long moment he opened them and said, *Does anyone have any rebuttal to Fredrika's comments?*

I do. Meerna, the tiny black-haired mermaid, was swimming to Mekkam. *How can we believe anything that comes out of her mouth? She was raised by bipeds, she admits it! And worse, she was fathered by he whose name we no longer speak. She could be leading us to treachery. It would not be the first time for her kin.*

I don't need to be treacherous to fuck you up nine ways to Sunday, Meerna, darling, Fred thought sweetly. *Anytime I wanted I could pull your head off and use your blood to make the sea that much saltier.*

You see? She thinks like a biped; all her reactions are that of a surface dweller. She is unkind, and prone to violence.

She is also "she who would be my wife," Artur said, coming up on Mekkam's left flank. *Do you dare question my judgment?*

Meerna opened her mouth—odd, for a telepath—and then closed it. She was silent for a long moment, until . . . *Highness, I do not.*

Well, naturally, Fred realized. What else could she say? Chickenshit. At least have the courage of your convictions.

No, Meerna's got a point, Fred added, cursing herself once again for being burdened with a conscience. *Why should you trust me? Not because of what my father did—I never knew the guy, so he's not likely to influence my actions today. And not because of what I said about what my father did. I could have been lying. Meerna's right: You don't know me. Which is why I couldn't advocate one course of action over another; all I could do was lay out your choices. You shouldn't trust me, and that's fine. You need to make up your own minds.*

So there.

Who are you to call anyone names, Meerna? Tennian said, out like a shot from her spot off to the side. *Fredrika took your insult when she could have done much worse. She does not know our ways but she has taken our rudeness without complaint . . . when she has the ear of the prince himself!*

Darn right, Fred thought. *The ear and pretty much any other part of him I want.*

She could have made any of our lives difficult whenever she wished. And what did she do? Stood up in front of everyone and gave her honest opinion!

Take that!

But even that did not satisfy you, and I suspect there are things in your *family's past that would explain that. Shall we explore your dark corners, Meerna, or will you remember your manners, remember you are supposed to be superior to the surface dwellers?*

I . . . meant no offense. This was a rather large lie, but Fred was feeling generous in her victory.

And God *damn* it if she wasn't getting kind of fond of Tennian. Girl wouldn't have said shit if she had a mouthful when they'd first met, but now . . .

That's all right, Fred said. *It's the elephant in the room. We were bound to trip over it sooner or later.* If she'd been speaking out loud, likely none of them would have had the vaguest idea what she was talking about. But they plucked her meaning from her thoughts, and many people were nodding.

Anyway, I guess that's all I've got to say.

Before she could pull away, or scream, Tennian had seized her hand and was pulling her over to a large knot of Undersea Folk, all of whom had much friendlier expressions on their faces than they'd had twenty minutes ago.

Damn, Tennian, remind me to never get on your bad side.

Small-minded, closed-minded, tiny-brained fools, Tennian was muttering, a constant stream of insults that flowed across Fred's brain. *As if we must be judged by the actions of one we had never met! Foolish, foolish . . .*

All right, calm down. Pay attention. Here comes more testimony.

The daughter of the surface dweller is right! an obvious Air Breather testified. *It is our land, just as it is theirs. Why should we hide? We have done nothing wrong! Why must we languish in brackish pools and never feel the sun?*

The Air Breather—Fred hadn't caught her name—went on in this vein for some time. Fred was amused to realize that when she'd heard "the daughter of the surface dweller is right!" she'd had no idea what the gal was going to argue until she'd said it. Because Fred hadn't really advocated either course of action.

This was made clear when several Traditionals spoke, also backing Fred up: we don't know how the bipeds will react; we can't trust them; it's safer to stay hidden as we have for centuries; we risk nothing and we lose nothing.

Oh, nuts.

What? Tennian sent back.

I don't think I've helped them resolve a damn thing.

Never mind. You did your job, which is all anyone could ask of you.

Then why did she feel like she'd let both parties down?

Thirty-four

Mekkam had asked Fred to remain after the Pelagic, so it was startling to see hundreds of Undersea Folk swimming off all at once . . . except for her. Several of them nodded to her, and one or two of the younger ones even waved.

Finally, they were alone . . . as alone as a mermaid and a king can be in an ocean teeming with life, anyway.

What can I do for you, Mekkam?

Only this. You were wise to commit to neither faction, but would you tell me your true thoughts.

If they'd been walking they would have fallen into step together; instead, she swam on his left, noticing he set a pace she could easily keep up with. Tactful, and then some.

That's just it, Mekkam. I really don't *know what you guys should do. I'd be fine whatever you picked. There's pros and cons to both.*

Indeed.

But you *must have a preference. Duh, of course you have a preference. In fact, the Traditionals are totally in your corner. You want to keep your people safe and I can respect that.*

But at what cost, Fredrika? To deny them their birthright? Smothering is not protecting, and I would rather not hurt my people while trying to help them.

Fred swam in silence for a moment. *Yeah, well, good luck with all of that.*

Would you really change your life if the Air Breathers swing the vote?

Sure. If all you guys will, it's the least I can do. Hell, all I'd have to do is show my boss my tail. It'd be all over Boston in a week.

That does not surprise me, since you would be changing your life a great deal should you come with us. I am pleased my son has chosen well. Mekkam smiled at her, keeping his sharp teeth well concealed, and Fred almost smiled back. *I hope you choose him as well.*

Well, we'll see what we'll see, I s'pose.

That we will, Fredrika.

They swam back to the beach, both lost in their own thoughts.

For her own part, Fred was thinking that if her mother hadn't remarried, she'd have introduced Moon to the king.

What's wrong with me? she thought, horrified. Being around Jonas has given me matchmaking on the brain!

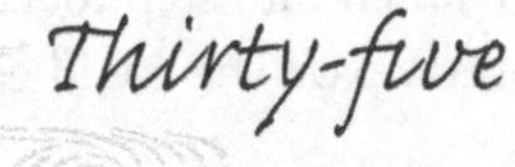

Thirty-five

"Great," Fred muttered as she stood up out of the surf, Mekkam beside her. "Here comes my boss."

"Hello, Dr. Bimm! Hello . . . er . . ." Dr. Barb, clad in a navy blue one-piece and an absurdly floppy straw hat, skidded to a halt in front of Mekkam. "You must be one of Dr. Bimm's family. I, ah, apologize for intruding . . ."

"No need, good lady. I am—"

"A nudist!" Fred burst out. "We're all . . . I mean, my family is all nudists. We like to be nude. All the time. That's why the private resort."

"Of—of course. I understand. I—I'm making you uncomfortable and I apologize. I'll—"

"Not at all, good lady. Will you dine with us? I would like to hear more about the New England Aquarium. Fredrika and I will clothe ourselves, of course."

"Of course," Fred added sourly.

Mekkam gallantly held out an arm. And without so much as a half second of hesitation, Dr. Barb latched on to it.

No doubt about it, Fred thought, trudging behind him. The old guy's still got it. Wouldn't Dr. Barb shit if she knew how old he was, never mind what he *really* looked like when he was naked?

"I think it's wonderful that your whole family can get together like this."

Mekkam forked another lobster claw onto Barb's plate. "Oh, we do not do it very often, good lady. This is a special occasion."

"I gathered. Dr. Bimm has never had a vacation in all the years she has worked for me, and then all of a sudden she took all her accumulated time at once!"

"The islands beckoned," Fred said sourly, polishing off another biscuit.

"We have much family business to discuss," Mekkam continued, refilling Dr. Barb's iced tea. "Perhaps we will need your help with some of it."

"And perhaps not," Fred said sharply.

"Oh, I couldn't presume to interfere," Dr. Barb said seriously. "It's bad enough I'm here at all."

Jonas kicked Fred under the table before she could form a suitably acidic reply.

Mekkam smiled, but it was an odd look: distant and almost unfriendly. "You never can tell," he said. "All things come together in the end, whether we wish it or not. Some might see your arrival here as a portent."

"And some might see it as a pain in my—Owwww, Jonas!"

"Sorry. My foot slipped again."

"My *fist* is going to slip if you don't cut the shit!"

"Fredrika," Mekkam said with absent authority. "Jonas. You have attained maturity; display it for us, if you please."

Embarrassed, Fred and Jonas stopped in mid-squabble. Dr. Barb's eyes went wide and, when Mekkam went out to see Artur, she leaned over and whispered, "He's the patriarch, isn't he? Your uncle, maybe?"

"Patriarch, yeah," Fred sighed. "Something like that."

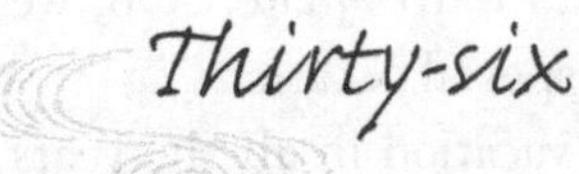

Thirty-six

"Oh my God! It's after me! It's gonna kill me!" Jonas was frantically thrashing his way back to her. His snorkel was askew and his mask was on crooked as he sputtered and flailed. "Get it away. Get it awaaaaaay!"

Fred saw the ray, a gorgeous specimen with a four-foot wingspan, and swallowed a sneer of disgust. "Will you calm down? It's harmless."

"Tell that to Steve Irwin," Jonas retorted. "God, I'm surrounded by living creatures! This sucks!"

"Well, it *is* the ocean, Jonas. And stop thrashing. You're doing a perfect imitation of a nice plump seal in distress."

"Aaaggghhh!"

"Oh, calm down. You're perfectly safe. We're not even thirty feet offshore." Dr. Barb was still sunbathing on her stomach, Fred was relieved to see, and there was no chance she could see Fred's tail, even if she was facing the right way and staring straight at them.

"That thing is huge!" Jonas accidentally took a gulp of salt water and coughed for five minutes. "I'm telling you, it's thinking about how I might taste."

The ray couldn't have given a shit about how Jonas might taste; it was swimming gracefully around them, either curious or looking for food or both.

She tried to distract him. "Hey, you know what another name for a ray is? Mermaid's purse!"

"How fascinating, now will you please kill it so that I may live?"

"I'm not killing it, Jonas." She grasped his arm, peeked again at the dozing Dr. Barb, and with a powerful flex of her tail, propelled them twenty feet in the other direction. "There, okay? Now you're surrounded by just fish and maybe a sea turtle."

Jonas coughed for another ten minutes. "You want to warn me before you turn the motor on?" he gasped after a long while.

"All you've done since we've gotten to this island is bitch. Well, that and have sex with Dr. Barb. What's the matter?"

"Are you kidding? You don't think it's a little stressful, spending all day on the beach wondering what you guys are talking about? Then worrying your girlfriend will figure out your best friend's biggest secret?"

"Lame," Fred decided.

"Drinking rum and Cokes all by yourself because your girlfriend is a scientist who just *has* to go poking around the local flora and fauna? She spent three *hours* feeding grapes to the iguanas yesterday—"

"Poor baby. Even when she's here, you're feeling ignored."

"—wondering if today's the day you're going to decide to beach yourselves all at once, preferably in front of CNN cameras? Do you know how stressful that is?"

"*You're* stressed? I've been freaking out ever since I found out my testimony might actually have an *impact* on the decision!"

A long, dark shape glided past Jonas, and Fred couldn't help it; her eyes widened. Unfortunately Jonas saw and spun around. "What? What? Oh my God, it's a great white, isn't it? *Isn't it?*"

"Could be," Fred said cautiously. "I don't think I can take one on by myself. Just . . . sit . . . still . . ." *I'm going to hell,* she reminded herself with an internal grin.

"Oh my God!" Jonas screamed in a whisper.

The dark shape surfaced . . . and blew a stream of water between Jonas's eyes. "Good evening, Jonas. Little Rika."

"You scared the hell out of me!" Jonas roared. "Don't ever do that again unless you want to be chopped into a hundred Filet-O-Fish sandwiches! I know the VP of marketing at McDonald's; I could make it happen!"

"Jonas is feeling a little hysterical this evening," Fred explained. "I think he's having his period."

"I did not know such things were normal for the males of your kind."

"They aren't," Jonas huffed. "I'm out of here. You two will have to find some other biped to torture." He began laboriously paddling toward shore. "And you both have split ends!" was his parting shot as a wave closed over his head, swallowing the rest of his insults.

"I didn't really think about it like that," Fred said, watching him go.

"Like what, Little Rika?"

"He said it's really nerve-racking, waiting to see what we decide."

"For us no less than him."

"Right, right. What's up?"

"Nothing is up." He pulled her into his embrace and nuzzled the top of her head. "I only wished to see you."

"Oh. Well, that's nice. Careful, Dr. Barb's onshore."

"I see her. Though I seriously doubt she sees me . . . or you, for that matter." He dismissed Dr. Barb with a shrug. "You did well today. I expected nothing less, of course."

"Of course. Well, it was definitely interesting. Never thought I'd see Tennian riding to the rescue, that's for sure."

"Yes, she is something of—you would call her a rebel."

"Tennian?"

"Oh, yes. She was the despair of her family for many years."

Fred started giggling and was afraid she wouldn't be able to stop. "Oh, right. I can see it now. They must have wept over her antics for days. Months!"

"Are you quite well, Little Rika? You seem in . . . unusually high spirits."

"I'm probably light-headed," she admitted. "Haven't had a chance to eat today."

"Then come along."

"Oh, more seaweed grazing?" she asked hopefully.

"If you wish."

"I really liked that place."

"As did I, and not only because you were pleased to join me."

"Artur, what if I have to tell you no?"

The smile slipped from his face. "I will have to devoutly hope you do not."

"But what will you do? Find someone else?"

"Ah, Little Rika. Were you not listening to your own testimony? There is no one else like you."

"How horrifying," she joked.

"But singularly comforting," he said, and leaned forward, and kissed her softly.

She kissed him back, and the waves rocked them, pushing them farther into each other's embrace.

"Rika, my Rika . . ."

"Not your Rika," she mumbled against his mouth. "Don't spoil this."

"Oh, never! Tell me, Rika, are you fertile?"

"You mean, right this second? No. But in general? Yeah. I'm pretty sure." She menstruated, which had to count for something. She assumed she was fertile because she had not had occasion to think otherwise. Funny how her own biology was of no interest to her at all.

But maybe that was just another way to hide.

"Oh, excellent."

"If your plan is to knock me up and force a shotgun marriage," she warned him, "it won't work."

"The thought," he assured her, nibbling an earlobe, "never crossed my mind."

Thirty-seven

Good morning.

Hi.

Hello.

Morning.

Good morning, Fredrika.

Hi, Tennian.

This is my friend, Bettan—I believe you met?

Sure. Fred shook hands with the lean, red-haired mermaid.

I hope you will not judge me by the company I keep, Bettan teased, no doubt referring to Meerna's anti-half-breed diatribe from yesterday.

Gosh, that would be terrible! Being judged by the people you're with instead of, you know . . . who you are.

An awkward silence followed that, and Fred had a rare twinge of conscience: had she gone too far?

But then Tennian, as usual, saved the day. *You are wise, Fredrika, as well as fearless. And yes, that would be terrible.*

I found your testimony quite interesting, a strange merman she'd never met spoke up in her mind.

As did I, a merman named Linnen added.

They chatted for a few minutes, Fred well aware she had Tennian's outburst the day before to thank for everyone's friendliness. And Artur, of course.

When the group broke up, Tennian whispered in her brain, *What's amazing is, Linnen is a Traditional and Coykinda is an Air Breather! And yet they both found something to take away from your testimony.*

In other words, I didn't help at all: things are exactly the way they were two days ago.

Someone with a grim view of things might see it that way, Tennian admitted.

That's me, baby. Grim View is my middle name. Well, names. Say, Tennian, can I ask you something?

Ask.

Which are you?

Oh, I'm an Air Breather! I do not wish to hide!

Fred snickered. *Why am I not surprised?*

But my family is Traditional. They think it is dangerous to expose themselves to the bipeds. And they side with the royal family in all things.

Not you, though, huh?

Artur understands, Tennian thought confidently. *We were babies together.*

Well, your family's not entirely wrong. It might be dangerous.

So is swimming alone in strange water; so is hunting in killer whale territory. Life is dangerous, and I do not care! It would be worth it to walk on the grass and not be afraid all the time.

If you break out into a rendition of "Part of Your World" I'm going to beat you to death.

Eh? Oh, see! It starts.

She was right; it did.

They will lock us up in their aquariums! Fredrika is right: they will use their knives on us to explore our bodies, and never once think they are hurting people who are as they are.

And:

Fredrika is right! The planet belongs no more to them than it does to us; we have as much right to a beach house as a—a—

Hollywood film producer, Fred added helpfully.

And:

The traitor's daughter is right! Her people foul the water; they will not respect our rights. Better to stay hidden.

That is not what the traitor's daughter is saying!

Uh, guys? The name's Fred, okay?

And:

We will never agree; I do not understand why King Mekkam has not called the question.

It has not been so very long; do you imply we are as the surface dwellers, never agreeing on anything?

Ask Fredrika; she would know. I do not. I only know I will not change my mind.

Nor will I!

Very well, then!

Yes, very well!

Fred rubbed her temples. Around her, testimony went on while minor arguments broke out on all sides. Mekkam called the place to order again and again, but chaos lurked. She wished for an Advil. She wished for a bottle of Advil.

Finally, the day's testimony was over. But this time, she was followed—chased, really—back to shore by several Traditionals and Air Breathers, all interrupting each other to be heard on the issue, all waiting for her to validate their opinions.

Guys—

Surely you can agree that the history of your mother's people speaks for itself.

Guys, I'm really—

Data does not speak for itself! Fredrika would tell you that her mother's people have goodness in them, too.

Guys, it's been a really long day.

Fredrika could use her science powers to protect us! She would not allow her father's people to be enslaved.

Guys, I've got a splitting headache.

Fredrika is only one person; how can she stand against millions?

A familiar silver orb floated into sight and Fred arrowed toward it so fast, she nearly knocked herself unconscious on a viewing window. She pounded on the plastic until the air lock slid open.

Later, guys. She gave the chattering mermaids a hurried wave, and darted into the URV with pure gratitude.

Thirty-eight

"They're after me, Thomas, they're after me!"

"Fred, calm down." Thomas handed her a towel, and a robe. He waved at the Undersea Folk who were still milling around outside the URV. "Long day, huh?"

"You have *no* idea. I went from being totally ignored to totally harassed." She shrugged into the robe and toweled her hair dry. "God, and the voices! You just can't get them out of your head, no matter how hard you try."

"If I didn't know better, I'd be prescribing you some tranqs right now."

"I could use some, believe me." She slumped against the galley counter. "Got any booze in this thing?"

"That bad, huh?"

"It's just—that's a lot of people to have in your head, you know?" She looked out the window. "I'm used to having my brain to myself."

"Does it hurt? The telepathy?"

"Huh?" She jerked her attention back to Thomas, who handed her a beer. "Oh. No. No, it doesn't hurt at all. It's just overwhelming.

Sometimes. Tell you what, I can see why exile is such a big deal to these people. If you grow up used to hearing all those voices . . . and then all of a sudden you're all alone . . . My father must have hated it."

"Your father sounds like a shitheel who had it coming," he said cheerfully.

"Well, yeah." She sipped her beer. "Boy, it's nice in here! Nice and quiet."

"Ah, my sinister scheme to get you alone has succeeded beyond my wildest dreams."

"Are you talking to me, or plotting your next romance novel?"

"Both," he said, and then kissed her spang on the mouth.

"Perv."

"Beer breath."

This time she kissed him, letting the towel drop from her hair as she put her arms around him, pressing against him as his arms came around her. She ran her fingers through his thick dark hair and stroked his teeth with the tip of her tongue.

"This is—what I'd call—a mixed signal," he gasped, coming up for air. "Usually now's the time you sock me in the eye."

"I'm really tired, though."

"Too tired to try out the bed?"

She laughed as he squeezed her to him. "I'm having an off moment as a result of a brain full of voices not my own, but I haven't taken total leave of my senses."

"Shit."

"Don't sulk," she teased. "You're hardly cute when you do that."

"Looking cute is the least of my problems," he growled, carefully setting her aside. "And stop doing that to my hair, it makes me feel like ripping that robe right off you."

"I see I'm not the only one under stress."

He went to a board of instruments, glanced at them without really seeing them, and closed the tiny door to the fridge which, in his distraction, he'd forgotten to do before.

"Not stress, exactly, but for a while there it looked kind of tense. As strong as you guys are, I'd hate to see you come to blows. Over anything."

"And they're even stronger than I am. No, nobody's coming to blows. But it's a charged issue, that's for damned sure. And I took the easy way out: I didn't pick a side."

"Yeah?"

She sighed and looked at her feet. "Yeah. Laid it out for them, pro and con, but didn't actually pick a side."

"Then came in here to hide."

"Pretty much, yeah. Dr. Barb's waiting for me on land, and those guys are all waiting for me the minute I swim out of here."

"Well, the URV's yours whenever you want it. I'm glad it's making a nice hidey-hole for you."

She quirked an eyebrow at him. "You wouldn't be calling me a chickenshit, would you, Doctor?"

"Not to your face," he replied, then laughed. "It wouldn't—uh-oh."

"What?"

She heard the click, and then the cycling of the air pump. "Great," she grumbled. "What now?"

She hit the button, and the door slid open to reveal, naturally, Jonas and Dr. Barb.

Thirty-nine

His scalp still sizzling from the glare Fred had given him as she and Thomas had left the URV, Jonas led Dr. Barb the few feet to the bedroom. Worth it, worth Fred's ire (which, frankly, he brought on himself at least twice a week) and then some, because he'd been positively—

"I've been *dying* to try this place out," he confided, while his lover looked around the small underwater RV, exclaiming and staring and, he could tell, wishing she'd brought her BlackBerry. "You know, the bedroom?"

"This thing is a wonder of design!" the scientist said, momentarily elbowing the lover out of the picture. "It must have cost your friend a fortune!"

"Yeah, well, he's loaded and he can spare it, now check out this bed."

"And he's been living in it?"

"Yes. No. I don't know." Best not to get into the whole "No, just tools around during the Pelagic taking pictures" thing. "Barb, will you get your delectable ass over here?"

"And to think, it's all contained in—yeeek! Jonas!" She giggled and slapped his hand away, but he stood his ground and, as he outweighed her by a good thirty pounds of muscle, was easily able to drag her toward the small bedroom.

"Jonas, you act like you've been denied . . . Now just let me get a closer look at the design . . ."

"I *am* being denied." He started pulling on the straps of her swimsuit which, since they were wet, fought him like a live thing. "Right this second I'm being denied. Ack! What are you wearing, titanium?"

She laughed at him, brushed his hands away, then wriggled out of her suit with a few grunts, exposing much pink and cream flesh as she did so. Eventually (finally!), she was nude and holding out her arms. "There, Mr. Impatient, satisfied?"

"Not even close," he growled, then picked her up and tossed her on the small bed. His trunks were much easier to get rid of, and then he pounced on her.

"I really should be studying this thing's schematics," she told him between kisses.

"What 'thing' are you referring to?"

"After a year, you don't know?"

"Very funny." He kissed her mouth, the slope of her neck, the tops of her creamy, cool breasts.

"Oooh, your mouth is nice and warm," she groaned.

"I missed you so much."

"I missed you, too." She shifted her weight, pushing her nipple farther into his mouth. "I'm glad you liked my surprise."

He kissed, sucked, nibbled. "I loved your surprise. Adored it! It was the greatest surprise I ever got in my whole life!" He thought briefly of Fred and quailed, then banished the thought. The quickest way to lose his hard-on would be to think of his childhood friend—practically a sister to him!—in a murderous rage. "I loved seeing you, loved the surprise!"

"I just thought—since you were stuck down here—with all of Fred's family—that you might like company." Each time he kissed her she had to pause. "I know—you like—to help her—in social situations—"

"I could use help in a social situation right now."

"Oh, yuck!"

They laughed together, as lovers will, and moved together, and kissed, and touched, and when he entered her she moved against him like a wave, and clung to him. And as her orgasm rippled through her she whispered in his ear, told him she loved him, told him he was for her and she was for him, whispered love, whispered, whispered.

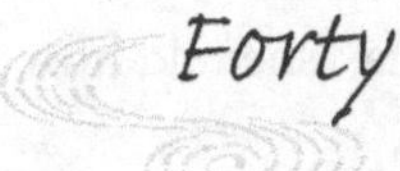

Forty

Jonas groaned as the love of his life bounded off the small bed, cleaned herself up in the smaller bathroom, then wriggled back into her swimsuit. He had just enough energy to roll over and take a nap.

"Why does sex energize you like this? My God, you're acting like you had a Red Bull IV drip."

"Physiology, my love." Barb snapped her straps into place. "Now: your base needs have been taken care of, and nothing is going to stop me from examining this thing."

Jonas groped for his trunks, found the pocket string, found the small hard object tied securely to the string. "Hey, Barb."

"Jonas, I already told you—"

"Be my wife?"

"—that nothing—What?"

He yanked, but he'd done too thorough a job tying the engagement ring to his trunks. "I want to get married. I think . . ." Yank, yank. ". . . we should get . . ." Yank! ". . . married."

Barb came over to the bed and after a final, futile yank, he presented her with his swim trunks. She did some sort of womanly thing and then the ring was free. "Oh, Jonas! It's a pearl!"

"From the ocean," he prompted the marine biologist.

"But—but you didn't know I was going to be here!"

"Are you kidding? I've been walking around with that thing every minute of every day for three weeks."

"For three weeks? Why did you—"

"Barb, is that a yes or a no?"

"What? Oh!" She slipped the ring on. "Yes, of course, yes."

"Really?" His postcoital lassitude vanished; he'd hoped she was going to say yes, but hadn't been one hundred percent sure. She had, after all, been married before. "You will?"

"Oh, sure, I've been waiting for you to ask." She smiled down at the ring. "This isn't going to make Dr. Bimm very happy."

"Yeah, well—"

"Wait until she sees the pink bridesmaid gown I'm going to make her wear!"

Jonas gaped at his betrothed. "You . . . are . . . *evil*!"

"Yeah," Dr. Barb said, and giggled.

Forty-one

All morning, Fred couldn't shake the feeling that something was hideously wrong. Something had happened, she was sure of it. Something that directly affected her in a negative way. Something repugnant and bloated, just off the horizon. Something waiting to eclipse her life.

She was so busy trying to figure it out, she barely paid attention to Pelagic testimony. And for hours she'd half-listened to Air Breathers elegantly savage Traditionals, and vice versa.

This was essentially a playback of the last three days, she figured. It was like any emotionally charged debate . . . abortion, politics, religion. You'll never change the other person's mind. Never.

And what was *wrong*? Why the feeling of foreboding? She felt like Custer . . . the day *after* the Indians landed.

About three hours later, after a Traditional stepped down, Mekkam stepped up.

I've just received word. Enough of our people have heard testimony; they wish to vote. In the tradition of the Pelagic, the royal family will abide by the vote, regardless of the outcome. As will we all. Voting will take place at once; I will let you know when we have a tally.

And that was that. Fred suddenly wished she'd been paying a bit more attention.

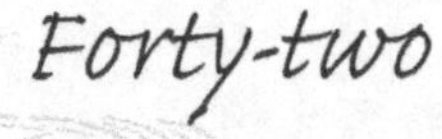

Forty-two

"So that's it?"

"That's it," Fred said. She, Jonas, Thomas, Tennian, and Artur were eating in the small dining room. Tennian, she couldn't help notice, had put away enough shrimp to repopulate two fisheries. "They'll vote, and Mekkam will tell us who won."

"Uh . . . don't take this the wrong way, Artur . . ." Jonas began.

"I have noticed that when a biped says that, something offensive will invariably follow."

"Well, maybe." Jonas cleared his throat and put his fork down. "Anyway, Mekkam is the super telepath, right? It's why he's king?"

Tennian, Artur, and Fred nodded in unison.

"And everybody's—what? Beaming their thoughts at him? Until enough of them vote?"

More nods.

"Well. Uh. You said he's a Traditional. What's to stop him from just *telling* you what the vote is? From telling you the Traditionals won?"

"You think of our king as you are used to thinking of your own leaders," Artur said, mildly enough. Fred knew enough now about her father's people to realize Artur was being quite self-restrained. Especially given that Jonas had just insulted the hell out of Artur's dad. "But our king would not lie for his people. That would—ah—would—"

"Pervert," Fred suggested.

"—pervert the whole system of the Pelagic."

"Oh. Well, thanks for answering my question. I don't know that I'd have that kind of self-control. I mean, if I really thought staying hidden would be best for my people, I'd be tempted to just tell them that's how the vote went."

"Well," Artur said reasonably, "that is why you are not a king."

"And thank God. I've got enough headaches keeping track of *one* mermaid, never mind eighty zillion of them."

"Har, har," Fred said sourly.

"How long until the returns come back, so to speak?" Thomas asked. He slid the bowl of shrimp cocktail closer to Tennian who, Fred noticed with rising nausea, was eating the tails, too. She tried to ignore the crunching. "Couple of days?"

"The last time the Pelagic voted, it took about a day. It all depends on how many of us vote."

"Well, I'd think you all would!" Jonas cried. "It affects all of you, doesn't it?"

"Do all of your countrymen vote in every election?" Artur asked.

"Yeah, good point, but you're supposed to be better than us. You guys don't have any Republicans, at least."

"Oh, don't even start," Fred snapped.

"Well, did they wreck the country or didn't they?"

"They absolutely did not." Fred jabbed her butter knife in Jonas's general direction. "If we left it up to you Dems, all the lifers would be out on the street and our taxes would be in the eightieth percentile."

"Like you even know what paying taxes is . . . you've worked for nonprofits your whole life!"

"I pay taxes," she said hotly.

"Yeah, for fun! The only reason you're talking like this is because Moon and Sam are rich. It's true," he told Artur and Tennian. "Fred's folks have more money than the Kennedys."

"Who are the—"

"They do not! And shut up. And—oh, shit. Here comes Dr. Barb." She checked; everybody had shorts on; Tennian was floating around in what she suspected was one of Thomas's T-shirts. "Watch the mermaid talk, you guys. And Tennian, will you stop *crunching*?"

"But they're so good," she replied in a small, wounded voice.

"Hello!" Dr. Barb trilled. She stopped short of the table and looked at Jonas. "Did you tell her?"

Jonas shook his head. "I was waiting for you."

"Tell me what?" Fred asked suspiciously, the feeling of foreboding back in the front of her brain.

Dr. Barb thrust her fist at Fred's face; she ducked. Then realized . . . "That . . . looks like . . . an engagement ring."

"Good work . . . Doctor . . . Bimm . . ."

"Oh, are you formalizing your mating?" Tennian asked, sneaking more shrimp onto her plate. "Congratulations."

"No!" Fred screamed. "You can't! Think of what it'll do to my personal and professional life!"

"There was that," Jonas admitted, "but aside from those benefits, we're also in love."

"Aw, fuck." Fred slumped over her plate and hid her face. "By which I mean, congrats."

"Thank you," Dr. Barb said. To Jonas: "That went much better than I expected."

"Believe it or not, Dr. Barb, I actually have bigger problems than this right now."

"Family reunions can be stressful," her boss said sympathetically.

There was a furtive crunch and Tennian looked guilty as Fred glared at her. "Tennian, please! Stop eating the tails!"

"You should not treat her so, when she does such a good job standing up for *you*. As, of course, do I," Artur added without a trace of braggadocio.

Trying to stomp on her rising hysteria, Fred managed not to yell, "Well, I don't need your help, or her help, or anybody's help!"

"Oh, here we go," Jonas said to his peas.

"No, it's not the usual independent rant. It's the 'I deserve to be heard based on who I am, not who my father is' rant. I can't believe I actually had to *say* that. I'm not the one in the wrong; your people are! In fact, I—I—"

She stopped talking, startled.

"Fred?"

Why hadn't she thought of it before?

"Fred?"

It was so simple! Why hadn't any of *them* thought of it before?

"Fred!"

She grabbed Artur by the collar (for a wonder, he was wearing a shirt, too). "Quick! Where's your dad?"

Forty-three

Little Rika, I must warn you, he is likely in meditation. It *is exhausting, catching all the votes with his mind like this. He—*

I don't care. I've got to talk to him. I've got it!

So you said, but you have not elaborated.

Bring me to the king, and I'll elaborate all you want.

There.

She could see the king floating in about forty feet of water. He was upside down, his long grayish red hair almost dragging through the sand.

Mekkam! Excuse me? Mekkam?

He cracked one eye open and observed her. *Yes, Fredrika? Is something wrong?*

Yeah, you're going about this totally the wrong way!

The other eye slowly opened. *Indeed?*

Yeah. Uh. Sorry to interrupt. In her excitement, she darted around and around him. *Listen: it's wrong to make a group decision on something that will affect every single person differently.*

Oh?

She mentally gulped at the dry voice. And thought to herself, *I'm the only one who'll talk to the king like this. I've got to try!*

I think rather than forcing everyone to comply with the group vote, you let each one of your people make up his or her own mind.

But if, say, a third of them wish to expose themselves—

Where's the rule that says you all have to? In fact, let the Traditionals stay in hiding, if they want. That way the Air Breathers will always have a home to retreat to. You're not exposing everyone to one decision. You're not exposing people who want to stay safe.

Mekkam closed his eyes again and thought it over.

I do not know, Rika, Artur said worriedly. *We are a people of tradition, and by tradition the Pelagic—*

If you guys want to show up in the twenty-first century, you've got to act like it. And that includes chucking a legal system that's four hundred years old. Heck, ours is almost that old and it's a fucking mess!

Artur began, *I do not—*

Enough. I have decided.

Fred realized she wasn't too crazy about living in a monarchy. Why should one guy be able to decide something like this?

Then she thought, *One day it might be me making these decisions! Disaster!*

Fredrika makes a good point. Further, she has shown me a way to help all my people, regardless of which side they are on. How annoying not to have thought of it myself. But we are a prisoner of our own societies, whether we live in the sea or in the suburbs. It will be as she said.

It will? Fred gaped and was nearly spun away from him when she stopped paying attention and let the current grab her.

We will tell everyone. Right now.

And then, a moment later: *It is done.*

Forty-four

But how will we—

Then I will return—

—couldn't be simpler—

—couldn't be worse—

And how can we—

But he said we could—

ENOUGH!

A hundred minds all shut up at once, and at least that many pairs of eyes were staring at Fred. She cleared her throat, remembered she didn't have to speak out loud, then added, *If you want to go up, go up. Just swim up to one of the public beaches and walk out. Or we could go hunt down the offices of* People *magazine. But one thing: Bipeds have a big-time nudity taboo. So if you want to hang out surface-side, you'd better love the idea of jeans and T-shirts.*

I will go. That thought, clear and cool, like a mountain spring. *I will go right now.*

Tennian. Shocker. Fred swam after her as she ignored the private beach and made for the public shore about five hundred yards away.

Uh, Tennian, they might be scared.

Who could be scared of me?

You'd be surprised. Just . . . no sudden moves, all right?

Fred could hear displaced water and looked; Thomas was chugging behind her and Tennian in the URV. She waved, then went back to following Tennian.

The blue-haired girl popped to the surface in full tail, a hundred yards offshore. There was a filthy boat staffed with sailors, all of whom started shouting and pointing at Tennian.

She waved.

Fred popped up beside her, squinting at the boat. There was something familiar about it, something she had read recently . . . it wasn't Navy, or Coast Guard. It wasn't a private yacht. It was—

"Pirates!" Fred gasped. Now she remembered, oh, yes. Modern pirates were popping up all over the place, robbing cruise ships and private yachts. "Tennian, don't—"

"Hello!" she cried, waving. Her tail was all too visible beneath the clear waves. "I am Tennian, of the Undersea Folk, wishing you—"

There was a crack, and Tennian disappeared beneath the waves.

Forty-five

Tennian!

I—don't—What happened?

Fred caught Tennian as she spun toward the sand bottom. Her blood was already darkening the water, which would bring the little guys: black tip reef sharks, white tip reef sharks, and grey reef sharks. They, in turn, would bring the big boys: makos, great whites, tiger sharks, hammerheads. Dammit!

You've been shot, Tennian. They shot you with a gun . . . a weapon.

But why?

Because they were scared of you.

But I did nothing!

Welcome to the wonderful world of bipeds.

She turned, feeling more displaced water, and saw Thomas had pulled the URV up right behind them, and was beckoning frantically toward her. And, like an answer to a prayer, Artur materialized on her other side and picked Tennian up out of the sand.

Come on, Thomas can fix this.

Do not be afraid, Tennian. Rika's Thomas is a most competent healer.

I'm NOT afraid. They were afraid of ME!

Fred saw a black tip reef shark circle toward them, waited for it to get closer, then punched it in the nose. It was either that or go for the eyes, and she didn't want to blind the fish for following its instincts. It spun away, sending a startled (and disgruntled) thought in her direction.

Three more came up on her blind side, but Artur bared his teeth at them and they darted away. In the ocean, she supposed the Undersea Folk were at the top of the food chain.

Remember where the boat was. We'll go back later and settle their hash, Fred thought.

Indeed. I look forward to that, Little Rika.

She saw a large shadow start toward them and thought it was probably a tiger shark. She started pushing and hurrying them along, never taking her gaze from the shadow. The three of them got through the air lock in record time, and then Artur was stretching Tennian out on the tile. Thomas had appeared, carrying a bulky first-aid kit.

"Finally. Took you guys long enough."

"Sharks," Fred said shortly.

"Great. Tennian, you doing okay, honey?"

"I did nothing!"

"Yeah, well, what can we say. We're a skittish and unpleasant race." Thomas pulled her into a half-sitting position and looked at her back. "A neat through and through. Probably a rifle. Did you see it, Fred?"

"It was long, that's all I saw."

"Rifle, then. Good. Small bullets," he told Tennian, "and not much damage. And they aimed high. Or hit high, anyway."

"That is good?"

"Very fuckin' good."

Blood was pooling beneath Tennian and Fred knew from experience that she had to be in pain, but the blue-haired mermaid only had eyes for Thomas, and seemed to hardly notice as he fixed her shoulder.

Déjà vu all over again, she thought. A year ago, she'd been on her back, bleeding like a pig and bitching to beat the band. Now . . .

Artur was looking at her strangely.

"What?"

"Can you not hear me, Little Rika?"

"Sure."

"I mean, before. Could you not hear me before?"

"Spit it out, Artur! What the hell are you talking about?"

"He said, 'This will not endear my people to yours,'" Tennian gasped. "You could not hear him?"

"Well, no. I guess my mer-telepathy only works when I'm in the water. Right?"

"Oh."

"You mean you guys can talk like that out of the water?"

"Of . . . of course. All of us can."

"Oh."

Artur and Tennian were looking at her with great sympathy, like she was missing a leg or something. "Who cares?" she asked impatiently. "Can we focus on getting Tennian fixed up, please?"

"Yes, of course," Artur said. He was having trouble meeting her gaze. "I was taken by surprise. I have never known anyone who could not—I mean, any Undersea Folk who could not—why, your *father* could—"

"Half-breed, Artur, remember? I didn't get the teeth, and I obviously didn't get the full ESP gene, either. Big fucking deal! Can we get back to Tennian now?"

"I am . . . well. I was just . . . surprised."

"Tennian, they *shot* you!"

"Yes. As I said. Surprised." She gasped as Thomas did something to her shoulder. "Very, very surprised."

"You got this?"

"I got it," Thomas said, not looking up.

"Then let's get up there and kick some pirate booty."

"I do not think that will be necessary," Artur said, but he followed her out the air lock anyway. And when Fred got to the surface, she got the surprise of her life.

So, she imagined, did the pirates.

Forty-six

The small, ugly boat was swarming with Undersea Folk. But the first thing to catch her attention was King Mekkam, who was holding the rifleman at arm's length and saying, "You do not harm one of my people without facing consequences, biped."

Two ladders hit the water and Fred scrambled up one. Artur was already on the ship. How did he *do* that? She saw three rifles on the deck, all of them with bent barrels. There were perhaps a dozen Undersea Folk and maybe eight pirates. No chance for the bipeds at all.

One of the Undersea Folk was Tennian's twin, who was standing on the captain's head. His teeth were being ground into the deck as he flailed and said, *"Mmmph gmmphh dmmmph!"*

"Oh, boy," Fred said. "So much for good race relations."

"They are thieves and law flouters, yes?" the king asked.

"Yes, Mekkam."

"Then we will turn them over to the authorities. Are there many like this?"

"Kind of," she admitted. It was tough to admit that pirates were alive and well in the twenty-first century.

"Then we can be of assistance to your authorities. We will be good at that."

"I guess," she said respectfully, trying to ignore the begging and screaming. "But are you sure you want to? Tennian didn't do a damned thing."

"Exactly so," her twin, Rennan, said, actually jumping up and down on the pirate captain's head. "So we, too, will try for the surface world."

"This is all my fault," she said glumly, sitting beside two unconscious pirates. "Me and my whole 'democratic process' speech. Me and my shitty advice."

"On the contrary, Little Rika. You did warn us. Many times. And Tennian is grown, and able to make her own decisions."

She looked up at him, realizing . . . "I would have known what they were up to. You organized and led an attack with your dad, from the URV. You did it all with your telepathy while at the same time you were helping us with Tennian. And I didn't have a clue what was going on, because I'm mind blind when I don't have my tail."

"It seems that is so." Artur knelt beside her. "But I do not mind, Little Rika, truly. I was surprised, true. But your differences make you the delight you are to me. And if you do not mind, I do not mind."

"Oh, the one-eyed person in the country of the blind and all that, huh?"

"What?"

"Never mind. What now?"

"Now the others have decided they will—"

"Come!" Rennan cried, and quite a few of them dived off the bow of the ship, shifted to tails, and began swimming for the public beach, which was crowded (as could be expected this time of year).

"But what about the bad guys?"

"They will sleep."

Fred looked. Yup. Pirates were all unconscious. Only she and Artur were left, conscious, on the ship.

Fred got up off the deck and stared after the swimming Folk. All she could see were their heads bobbing in the surf. "Are they *still* going to the public beach?"

"We can be a stubborn, implacable people, Little Rika."

"Oh." She nibbled her lower lip. "I see. Kind of a knee-jerk 'they can't scare us off' type reaction."

"Exactly so."

Artur and Fred dove off the stern and swam after the other Undersea Folk. One by one, the Folk swam up to the beach, shifting from tail to legs in full view of at least two hundred tourists.

"Hello," Rennan was saying to a delighted little girl. "I am Rennan, of the Undersea Folk."

"Becky."

Biped and merman shook hands.

"Becky!" Mama wasn't happy at all, and came running over, jiggling everywhere in her too-tight black one-piece. "You get back here!"

"Hello, madam. I am Rennan."

His outstretched hand forced her to remember her manners; she hastily shook his hand.

"Did you see, Mom? He's a merman! He had a tail!"

"Are they shooting a movie around here?"

"No, madam. Come and meet my friends."

Fred watched, amazed, as tourist after tourist came down to the water, some trying to cover the Folk with towels, most amazed at the transformation. Only the children were unrestrainedly delighted.

"Wow," Fred said. She waved as Jonas screeched up to the beach in the resort van. "Never thought I'd see the day."

Jonas was now hopping up and down on the sand, shaking a fist at her.

"What is he screaming?" Artur asked.

"Oh, the usual. 'You didn't tell me.' 'You left without me.' Yak-yak-yak."

"He seems agitated. Even for Jonas."

"Hey, now he gets to go home and start planning his wedding."

"Ah, a noble goal."

"Speaking of which, where the hell is Dr. Barb?"

By now Jonas had hopped back in the van and driven right up on the beach, a huge no-no. Jonas hit the brakes as the passenger door opened and Dr. Barb jumped out.

"What's going on?" she cried. "Are you all right, Dr. Bimm? Did you see the pirates?"

Fred, still knee-deep in the surf, abruptly sat down.

"Dr. Bimm? Are you well?"

And shifted to her tail.

Dr. Barb stared down at her. At her tail. Blinked. Rubbed her forehead. Blinked faster. Meanwhile, Jonas came up and put his arm around her. "Anybody get hurt?" he asked quietly.

"Tennian. And all the pirates."

"Dr. Bimm."

"Yeah, Dr. Barb?"

"You're a mermaid."

"Yeah, Dr. Barb."

Dr. Barb was blinking so fast, Fred wondered if the woman was going to have to sit down. "Then this," she said at last, "this explains all those late nights when you'd insist on feeding the fish on your own."

"Yeah."

"This explains rather a lot, actually."

"Okay."

"Including your hair."

"Yep."

"This isn't a family reunion, is it?"

"No, Dr. Barb."

"Okay. I just wanted to get that cleared up." Her boss knelt and tentatively put a hand on Fred's tail, where her left calf normally would have been. "Dr. Bimm . . . you're really quite beautiful."

"Thanks, Dr. Barb. You can go ahead and have a heart attack now."

"Oh, no." Dr. Barb was scanning the beach, taking in the tourists and the other Undersea Folk. "There's going to be far, far too much to do." She was absently patting Fred's tail. "This changes everything."

"Think so?"

"This is our prince," another Folk was saying. "Prince Artur, and our friend, Fredrika."

"Hi." Fred shifted to her legs, stood, and shook hands with a strange, chubby male tourist who hadn't used enough sunscreen on his bald head. "My name's Fred, and I'll be your mermaid today."

Forty-seven

Much later, she and Artur went back to the URV to check on Tennian, who was drinking her third Coke and chattering to Thomas.

"Ho, my prince! Fredrika!"

"Your twin's up there kicking ass and taking names."

"Yes, I have been following the events."

Right. That darned telepathy . . . In full-blooded Folk, it worked wherever they were, not just in the water. Dammit. She'd never felt more like just a half in her entire life.

"And see! Thomas has healed me."

"Not quite," he cautioned. "I think you should take it easy for at least a day. I know Fred heals quickly, but I've never treated a non-hybrid before."

"Well, super," Fred muttered.

"I am grateful you were here," Tennian said.

"Oh, it was my pleasure. Really."

Fred watched the two of them stare into each other's eyes.

Dammit! That fucking Florence Nightingale syndrome! He'd fallen in love with Fred after patching her up, then left for a year. Now here he was, slobbering all over Tennian and making a damned fool of his damned self, dammit!

Well, she didn't care. She absolutely did not. In fact, it made things an awful lot easier. Yes, it did.

She turned to Artur and abruptly said, "I've decided. I'll come home with you. I might even marry you. But one thing at a time. First, a visit."

Artur yelped with delight and swept her up in a rib-cracking hug. "Oh, Rika! You have made me very, very happy. I have so many things to show you!"

Fred submitted to the embrace, and couldn't help but notice that Thomas didn't look up. Not once.

Oh, well.

That was that, then.

Dammit.

Forty-eight

"You guys, you guys!" Jonas was yowling and Fred, Artur, Thomas, and Tennian ran the last few steps to the bar.

Dr. Barb darted out of the main lodge and frantically beckoned. "Hurry, Dr. Bimm! Prince Artur! You're on again!"

They had the television above the bar tuned to CNN, where the stream informed them of stock prices, and the talking head was saying, "—actual mermaids!"

"Undersea Folk," Tennian corrected.

"You knew and you didn't tell me," Dr. Barb was saying reproachfully to Thomas. "I think as your supervisor I had a right to know." She raised an eyebrow at Fred. "And as *your* supervisor I definitely had a right to know."

"Tough nuts."

"Yes," the talking head was saying, "actual mermaids."

"Undersea Folk!" Tennian almost shouted.

"See, if you're already yelling at the TV, you're halfway to fitting into our world."

"No, it's not a new movie, and no, we're not pulling your 'tail.'"

The group groaned in unison.

"It seems several tourists in the Cayman Islands spotted these mermaids—and mermen!—and although the sightings have yet to be confirmed, too many statements sound alike to be easily dismissed. Whether it's true or not, one thing remains certain: it'll be a whale of a sea tale. I'm Margaret Bergman, CNN."

"That's it?" Fred practically screamed. "Tennian gets shot by pirates and you guys storm the beach like the kids took Normandy, and all CNN coughs up is that it's an unconfirmed sighting?"

"Hey, one thing at a time. I'm amazed they broadcast as much as they did. And one of you guys will stand still long enough for a confirmed sighting, I've got no doubt about that. But never mind all that junk." Jonas pointed a bony finger at her. "What's this crap I hear? You're taking off? You're not coming back?"

"Not right away. Dr. Barb can find someone else to feed the fish."

"Not someone with your unique qualifications," Dr. Barb protested.

But Fred recognized the look in her eye, in any researcher's eye, and figured it was just as well she wasn't headed straight back to the NEA. "And my mom vastly prefers your company to mine, anyway, Jonas. I'm just heading down to the Black Sea with Artur to find out a little more about my heritage."

"For how long?"

She shrugged.

"But—" Jonas glanced at Thomas, who was hand-feeding Tennian shrimp. "Oh. Never mind."

"It'll be fine."

Her friend gave her an odd look. "Will it?"

"Sure."

But deep down, she had no idea, and was as afraid to see Artur's home as she was anxious.

Because everything was different now, and she had to take responsibility for that. For these people. If that meant being the queen, then that's what it meant.

As for Thomas—

She'd never really liked him anyway.

"But what am I supposed to do in Boston with you gone?" Jonas was whining.

"Have sex with my boss? Whoops. Former boss."

Dr. Barb moaned. "I can't believe you're doing this to me. You work for me for *years*, you finally tell me about your heritage, and then you quit, all in the same day."

"I'm sorry that my being a mermaid is making things stressful. For *you*," Fred added pointedly.

"But you'll visit, right? You'll have to visit," Jonas pleaded. "You're my best man. So to speak."

"Sure, I'll visit." Fred was thinking of Ellie's file, snugly tucked into her desk drawer back in her Boston apartment. Sure, she'd visit. At least once. She needed to have a nice, long chat with Ellie's father.

"Let us tell my father the good news," Artur said, and she smiled—she didn't have to force it, for a change—took his hand, and fell into step beside him as they hurried toward his father.

The king was shaking salt water out of his hair, and beamed at them when he saw them.

This is my life now, Fred thought. *These are my people. Who's better equipped to help them with the transition than me?*

After what happened to Tennian, I couldn't just turn my back on them and go back to my boring, lonely life.

I've got to help them. I will help them. Even—

"—but that is wonderful!"

—even if it kills me.

Fish out of Water

For William Alongi: father, grandfather, husband, brother, uncle, friend. Things aren't as exciting without all the grumbling, big guy. And for Cindy Hwang, who, in the face of enormous personal tragedy, never once lost her kindness, humor, skill, empathy, or professionalism.

As Andrew Vacchs, the finest writer of noir fiction in the twenty-first century and tireless champion of the helpless, once said (and I'm paraphrasing), "If love died with death, this world wouldn't be so hard."

That's just right, sir. That is 100 percent correct.

ACKNOWLEDGMENTS

This is the last book of the Fred the mermaid trilogy; the other two are *Sleeping with the Fishes* and *Swimming Without a Net.* (There's also a mermaid novella in my anthology *Dead Over Heels*, which takes place just before the events of this book.)

Although Betsy the vampire queen made me semi-famous (infamous? delusionally famous?), I actually thought up Fred long before I ever wrote *Undead and Unwed.* So it's a little strange to me that I'm putting paid to Fred while Betsy goes on and on and on.

("And on," the critics added snidely, "and on, and on.")

Well, hell. She *is* a vampire. And that's what they do, I s'pose. Fred, however, is mortal.

Anyway, I wanted to thank Cindy Hwang, my editor, for going along with my idea for a grumpy mermaid, and for never asking, "What, exactly, is wrong with you?" At least, not out loud.

My agent, Ethan Ellenberg, for making the deal happen.

Leis Pederson, who catches many of my boneheaded mistakes and never gets the credit.

My Yahoo! group, for their support.

Charlaine Harris and her fan group, three of whom dressed as Fred, Dr. Bimm, and Jonas for the *Romantic Times* 2008 convention, forcing me to pretend my eyes were leaking because of allergies.

And, always, my friends and family, for tirelessly listening to my near-constant bitching.

MaryJanice Davidson
www.maryjanicedavidson.net

AUTHOR'S NOTE

Although there is a Florida Aquarium, I have no idea if it's open at the top or if it's possible for people to fall into Shark Bay. It's quite possible (more like probable) I took some liberties. Sorry, Florida Aquarium.

Also, although there are many fine naval bases in Florida (in the country, actually), the Sanibel Station is 100 percent made up, as were the actions of the sailors stationed there. Got that? Fiction. Not true. Please don't ask me why I hate America, okay?

Also, salmon pink bridesmaid gowns do clash terribly with green hair.

I love treason but hate a traitor.

—Julius Caesar

It's silly to go on pretending that under the skin we are all brothers. The truth is more likely that under the skin we are all cannibals, assassins, traitors, liars, hypocrites, poltroons.

—Henry Miller

A mermaid's not a human thing
An' courtin' sich is folly;
Of flesh an' blood I'd rather sing,
What ain't so melancholy.

—E. J. Brady, "Lost and Given Over"

A reporter meets interesting people. If he endures, he will get to know princes and presidents, popes and paupers, prostitutes and panderers.

—JIM BISHOP

Time magazine: "Is it true that if you help a mermaid, you get one wish?"
Fredrika Bimm: "Shut up."

Fuck the fathers. They should know better.

—PAT CONROY, *The Prince of Tides*

THE STORY SO FAR

Fredrika Bimm is a hybrid—her father was a merman who got her hippie mother pregnant one night on the beach and then disappeared forever. Part of both worlds and feeling out of place pretty much everywhere, Fred's dearest wish is to keep herself to herself and stay under everyone's radar.

Circumstances, however, make that impossible. In the last year and a half, she has helped Prince Artur of the Undersea Folk (what the mer-people call themselves) figure out who was dumping toxins into Boston Harbor, fallen for a fellow marine biologist (Dr. Thomas Pearson, who writes romance novels on the side), fought pirates (yes, pirates), attended a Pelagic (don't ask), met the king of the Undersea Folk (who is obsessed with the HBO series *Deadwood*), walked in on her mother and stepfather having sex, walked in on her boss (Dr. Barb) and her best friend (Jonas) doing their impersonation of the Thing That Can't Stop Kissing, visited the Cayman Islands, and watched as several of her father's people showed themselves (tails and all) to the world.

Also, she's taken a leave of absence from her job at the New England Aquarium. So, she's been busy.

Now, six months after the first of the Undersea Folk were seen on CNN, the world is transfixed by the idea that mermaids are real . . . have always been real . . . and there could be one living right next door.

Also, she has to house hunt in Florida. During tourist season.

Oh, the humanity.

Prologue

He stared, transfixed. His people were showing themselves to the world! How could the royal family—the *king*—go along with this? It went against centuries of tradition and ingrained behavior.

He instantly started figuring how he could turn the situation to his advantage.

One

"Excuse me, but are you a mermaid?"

"Why?" Fred was poking through the large, airy kitchen and trying not to show how impressed she was with the ocean view. She knew the Realtor would pick up on it like a bloodhound to sweat. "Do I get a discount? 'Show us your fin and we'll show you ten percent off.' Like that?"

The Realtor colored, which, given that she had the creamy complexion natural to most redheads, gave the impression that she was about to have a stroke. Fred wondered how long it would take for the paramedics to show.

"I didn't mean anything by it." She coughed. "It's just—your hair."

"I know, don't tell me. I fired my stylist." Fred fussed with the ends of her green hair, which were now chin-length as opposed to tumbling halfway down her back. Much easier to take care of, though her friend Jonas had shrieked like he'd been stabbed when he'd seen it. "And I'm still getting grief about it from my friend. My stupid, irritating friend."

"But it's blue."

"Technically it's green." She opened a cupboard to see how deep it was. "You know how the ocean looks blue but it's really green? Same with my—Does the garbage disposal work?"

"Wha—Yes. And the house comes with all the appliances, as well as lawn maintenance. So are you?"

"I dunno. It's pretty expensive. And what do I need four bedrooms for? You know what that'll mean for me? Drop-in guests. 'Say, Fred, you've got plenty of room, we're staying here for a month.' Any idea how much I hate drop-ins? I hate them like a fat kid hates Slim-Fast. Besides, I live in a Boston apartment most of the year. Mowing a lawn would actually be a treat for me."

"No, I meant, are you a mermaid?"

"The term is Undersea Folk."

"Yes, are you?" The Realtor was actually leaning toward Fred with the urgency of her question. Fred found she was backed up against the dishwasher, close enough to count the threads in the buttons on the Realtor's blouse. "Because I know I've seen you on TV. On the news. I'm sure of it. So are you?"

"Why, are you afraid you won't be able to track down all my references?" Fred sidled away from her and walked through the dining area.

This entire side of the house had enormous windows, all of which boasted ocean views of the Gulf side. It was 2:30 p.m. on Sanibel Island, Florida, February 11, and she was walking around inside a house that would sell painlessly for five million dollars, even with the housing market deep in the shitter as it was. The Realtor was asking five thousand a week to rent it out.

"Also, you swam in from the ocean side. Most people drive to the house."

"Is this your not-too-subtle way of bitching about me tracking salt water all over the floors? Besides, I had to work off the brownie sundae I had for breakfast. What about the washer and dryer?"

"Right through here." The Realtor, whose name Fred had forgotten, opened a door off the kitchen and gestured. Fred peeked around the corner and observed a full-sized washer/dryer combo in a spotlessly clean laundry room.

"Hmmm."

The entire first floor (except for the bathroom) was one gigantic room, the front hall leading to the dining area leading to the kitchen leading to the living room leading to a large porch that ran nearly the length of the house. The walls were the color of Coffee-Mate; the furniture and décor were done in Modern Millionaire. All the windows were thrown wide and a fresh breeze made the curtains billow.

Upstairs were several bedrooms and three more bathrooms, one with a Jacuzzi big enough for a soccer team. Two of the bedrooms boasted ocean views as well. The cream-colored walls made the large house appear even more spacious.

Fred stared thoughtfully out over the lawn, eyeing the outdoor Jacuzzi and swimming pool. Her boyfriend/suitor/someday-sovereign, Prince Artur, had encouraged this move. And she had to admit, it wasn't the worst idea she'd ever heard.

Ever since Undersea Folk had started coming out of the water closet (heh), she'd been fielding interviews and handling the press and in general acting as go-between for the royal family, the Undersea Folk, and surface dwellers. As a result, the world was assuming the Undersea Folk's primary residence was here, just off the coast of Sanibel Island.

They were wrong.

Which suited the king just fine.

But Fred craved her own space to retreat to, and never mind Artur's argument that she could use the ocean as an escape hatch. The ocean—yech! Seaweed and barracudas and mouthy fish (mouthy telepathic fish, anyway) and silt and frankly, she vastly preferred a pool to the large, messy ocean.

Yes, she needed her own space and perhaps this zillion-dollar mansion was it. Although her stepfather was wealthy, he hadn't flaunted it when she was a kid, and although she had a healthy trust fund, she'd always been content with her little one-bedroom apartment in Boston.

This place, though . . . Artur had pointed out that, as the girlfriend of the prince, she needed more than a teeny Boston apartment. How had he put it? *Someplace worthy of our future queen.* Amazing she even remembered what he'd said, she'd been laughing so hard.

"I dunno," she said. "It's really big. And—"

The front door boomed open and there stood Prince Artur, well over six feet, with shoulder-length hair the color of smashed rubies, and eyes almost the same shade. He hadn't shaved for a couple of weeks and his beard was also a deep red. His shoulders were so broad, and he was so tall, he barely fit in the doorway. He was shirtless, and barefoot, and clad only in a pair of denim shorts.

"Ho, Little Rika! Is the cottage to your liking?" He frowned, glancing around. "It looked more fitting from the outside."

Fred smirked at the gaping Realtor. "Now, him? *He's* a mermaid. So to speak."

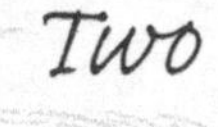

Two

"I was told this would be a suitable residence for my little Rika," Prince Artur said with a frown.

"It's plenty suitable; don't be such a royal snob."

"I do not think it is fitting for one who will one day be queen," Artur persisted with maddening stubbornness.

That did it. "I'll take it," Fred told the astonished Realtor, who was staring at the prince as if she were in some sort of sex trance. "And I'll pay asking and all the fees and sign whatever I need to sign, but I need to move in by the end of the week. Open-ended lease, six-month minimum, whatever security deposit you need. Okay?"

"Neh," the Realtor said.

"Great. And quit that 'one day will be queen' talk, Artur, I've told you before. Just because I'm with you doesn't mean I'm—you know. With you." *Which, technically, makes me a tease. Hmm. Not sure I care for—*

"Ah, Little Rika." Artur snatched at her but she managed to dodge out of the way, nearly braining herself on the cupboard she'd left open. "One day you will see the wisdom of our love match."

"And don't call me that. It's Fred. Or Fredrika. Or Dr. Bimm. Or Bitchcakes. Or—"

"I've seen you on TV, too!" the Realtor exclaimed. "You're the prince of all the mermaids!"

"Undersea Folk," Artur and Fred said in unison.

"You look just like your dad!"

Artur inclined his head, the closest thing to a bow he bothered with. "That is my honor, good lady, and you are kind to point it out."

"Vomit, vomit, vomit," Fred mumbled.

"Let's see, you were on CNN . . . and *People* did that big cover story on you guys . . ." The Realtor snapped her fingers and pointed at Fred. "I knew you looked familiar. The hair threw me—it was longer in the pictures."

"Congrats, Nancy Drew. Why don't you scamper on back to the clubhouse and draw up my damned contract?"

"Forgive the lady," Artur said, gallantly offering the dazzled Realtor his elbow and walking her to the door. "She has been seeking a temporary home on land for many days and it has left her in ill humor."

"Being saddled with a stupid nickname has left me in a worse humor!" Fred bawled after him.

"More so than usual, though the thought makes me tremble," he added in a mutter. "How kind you were to show her this small and charming cottage; we are sure you will be as efficient in the rest of our business dealings."

"Yeah, thanks a heap," Fred called. "Bye."

"Oh. Oh! Yes, of course. Good-bye! Oh. But I can't leave you here, since technically this isn't—"

"The lady and I will be leaving as well."

"Oh. You're going to jump back in the ocean, aren't you?"

"It's quicker than calling a cab," Fred said, taking a last look around her new home before following Artur out the back door.

Three

Fred stripped out of her shorts, T-shirt, and panties and left them on the lawn. What the hell . . . in a few days this was going to be her home, anyway. She wondered who had left the clothes for her on the lawn in the first place—it's not like she could swim with a tail in a pair of shorts. One of Artur's crew, probably.

She shouldn't have been surprised that he'd be underwhelmed by the house—he was used to enormous underwater palaces. When the Undersea Folk built something, they thought big. And why not? Wasn't most of the planet covered with water? They were used to having three-quarters of the planet to spread out in.

There was no beach leading to the Gulf; instead there was a sharp drop-off and a long dock. She trotted to the end of the dock, cast an amused glance at the shit-caked plastic owls perched on the pier, and dove off, shifting immediately to her tail form. Artur was several feet ahead of her, effortlessly moving through the water with powerful thrusts of his tail.

As a hybrid, her tail wasn't as long as his, nor as wide, nor as beautifully colored. Artur's reminded her of a peacock's, all greens and blues, while hers seemed less magnificent, almost dull. *Be grateful you have a tail at all,* she reminded herself. She might have taken after her human mother, after all, and not have been able to shift. Bad enough she couldn't swim in her legs . . . imagine not being able to breathe underwater.

She caught up with him after a few more strokes, glaring at a barracuda that was swimming annoyingly close. The fish sneered at her and darted away, the predator's thoughts

(big thing can't bite the big thing hungry not big thing)

setting up an echo in her mind.

Hey, Artur.

Yes, my dear one?

I gotta say, it was pretty smart of your dad to let the world think your HQ is here.

HQ?

Headquarters. The seat of the government, or power, or the capital—everyone thinks it's here instead of the Black Sea.

He flipped over and floated on his back, a good thirty feet beneath the waves. She swam beneath him and then over him, waiting for his response.

It will take some time before we can completely trust your mother's people, Little Rika. I hope this gives you no offense.

Offense? Who warned you about them in the first place? Hmm, lemme think—oh yeah! It was me. You know how many people have been fucked over in the name of scientific advancement? It's pretty damned smart, actually, letting the world think we all hang out here. But one thing your dad's got to spare is brainpower.

Artur laughed in her head. *So true, my Rika!*

They passed two more Undersea Folk—a man and a woman, the man with hair the color of daffodils; the woman with hair so pure a black it seemed to swallow up the light.

Greetings, my prince.

Ho, Prince Artur! Fredrika.

Fred nodded to them both. It didn't escape her notice that only one had acknowledged her and called her by name, though she knew damn well she was notorious enough that all the Undersea Folk knew her on sight.

Notorious.

Shit.

She was somewhat mystified that it bugged her—she'd never been one to sweat what strangers thought. But dammit, the Undersea Folk who didn't like her didn't know her. They didn't like her because Dear Old Dad had been a traitor. Big believers in the whole "the guppy doesn't fall far from the frog" school of thought.

And dammit, it wasn't *fair.* It was fine if someone didn't like her based on her own merits—and the list was long and distinguished, both of her odious faults and the people who didn't like her—but they ought to at least get to know her before they decided she was a shit.

I know your thoughts, my Rika. Shall I thrash the one who dared ignore you?

Don't make it worse. It's no big deal.

Ah, Little Rika. Your lady mother did not teach you to lie. How unusual for a surface dweller, even one as noble as your mother.

Fred had no answer to that.

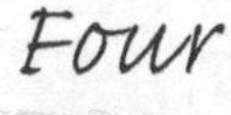

Four

She spilled her tea when the front door was thrown open. More mermaids? Her stepfather? Another guy who wanted to shoot her for profit? *Time? Newsweek? People?*

"Dum dum dah dum!" Jonas cried, arms spread, suitcases at his feet. "Dum *dum* dah dum!"

"Something nutball this way comes," Fred muttered, dabbing the tea off her shorts and slowly getting up from the couch.

It was moving day and she had been in the house less than three hours. She cursed the impulse she'd followed last week to (a) give her best friend her new address and (b) send him a spare key. Stupid force of habit. He'd had spare keys to her homes for years.

Did this mean on a subconscious level she actually *wanted* him to show up in her life?

Stupid subconscious.

"Ooooh, nice digs," Jonas said, lugging his suitcases inside, listing radically to the left under the weight of the two in his hand. "Are you finally going to live in the manner to which your stepfather and hot mom are accustomed?"

"Shut up," she said automatically, but, as she'd known, he wasn't deterred.

He was an exhaustingly cheerful blond, taller than she—about six-three—with the mind of an engineer (he designed shampoo for the Aveda corporation) and a black belt in aikido. He was also the most metrosexual guy on the planet—continually being mistaken for gay (mostly because he insisted on drinking appletinis)—and a loyal friend.

They had been best friends since the second grade.

"So, check it," he said, kicking one of his suitcases out of the way and crossing the room to plop down on the chair opposite Fred. "Barb has given me carte blanche to plan our wedding."

"Barf," she muttered.

"Because, as you know, she's been through this before."

Fred knew. Dr. Barb, her boss at the New England Aquarium, had been married to a real shitheel several years ago.

"And I've decided, since you're stuck down here playing go-between for Artur's folks and us lowly humans—"

"To burst in on me and make me spill my tea?"

"—to have the wedding here. On Sanibel Island."

Fred tried not to, but she couldn't help it: she groaned.

"Aw." Jonas beamed. "I knew you'd be pleased." He propped his sandaled feet up on the coffee table, admiring his no-polish pedicure for a moment. "So as my best man, so to speak—"

Fred groaned again. "Don't you think I've got enough on my plate right now?"

"Oh, who cares. Also, I bring a message from my blushing

bride-to-be, who wanted me to remind you that she's still refusing your resignation."

"For God's sake," Fred said crossly. "I haven't set foot in the aquarium for ages."

"Hey, don't shoot the messenger, doll."

"I'd like to *throttle* the messenger."

"Barb says you're the best marine biologist she's ever hired. Also, since you outed yourself to her as a mermaid, there's no way in hell she's letting you quit." He yawned. "So which room should I take?"

"And so it begins," she muttered. "I told her. I told that Realtor. Drop-ins. I hate drop-ins."

"Anyway," Jonas said, well used to ignoring her bitching, "I'd like the wedding to take place on a private beach, so I'll need your help with that, and also with other wedding minutiae. Can you clear your calendar this week to help me with cake tasting? Also, you'll need to buy a ridiculously classy and expensive bridesmaid dress—unless you want to get a tux instead."

"Can't you just whip out a gun and shoot me in the face?"

"Maybe tomorrow," he said comfortingly.

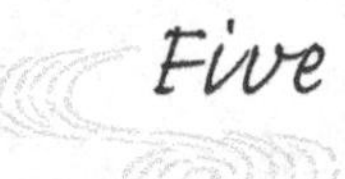

Five

Fred was trying hard not to glare at the reporter from *Time* and having her usual degree of success. For the hundredth time, she questioned the king's wisdom in making her the go-between between surface dwellers and Undersea Folk. The king's argument—

that she was the only half-and-half on the planet—had seemed so logical at the time . . . Clearly he had paid no attention to her poor interpersonal skills.

"Several countries are offering citizenship to the mermaids—"

"Undersea Folk."

"—how do you feel about that?"

"I feel they don't need land citizenship. They've got the run of the oceans. I also think it's typical of humans to assume Undersea Folk would jump at the chance for U.S. citizenship. Because that's where you're going, right? It's not altruistic in any way. America wants dibs on the finned."

The reporter, a slender, balding man with warm brown eyes, smiled. "Interesting point."

"Insulting point, actually. But have it your way."

"So tell me about yourself—your mother's human, and your father—"

"Next question."

The reporter blinked. "I understand that some of the Undersea Folk don't care for you because your father—"

"Next question."

"Is it true that if you help a mermaid, you get a wish?"

She stared at him. He chuckled nervously under her gaze and added, "Or have I been watching too many movies?"

"It's not true. If you help a mermaid, I get to punch you in the teeth. That's the rule."

"You're an, ah, unusual diplomat."

"Take that back!"

"All right, all right, you're a lousy diplomat."

"Thanks," she said, mollified, thinking: *How did I end up here? Now? Doing this job? With these people?*

"So would you say the Undersea Folk are less—ah—warlike than humans?"

"Less warlike?" she asked blankly.

"There's been some talk about the comparisons, and several Undersea Folk have made no secret of the fact that they don't trust—what do they call us? Surface dwellers?"

"Can you blame them?"

"So you're not denying it?"

She stifled a sigh. More Homo sapiens arrogance. *They're not like us, but we'll find a peg to jam them into anyway.* Ugh.

"Undersea Folk are like anyone else. There are saints, there are assholes, but most of them are somewhere in between. Like anyone else on the planet, you need to get to know one before you decide what kind of person they are. And like anyone else on the planet, you can't say every member of the species acts or talks or thinks the same." Duh. For a moment she'd thought she'd said it out loud. What she *had* said out loud was probably bad enough.

"Oh, this is dynamite," the reporter enthused. "Do you mind if I change 'assholes' to 'jerks'?"

"Censorship," she observed. "Alive and well in the home of the free."

Thick-skinned, like most journalists, he ignored that. "And we'll be sending a photographer over to take your picture—say, two o'clock?"

Fred grimaced, which the reporter took as a strained smile of acquiescence.

"And say, how about a demonstration? Can you—I mean, we see the mer—the Undersea Folk with their tails, or with legs, but nobody's ever seen them shift form. Maybe you could—"

"Do I *look* like a performing seal?"

"So, no." He slapped his notebook shut. "Well, thanks for your time, Dr. Bimm."

She grunted.

"Say, could I get your autograph for my little girl? She's crazy about mermaids."

Oh, Lord, this is punishment for all my sins.

Six

She was resting on the bottom of the pool when she saw Jonas appear, squatting beside the deep end. He looked wavy yet distinct, and he was wearing a pair of shorts so orange they hurt her eyes. He was gesturing impatiently to her.

She ignored him.

His gestures became more urgent.

She yawned and stretched her arms out over her head, a lazy flick of her tail propelling her halfway to the shallow end.

Now he was pointing both middle fingers at her, jabbing the air. She snorted, a stream of bubbles popping to the surface.

He leapt in, swam busily for a moment, then tried to grab her arm and haul her to the surface.

Oh, pal. Mistake.

Jonas must be really agitated, or he'd have remembered she was three times stronger and faster. She wriggled easily from his grip, spun him around, grabbed his ankle, and propelled him through the water with a healthy shove. He nearly brained himself on the steps leading into the shallow end, then bobbed halfway to the surface.

In fact, maybe he *did* brain himself, because he was floating face-down in the water.

Don't fall for that one again.

He still wasn't moving.

He gets you every time with this one.

Maybe she'd pushed it a little far with the roughhousing.

Moron!

She agreed with her self-assessment, but nonetheless reached him in half a second, seized him by the shirt, and flipped him over. They both bobbed to the surface.

He opened his eyes and spat a stream of water at her forehead. "We were supposed to be at the caterer's ten minutes ago."

She let go of him in disgust and wiped her face. "Must have slipped my mind."

"Sure. Now get your fishy butt out of this pool, get dressed, and haul ass to the car."

"You don't need me," she whined. "You're way better at this stuff than I am."

"We're the Team Supreme, dumbass. Now get going."

"Shouldn't you be shielding your eyes at the sight of my breathtaking nudeness?"

"Oh, like I haven't seen your knockers every week since the second grade."

She giggled in spite of herself. "I'm pretty sure I didn't *have* knockers in the—"

"Out. Dress. Car. Caterer."

"You know, I'm under a lot of pressure," she grumbled, shifting from tail to legs and stomping up the shallow-end steps to the patio. "I don't need to take shit from Groomzilla."

"You'll be taking a smack in the mouth from Groomzilla if you don't haul ass. Tail. Whatever."

She laughed at him; she couldn't help it. Jonas was never more hilarious than when he was pretending to be a badass.

Seven

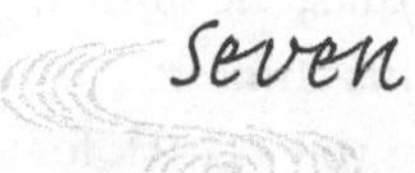

"Well, how about this one?"

"If I have to jam one more piece of cake down my gullet, I'm going to vomit all over your baker."

The baker, a cadaverously scrawny fellow Fred distrusted on sight (Did he never sample his own product? Why wasn't there an ounce of fat on him?), grimaced but hauled out more slices on napkins.

They were seated practically *in* the front window at a small table set for two. A small, romantic table: silver candlesticks, snow-colored linen napkins, real china. Jonas, of course, was loving it. Fred, not so much.

"This is one of my favorites," the baker said with quiet insistence.

"I can't."

Jonas remained undaunted and said, between chomps, "But it's chocolate!"

Fred moaned. Chocolate with ganache filling. Vanilla sponge cake with raspberry filling. Carrot cake—blurgh! German cake with coconut cream filling. Strawberry cake with strawberry jam filling. Lemon chiffon with Meyer lemon curd filling. Angel food cake with no filling. Angel food cake with coconut filling. Red velvet cake with vanilla buttercream filling. Coconut cake with chocolate fondant. Marble cake with chocolate buttercream frosting. Orange cake with (yurgh!) marmalade filling. Orange poppy seed (double yurgh!) with no filling. Banana cake with coconut filling. Spice cake with (vomit) lemon poppy seed filling. Mocha cake with coffee buttercream filling.

"I can't," she said again, positive she'd put on five pounds in the last half hour.

"Well, *I* can't decide between the lemon chiffon, the mocha, or the vanilla sponge cake." Jonas chomped busily, then said, spraying the spotless tablecloth with crumbs, "Nope. Too rich."

"Have all three, then," she said crossly.

"We're not *all* made of money, Madame Grouchypants," he sniffed, unaware that he looked ridiculous with frosting on his chin.

"Jesus, *I'll* pay for them, okay? Just pick. I'll write you a check for ten grand right now if I can just leave."

"You're supposed to help me pick. That's why you're here."

"And I thought I was here to clog my arteries and flop facedown into buttercream frosting during my heart attack."

"We also have apple," the scrawny baker added.

"Twenty grand," Fred begged. "Anything. My checkbook's right here."

"Oh, all right, you can buy the cakes. But we still have to go see the caterer."

"I *can't*," she cried. "You're not listening: I will vomit. Puke. Yark. Blurgh. Spew. Shout at the floor. Whatever. I'll do it. I'm so close to tilt right now, I could be a Vegas slot machine. I—"

"Say," Skinny Baker said, "haven't I seen you on TV?"

She fled.

Eight

Then—then! Not only is my best friend (and worst enemy) *marrying my boss, the wedding's happening here. On Sanibel. And I have to help him pick out cakes and food and tuxes and flowers. All because he's so hot to get hitched the damned wedding's happening in two months. Two! Months! Like I don't have enough things to worry about!*

You have many trials, Little Rika.

Artur's tone sounded right—sympathetic and warm—but he was having a terrible time hiding his smile. Much more so than, say, the average human: Artur had the typical dentition of full-blooded Undersea Folk, and had teeth to rival a great white.

They were a few miles out into the Gulf, swimming about thirty feet below the surface. Although Fred normally wasn't a fan of ocean swimming, she couldn't fault the more-or-less beautiful waters of the Gulf of Mexico. You just had to avoid the areas her mother's people had cheerfully polluted the hell out of. And ignore the sneers of the occasional passing nurse shark.

She had fled the bakery and, since Jonas had driven, ran to the first beach she could find—and on Sanibel, they were plentiful. She was out of her clothes in seconds (how many outfits had she left scattered on various beaches around the world?) and into the water, flailing helplessly until she switched to her tail. Then she'd arrowed beneath the waves and put major distance between her and the shore, as quickly as she could.

The irony: if she was home, if she was in Boston, she would have retreated to her tiny apartment and barred the door for a week. But her rental down here was too big, too open, and didn't feel like hers. She was too easily tracked down in the swimming pool. And here, in the ocean, she chanced running into Undersea Folk who hated her because of what her father had done before she was conceived, never mind born.

I am the unluckiest hybrid on the planet.

Oh, stop it, she scolded herself, zipping past a school of snook that were busy trying to stay the hell out of her way. Their panicked thoughts raced across her brain like confetti: *big one eat no eat do not eat no big one* no eat!

Knock it off, she sent back. *I'm stuffed; you don't have to worry about a thing.*

First off, she was the only hybrid on the planet (probably). Second, zillions had it worse. No money. No idea where their next meal was coming from. No way to breathe underwater without scuba gear. Next, she was at the top of the food chain—on both her mother's *and* her father's side. Unlike, say, anything else that swam in the ocean.

And finally, nobody twisted her arm to do any of this crap. She wasn't a victim—far from it. She could have said no. It's not like she didn't know how.

Then why do I feel like everything's spinning out of my control?

Well. There was the small fact that two years ago, only a handful of people knew she grew a tail when she swam. Two years ago, her love life was not at all complicated. (Nonexistent would be the more accurate term.) Jonas wasn't dating Dr. Barb. The world of surface dwellers had no idea mermaids (as they insisted on referring to her father's people) existed. Oh, and thousands of Undersea Folk hadn't decided to hate her because of her shitheel dad.

I prob'ly just need a nap.

She darted past a few goliath grouper, slowing to watch them—she'd never seen that particular species outside an aquarium. She knew it was illegal to keep them if you caught them—the rule down here for goliath grouper was strictly catch and release. Pity. She'd heard grouper were delicious.

She was so absorbed in indulging her inner science geek she didn't see the two Undersea Folk until they were swimming right above her.

Hi, she sent cautiously.

Hello, one of them sent back. It was a male, with a tail much longer, broader, and prettier than hers, all peacock blues and greens. His hair was also green, the color of mashed peridots; his eyes exactly matched. His shoulders were broad, tapering to a narrow waist, and she realized yet again that male Undersea Folk had no chest hair.

Did they shave, the better to be more aerodynamic? Naw. Just something else that set them apart from surface dwellers.

Hello, Fredrika Bimm, the other one said, a female with a narrow, bright yellow tail. Her hair floated around her in a cloud—a literal cloud, as it was perfectly white. *Are you well?*

Hallelujah. Undersea Folk who were going to wait to get to know her before hating her.

As can be expected, I s'pose, she replied. The three of them circled one another. *I didn't catch your names.*

I am Keekenn, the male said, *and this is my mate, Rashel.*

Rochelle, Rochelle, Fred thought inanely. A young girl's strange erotic journey from Milan to Minsk.

I've got to stop watching all those Seinfeld *reruns.*

What? Rashel asked.

Nothing, Fred sent back hastily. *Thinking about something else. Do you guys live around here?*

Not at all. Our home is off the coast of Greenland. We came down here to show numbers to His Majesty the king.

Ah! The better to fool you with, my dear.

Pardon? Keekenn asked.

You know. So the surface dwellers think you guys mostly live here. As opposed to being all over the world, and/or the Black Sea.

I have never seen a surface dweller up close before, Rashel admitted, arching her arms over her head and zipping past Fred. There was a spray of blood and scales, and then the woman was chomping on the head of a grouper and offering the body to her mate. Fred, who was allergic to fish, managed not to vomit and pawed the scales away from her face. *I am most curious. Perhaps it will be an agreeable experience.*

They're not all bad, Fred agreed.

Forgive my mate, she is in pup. Would you like some?

Fred's hand shot up and she pinched her lips together to forestall the barf reflex. *No, no, I've already eaten. You guys knock yourselves out.* In pup? What the hell did that mean? Pregnant?

Hmm. Her inner science geek surged forward with a hundred questions and Fred ruthlessly stomped it. She debated mentioning that it was illegal to devour grouper, then decided that surface dweller fishing rules probably didn't apply to your average pregnant mermaid.

I don't s'pose you guys know where Artur is?

The two exchanged glances, and when Rashel answered it was quite cautiously: *He is several miles from here, in meet with the king. Can you not call him?*

This wasn't the time to explain that, as a half-and-half, her underwater telepathy was quite limited. Her range was poor, to be perfectly blunt. And out of the water, unlike pure-blooded Undersea Folk, she had no telepathy at all. That had been difficult for Artur to get used to. Apparently, it made her borderline retarded in the eyes of many of her father's people. Hurdle number twenty-nine to vault before things ran smoothly.

I didn't want to bother them, she lied.

We did run into another friend of yours, Rashel added.

Oh, yeah?

Indeed. We must be going, but you will see her very soon. It was agreeable to meet you.

Likewise. Her? What friend would they know of who was a *her*?

Rashel and her husband swam away—not one for long good-byes were the Undersea Folk—leaving Fred momentarily alone. The presence of three predators had cleared the area of every single fish, and even a couple of sharks. She had no idea what to—

Ho, Fredrika Bimm!

She spun. And gaped. *Tennian?*

Of course, her blue-haired rival replied, sounding pleased. *Perhaps you were expecting my irritating brother?*

No. That, Fred didn't need.

Rival? Where had *that* come from?

But Fred, a lousy liar, was even worse at lying to herself, and she knew perfectly well where that had come from.

Nine

Tennian, cousin to Prince Artur and girlfriend of Dr. Thomas Pearson, swam close and squeezed Fred's arm in what she probably thought was a warm greeting, but which actually made Fred's arm go instantly numb.

How nice to see you again, Fredrika! I had hoped to run over you.

Into me. And that's super. I s'pose Thomas is around here somewhere. It took a great deal of effort to sound casual and not terribly interested in the answer.

Tennian shrugged. *Very likely. You will see him soon, I am sure.*

Great.

Is it not marvelous in these seas? So warm, and such life! Too many boats, though, she added thoughtfully, looking up as a fleet of Jet Skis went by fifteen feet above their heads.

Tourist season, Fred explained. *So you guys came down to answer the king's call?* As soon as she asked, she realized what a dumb question it was. The king didn't have to call. Tennian was by far the most curious mermaid Fred had ever met, and the girl was absolutely fascinated with surface dwellers. If there was a gathering, a meeting, a boat full of tourists hoping to catch sight of a mermaid, a press conference, a pirate ship, a—a Tupperware party, Tennian was there.

She was a striking woman—annoyingly, all the purebred Undersea Folk were easy on the eyes, not a pimple or cross-eyed mutant in the bunch—with dark blue hair and eyes that were even darker, the way small sapphires sometimes looked black.

When the Undersea Folk showed themselves to the surface for the first time, Tennian had been shot.

It hadn't done a thing to squash her curiosity.

And that had been, of course, when Dr. Thomas Pearson, that cheating shallow wretch, had fallen for her. And off they'd gone into the wild blue yonder . . . or wherever a mermaid and a human went to bang their brains out.

Cheating? That wasn't fair, she had to admit. It's not like she'd told him she'd loved him. It's not like they had ever even dated. *He'd* been the one to say he wanted to stick around. And then left for a year.

To finish his fellowship, her conscience reminded her. *Not to abandon you.*

Never mind that. It wasn't the leaving. No, what stung was how quickly Thomas had shifted allegiance. He'd thought she was the bee's knees, but Fred should have kept in mind Thomas had become a marine biologist *because* he was a mermaid freak. He'd been perfectly happy to go off with Tennian and leave Fred yet *again* . . .

Oh, quit it.

What? Tennian asked, her dark blue hair floating around her as she peered, in vain, for something to catch and devour. Girl had a healthy appetite, among other things.

Never mind. So how've you been? All healed up, I guess?

Indeed. Thomas tended me quite well.

Oh, I have no fucking doubt about that.

And here you are, Fred sent politely.

Yes, yes! Already today I have spoken to a man from the land of Texas, two women on their way to 'bridge,' although whether that is a noun or a verb I cannot say, and six children who swam out when they saw me just off their beach.

Just be careful. You don't want to get shot again.

No, I do not! But they were all very nice. I have also seen you on the television machine many times.

Don't remind me.

The king was wise to appoint you our representative.

That's open for debate. Speaking of royalty, you seen your cousin around?

Oh, yes. Unlike some others, Tennian didn't hold Fred's poor-range telepathy against her. Tennian didn't hold anything against her. It made her awfully hard to dislike, even if she was boning Thomas. *He comes now—shall I call him for you?*

That'd be great.

Dammit. The girl was just too nice. Dammit!

Ten

So Artur had come darting through the water toward her and Tennian had gone off somewhere and they'd swum together and she'd bitched about her morning. She was careful not to mention Thomas was back in town; Artur made no secret that he thought of the man as the one rival for Fred's affection.

It seems your mating rituals are grueling to the extreme, he teased, and she laughed in spite of herself.

No, anything Jonas is involved with is grueling to the extreme. You'd think I'd be used to it by now.

You would think.

Oh, and I met with that reporter from Time.

Ah, thank you. I have no liking for your press and nor does my good father the king. It is best left to those who understand them.

Fred snorted.

I know that sound! You think my father has chosen wrong. You always think, when complimented, that the other is wrong.

Fred had to admit the redheaded SOB understood her pretty well. It was as irritating as it was flattering.

I just wish it was over with, you know? The wedding. All the press junk. I wish we could go back to our lives.

So do all who are called to greatness, Little Rika.

Called to greatness! she shrieked in his head, giggling like a madwoman. *Oh! That's too good, Artur! That's too damned funny!*

He seized her by the hands, surprising her into choking off her laughter. He was gazing down at her with his intense, ruby gaze. His chest was so broad it filled her world; his face, so handsome and intent, filled her heart. Or someplace lower.

Little Rika, it has been my honor to have you at my side these many months. You have done—as I knew you would—great things for my people. You have given up much to be our liaison. And I have watched you with great pride. But I must press for a more formal arrangement. I ask—I need*—you to be my mate, and One Day Queen.*

One Day Queen? Her thoughts were such a whirl, she sought refuge in sarcasm. *Does that mean I'd be the queen one day, or queen for only one d—*

He stopped her thoughts—no easy trick—with a kiss. A long one. A kiss that left her bruised and wanting more and confused and horny and sad and lonesome, all at once.

Artur! Haven't you been listening to a thing I've said? I hate wedding planning! My litany of bitching prompted you to ask me to marry you? How the hell does your mind work, anyway?

I have long wanted to ask you, my Rika. I do not think this comes as a surprise to you.

Well. Not really. He certainly hadn't made any secret of the fact that he wanted to marry her, that he loved her

(like Thomas, he said the same thing and then he left)

and wanted to be with her, always. She had just made the natural assumption that the more he got to know her, the less he would want her. It was perfectly logical.

Artur, I don't know what to say. I mean, I'm really flattered. And pretty much any woman on the planet—tail or legs—would be lucky to get you. I just—I'm not sure I'm the right girl for you. Although, now that she was in her early thirties, "girl" wasn't quite accurate. Except maybe it was, because Artur, who didn't look a day over twenty-five, was actually well into his sixties. Undersea Folk lived long and aged slow.

I beg you to think of it, at least. I do not require your answer this moment, though it would please me as nothing else has. I will wait for you, my Rika, as long as you require.

If you're willing to wait, then I'm willing to give it serious thought, she told him, abruptly squeezing him around the waist. She rested her head against his shoulder and he stroked her short green hair. *Serious thought.*

Then I remain content, he said and kissed her again.

A new start, she thought, kissing him back, and why not? Thomas had Tennian, Jonas had Dr. Barb—where was her chance for happiness? Right in front of her?

Maybe so.

Eleven

Fred popped out onto the deck and walked through her backyard to the pool area, where Jonas was lounging on a patio chair with *Modern Bride* and carefully ignoring her.

She sighed. Jonas in a sulk was about as fun as curdled milk.

She coughed. "Hi."

"Not speaking to you," he said, angrily flipping pages. "As best men go, you suck."

"I know."

"Suck, suck, suck." Each "suck" was punctuated by another turn of the page. "In every possible way, you—Oooh! Now there's a floral arrangement I can live with."

"Jonas—"

"Not speaking to you."

"Listen, I really need to talk to you."

"Listen, I really am not speaking to you. And put some clothes on, wouldya? You've got neighbors."

"Artur asked me to marry him."

Modern Bride went flying in one direction, Jonas's sandal in another as he lunged out of the chair. "What? He did? When?" He clutched his temples and writhed as if on the receiving end of a shock treatment. "Oh, my God! *Two* weddings! I get to plan *a royal frigging wedding*! The guest list! The location! The clothes! And your *mom*! Moon Bimm is going to *freak out*!"

"Jonas—"

"Let's see, it'll have to be somewhere regular people and Undersea Folk can go to, and the food will have to—"

"*Jonas.* I haven't said yes yet," she said, rummaging around in the large plastic chest beneath the porch and extracting a robe. She shrugged into it and plopped down in a poolside chair. "I'm not sure it's the right thing to—"

"*Grab him, you idiot!*"

"You don't have to scream."

Jonas groaned and nearly plummeted into the deep end. "Fred, today's the day. It's finally happened. I'm officially going to kill you. And it's not going to be quick and painless, either, the way I always imagined it. It's going to be long and hideously drawn out, like a bingo tournament."

Fred stifled a yawn. Not even lunchtime, and she was already exhausted. Also, Jonas informed her "today was the day" about every other week.

He was now pacing back and forth in front of her, limping a bit as he was wearing only one sandal. "Let's see, you don't want to marry Artur because . . . um . . . let's see, you don't want to be a princess? And eventually a queen?"

"Actually, no."

"Moron!" he hissed. "Think of all the people you could help! You could change the world, dumb shit! And the jewelry, think of the *jewelry*."

"Because I care so much about the perfect charm bracelet."

"Let's see, what else? You . . . *don't* want the love of a gorgeous hunk who thinks you're beyond swell? Who'll literally treat you like a queen? You *don't* want all the Undersea Folk to *have* to be nice to you, even the ones who have been real assholes? You *don't* want to settle down in time to have kids? You *don't*—"

"You're going supersonic and shrieky. Soon only dogs will hear your litany of abuse."

His teeth came together with a click and she knew, in his mind, he'd just chomped on her nose. "You know what your problem is?"

"I have tons," she admitted.

"Goddamned right! The big one right now is that you're a commitment-phobe."

"Well, yes."

"Don't try to deny it! You—Oh. Okay. Well, admitting you've got a problem is the first step."

"I'm not sure I see myself marrying a merman and living in the Black Sea and being a queen and giving birth to princes and princesses and—I just don't know if that's the life I'm supposed to have."

"Oh, no. You're supposed to die smelly and alone, mourned only by your forty cats."

"I hate cats."

"When you're an old lady (and alone) you'll love 'em. Think *that's* the big plan for your forever after?"

"I don't know the plan," she said patiently. "That's the problem."

"That's not the only problem," Jonas muttered. He stopped in mid-pace and spun to face her. "Waaaaait a minute. This doesn't have anything to do with Priscilla D'Jacqueline, does it?"

"Don't be a dumbass."

"It does! It totally does!"

"And don't call him that."

"Hey, it's not my fault he writes romance novels under a silly-ass pen name."

It was true. Thomas Pearson, M.D., Ph.D., marine biologist, and bestselling romance novelist Priscilla D'Jacqueline. He carried Strunk and White's *The Elements of Style.* And a switchblade.

Complicated fellow.

"Artur's proposal and Thomas are separate issues."

"Ha-ha-haaaaaaa."

"It's true," she insisted. "Thomas made his choice. He left . . . more than once, if my math is correct—and you'll recall it's always correct."

"Don't be showing off, *Dr.* Bimm."

"You know I pretty much wrote him off after Tennian got shot and he went all Florence Nightingale on her. They deserve their Happily Ever After."

"I know you *said* you wrote him off. You also say you're a lousy liar, but I'm not so sure about that one. Especially when it comes to your love life. Anybody can lie to themselves."

"Not only am I not in love with Thomas Pearson"—she sighed—"I'm not even sure we're friends. And even if I was in love with him—which I'm not—he's not free to make a commitment. And I'm not sure I'd trust him to stick around if he was. He's really bad at it."

Then, like a genie conjured from a bottle, Thomas Pearson strolled around the side of the house, whistling. He brightened when he saw her and said, "Who's really bad at what?"

"Awesome!" Jonas chortled. "Now it's gonna get good."

Twelve

Fred stared at the apparition dressed in a blue oxford shirt with the sleeves rolled up; khaki shorts; loafers without socks (hi, folks, remember the 80s?); diving watch; and no other jewelry (Tennian hasn't dragged him to the altar, or the Undersea Folk equivalent?). Ridiculously tan—but then, Thomas was never one to skulk in a lab. He was an outdoor boy, which she couldn't help respect despite the—

Oh, stop it!

And tall, very tall—he had a good three inches on her, and she was a healthy six feet—with what most people would call brown hair. She called it russet with gold and red highlights. Never to his face, of course. Hardly ever even to herself, but she had to admit that in his own way, his hair was as interesting as hers . . . and he, at least, didn't have hair of a freakish hue.

The more time he spent in the sun, the lighter it got, and from the way the sun was glinting off his hair, he'd been spending a great deal of time outside indeed.

Sure. Following Tennian's luscious butt hither and yon.

It was longer than usual—he normally kept it short and neat, but now it curled almost to his shoulders, and his golden-brown bangs hung in his face. He flipped them back with a jerk of his head and grinned at her.

Brown eyes—again, not just brown. Brown with (*sigh*) gold flecks. Flecks that twinkled at her whenever he was grinning, just as he was now. Flecks that—oh, Christ, now she sounded like one of his silly-ass romance novels! (Fred was a fan of science journals and true crime stories; *Small Sacrifices* was, in her opinion, one of the finest glimpses into the mind of a sociopath she had ever seen.)

To compensate for the mad feeling that things were still spinning beyond her control, she took refuge behind her temper. "What the hell are you doing here?"

He burst out laughing. "I had a bet with myself—you'd either say, 'What the hell are you doing here?' or, 'How the hell did you find out where I live?' Or possibly, 'Aren't you supposed to be the hell in the Black Sea?'"

"Hey, Thomas." Jonas stuck out a hand, and Thomas crossed the patio in three long strides and shook it. "Long time no, et cetera. Should've guessed since Tennian's around you wouldn't be far behind."

"Oh, she is?" he said vaguely. Then, more briskly, "So what were you two talking about? Looked like life and death from your expressions."

Fred waved a hand, her pulse finally getting back under control after the shock of seeing him. She'd hardly heard what he said . . . only the last comment had really penetrated. "More interviews and crap. Jonas is the wall I wail to."

Jonas leered and looked pleased at the same time, like a man with a bellyache who'd gobbled five antacids.

"Yeah, I saw your picture in *People* last week. You cut your hair!" He was staring, and smiling, at her chin-length strands.

"All of 'em," she replied. "Also, Jonas is planning his wedding down here."

Thomas rolled his eyes and plopped into a patio chair opposite her. "Oh-oh! That makes you—what? Best—let's see, not best man . . . best woman? Best grump? Best bitch?"

Ignoring Jonas's haw-*haw*, she snapped, "How'd you like to get knocked into the Gulf?"

He propped his tanned legs up on a patio table and stretched his arms behind his head. "Ah, any excuse to have your hands on me."

"I forgot what a big bag of flirt you are."

"But I didn't forget what a cutie *you* are."

"Oh, gawd!" Jonas groaned. "Can't you two just do it and get it over with?"

Thomas laughed long at that one, as if it were the funniest thing he'd ever heard. Fred found it less amusing. Okay, not amusing at all. Okay, the polar opposite of amusing.

"Anyway," Thomas continued, as if she had the teensiest care about what brought him to her rental, "since I can't turn on a television or pick up a newspaper without reading about Undersea Folk or seeing your picture, I thought I'd head down here once I finished my last book. And here you are! Also, this is a small island and everybody knows you're staying here."

"Great," she grumped. "Just what I need."

"Aw, you know you're a Miss Congeniality at heart." He yawned. "So, can I crash here? What does this place have, nine bedrooms?"

"Hardly." Oh, this was too damned much. Stress upon stress upon stress and Thomas fucking Pearson as her new roommate. Not to mention Tennian. Fred could already picture finding long blue strands in her hairbrush. "It's smaller than it looks. On the outside."

"The soul of hospitality, no matter how heavy her duties."

Jonas cleared his throat, which did nothing to alleviate the tension Fred was drowning in. "Hey, check this. I might not be the only one getting married—Artur proposed!"

"To Fred?"

"No, to Dick Cheney. Yeah, to Fred."

Thomas stiffened in, Fred assumed, genuine surprise. "Artur asked Fred to marry him?" He looked right at her, no twinkle at all in those big brown eyes. "What'd you say?"

"I'm still thinking about it."

He chewed on his lower lip for a moment. "So. I'll just go inside and pick a bedroom, then. My stuff's around the front of the house."

"But I haven't said you could—"

He got up out of the chair and stalked around the corner of the house.

"Well." Jonas coughed again. "And here I thought things might start to settle down a bit." Then, "Dammit! I completely forgot I'm not speaking to you."

"You always do." She sighed and wondered which was the more practical decision: kick Thomas out of her house, hide on the bottom of the pool, or jump into the Gulf and head for Cuba.

Well, shit.

She followed him in.

Thirteen

She had thrown open her (rented) front door and caught Thomas halfway up the steps.

"Look, Pearson, I never said you could—"

"Are you really going to be a princess? And eventually a queen?"

"Actually, the queen's been dead for several years, so—"

"Fred. Cut the shit."

She stared at him and tried to find an answer. Good damn luck. "I'm thinking it over." *Not that it's any of* your *business.* "Jonas reminded me that Artur would treat me, quite literally, like a queen." Not that it's any of your business. "Guys like that are hard to come by."

He smiled sourly.

"Well." She bristled. "They are."

He squinted at her from the sixth stair. "And that's what you want? Royalty? A title? A kingdom?"

"I don't know. I don't know what I want," she admitted. "But Artur and I—we get on, you know. He's shown me things I could never have seen—Shit, I don't have to tell you, I'm sure you've seen plenty of things with Tennian." Besides her tits. "And I won't deny that it's tempting."

Sure. You bet it was tempting. If for no other reason than she wouldn't have to watch Tennian and Thomas slobber all over each other and make li'l hybrids.

"Can't blame you for that one. He's a good man," Thomas said slowly. He had stopped his upward descent and now sat on the stairs, chin cupped in one hand. "It's a good offer. And like you said, he can show you things, and give you things, no one else on the planet can."

"Yes."

"No one would blame you for saying yes, least of all me."

"You've always liked him," she admitted, shutting the door. Jonas, no doubt, would sulk by the pool, giving them the privacy they needed. Or he'd pretend to sulk, which resulted in the same thing.

"Yes. Liked him, admired him, resented him, wanted to beat him, respected him, tormented him, fed him." They both grinned, remembering the trip to Faneuil Hall two years ago when Artur had ordered one of everything—or so it had seemed.

Thomas's smile faded and he sighed, a dreadful sound like dead leaves careening down into a sewer. "You should give it some thought."

Why did he sound so strange? "I am."

"Well." He wouldn't look at her. Why wasn't he looking at her? "That seems pretty sensible."

"Sensible was never my problem."

He smiled. "No."

"Saying 'no' these days seems to be my problem."

He laughed at her.

"I'm serious. I've talked to so many reporters, when I had better things to do, that I've lost count."

"Well. The king will be pleased."

"Yes. How long," she said, "were you planning on staying?"

"I dunno," he said vaguely. "Until there's nothing left to see or hear, I s'pose."

"Thanks for being so specific. And Tennian? Will she be shacking up in your room?"

"Tennian is a darling." Fred tried not to flinch. "And will do what she likes; it's her nature. She's an amazing mer—uh, woman."

"Yes." She sought desperately for a change of subject. "I'm guessing your fellowship is done."

"Oh, yeah. Scotland was the last stop—thank God! Did you know I make more money with one book than in two years of being a marine biologist?"

"Great, Priscilla."

"Tennian and I have spent the last few months exploring the planet. She's shown me things." He shook his head and she could see the scientist behind his eyes scheming, scheming. "Things I never dreamed I'd see, not in a hundred lifetimes."

"Well," Fred said stiffly. "How nice for you both."

"And like we've been saying, Artur could do the same."

"Probably."

Thomas sighed. "I'll take the second bedroom on the left."

"That'd be peachy keen."

Oh, sure. Keen. Like an unwanted roommate. Like plague. Like famine.

"I'm not sharing a bathroom with you!" she bawled as he vanished up the steps and down a hallway.

Fourteen

A night later, Fred was forced to play hostess. Not that she was having to do any of the actual work, thank God. Jonas had bought the food, Thomas had fired up the grill, and Tennian had shown up with her twin brother and a half dozen fresh lobsters.

"Ho, Fredrika Bimm! You recall my brother, Rennan?"

"Vividly." They shook hands gingerly. Rennan wasn't nearly as friendly or open-minded as his sister and was wary of Fred because of her family history. He was a male version of Tennian, with the same blue hair and sapphire-colored eyes. But if he wasn't civil, his sister would kick his ass. She'd done it before. "How'd Tennian drag you here, anyway?"

"It was my honor to come," he replied stiffly.

"Aha! Word's getting out that Artur proposed, I'm guessing. Tsk, tsk, Rennan . . . hedging your bets? How . . . courageous."

He scowled at her, then at his twin when she snickered.

"Well, come on in. Thomas is in the back, trying to fry his eyebrows."

"Fry his—?"

"Hi, Tennian!" Jonas managed not to leer; for a change, Tennian was fully clothed.

Not for the first time, Fred wondered where Undersea Folk got their clothes. The Gap? A mall? An underwater mall? She knew they had gobs of money—every doubloon, antique, gold bar, or what-have-you since man first built ships and lost them to the sea was the property of the king and his people.

"Glad you could make it," Jonas was still yakking, "and—oh, my God, look at the *size* of those things!"

Reasonably sure he meant the lobsters and not Tennian's boobs, Fred relieved her of them and stuffed the wriggling creatures into her fridge. She couldn't eat them, of course (her allergy had been a source of great hilarity to Tennian), but the others would love them.

"I've noticed you don't seem to mind vocalizing so much anymore." This was more scientific curiosity than polite conversation; when they had first met, several months ago, Tennian would hardly say two words out of water, but was quite chatty with her telepathy.

"I practiced with Thomas," the girl replied, inspecting the tablecloth and cloth napkins and dining-room chairs.

I'll bet.

"His Highness regrets," Rennan said, watching his sister with a bemused expression, "he cannot join us for this meal. The good king his father required him to tend to some family business."

"Too bad," Thomas said, sliding open the deck door and popping inside. "He's gonna miss a spread. Hey, Tenn. Hi, Rennan." He embraced Tennian and shook Rennan's forearm, an Undersea Folk–style handshake. "Glad you could make it."

"Oh, I love looking at surface-dweller homes, and I had heard Fredrika was residing in quite a nice one." Tennian flipped a dining-room chair upside down, examined it, and righted it. "And I see I heard correctly!"

"She's so *adorable*," Jonas whispered to Fred. "I'm in love with someone else and I'm still having a hard time resisting her . . . Say, Tennian, could I take a look at your hair?"

Tennian blinked. Fred lied, "Surface-dweller custom. We also inspect each other for ticks," so the smaller woman agreed.

Jonas fussed with the woman's long blue strands for a few moments. "Great body. Not too many split ends. What you need is some good conditioner and maybe some gel. I've got both in my rental car."

"Jonas is a scientist, like Fred and me," Thomas explained.

"Ha!" Fred sneered.

"Only he works for a company that makes hair products. He helps think them up."

"I do not wish to put chemicals in my hair," Tennian said soberly. "They would get into the seas. I do not wish to dirty the seas."

"How about a trim, at least?"

"But I don't—"

"I'm taking grill orders," Thomas interrupted. To Jonas: "Give it up." To the group: "So who wants what?"

Tennian and her brother were quite familiar with cooked food, as Undersea Folk frequently held banquets on various deserted islands. They both opted for steak and lobster. Fred decided on a burger and salad. Thomas and Jonas wanted lobster. So Fred found a large pot—hooray for furnished rentals!—and started the water boiling. Thomas disappeared back outside to start grilling.

They sat around the dining-room table, enjoying the sea breeze and gossiping about current events. Unlike his sister, Rennan wasn't keen on being pestered by tourists who wanted to see his tail. If not for his sister's choice, he would have elected to remain hidden from the surface world. The king had given that choice to every one of his subjects, and several thousand of them (Fred had no idea of the exact number) remained off surface-dweller radar . . . literally.

But many, like Tennian, had been curious too long to stay out of sight. And despite being shot by pirates, the smaller woman's enthusiasm for all things surface remained undiminished.

"Water's boiling," Jonas said, peeking into the pot.

"Then drop 'em."

"Chickenshit," he said, not unkindly.

"Can't stand the noise they make," Fred admitted.

"But I thought you couldn't hear us or them outside the water," Rennan said, then *oof*'d as his sister slammed an elbow into his side. "I wasn't being rude," he said, gingerly rubbing his ribs.

"Yes, you *were*; we're not supposed to *tease* her about that. She can't help it if her lady mother is a surface dweller."

"I was only asking," Rennan said, sounding wounded.

"It's okay, Tennian, don't beat him up anymore. I'm not offended."

"Just offensive," Jonas said cheerfully, extracting the wriggling, depressed crustaceans from the fridge.

Fred was momentarily taken aback. No, she had no telepathy on land, couldn't hear a mermaid or a goldfish. But purebreds could. What in the world did a lobster sound like to them as it was being plunged into boiling water? Dear God!

"I meant the *'eeeeeee'* noise when they hit the water. That's what I can't stand."

"That's just the air being shoved out of their shells by the force and heat," Jonas explained for the zillionth time. "They're not actually, y'know, *screaming*. You'd think a marine biologist would know this stuff. Also: gross."

"Well," Tennian began awkwardly, then glanced at her brother, who shrugged. "Well, they do. Ah. Scream. But for less than half a second. They don't like going near the pot, but once they are—ah—inside, they are done."

The dinner party from hell, Fred thought, having no clue what was in store for her in the next half hour. *That's what this is.*

Twenty minutes later, they were all eating with varying degrees of enthusiasm. Tennian and Rennan made short work of their lobsters but took the steaks slower. Thomas was ravenous—he'd been gone all day; Fred had no idea where and was too proud to ask—and wolfed down his meal. Jonas ate methodically and neatly, peppering the twins with questions between bites. And Fred ignored her meat and picked at her salad.

"I met the most charming young surface dweller this afternoon," Tennian said, slurping the meat out of a lobster leg. She bit off the joint and chewed noisily for a few seconds. "She had perhaps . . . four seasons? Five?"

"Years," Thomas corrected her gently.

"Of course. She had been caught in the riptide and I pulled her back to shore. Poor little one, so frightened! She petted my tail all the way back to shore. Her lady mother was very kind also."

"Well, jeez, I'd hope so," Jonas said, used to Tennian's habit of devouring shellfish, shells and all. "Good for you."

"They all seem very nice," Tennian added. She bit through a lobster claw and extracted the meat, ignoring the melted butter Jonas had placed before her. She squeezed, and the claw shattered and pieces littered her plate. "Other than the ones who shot me, of course."

"Of course," Thomas said, then caught Fred's eye and they snickered together. "Nobody's perfect, though."

"And if anybody'd know, it'd be those two," Jonas teased. "In fact, I—"

There was a sharp rapping at the front door. Fred groaned inwardly and got up. "Maybe Artur could make it after all."

The twins shook their heads in unison. "He would have told us on his way."

"God, I'd *love* to be telepathic," Jonas was saying as Fred made her way to the door. "Way more efficient than flapping my gums all day long."

"Yes," the twins said in unison.

Another hard rap, and Fred pulled the door open. "All right, no need to knock it down." She stared at the man. "Who the hell are you?"

He was almost exactly her height—perhaps an inch taller. His hair was the exact color of hers, only it was shoulder-length. His eyes were also a vivid green, the color of the ocean in high summer. His face was smooth and unlined; he looked like he was in his mid-twenties.

Fred wasn't fooled; with that coloring he had to be Undersea Folk. And they aged beautifully. He could have been in his fifties, or barely drinking age.

He was wearing jeans, tennis shoes, and a red polo shirt. His fingers were long and, as he stretched out his hand for her to shake, strong. He was lightly tanned, and really pretty good-looking.

"Crashing the party?" She managed to extract her hand before he broke any bones.

"Yes, several years too late, Fredrika. Do you not recognize me?"

"Should I?"

"Has your lady mother never described me?"

Fred blinked.

The hair.

The eyes.

Oh man oh man ohmanohmanohman.

Her insides seemed to lock up and then slither to the bottom of her stomach. She felt her left eye twitch in a stress spasm. Oh, this was perfect. Icing on the wedding cake, so to speak. Christ.

"Don't even tell me."

"I'm—"

"I said don't tell me!"

"—your father. My name is Farrem."

From behind, a baritone yowl from Rennan: "Traitor!"

And also from behind, Tennian: "Get away from her right now, you filth!"

A chair fell over and she could hear rapidly approaching footsteps. Tennian, with the height of a pygmy and the courage of a rabid ape, launching herself, no doubt.

Fred turned, braced herself, and caught the woman by the elbows—barely. They both toppled backward, into Fred's father, and out the door onto the sidewalk.

Fifteen

For a few minutes Fred felt like a character in a Bugs Bunny cartoon—everything was whirling fists and rolling around on the lawn and kicking feet. All that was missing was the cloud of dust and the darting stars.

Finally, *finally* she was able to get to her feet and between her (groan) father and Tennian, making the time-out sign from football and instantly realizing neither of them probably knew what it meant.

"Cut it *out*!" she shrieked, booting Tennian in the ankle and hooking an elbow into her father's gut. It was like elbowing plywood.

Tennian lunged and Fred backed up fast, forcing her father to back up as well. "You remove yourself from the lady's property this moment or I shall—"

Fred was shoved forward as her father first planted his feet and then started forward. It occurred to her that both of them had at least twice her strength. "I have a perfect right to see my daughter on land, you pious—"

"I mean it, you guys. Not here, not on my front lawn; I'm getting dizzy and my damned dinner's getting cold!"

"But he is a most foul—"

"I did not wish for this and I—"

"Cut it out!"

Sulky silence. Not to mention staring eyes . . . everyone else had piled out the front door to watch the fight. Jonas and Thomas seemed fascinated. Rennan looked horrified and amused at the same time; it was well known that his twin was the hard-ass.

Fred sighed. Pushed her hair out of her eyes. Glared at them both. "You guys better come inside."

"I am grateful for your hos—"

"But, Fredrika! He is a most loathsome—"

"Tennian, he's coming in. You can come in, too, or stay out here on the lawn. Or go jump in the ocean. But he's coming in."

"So . . . he's coming in?" Jonas was grinning, looking from father to daughter to father. "Hey there, Fred's Dad. Nice to meetcha. You want a burger, a lobster, or a steak?"

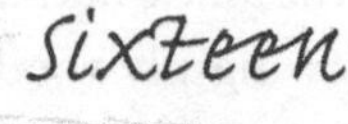

Sixteen

Rennan and Tennian wouldn't stay.

"Oh, come on," Jonas, ever the peacemaker, coaxed. "Look how much lobster's left! Without you chewing on the things, all that shell is going to go to waste."

"We cannot remain under the roof with a traitor to the royal blood," Tennian said stiffly, and Fred remembered that Artur was her cousin. She, probably more than the average Undersea Folk, took Fred's father's betrayal more personally than most. "I do not mean to give offense, Fredrika."

"Farewell," her twin added, holding the door for his sister. "The food was very fine."

"Run along, children," her father said. Fred had to admit, he seemed pretty unruffled at the snub. Almost . . . amused?

She sort of liked him for it.

The twins stomped out looking (Fred had to admit it) exactly like kids throwing a tantrum.

"So!" Farrem said brightly, sitting down in Tennian's chair. "Are you going to eat that lobster?"

Seventeen

"This is a little awkward—" Fred began, only to be interrupted by Jonas.

"No, it's cool! It's so cool that you showed up now! My God . . . so . . . many . . . questions . . ." Jonas clutched his temples. "Let's start with the big one. Does inherent grumpiness run in your side of the family? Because she sure didn't get it from her mom. And do you take pleasure in looking as unattractive as you can at every opp—"

Farrem laughed, an easy, deep sound. "I will gladly answer your questions, good sir, but perhaps introductions could come first?"

"If you're expecting your one and only daughter to remember protocol, you're gonna have a long damn wait," Thomas said, smiling a little. Fred wasn't fooled. Thomas might look and sound casual, as if this were any other get-together, but she knew the scientist in him wanted to stick Farrem in a lab and run several hundred tests. And right now!

"Am I?" Fred asked.

"Are you what, my own?" Farrem bit off a lobster claw and crunched contentedly.

"Your one and only daughter."

Farrem laughed. "As far as I know! Certainly you're the most famous of my offspring, even if I had several dozen to keep track of. I saw you on the television box and thought, could that be the product of that delightful night on a Cape Cod beach? You must admit . . ." *Crunch. Crunch.* ". . . we look a great deal alike."

"Yeah, I was noticing that, too." One thing about Undersea Folk . . . the only ones who shared the same coloring were blood relatives, like Artur and the king, or Tennian and her brother. "Well, you asked about intros. This is my best friend, Jonas, and this is my colleague—"

"Colleague?" Thomas cried with mock hurt. "Is that all we are to each other, you heartless harpy?"

"—Dr. Thomas Pearson. Guys, this is—well—Farrem." She wasn't ready to call him "Dad." Shit, her stepfather, Sam, had raised her (he'd married her mother, Moon, while she was knocked up with Fred) and she didn't even call *him* Dad. "My, uh, biological father."

"It pleases me to meet such gentlemen over my daughter's table." *Crunch.* "Fredrika, tell me—how is your lady mother?"

"Hot," Jonas said.

Fred glared. Jonas's crush on her mother got more disturbing every year. When they were nine it wasn't too creepy, but now . . . "Moon's fine." *In fact, I'm going to have to make a phone call. Right now.* "She thinks you're dead."

Farrem's smile dropped away like someone had snatched it. "To many of our folk, I am. Or as good as."

"So why are you here now?" Thomas asked.

"Is it not obvious, Dr. Pearson? The king could banish me from his kingdom . . . but not from the surface. I confess I could scarce believe my eyes when I started seeing the news reports."

"You and most of the rest of the planet."

"Indeed! And now that my folk have begun making themselves known to surface dwellers . . ." Farrem shrugged and crunched into a claw. "It seemed an opportune time to reemerge."

"I'm sure the others will be thrilled," Fred said dryly, remembering the reaction of the twins.

"That," Farrem said coolly, "is their problem and not mine. Besides, how could I stay away when every time I turned on the television box my own eyes were staring out at me?"

Fred could feel herself start to blush, and fought it. Still. A nice thing for him to say. Gracious, even, because she was no beauty, and *he* was really handsome.

"I must admit, I was astonished—not only to see you, but to see my own people coming out of the sea. Astonishing. Truly." He shook his head. "After centuries of hiding . . ."

"But what's your plan? I mean, Fred says you got kicked out—banished or whatever—after, uh . . . So what's your plan?"

"I was intemperate and willful in my youth," Farrem said evenly, "and reached too high. I was deservedly slapped down and have been paying the price for over three decades. I earned my banishment. But the king cannot keep me from the surface, and now that my people are out *here* . . ." He shrugged. "My plan is atonement. I wish to show the royal family I am no threat . . . Not that, after defeating me, they need such assurances! And eventually . . . maybe . . . acceptance."

Fred thought about the twins and didn't think dear old Dad should hold his breath on that one.

"It will take time," he said, practically reading her mind. "But then, if you know our people, Fredrika, you know that time, at least, is something most of us have much of. Comparatively speaking," he added with an apologetic glance at Thomas and Jonas.

"You should stay here while you put Operation Atonement into action," Jonas said. "Fred has tons of room."

Fred, who had raised the can of Coke to her mouth, nearly crushed it. "What?" Oh, this was too much!

"Of course, I would never impose," her father said hastily, which made Fred feel bad, which made her mad.

Which made her *furious* at Jonas. Tons of room, her scaled ass! If her math was correct, there was exactly one empty bedroom left . . . which she was about to offer to her long-lost father. She knew, knew, *knew* renting a four-bedroom house was an exercise in madness.

On the upside, with no more bedrooms to offer, that'd be the end of drop-in guests. Probably. Maybe.

"It's no imposition," she lied, wishing she dared toss Jonas into the pool. "We can—uh—" What did fathers and daughters *do*, exactly? Go to father/daughter picnics? Was he going to teach her to drive? Would she share her dating debacles with him? God, he wouldn't think he had to tell her about the birds and the bees, would he? "Upstairs, last door on the left."

"Then if you will excuse me, I will get settled." He stood so quickly they hardly saw him move, and bowed to them. "My thanks for the welcome, the meal, the conversation, and the very fine hospitality."

They watched him climb the stairs, and then Thomas leaned in and murmured, "Your old man's got style to spare."

"I wonder if he was so polite when he tried to kill the king."

"C'mon, Fred." Jonas snatched her Coke and took a healthy guzzle. "He said it himself—he was a jerk when he was young. Seems to run in the family."

"How'd you like to hit the pool? From the second story? Through a closed window?"

He ignored her threats, as he had for decades. "It was thirty years ago. He's sorry now, I bet. But that's not even the important thing."

"Oh, do tell, Jonas." She grabbed her Coke back. "What's the important thing?"

"Deciding whether or not to call Moon."

Her mother! Ack. Jonas was right, curse his eyes. She cringed, picturing the call.

And then the visit.

Better get it over with.

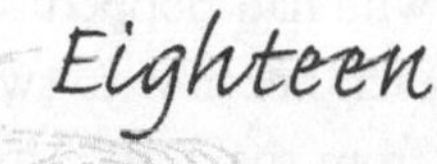

Eighteen

"Now!" Moon Bimm said briskly. She and her husband, Sam, had taken a cab from the airport and had only now arrived at Fred's house. "What's this all about, Fred? Why so mysterious on the phone? If you're trying to get out of helping Jonas plan his wedding, you can just stop it right now."

"But how'd you even know Jonas—"

"He called me."

"What?"

Moon blinked. "He calls almost every week."

"Oh, for the love of—"

"Do you have any herbal tea?"

"No, I have beer and soda."

"Fred, how can you treat your body so badly? It is a sacred temple, a gift—particularly yours! Vitamin water and salads, that's how you could best show your body how grateful you are for the gift of such a hallowed vessel."

Fred ground her teeth. Moon had never quite let go of the hippie thing, and it was maddening. Also, she was a *rich* hippie, like that wasn't a weird-ass paradox. Sam came from tons of money.

And, though she wasn't about to admit it to Jonas, her mother was in damned fine shape for a woman in her fifties. A short, good-looking blonde with silver streaks running through her shoulder-length hair, Moon was plump where women are supposed to be plump, with laugh lines and a near-permanent smile. She didn't dress like the wife of a millionaire, preferring faded T-shirts and jeans.

Sam, Fred's stepfather, was as mild-mannered as Fred was not. Tall, balding, with a gray-streaked ponytail, he, also, didn't dress like a millionaire. More like a struggling artist.

Although she could never tell him so, she loved him and honored him for not fleeing when he realized his new wife had popped out a mermaid. He had even, memorably, tried to teach her how to swim.

It had gone badly. He'd had to be rescued from the YMCA pool. But that wasn't the point.

"Mom, I didn't call you guys down here so you could lecture me about my Coke habit. The thing is—"

"Are you nervous about *60 Minutes*? Because you'll be fine," Sam said, opening the fridge and peering inside. "You've been doing fine in all your interviews."

"Thank goodness for TiVo," Moon added. "Otherwise we couldn't keep up with all your appearances."

"Your mother is keeping a scrapbook," Sam said, popping a beer. He, unlike Moon, didn't mind polluting his sacred temple with the occasional can of Bud.

"Don't even tell me."

"It's getting huge."

"Sam, seriously! Don't tell me. Listen. Mom. And, uh, Sam. Now don't freak out."

"Oh, my God!" Moon darted forward and seized Fred's cold hands (they were always cold) in her warm ones. "You're pregnant!"

Fred, a full head taller than her petite, sweetly plump mother, blanched and tried to pull away. Weirdly, it was difficult—Moon had quite a grip when she wanted. "Mom, I'm not—Jeez, ease up, will you? My fingers are going numb. I'm not pregnant. You have to have sex to get pregnant and I'm in the middle of a three-year dry spell."

"Oh, now that's just ridiculous! Prince Artur would have sex with you in half a second, and I'll bet that nice Dr. Pearson would, t—"

"Mom, we are not. Discussing. My arid. Sex life."

"But it's not wrong to share what God has given you with a man you—"

"Mom!" Fred nearly howled.

"Try not to scream, hon," Sam said, sipping contentedly at his Bud. "It's not even noon."

Fred extracted herself from her mother's grip with no small difficulty, took a swig of Sam's beer, then sucked in a breath and tried again.

"Thanks for coming so fast. I've got some news and I wanted to tell you in person."

"Well," Sam said reasonably, "don't keep us in suspense."

The front door opened and Jonas called, "Hey, new rental car in the driveway—is your hot mom here?"

Fred moaned. Sam grinned, got up, pulled out another beer, and handed it to her. Moon turned to greet Fred's unbelievably irritating friend.

"Jonas, you bad boy, like I don't know you're in love with a perfectly beautiful woman."

"Ah, Moon." He hugged her mother so hard, the woman's feet left the floor. "You never forget your first crush. So, what d'you think of the news?"

"We were just—"

"*I* think she should say yes. Don't you want to have a princess in the family?"

Fred finished her beer in four gulps.

"*What?* You mean Prince Artur finally asked you to marry him?"

"Mom . . ."

"But that's wonderful! You can settle down and have children and help the Undersea Folk and—and—"

Shocking everyone in the room, Moon burst into tears.

Nineteen

Pandemonium. Shouts. Threats. Tears. Kleenex. More shouts. More tears.

"Mom, what *is* it?"

"I'm so sorry," she sobbed. "I'm happy for you, I swear I am."

"I can tell," Fred replied, moderately horrified.

"Only . . . you'll have to go live with him. In the castle under the Black Sea. And I'll never see you. Not like I do now. How can I?"

"But I hardly ever visit unless—"

"I can't even visit . . . Dr. Pearson told me the pressure alone would kill a surface dweller; that's why they built their home base there. This—" She waved a hand, vaguely indicating Sanibel Island. "This isn't real. It's a fake castle; the king's playing it safe, you explained it to me. And I understand. I truly do."

"You don't look like you understand," Fred said doubtfully.

"But if you got married—if you were a member of the royal family—you'd have to move. To the other side of the planet. *Beneath* the other side of the planet. And I don't want—you're my only—"

"Mom, for God's sake." Fred could count on one hand how many times she'd seen her mother cry. It was frightening and frustrating and weird, all at once. "That's not even my news, thank you very much, *Jonas*."

"Well, how was I supposed to know you wouldn't mention, oh, I dunno, *a royal marriage proposal* to your mom?"

Moon sniffed and blinked up at her daughter. "You mean he didn't propose?"

"Oh, he proposed. I just haven't made up my mind."

Moon looked horrified even as Jonas was busily blotting her cheeks with Kleenex. "But then I've messed it up! You'll factor my reaction into your decision-making!"

"When has she ever, Moon?" Sam asked mildly, which was just the right thing to say. Everyone calmed down.

She sniffled again. "But then what *is* your news?"

"Well. It's like this. My father—my biological, Undersea Folk father—is alive."

Moon and Sam stared at her.

"Blow," Jonas ordered, and Moon blew into the Kleenex.

"And staying here. With me."

More staring.

"And he was hoping to see you again. If your—uh—" She turned to Jonas. "How'd he put it?"

"'If he who is her mate in no way objects,'" Jonas parroted. "Guy talks like a book. A good book," he added hastily, "but still. A book. I mean, I've got a degree in chemical engineering and *I* don't talk like a book."

"More like a comic. Anyway, 'he who is her mate'. . . that'd be you," she told Sam. "He'd like to see her again if you don't mind."

"I don't mind," Sam said. "I'd like to meet him myself."

"Awww. Just like a family reunion," Jonas said. "Actually, it *is* a family reunion. Here," he added, handing Moon more Kleenex. "Keep the box."

Twenty

Before things could settle down, the front door opened and Farrem walked in. Limped in, actually, and he had the beginning of a gorgeous black eye.

Fred was on her feet before she knew she was going to stand. "Jesus Christ! What happened to you?"

"Ran into three or four of the old guard," he said with dry good humor. "They reminded me that the rash actions of my youth have not been forgotten." He touched his swelling eye and grinned, showing the exceedingly sharp teeth common to Undersea Folk. Sam nearly choked on his beer—Fred had inherited her mother's teeth. "Forcefully. But who is this? Not Fred's lady mother and he who is her mate?"

"H-hello," Moon said, wiping her face. Then she got a closer look as Farrem closed the distance between them and gasped. "My God! You haven't aged a day!"

He laughed and took her small hands in his. "If only that were true, Madame Bimm."

"Please." She smiled wryly. "I think you can call me Moon."

"With your mate's kind permission," Farrem said, bowing slightly in Sam's direction. Sam looked nonplussed for a moment, then nodded back.

Moon cleared her throat. "Are you—are you in trouble? Because you've come back?"

"Of course," he replied easily. "Deservedly so. I hope to win my people over in another decade or so."

Fred was struck, once again, at how Undersea Folk thought nothing of a task that might take twenty or thirty years. By comparison, surface dwellers were fruit flies running around trying to accomplish everything in a nine-day life span.

Did I just refer to my mother's people as flies?

Eesh.

"—enough of my nonsense. What have you been doing these past decades?"

"Well, raising your daughter, of course." Moon laughed. "Though once she was about thirteen or so she stopped listening to me."

"Yes, that is typical among our kind."

"Our kind, too," Sam said, smiling a little.

"And it is on just this basis that King Mekkam decided to let his people reveal themselves, I suspect. In many ways, we are not so different."

"If you say so, pal," Jonas said, sounding fairly unconvinced. Fred jumped; he'd been so uncharacteristically quiet she'd forgotten he was there. "I guess anyone can get past the tail. And the teeth. And the breathing underwater thing. And the—"

"Don't you have a wedding to plan?"

"As a matter of fact," Jonas said with stiff dignity, "I'm late for a tux fitting right this minute."

"So run along."

"I will. See you guys later." And right before he went out the door he said, "Also my fiancée will be here tonight and I don't want to hear any bitching about it, good-bye!"

"Wait!" Fred yelled, and the door slammed.

She cursed vividly enough to make Farrem raise his eyebrows.

Twenty-one

"Well, that's just great," Fred fumed. "I knew I should have just gotten a room at the Super 8."

"You remind me of my mother," Farrem commented. "She often complained about events that did not truly upset her."

"You stay out of this. Dr. Barb. Great! Well, I guess I can try to quit again."

"Pardon, what?"

"Never mind, Farrem."

"She keeps trying to quit her job in Boston, and her boss keeps not letting her," Moon offered.

"Never *mind*. Suffice it to say I lead a stupidly complicated life."

The front door slammed open hard enough to shake part of the house, and a furious Prince Artur stood in the doorway.

"Case in point." Fred sighed as the prince stomped toward them. "You know, surface dwellers do this thing called knocking. If you're going to hang out on top of the planet as opposed to beneath the waves, you might want to—"

"So it is true," Artur hissed, eyeing Farrem the way you'd look at a cockroach in your cereal bowl. "I would never have believed it to be had I not seen it myself."

Farrem turned slowly. "My prince," he said calmly.

"You will remove yourself from the home of she-who-will-be-my-mate at once."

"How can he?" Fred asked. "He's staying in one of the guest rooms upstairs. His stuff's probably all over the bathroom."

Artur actually clutched his head. "I had heard that as well, but put it down to uninformed rumor."

"And that's quite enough of telling my houseguests what to do. That's *my* job."

"Fredrika, I insist this man leave your home at once."

"*This man* is my father, so tough nuts."

"I do not wish to be the cause of strife between you and the prince," Farrem said. "I shall go."

"Sit your ass back down," Fred ordered. Farrem arched his eyebrows but obeyed.

Then she turned to Artur. "And you! Don't come barging into my house without knocking and then start ordering people around. In case you haven't noticed, *Prince*, this isn't your domain. It's mine!"

Sam cleared his throat. "Technically, that's not—"

"You want to boss people around in the Mariana Trench, fine. Don't pull that shit in my house."

Artur blinked, scowled, and blinked harder. Farrem brought a hand up to cover his mouth; his eyes were wide and Fred suspected he was hiding a smile.

"Rika, this man is—"

"My father. Whom I've never met. Whom I'm getting to know. Who is a guest in my house."

"I think you might like him," Moon piped up, "if you gave him a chance, Artur."

"He tried to kill my father, good lady."

"Oh. Well, that's harder to forgive," Moon admitted. "But he said himself, he was just a kid when—"

"—he committed treason."

"I will go," Farrem said.

"Freeze," Fred ordered. Thinking, *Why am I fighting so hard for this? Because it's going to stick in Artur's craw? So my mom can get to know my dad? So I can? Why?* "I suppose Tennian practically broke a leg getting to you to blab."

"Tennian did her duty."

"Yeah, she's not biased or anything."

"Fredrika," Farrem said quietly. "The royal family has every reason to distrust my motivations."

"I get it, I get it. Listen, Artur, it was thirty years ago, okay? He was just a kid. Your dad banished him. *Banished* him. For three decades he hasn't seen another member of his own species. Doesn't that count for anything?"

Scowling silence.

"Besides, all this high-handed stuff is no way to get me to agree to marry you," she teased, hoping he'd lighten up.

Farrem's green eyes opened wide. "*Marry?* By the king, of course!" He literally slapped himself on the forehead. "When you came in, you called her she-who—but I admit I was much more occupied watching your hands than listening—so you'll be my princess, and one day my queen?" He shook his head so hard, green strands flew. "Astonishing! O irony, how she makes slaves of us all!"

"That's beautiful, Farrem," Moon breathed.

"I haven't said yes yet, so calm down. And you!" She turned back to Artur, who was looking sulky as well as annoyed. "I can read you like a book, Artur. You're thinking now that my dad has turned up alive and well, even *more* of the Undersea Folk won't like me. It was one thing when everyone assumed he was dead. But him showing up . . . it might make marrying me a bit trickier, especially if the court of public opinion doesn't come back in your favor."

"I would hope," he replied stiffly, "I am not as shallow as that."

"Well, Artur, so would I."

"Fred!" Moon gasped.

She turned. "Don't you think you and Sam should—"

And then, for the dozenth time (at least), her front door opened and Thomas was racing into the room. "Fred, Artur found out your father's in town and he's coming over here to—oh." He screeched to a halt, narrowly avoiding slamming into the table. "You, uh, already know."

Fred was resting her forehead on the table. "I want all my keys back," she said into the wood.

Twenty-two

An hour later, her parents had departed for their hotel, Artur had dived off the dock in a sulk, Farrell had retired upstairs, and Fred and Thomas were drinking the last of the beer.

"What a day," she moaned. "And it's barely half over!"

Thomas grinned at her. "A week with you is more exciting than a year anywhere else."

"Cut the shit," she said morosely. "I'm in no mood for idle flattery."

"Who said it was idle?"

"Idle is your middle name. I s'pose Tennian blabbed that Artur was coming."

"Tennian?" Thomas looked puzzled. "I haven't seen her since dinner last night."

"What are you talking about? Aren't you staying with her? Or she with you? Or however you guys worked out the details? Are you shacked up in the URV, or what?"

"What are you talking about?"

"You know what? Never mind, I don't want to know."

Thomas was looking more and more mystified. "Fred, what the hell are you babbling about? Tennian and I are just friends."

"I don't babble, and what the hell are *you* babbling about? You guys sailed off together last fall to live happily ever after."

Thomas laughed at her. "The hell we did! I mean, we went off together, but I went with her first strictly as her doctor—she *was* shot, you'll recall."

"Well, she *did* board a pirate ship."

"True," he admitted.

"And you two were making goo-goo eyes at each other."

"No, we weren't."

"I was there!"

"I'm really fond of her, okay? I thought—think—she's a fascinating individual. But I was never in love with her."

Fred tried to digest this, but he wouldn't stop talking, so it was a lot to take in.

"And don't forget about the new book I've been working on."

"*Love in the Time of Fish?*"

"*The Anatomy and Physiology of Homo Nautilus.*"

"Oh," Fred said. "That." Luckily, this time she managed not to go off into gales of humiliating laughter when he told her.

And he was *still talking*. "So far as I know, I'm the only doctor on the planet who's treated surface dwellers *and* Undersea Folk. You should do it, too, Fred."

She was having major trouble tracking the conversation. "What?"

"Write a book. You could write your life story—or at least, a book about the Undersea Folk. Or best of all, a book about the Undersea Folk through the eyes of the only hybrid on the planet. It'd sell in about two seconds. You'd be a bestselling author!"

"I've got enough fame, thanks. But about you and Tennian—"

"Well, like I said, Tennian's been a big help with my book. And to pay me back for taking care of her, she showed me some unbelievable things."

"I'll bet."

He ignored the jibe. "I mean, just knowing you, I thought I'd seen things, but she—" He shook his head. "You know, you really need to get over to the Black Sea and see all the underwater castles. Thanks to the URV, the pressure didn't squash me like a caterpillar."

The URV—Underwater RV—was the submarine Thomas had had built eighteen months ago . . . it had allowed him to observe various Undersea Folk gatherings. It was also ridiculously comfortable, tricked out with a kitchen and a bedroom, among other things.

"So you broke up?" Fred said through numb lips.

"What, broke up? We were never dating."

Fred did her famous impersonation of a goldfish; her mouth popped open, then closed, then popped open again. Her thoughts, chaotic enough this week, were whirling.

Stop the roller coaster, I want to get off!

Why hadn't he—why had she assumed—what did this mean for her relationship with Artur—why hadn't she known this before Artur proposed—why had she so stupidly jumped to conclusions—why why why ?

"Are you all right?" Thomas asked, polishing off the last beer. "You look a little green. Even for you."

"It's just—it's just that kind of week," she managed, thinking, *He must never, never know what I assumed, or what I hoped, or the effect his little announcement had on me. Never.*

If he really loved her, he wouldn't keep going off on months-long trips. If he really loved her, he would have stayed in touch while he was in Scotland, the Black Sea, wherever.

And that was fine . . . he had never promised her a damned thing. But it was clear to her now what her answer to Artur must be.

Twenty-three

Later that night, Fred sat quietly on the couch, pretending to read about herself in *Time.* Around her, the bustle of an impromptu dinner party went on. And on.

Her mother and Sam had come back with groceries, and once again Thomas was manning the grill. Jonas had returned with a catalogue of tuxes, the one he'd chosen clearly marked. Black tuxedo, red cummerbund, yak-yak-yak. He'd also informed her she would be trying on bridesmaid dresses the next day at ten.

And the hell marches on . . .

Dr. Barb, Jonas's fiancée and Fred's (former?) boss at the New England Aquarium, was also at the house. She had arrived promptly at four, refused both a written and verbal resignation, then pretended she wasn't dying for Fred to shift to her tail.

Fred had given in, diving into the deep end of the pool and shifting to tail form more or less without thought. There was a method to her madness; she'd tried to resign yet again while Dr. Barb was fairly dazzled, and it hadn't worked. Yet again.

"Dr. Bimm, if I may—" Dr. Barb was always perfectly polite, even squatting beside a pool dressed in madras shorts and a white button-down, talking to a mermaid. "How do you breathe underwater? Do you have internal gills? And if so, do they—"

"No. I just pull oxygen from the water through my cells. I hold my breath, of course, but I still get plenty of air, so to speak."

"But you don't know for sure?"

"Well, I've never seen a post on a fellow Undersea Folk, so I couldn't say for sure . . ."

"But, Dr. Bimm, you're a marine biologist."

"Really? I forgot all about that. So that's what that diploma is for . . ."

"Surely you're curious about your own . . . ah . . . unique physiology. Blood tests at the very least could . . ."

"I didn't want to call attention to myself in college. Or grad school. Or anywhere," she said shortly, and that was the end of that. At least, Dr. Barb was too polite to bug her further.

But Fred knew the real reason she, an alleged scientist, knew so little about her own body: she had been a freak all her life. She had no interest in running tests that confirmed her freakishness. She wanted to blend, not call attention to herself. (How annoying to find that hair dye never took; it washed out the moment she grew her tail . . . thus, cursed with green freak hair.) Ignorance, at least in this one case, was bliss.

Well. Cowardice, really. But dammit, she was fine with that. She'd had a loaded gun in her face, for Christ's sake. She'd been *shot*, even. She was entitled to be a coward in the minor area of her extreme freakish appearance.

Now, Dr. Barb and Jonas were snuggling at the dining-room table and tossing the salad. Or snuggling the salad and tossing each other; Fred was careful not to look too closely. The scenes she'd walked in on starring the two of them . . . *yurrgh*.

And now what the hell was this? There was a funny sound reverberating through the house. Fred looked up from reading about herself

("That's the dumbest question you've asked so far.")

and listened, puzzled. It sounded both familiar and strange at the same time. She'd heard that sound before in her life, but under which circumstances? So hauntingly familiar . . . it was on the tip of her tongue . . . it was . . . was . . .

The doorbell!

No wonder she couldn't place the sound, she thought as she got up to answer it. Nobody ever used it! Most of them didn't even knock.

"Someone's at the door!" Jonas yelled, showing Moon a picture of his tux.

"I've got it," she called back. She opened it and saw Tennian standing with another Undersea Folk. This new mermaid had such striking coloring, she made Tennian seem almost drab: waist-length, deep purple hair, and eyes the color of wet violets. Pale skin, almost milky—the complexion of an Irish milkmaid, with the faintest blush at her cheeks. She came up to Fred's shoulder and was, without question, the most beautiful woman Fred had ever seen.

"Whoa," she managed before she could stop herself.

"Good evening, Fredrika Bimm. This is my friend Wennd."

Wennd said nothing, merely bowed her head in greeting.

"Well, hi. What brings you two here?"

Wennd shot an anxious glance at Tennian, who said, "Wennd is really very curious about surface dwellers. But word of what happened to me has spread and she's somewhat . . . apprehensive. I was hoping you would perhaps introduce her to your friends and family, who are really very nice surface dwellers and won't shoot anyone."

"Probably," Fred said. "You sure, Wennd? Haven't you heard? I come from a short, undistinguished line of traitors."

Wennd's gorgeous purple eyes widened. "That was your sire. Not you."

Fred knew, then, that Wennd was young. So damned hard to tell with these guys; she could have been twenty or fifty. She'd noticed the real grudge holders were the ones who had been around during her father's disastrous attempt at a coup. But the younger generation . . . the ones who hadn't had to fight, hadn't had to choose sides . . .

"Sure," she said, stepping back. "Come on in. This place is crawling with unwanted g—uh, surface dwellers."

Twenty-four

Fred led the two women into the main dining area. "Guys? Guys! Jonas, put that catalogue away before I make you eat it. Thomas, the grill can wait for ten seconds. Sam, we're out of beer so stop looking."

"But you should take another look at the tux so when you try on—"

"But the temp on the grill is just right, I need to put the burgers—"

"How can you possibly be out of beer?"

"*Guys.* Most of you already know Tennian. This is her friend Wennd. She thinks surface dwellers are dangerous sociopaths and I admit, I couldn't think of much to say in our defense."

"I didn't say that exactly," Wennd almost whispered. Even her voice was beautiful, tinkly and sweet. Fred was ready to smack her. It was positively sickening when one person got every single fabulous attribute available. Probably a tomcat in the sack, too. "It's quite nice to meet you all."

Jonas and Thomas managed to close their mouths long enough to shake her forearm, the traditional greeting for Undersea Folk. Moon gently bullied her into having a seat at the table, and Sam offered her a large glass of water . . . the beverage of choice for most Undersea Folk, who got terribly thirsty after being out of the water for any length of time.

Out of all the men, he was the only one not staring at the beauty.

This surprised Fred not at all. Sam had never, ever looked at another woman since he'd hooked up with Moon. It was touching, yet creepy.

"So where are you from, Wennd, dear?" Moon asked.

"I live in the Indian Ocean, mostly," Wennd whispered.

"Oh! That's . . . er . . ."

"Third largest ocean in the world, Mom," Fred said. "North border, Asia."

"West border," Thomas piped up, not to be outflanked, "Africa, bordered on the east by Indochina, the Sunda—"

"—Islands and Australia," Fred finished triumphantly. "How about *that*?"

"Wow," Jonas said. "It's the Battle o' the Geeks. I think I nodded off around Indochina."

"But I already know those things," Wennd practically whispered. Fred felt like giving her a megaphone.

"She was enlightening *me*, dear." Moon laughed. "Geography was never my strong point."

"So what brings you here?" Jonas asked.

Wennd looked around cautiously, then replied, "As you all seem to have the ear of the king or the prince, I will guess it is all right to confide. I was one of the citizens the king asked to come here."

"Right!" Thomas snapped his fingers. "To preserve the illusion that your headquarters are here, not the Black Sea."

"Yes, Dr. Pearson, that is correct."

"How'd you know my—"

"Tennian described all of you."

"No doubt," Fred muttered. A thought struck her: "The illusion is working great. You know, other than Artur and King Mekkam, I don't think I've met anyone who lives in the Black Sea, where the real castles are."

"Well, who's fault is that, Miss I Haven't Made Up My Mind?" Jonas said. "You marry Artur and you'll probably be there in forty-eight hours."

"Doubtful," Fred said. "I can't swim as fast as he can."

"Yeah, but *you* have frequent flyer miles."

Fred snickered. *Good one.*

"You will join us for dinner," Moon said, pretending it was a question. Wennd must have had a mom much like Moon, because she didn't even try to demur.

"Hello," Dr. Barb said. She'd been gaping at the violet-haired mermaid during the entire discussion. "I'm Dr. Barbara Robinson. I run the New England Aquarium. May I ask a personal question about your species?"

"Yes."

"Does your coloring run in your family? Or is it natural to, say, a country of Undersea Folk?"

Wennd's big eyes widened. "Do you mean, does my mother have purple hair, or does everyone who lives in the Indian Ocean have purple hair?"

"Yes, it's a matter of—"

But Dr. Barb had to quit, because Wennd had burst into a loud, honking laugh. It was such a contrast to her shy demeanor and whispery voice, half the room flinched. She sounded like a Canadian goose chasing away a predator.

"So . . . no?" Sam asked.

Wennd was actually clutching her stomach and honking away.

"Wennd," Tennian said reproachfully. "Please don't laugh at my friends."

"Why not?" Fred asked. "I do it all the time."

"I beg your pardon," Wennd gasped. "I am so sorry. Truly. I just—does everyone in the American state of Florida have yellow hair and blue eyes? Because they are in proximity with each other?"

"Point," Jonas admitted. "Or assuming that if your mom is a redhead, everyone she's related to would be, too." Pause. Blond Jonas added, "*My* mom's a redhead."

Thomas was spinning the spatula in his grip like it was a six-shooter. "Hamburger or hot dog?"

"Just more water, if you please." When Moon opened her mouth to bully Wennd into eating, the mermaid added, "Tennian and I ran into a bull shark on the way here. I'm really not hungry at all."

"You two took on a *bull*? By yourselves?" Thomas looked horrified and Fred couldn't blame the ignorant sap. He still didn't comprehend how strong, fast, and predatory full-blooded Undersea Folk were. "Tell me it was a baby. Or an immature female. Or—"

"It was a male, about—what? Six feet? Two hundred pounds?"

Moon's and Sam's eyes were big with admiration; Jonas yawned. He'd seen Fred fight off a school of barracuda with no trouble at all when they were freshmen in high school (Moon had treated them to spring break in the Bahamas that March).

"But Jesus! They're so aggressive! Not to mention unpredictable. You do know that because they can tolerate shallows, and fresh water, that they're probably more dangerous to humans than great whites?"

"Thomas," Tennian said gently, "we're not human."

A short, embarrassed silence. Fred hid a smile and thought, *More Homo sapiens arrogance. Or is it chauvinism?*

"You are kind to be so concerned for our welfare," Wennd said, giving him a dazzling smile in which there were about a hundred razor-sharp teeth. At least, that's what it looked like. "We were perfectly fine. Not so much as a scratch on either of us."

"*That's* the stuff you should be telling *Time* and *Us Weekly*," Jonas said. "'Gorgeous mermaids eat giant shark and live to tell the tale.' Get it? Tale?"

"They're too busy asking me about my freak hair," Fred said irritably. "And do you really want PETA and Greenpeace weighing in? They'll decide Undersea Folk are abusing natural resources and exploiting sharks and smoking kelp or what have you."

"You were right," Wennd said to Tennian. "She *is* wise."

This time, everyone was laughing—except for Fred, who glared.

"I just know a few things about fanatical surface dwellers," Fred said defensively. "That's all."

"So how did you arrive? Migrate? Whatever," Thomas asked. "It's not like the Indian Ocean is just a hop and a skip away from the Gulf."

Wennd gradually lost her nervousness and, as she talked with Thomas and even followed him outside to observe the grilling process, chatted amiably about her migratory habits, among other things.

Fred watched them getting along like super swell pals, wishing she didn't care and remembering wishing never helped anyone.

I've got to put him out of my head, is all. If he really loved me, he wouldn't keep chasing other mermaids. And if I really loved him, I wouldn't tolerate it. Or, at least I'd tell *him I loved him.*

But, oh, that felt like such a lie.

One thing was certain. If she married Artur, she could focus on an entirely new life. A fresh start . . . and she'd see to it that Moon could visit whenever she wanted. Shit, *she* would visit *Moon* whenever Moon wanted. Marrying the prince of the Undersea Folk didn't mean she had to turn her back on her life. It was just time for something new. That was all.

And why did that feel like another lie?

Twenty-five

Fred dove off the dock, automatically shifted to her tail, and went in search of lunch.

This was always accomplished quite easily. Although she was allergic to fish and shellfish, the ocean teemed with probably five times the plant life that dry land had. And she liked how quite a bit of it tasted. More than once she thought she should have gone into botany, because it would have been nice to know more about different underwater plants . . .

Time to mull that over later. She wanted to eat, and then she wanted to find Artur and tell him yes.

She found an underwater meadow and pulled up some stalks and leaves. They tasted mildly salty, almost bland (as opposed to some types of seaweed that fairly burst with flavor), and she ate until she felt about as svelte as a manatee.

Artur, she had been told, was in yet another meeting with his father, King Mekkam. Having thousands of their subjects "come out," so to speak, must require a lot of jawing back and forth between the king and his heir. But she knew he would head to her house when he finished and hoped to intercept him underwater, where they'd have a bit of privacy.

And behold! As though the thought had conjured him like a genie out of a bottle, here he came, swimming steadily toward her, his expression fixed in a worried frown.

Hi, Artur.

He kept swimming. He was less than fifteen yards away. What on earth could he be thinking about? Not that she thought she was a raving beauty or a phenomenal intellect, but he *had* made it clear he wanted her for his wife and wasn't interested in taking no for an answer.

In fact, she was used to fending him off, not seeking him out. Could this week get any more fucked up?

Artur! Hey!

He blinked, saw her, and smiled. *Ho, Little Rika. It pleases me to see you waiting for me.*

Eh, don't flatter yourself, I was hungry and my house is full of uninvited guests. Also, I walked in on Jonas and Dr. Barb doing it on my living-room carpet this morning. What a way to wake up! I had to Clorox my eyes.

Your life is difficult, Little Rika. The words were right, but she could feel he was only half listening.

She turned as he passed her and they swam in silence, side by side, for a few seconds. Then:

I wanted to let you know I've decided.

Hmmmm?

Oh, this was not happening. She'd been fretting and wondering and agonizing, practically, and now she was going to give him what she assumed was going to be the best news of his life (and yes, she was aware of how conceited that was) and he was barely paying attention.

What had her father said? *O irony, how she makes slaves of us all.* Well, that was pretty damned close to the truth, wasn't it? That'll teach her to assume a man's just hanging around waiting for her to deign to marry him.

Artur, don't take this the wrong way, but will you snap the hell out of it? I'm trying to have a conversation!

He slowed and circled her, tail flexing powerfully, muscled arms behind his back. *I beg your leave, my Rika. My father and I have a problem . . . we think.*

Well, lay it on me. Maybe I can help.

He smiled at her. *For one who professes anger and irritation much of the time, you do a fine job hiding your generous nature.*

Flattery will get you, et cetera. She reached out and snatched at the base of his tail and managed to hang on—just. God, he was strong! She shook it, trying to get his full attention. *What's wrong?*

He instantly spun away and started heading back out to open sea; she managed to hang on—barely—to his back fins. She felt like a water-skier being hauled behind a speedboat with a jet engine.

My good father has noticed the disappearance of several of our people.

Really? You mean, they were supposed to be here pretending this was HQ, and they never showed? Or—

Yes. That, and my father has simply lost contact with some of our people.

Fred mulled that one over, still hanging on to Artur's tail for dear life. Fish flashed by so quickly she couldn't identify the phylum, never mind the specific class.

She had discovered last year that Mekkam, as king, was the most powerful telepath of his people (in fact, the greatest telepaths were all members of the royal family . . . and her father had tried his coup in part because he was extraordinarily gifted in that area as well).

Mekkam could be in contact with any one of his subjects at any time. He could project his thoughts to *all* his subjects at any time. And, like all purebred Undersea Folk, his telepathy was just as powerful on land as it was beneath waves.

So it made sense that, if Undersea Folk were disappearing, he would be the first to notice.

Thus, all the frequent and secret meetings, she mused.

Indeed, Artur thought soberly.

Does he think they're dead? she worried.

We cannot be sure, which is why this matter is so troubling. Usually, when one of us dies, my father can feel their death throes. He has felt none. Only—only—a blank silence where once there was a vibrant mind.

Jesus. She mulled that one over, troubled. *That's fairly sobering.*

Indeed.

So what's the plan?

We do not know.

That sucks. Maybe it's nothing. Maybe your dad's, uh . . . She coughed, sending up a stream of bubbles . . . *getting old.*

Our telepathy gets stronger as we age. Not weaker.

That ruled out her theory of Undersea Folk Alzheimer's.

And her mind seized upon the fact he had so casually dropped: they get stronger? Stronger as they age? What other species on the planet got *more* powerful as they aged? She had to stifle the urge to kidnap Mekkam and do experiments on him.

Then a nasty thought hit her. *You don't think my father's up to his old tricks, do you?*

Silence.

Well. Do you?

Twenty-six

It seemed a long, long time before his answer came, and when it did, it was full of reluctance. *It has been suggested.*

Oh, that was subtle. Since Artur and Mekkam were the only ones in these super secret meetings, one of them had "suggested" it. Tricky, tricky, Artur.

Well. I guess I can't blame you. But he's only been here for a couple of days. How long have people been disappearing?

For half a year.

There you go. My dad's been too busy skulking in banishment to be disappearing unsuspecting Undersea Folk. Doncha think? Plus, he's been on land for most of the last thirty years. Hardly in a position to be ambushing unsuspecting mermaids.

There is another theory. Now Artur's reluctance was coming through so heavily, she could practically feel it crawling across her brain. *Perhaps . . . perhaps soldiers of the planet's land countries have been . . . doing things. Secret things.*

Okay. That's not altogether implausible, she admitted. Hell, she'd warned them, hadn't she? Her mother's species, in their own way, were even more bloodthirsty than Undersea Folk. At least the UF only killed to feed themselves or defend themselves. The same, unfortunately, could not be said for Homo sapiens.

I am relieved my theory has given no offense.

Tough to be offended by the truth . . . at least, this time. Frankly, it's pretty plausible that, I dunno, some secret government agency has been stealing Undersea Folk and doing experiments on them. How can we check it out?

I was hoping your friend Thomas might be of assistance.

How could he— She trailed off. Because of his money? No. Artur had tons of it. Because of his education? No. Fred was technically Artur's subject (though she'd eat a pound of sushi before bowing or referring to him as "my prince" or any of that other nonsense . . . she was an American, dammit!), and her background was as extensive as Thomas's . . . He didn't have to seek out a surface dweller. Then what—

It hit her. *His dad.*

Yes.

Thomas had been a navy brat. His father was some high-up mucky-muck in the U.S. Navy.

Do you think he would assist us?

Let's ask him.

Artur abruptly stopped swimming, but Fred's forward momentum shot her past his tail and into his arms.

I was mightily pleased to see you waiting for me.

And I was mightily pleased to have a fraction of your attention.

Only my father's displeasure and the welfare of my people could blot you from my mind for the merest instant!

Daddy's boy.

Laughter. Laughter in her head. And with his arms around her, with that rollicking laughter echoing through her brain, she said before she could chicken out, *I've been thinking about it. I'll do it.*

Do what? he teased. *Insult my mighty intelligence? Throw Jonas into the pool yet again? Be disrespectful to your people's newsmakers?*

Reporters, she corrected automatically.

More laughter in her head. *Oh, no, you don't, Little Rika! I have watched much television. When there is no news, your "reporters" make the news.*

Can we debate the merits of modern journalism any other time but now? And no, numb fins, none of the above. What I meant was, I'll marry you. I'll be your wife.

Oh, Rika! He hugged her so hard that, if she'd had to breathe, she would have been in serious trouble. *Truly, you have made me the happiest man in the seas! Now, without doubt, you are she-who-will-be-my-wife.*

She snuggled into his embrace, hoping he wasn't cracking her ribs. *You know, for a bunch of telepaths, you've got a remarkably bloated language. Try fiancée. Fee-on-say.*

It matters not, he said, and kissed her four miles out in the Gulf, forty feet below the waves, her green hair fanning out like an undeserved halo. Their hair was entwined, their arms were around each other, they were hungrily exploring each other's mouths, and Fred could feel the kiss all the way to the bottom of her tail.

There, she thought. That's settled.

Okay. Back to business.

Twenty-seven

"Awesome!" Jonas screamed, badly startling the saleswoman. "Princess Fred! Ohmigod! I can't stand it!"

"I can't stand it, either. Stop yelling." Fred, standing in front of the full-length mirror, scowled at her reflection. The dress was salmon-colored, had a mermaid skirt (doubtless Jonas's idea of a subtle joke) and a low-cut bodice and beading on the sleeves, and it clashed horribly with her hair. Odd. Jonas usually had much better taste than this. "And I'll bite your ears off if you make me buy this one."

"It wouldn't be in *that* color. Be serious. I told you: apple red. Dr. Barb's sister and cousin and you are all wearing apple red. Just like my tie and cummerbund are apple red—don't you remember?"

"No."

"Oh, look who I'm talking to."

She nodded in agreement. The small bridal shop was jammed with dresses of every size, shape, and color. An entire wall was devoted to white satin shoes. Another wall: clutch handbags in every style and color you could imagine. Playing over the speakers: *Trumpet Voluntary.* Well, that part wasn't so bad.

"So! When should I throw the party?"

"Party?" She had disappeared back into the dressing room to try on dress number four. She couldn't get dress number three off fast enough—she thought she heard a seam tear. Fuck it. "What party?"

"Your engagement party, dumbass! Let's see . . . we should probably have it at your rental house, since it's the—"

Fred groaned. Slipped number four over her head. Hmm. This one didn't entirely suck.

She stepped out. "Forget it. Artur and I have some Undersea Folk junk to look into. After the dust clears you can throw your stupid party."

"And don't forget, I'm planning your wedding."

"I wouldn't have it any other way," she said with complete and total sincerity.

"Now *that's* not bad," Jonas said, eyeing her up and down critically. She knew his taste was quite a bit better than hers and was happy to follow (fashion-wise) where he led. But she couldn't help agreeing. Strapless, with a tight-fitting bodice. A-line, with the skirt falling straight to the floor, just past her ankles. And the color was right: apple red. It made her hair seem even greener, almost the color of pine trees. And her eyes—the color did wonderful things to her eyes!

"We're done," Jonas told the saleslady. Then, to Fred, "See, see? Not even half an hour. You should trust me more often."

"I'm still digesting cake, you awful man. Never," she vowed, popping back into the dressing room to get back into her shorts, ratty T-shirt, and flip-flops.

"Behold," Jonas said mockingly as she stepped out. "The future queen of the Undersea Folk. At least they won't care if you don't wear a bra in the Black Sea."

"I hate bras," she muttered and stomped toward the front of the store to pay for the damned dress.

Twenty-eight

Thomas had left a note saying he was meeting some colleagues at the Florida Aquarium in Tampa Bay. Fred suggested to Artur that she drive them there and he readily agreed.

That was how she found out Artur hated being closed up in automobiles.

"For God's sake," she said, amazed, "you're perfectly safe."

Artur had his legs drawn up under his chin. His seat belt was tightened to the point of asphyxiation. He was trying not to huddle and failing. "All these metal boxes, hurtling by at ridiculous speeds. Madness, madness."

"You've never been in a car before?" She was dumbfounded. Then remembered this was a merman who lived at the bottom of the Black Sea. Okay. Not such a ridiculous idea, but still . . .

"No. I was on a train, once . . . in Boston. There was more room on the train. I could walk around on the train, although the king of the train did not like that."

She managed not to groan. "Don't tell me. You're claustrophobic."

"I don't know that term," he said, and she didn't think he'd ever been so white before.

"It means that you don't like small, enclosed spaces, um, mighty prince who conquers worlds and women with green hair."

He laughed hollowly, then cringed when a semi zipped by them, blaring its air horn. Fred flipped the driver the bird with both hands.

"Keep your hands on the steering device!"

"It's fine, see? I'm steering with my knee."

"Please don't," he moaned.

"Artur, for God's sake. You've taken on pirates, great whites, survived a coup, and you're marrying me. I can't believe you're scared of anything, much less being in a car."

"I am not scared! I am . . . cautious."

She snorted. "Look, here's the exit. We're almost there, so don't pee your shorts just yet."

"You will show me the nearest body of water when we leave this place. I will swim back. You should join me."

"And abandon my rental car? Forget it. Think of the paperwork!"

"Paperwork?"

"I signed a contract," she said solemnly, trying not to laugh at him. "It's a very serious thing among surface dwellers, you know. Rental-car contracts."

"I know of contracts. I would not want you to break your word. That would not befit my princess."

"And it would wreck my credit rating, too."

They pulled into the parking lot, picked up their visitor passes from a ticket seller, and went looking for Thomas.

Artur cheered up considerably once he was out of the compact car, and eyed the exhibits with great interest.

"Cheer up, brothers," he said softly, standing in front of an exhibit of manta rays. "You are safe here and well fed. Were you free, you would be meat."

"Stop talking to the rays," Fred muttered, noticing the odd looks they were getting. She absolutely did not, *did not*, want to be recognized today. She and Artur had urgent business with Thomas. The business of her people.

My people, she mused. *Huh. Always before I've said my father's people. But they're just as much mine. Why didn't I see that before? Too busy hiding from myself, I guess. Poor Artur has no idea he's marrying a coward.*

"I could not help it," he said, sounding wounded. "They spoke to me first. Besides, you cannot speak to them on land, so it seemed rude to indulge in an ability you do not share."

Fred raised her eyebrows. That had come up before, her lack of telepathy on land. Artur had been almost embarrassed when he'd realized it. Was that going to be a problem for them?

She'd worry about it later, and for now led him away from the exhibit. She thought she heard someone say her name and she turned. But Thomas wasn't there.

They continued their search, separating so Artur could have a good long drink at the water fountain while Fred continued looking, eventually finding herself standing at the top of Shark Bay.

She peered in and saw sand tiger sharks, blacktips, zebra sharks. An impressively large sea turtle. Lionfish—big-time poisonous. Triggerfish. Dragon moray eels. Jellies. It really was—

"It's you! You're that mermaid I saw on TV!"

Stifling a groan, Fred turned. Several teenagers were standing behind her, all with gaping jaws and reeking of Stridex. "Hi," she said.

"Ohmigod! This is, like, rilly, rilly cool," one of the girls said, chewing a piece of gum roughly the size of her fist. "Like, you're a mermaid 'n' stuff! Cool!"

Fred mentally groaned. The girl sounded awfully like Madison, the twit intern at the New England Aquarium. An hour with Madison felt like a week; a week felt like a century. And Madison wore pink. Every day.

Even if she hadn't needed to spend her time as a press liaison, never having to lay eyes on Madison again would have been reason enough to quit her job.

"Ohmigod, it's really you!"

"Yeah, it is, but I can't really talk right—"

They were getting closer, pattering her with inane questions, and she automatically backed up.

"—how do you have sex with a tail?"

"—true your mom isn't a mermaid, so you're, like, both?"

"—howcum all the mermaids are rilly, rilly hot? It doesn't make sense. You mean there's not one fugly mermaid in the whole world? Not *one*?"

"Apparently not," one of the boys said, "and it's awesome!"

"Hey!" she snapped, feeling her thighs touch the rim at the top of the shark tank. "Back off, annoying adolescents, like that's not redundant."

But just then, worse luck, a classroom of teeming third graders (she guessed, given their height and general grubbiness) burst onto the floor, pushing into the teenagers, who in turn pushed into Fred.

Who in turn toppled backward and fell into Shark Bay with a most undignified splash.

Twenty-nine

Getting oxygen was no problem, of course, but she couldn't swim without her tail. She couldn't even dog-paddle. She was as graceless in the water with legs as a penguin was on land.

So she flailed and wriggled and found herself upside down and batted aside the sea turtle and in general thrashed about like a dying seal.

She could see them.

She could see them *looking* at her, their noses pressed against the glass, their mouths open as they jabbered excitedly.

And damned if she was going to shift to her tail in front of a bunch of Florida tourists. She wasn't a goddamned sideshow freak. She'd prefer the humiliation of graceless thrashing to giving the tourists a better show than Slappy the Seal.

She heard the hollow boom of water being displaced several feet above her head—someone diving into the tank. Ah, the final humiliation . . . rescued by a staff member and then hustled off the property by security. Must be Tuesday.

A strong hand seized her by the bicep and she felt herself being pulled toward the surface. She kicked, trying to help, and nearly got stung by a lionfish for her trouble. She had no idea if she was immune to their venom, so that was the end of the kicking.

They broke the surface and her rescuer took a deep breath.

"Hi, Thomas." She wiped limp green hair out of her eyes. No, that was seaweed. Yech. She tossed it behind her. "I've been looking everywhere for you."

He grinned at her and she noticed he hadn't taken off any of his clothes, just jumped in after her. "You thought I was in the shark tank? Come on."

He climbed up the ladder, stretched down a hand, and hauled her out of the tank.

Everyone was *looking.*

"Please," Fred said, and to her horror, she was near tears. "Please make them go away."

And she sank to the floor, miserable and drenched, and Thomas signaled someone and held her while the top of the tank was cleared of tourists.

Thirty

"Little Rika, what in the name of the king . . . ?"

She was still huddled in Thomas's arms like some pathetic romance-novel heroine, but the threatening tears had abated. Now all she wanted was a towel and a Cobb salad. Oh, and to pretend that the last five minutes hadn't happened.

Meanwhile, Artur was standing over them, hands on his hips, looking astonished and worried.

"What did you do?" he asked again.

"I fell in."

Artur squatted beside her and Thomas. "Clearly. But why in the world did you need Dr. Pearson to help you?"

Fred said nothing. She liked Artur fine, and was more than a little horny for him, and was looking forward to

(running away)

starting a new life in the Black Sea with him. But she couldn't tell him. He would never, ever understand. No one would ever under—

"Are you kidding?" Thomas snapped. "D'you think she wanted to nude up and shift to her tail in front of two hundred gaping tourists? Bad enough she can't go anywhere without being bugged. She's not a goddamned exhibit."

Aw, rats. Here came the tears again . . . tears of sheer gratitude. She would have done anything for him then.

Anything at all.

"You are wrong." Artur's face—his expression bothered her—

annoyed and disbelieving and something else, something she could almost put her finger on, something like

(shame)

embarrassment. For him? Or for her?

"You are wrong. My Rika cares not at all about what strangers think."

"He's right," she said quietly. "Thomas is, I mean. I didn't want to do that. Change in front of everybody."

Artur's brow furrowed. "But—but, Rika, why? Surely you're not shamed by your beautiful breasts and tail. Although," he added thoughtfully, "the nudity taboo surface dwellers insist on could be problematic, in addition to being quite silly. But you need not keep your hybrid nature a secret . . . Why, much of the country knows!"

"Look, I'm not a circus act, okay? They were all staring. I hate being stared at."

"I do not understand," he said flatly, mouth a grim slash. "It is not behavior that becomes one of the royal family."

"Well," she said. "I guess you're wrong about that one."

"Your behavior is senseless."

"Oh, shut your piehole, Artur!" she snapped, straightening. She realized that Thomas had been holding her the entire time Artur had been nagging her. The big lug didn't mind *that*, oh, no. But her tail shyness, that was the big problem.

For the first time, she truly understood the chasm that lay between her upbringing and his.

"I do not know what that means," he said flatly.

"It means get off my back. You're not the one being stopped on the street damned near every day. You're not the one who has to talk to insipid reporters every week. You're not the one on the cover of the *National Enquirer* with the so-flattering headline, 'Freak Mermaid Pregnant with Alien Baby.'"

"But you agreed to all this."

"I know! But sometimes it's a little much, that's all. You don't have to act like I stuck a knife into the worldwide morale of Undersea Folk."

"Uh, guys?" Thomas cleared his throat. "Listen, sorry to interrupt, but why don't we go somewhere a little more private? You said you needed to talk to me about a big problem with the Undersea Folk?"

Artur and Fred glared at each other for a few more charged seconds, then Artur cut his glance away and said, "You are correct, Thomas. We require your help."

"Aw." Thomas beamed. "The Team Supreme, together again."

"Let's hope nobody gets shot this time," Fred said sourly.

Thirty-one

"What do you mean, disappearing? They're not showing up where they're supposed to, or dead bodies are showing up, or what?"

Thomas had asked, very politely, if he could introduce her to his colleagues at the aquarium, and she had agreed. They seemed pleasant and professional, if a little wide-eyed, and asked no weird or deeply personal questions. For marine biologists face-to-face with a mermaid, Fred admired their self-control. She doubted she would have been able to equal it.

And then, after handshakes all around (and a formal presentation of a lifetime pass to the Florida Aquarium . . . Fred imagined it was their equivalent to the key to the city), they graciously withdrew, and the director said they could use her office, which is where they were now.

Artur was answering Thomas's question, and thank goodness, because Fred had forgotten what it was, so busy was she studying her lifetime aquarium pass (laminated!).

"My father cannot find them. They have disappeared from his mind."

"Bummer," Thomas commented. Fred knew he wasn't being flip. At least, he didn't *mean* to be flip. He just had no idea how to process the information at this time, but still felt he had to contribute to the conversation. "I know your dad's a pretty powerful telepath—"

"The most powerful," Artur corrected, not without pride. "It is that to be king. I, the heir apparent, am second most powerful."

"Whoa, wait," Fred interrupted. "So how come you didn't notice any of this?"

"Second powerful is still much less powerful than my good father," Artur explained. "He is much, much older than I."

Fred nodded. Artur, though he didn't look it, was in his early fifties . . . fully two decades older than she was. Mekkam was over a hundred.

"Okay, so that answers that. Is it possible a bunch of them got—I don't know, the Undersea Folk equivalent of the bubonic plague and died all at once?"

Artur was already shaking his head. "No, Thomas. Were they dying, my king would feel it. They are simply . . . vanishing from his mind. Where once he could sense a vibrant, living being, there is now only silence."

"How many?"

"Four hundred seventy-eight."

Fred met Thomas's dismayed gaze and felt a similar expression on her own face. Almost five hundred! In less than a year!

"What—what do you want me to do? How can I help?"

Artur smiled for the first time in a long, long day. "Thomas, my people have a saying: we are made stronger by the honor our opponents hold. And at this moment you have made me strong indeed. We *do* need your help. We were hoping you might get in touch with your sire."

"Dad?" Thomas frowned, and then his dark eyes lit up. "Right!

Navy Intelligence. You think the government's being sneaky, don't you?"

Artur looked at the floor, unwilling to offend a former opponent whom he had always respected. Fred had no such compunctions. "It's happened before, Thomas. It's been happening since there *was* a government."

Thomas ran a hand through his shaggy dark hair and nodded. "Yep, can't deny that one. Well, Dad's been retired, but he still holds the rank of captain. And he's got a whole bunch of buddies still on active duty. I'll call him right now." Thomas laughed. "He'll be thrilled his sissy son needs his help."

Fred's mouth fell open. "Whaaaaat? The captain thinks Switchblade Pearson is a sissy?"

"I didn't go into the military," he said simply.

"I regret asking you to do anything that will put any strain on your relationship with your sire."

"Forget about it, Artur. This is a shitload more important than Dad and me."

"I thank you."

"But you're a doctor," Fred said, dumbfounded. "And a Ph.D.! And you've got street smarts and you designed the URV and you're a bestselling author and—sissy?"

Thomas grinned. "Bestselling *romance* author, don't forget."

Fred made a mental note to slug Captain Pearson when she met him. Who *wouldn't* want their kid to be so brilliant he could turn his back on medicine and study an entirely new field? And kick-ass in *both* fields? Military-minded moron.

"Well, thanks. Should we go to him, or will he come down here?"

"I happen to know that since retirement he's been bored out of his tits."

"Pardon?" Artur asked.

"Never mind. He'll come down here. He'll pretend it's a huge inconvenience, but he'll be here. And then I guess we'll try to get to the bottom of this." Thomas lost his habitual wiseass expression and sobered. "I hope your people aren't dead, Artur. I'll do everything I can to help you find them."

They shook hands, surface dweller–style.

Thirty-two

Later, Fred was sitting thoughtfully by the pool. The sun had gone down about an hour ago and she had a lot to think about. Thank goodness she finally had a little bit of—

"Okay, that's enough sulking, Fish Face. What's the matter?"

Jonas. Of course. Her mouth said, "Die painfully, Jonas, and preferably quietly." Her mind said, *Thank God. I really need to talk to him. He'll understand and he'll tease me and he won't judge and then I'll feel better. God, if you're paying any attention at all up there, thank you so much for dropping Jonas in my life when we were in elementary school.*

"C'mon," he was coaxing. "Spill."

"Don't you have bouquets to sniff or china to pick out?"

"Done and done . . . Barb and I registered today. Feel free to buy us many grossly expensive gifts at Macy's, Crate and Barrel, and Tar-jhay."

"It's Target, numb wad, and I've got up until a year after the wedding to cough up a gift."

"You *did* read that copy of Miss Manners I left in your room!"

"Shut up." She sighed, cupping her chin in her hand. She was sitting on a lawn chair and staring into the pool. "Something bad happened today."

"You wore white after Labor Day?"

"Hilarious. I fell into the shark tank at the aquarium."

Jonas coughed, except it sounded oddly like a muffled laugh. "Oh?" he managed.

"Yeah, and never mind how it happened. The thing is, everybody was staring at me. And I didn't—"

"—want to shift to your tail in front of the whole damn aquarium, sure. I get it."

"Artur didn't."

"Oh. You guys have a fight?"

"Not really. It's just—he didn't get it at all. He was almost . . . I had the impression . . . I felt like he was sort of . . ."

"Ashamed of you?" Jonas asked quietly, sitting cross-legged at her feet.

"Well. Yeah."

"He's under some pressure," Jonas reminded her. "The missing mermaids and all, like you were telling me."

"Yeah."

"And he wants to marry you *because* you do weird-ass stuff like flailing around in a tank in your flip-flops instead of stripping to your birthday suit and growing a tail. You think you're the only engaged couple who come from radically different backgrounds?"

"I didn't think about it like that," she admitted.

"'Cuz you're stupid," he informed her cheerfully.

"Thanks so much."

"So what was Thomas doing while you guys were working out radical cultural differences?"

"Uh. Holding me."

Jonas groaned and stretched out on the concrete. He lay there, corpse-like, for a few seconds, then propped himself up on an elbow and went into scold mode. "Fred, Fred, Fred! You've made your choice. You strung both of them along for . . . what? Two years? And now you're engaged . . . to—are you listening?—Artur! Enough with the dancing! Ow, I think I just scraped all the skin off my elbow."

"I didn't string them along," she protested, stung. "They're the ones who kept disappearing. At least Artur made it clear from day one that he wanted to marry me."

"Ahaaaaa!" he yowled. "What you meant is, *Thomas* kept disappearing on you. So you picked Artur."

"Yes, and my choice had nothing to do with the fact that he loves me and will make me a princess and show me things I could never, ever have discovered on my own."

Jonas held up his hands, as if he were being robbed. "Fair enough. I'm not arguing any of that stuff. But my point is, you made your choice. So enough with the wishy-washy bullshit."

"Artur was embarrassed. But Thomas pulled me out of the tank. He jumped right in and hauled me out. And he *knew* why I didn't pop my tail."

"Big surprise, you were raised by surface dwellers and another surface dweller gets you. *I* get you. It doesn't mean Artur's embarrassed, or ashamed, or regretting anything. You've got years to work all this crap out. Why is it bothering you so much tonight?"

"I don't know. I absolutely don't. It's been a weird week."

Massive understatement.

"And you've got another weird-ass mystery to solve. You're the Daphne to their Shaggy and Fred."

"The hell! I'm Velma, dammit."

"And you're on television and in papers and you hate the attention."

"So?"

"So. Give Artur a break. You're not exactly at your best right now. And he was *still* glad when you said yes."

"That's true."

Jonas leaned over and gave her a friendly slap on the leg. "See? All is well when you listen to your uncle Jonas."

"Just when I thought you couldn't get any creepier."

"You can't imagine my levels of creepiness. Now if you'll excuse me, I'm going upstairs to bone your boss."

Fred shut her eyes, but the awful images wouldn't disappear.

Thirty-three

Fred didn't dare go in the house, which was a shame, because the mosquitoes were a real bitch tonight. But Jonas and Dr. Barb could get pretty loud. She prayed they were at least doing it in their bedroom.

"Fredrika?"

She turned and looked. Her father had stepped out onto the patio. "Oh. Hi, Farrem. What's up?"

"Nothing is up. Only . . ." He hesitated. She had the odd feeling he was shy, or embarrassed. "I have not had the chance to speak with you in private. Do you mind?"

"Mind? I'd love the distraction, *believe* me. Have a seat. Hope you brought a can of Off!"

He chuckled. "You poor thing! Mosquitoes don't like how Undersea Folk taste. What an awful heritage to inherit from your lady mother."

"Thank God!" Fred exclaimed. "A UF who understands a surface-dweller reference. Usually I get a blank stare."

Farrem's laughter cut off abruptly. "Yes, I know that Off! is an insect repellant. I know many things about the surface world, as I have had to spend much time here."

"Uh. Yeah. Sorry. Didn't mean to bring the party down."

He sat in the patio chair beside her. "You did not. I will carry my shame for the rest of my days, and deservedly so; your comments have no effect on what I have done. But there have been compensations for banishment. I am sitting beside one of them."

"Aw," Fred teased. "I'm blushing."

"It is too dark for me to tell," he replied.

"Farrem, can I ask you something?"

"Because I was arrogant and thought my wishes were more important than sparing lives. Because I was cruel and foolish."

"Um. I was going to ask where you've been living all these years."

"Oh! Awkward," he said wryly, and Fred laughed again. Damn! It was great to talk to someone who didn't sound stilted, or from another *(species)*

country.

"I have seen much of the planet. In my despair, I traveled much of the world during my first decade of banishment . . . starting, of course, with the East Coast of this country. Specifically, Massachusetts."

"Specifically, Cape Cod," Fred said dryly, knowing well that she was conceived on one of the beaches there.

"Indeed! My encounter with your lady mother was the one thing that kept me from despair. I had forgotten a very basic fact. Although my own people despised me, there were many people who would not know of my shame. She was kindness itself. She . . . saved me."

Fred said nothing, but her thoughts were awhirl. She and Jonas had long ago agreed never to tell Moon that Farrem had only taken her out of despair, had come ashore because he had, literally, nowhere else to go. But Fred was having second thoughts.

She . . . saved me.

Moon deserved to know the wonderful thing she had done for a man she didn't know.

How often, Fred mused, had she taken her mother's generous nature for granted?

Since day one, of course. Did anyone ever *really* appreciate their mom?

Farrem had been silent while she pondered these things, and when he continued, it was in a low voice. "I had been planning my own destruction. I had planned to find land, get as far from water as I could, and die by dehydration."

"Jesus!"

"It is very difficult," he said simply, "for one of our kind to kill themselves. I supposed I could have let myself be eaten by a great white. Messy, though, and quite painful. But!" He sounded more brisk. Slightly more cheery, thank God. "Your lady mother made me rethink my course of action. So I went a'traveling. I saw many things."

"How did you—you know . . . Live? Make money? Whatever?"

"At first, I caught and sold fish at various coastal markets. When I wound up in Tokyo, I realized how very expensive sushi quality fish are—tuna, whitefish, squid—"

"Yerrggh! Stop, you'll make me barf."

"What?"

"I'm allergic."

"Stop that. You are teasing me."

"I'm absolutely not. I can't eat any kind of fish."

Her father went into gales of laughter at her confession. Most Undersea Folk did. They thought her hideous affliction was hilarious. "Oh! Oh, in the king's name! A child of mine, allergic!"

"I'm thrilled you're getting such a kick out of this."

"I do beg your pardon, Fredrika. But it *is* funny. I noticed you have your mother's teeth; it's actually quite a good thing you can't eat fish. Frankly, you don't have the dentition for it."

"Good point. So, you were in Tokyo . . ."

"And eventually made enough money to buy a fishing boat. And due to my . . . ah . . . affinity with the sea—"

"You always knew where to find the fish!"

"Just so."

"How many boats," she asked slyly, "do you have now?"

"Twenty-two. And homes in Tokyo, Greenland, and Perth."

She laughed. "Perth, Australia? Get out of town!"

"I assure you, I will, and quite soon. I also," he went on with what she felt was justifiable pride, "supervise a staff of several hundred."

"So you did sort of get your own kingdom, after all."

"I had not thought of it that way. You are wise for one so young, Fredrika."

"I s'pose you're going to tell me you're eighty years old or whatever— Never mind, I don't want to know. Tokyo, Greenland, and Perth, hmm? Lots of water in those areas."

"Not to mention saltwater pools on all my properties."

"That's great, Farrem." She meant it. She was proud of him, despite what he had done. At least he'd learned. He hadn't let it get him down and, by God, he'd grown. Made something of himself. She'd known plenty of humans who couldn't let go of the past. Who *wallowed* in the past.

Shit, who *hadn't* fucked up when they were younger?

"I think you did really well in a pretty difficult situation. And I'm glad you found me. I admit, I've been curious about you."

"And I, once I saw your picture, about you. You are the only hybrid I have ever known. It never occurred to me that I might have left your lady mother in pup. I am embarrassed to say I never came back to check on her."

"Well, like you said. You couldn't have known. Frankly, I'm amazed myself—two species usually can't mate successfully. You don't see any tiger/monkeys or seal/dolphins around."

"Ah . . . no. I sometimes wonder," he mused, "if the fool things I did in my youth had a purpose. One beyond my selfish desires. Because they led to you. And look what you have done, for your mother's people and for mine. You have changed . . . everything. Everything."

"Oh, it wasn't me," Fred said, startled and embarrassed. "The king's the one who said his subjects could choose to show themselves or not. I'm just . . . trying to help with the transition."

"And I am certain you had nothing at all to do with that decision," he said slyly, and she laughed.

"You should hang around," she said. "You're good for my ego."

"That is part of why I wanted to speak with you. I dare not hang around. At least, not much longer. I will not jeopardize your standing among my people. We are an old race, and a stubborn one. And we blame the children for the deeds of their parents. Illogical, yes, but part of who we are. Surely you have already run into prejudice because I am your sire."

"Nothing I can't handle."

"You are kind. But if you are to rule, you must not have me forever reminding our people of the terrible danger I once placed us all in."

"Danger—for them?"

"I was never meant to be king," he said simply. "If I had succeeded in my foolishness, all of our people could have been in jeopardy. No, Mekkam's line has been ruling us for a reason. I was too stupid in my youth to understand such things."

"Well. Uh." Fred cleared her throat. "Why did you think you should take over?"

"I once thought that just because your father, and grandfather, and great-grandfather had been king, that didn't mean that *you* should be king. I thought it was more about ambition, and ability, than heredity."

"You must have been studying the Windsors," Fred said dryly. "Because you're sure not alone in that. But that's neither here nor there—you don't think so anymore?"

He laughed. "I was defeated, was I not? That in itself proved me wrong. But what it took me thirty years to understand was that—and this is what you might call my 'duh' moment—Artur's line rules *because* their formidable telepathy is hereditary. It is through that ability that he safeguards our people. I had no right to attempt to usurp him."

"The way I heard the story is, you're pretty formidable yourself. In the telepathy area, that is."

"That was both my gift and my curse, yes."

She understood: if not for his power, he never would have tried the coup; he never would have been banished.

"That must be amazing. I can only hear the UF and fish and such when I'm in water, with my tail."

He frowned and cocked his head. "Beg your pardon?"

"I can't talk to Undersea Folk on land like purebreds can. I can't hear fish on land, sense them—nothing like that."

"You—you're mind blind when you have legs?" He was trying hard not to sound horrified, and failing.

"Hey, it's okay, Farrem. I've always felt

(like a freak)

different because I could hear fish. I didn't even know about UF telepathy until I met Artur. So I never knew what I was missing. It doesn't bother me."

He was—why was he looking at her so strangely?

"Fredrika," he said quietly, and knelt by the pool, and dipped his finger in the water, and drew some odd, complicated symbols on the dry cement, "can you tell me what this word is?"

She stared at the squiggles and lines. "It's a word? It looks like abstract art to me."

He sat back on his haunches, and why in the world did he look so *sad*?

"What's wrong?" she asked, nearly gasped. Suddenly it was hard to get a breath. "You look—what's wrong with me?"

"This is your name in our language," he said quietly, gently. "You can only speak our language in your mind, in water."

"I can't speak your language at all! When I talk to fish and—and Artur and Tennian and those guys, we're speaking English."

"You are not. You are speaking the ancient language of all the seas, the tongue that was common long before a fish who wanted to be a man crawled out of the ocean and grew lungs. We—the Undersea Folk—we know it through ancestral memories. We are all born knowing it. When you communicate with us telepathically, you are speaking our ancient tongue. It cannot be taught; you must have the memories for it, the ancient memories. But your mother's blood is strong in you, and—it's not just your teeth, daughter."

"What—I—what?"

"You can never read our legends. You can never communicate with us on land in our language. We can learn English . . . or French . . . or Italian. Those chatterings are ludicrously simple compared to the much older language of the sea. That is why we can speak with you on land. But you never can speak our tongue, hear those thoughts, read those stories, learn those legends. And you might pass on that—that surface-dweller trait—" My, how diplomatic he was! "You might pass that on to any children you give the prince."

Fred sat, frozen, and digested everything he had told her. "Why—why didn't Tennian tell me? Why didn't Artur?"

"I suspect," he said softly, "they could not bear to."

"Well." She mulled the shock of the day over for a minute or two. "That explains why Artur acts so weird whenever I do an un-mermaid-like thing."

"With all respect to the prince, your—ah—genetic inability to understand our language presents a considerable handicap." Farrem paused, then added, "He must love you a great deal to wish you for his queen."

"Yes," she said sharply, "he managed to overcome his repugnance at the thought of my gross defect." Which wasn't far from the truth. Certainly when Artur had first realized her limits, he and Tennian had acted as if she'd been born blind or something. Sad, and sympathetic, and slightly weirded out. It had been—

"Forgive me. I—I was thoughtless and—and cruel."

She waved a hand. "No, no. It's just—the shock, is all. And the thing is, I think my, um, handicap or what-have-you bothers him more than he lets on."

"It matters not, if he loves you, and he must—a great deal! I truly meant no offense. I was surprised. I naturally assumed one of my blood—Oh, Fredrika," he said sadly. "I am so very sorry."

"For God's sake, what are we, at a wake? I told you, it's fine."

But was it?

She was amazed that Artur would chance her polluting the royal family with—to be brutally honest—surface-dweller retardation. What good was a future king *who couldn't speak or read the fucking language*?

Did Artur perhaps feel that, after pursuing her for two years, he could not back down? Could not take back his proposal when she told him she'd marry him?

"It's fine," she repeated stubbornly.

"Then you are truly of my blood, Fredrika, because we have both acquitted ourselves in difficult situations."

"If you say so. Listen, I get your remorse and everything, and I probably wouldn't be the only one. Maybe if some of the, uh, old guard heard you talking like that, they might—"

She quit when he laughed.

"All right, maybe that's naïve. But here's something you might not know—people from my generation don't blame me for what you did. They weren't around for what you did. My friend Tennian doesn't blame me, and her friend Wennd doesn't, either—it's a story to them and that's all."

"Wennd?"

"Oh, just the most beautiful woman in the world. Don't get me started. Anyway, that's the generation I'll be ruling. Maybe I could un-banish you when I become queen."

He looked at her for a long time. Finally he said, "You are your mother's daughter. Which is more than I deserve. I will not hold you to what you just said, and I will not repeat it, ever, because I would not jeopardize your throne for anything. But I will never forget it."

He leaned in. Touched her hair. Turned.

Left.

Thirty-four

Jonas opened the door to the guest room and stepped inside. His ridiculously hot fiancée, Barb, was barefoot, in her linen capris and a navy blue bra. Her blonde hair was out of its habitual ponytail and streaming past her shoulders. She was looking at herself critically in the mirror, her almond-shaped brown eyes narrowed in concentration.

"What's up, sexy?"

"I've decided you're marrying a crone."

He groaned and flopped, face-first, onto the bed. Then he rolled over so he could ogle her. "Not this again, Barb. I swear, you got progressively more neurotic about your age the moment we got engaged."

"A crone," she repeated, examining her laugh lines.

"Fifteen years, Barb. BFD."

"What?"

"Big. Fucking. Deal."

"You kids and your slang," she teased.

He wasn't about to be diverted. "So what if you're older than me? You're *supposed* to be older, remember? As in, I'm not attracted to women my own age? I've got the hot schoolteacher/older woman fetish? Any of this ringing a bell?"

"Some of it," she admitted and smiled at him.

"I wanted you the second I saw you in that starchy lab coat, all strict and hot and hot."

"You said hot twice."

"Well. You're twice as hot as anybody else."

She laughed at him. "You can say that with a straight face, surrounded by all these ridiculously beautiful mermaids?"

"What can I say?" He sighed. "Love is blind."

"Mmmm." She stripped off her pants and hung them neatly over the chair before the mirror. "Did you get a chance to talk to Dr. Bimm?"

"Barb, since you're marrying her best friend, and since she keeps trying to quit and thus doesn't consider herself your employee anymore, I think you can start calling her Fred."

"She will not quit. I will never allow her to quit," she said firmly. "Even before I knew of her—ah—her unique heritage, she was the finest employee I ever had. She is on a leave of absence. She has *not* quit."

Jonas wondered why he surrounded himself with the most stubborn women on the planet.

Oh. Right. Because they were super damned sexy.

"I love how you're all formal and stuff."

"And I love how you're not." She smiled at him in the mirror. "But back to Dr. Bimm. Did you get a chance to talk with her?"

"Yeah. She had a rough day. All kinds of shit going on. I think I cheered her up a little. Or at least made her feel better."

"Can I help?"

"I don't think so, hon. She and Thomas and Artur have some sort of plan to fix the problem of the year, and the three of them make a good team."

"So my late ex-husband will attest," she said dryly. Then: "I worry about the stress she's under." She disappeared into the bathroom and Jonas heard running water. "Shhhzz gnnn mmm mmmms."

"Spit out the toothpaste and try again, hon."

Spitting. Rinsing. Then: "She's got too many problems. It's not fair that so much should be on her shoulders, and in such a short time."

"Haven't you been paying attention, gorgeous? We don't live in a fair world. Anyone who says differently is selling something."

"You stole that," Barb accused, "from *The Princess Bride.*"

"Sure I did. But it doesn't make it less true."

Barb came out of the bathroom naked. She sighed and said, "I wish Dr. Bimm was the type of person who would ask for help."

"What?"

"I said, I wish—Jonas, I know that look."

He'd gotten off the bed and was battling with his belt. "What look?"

"Your I-must-be-sexually-satisfied-right-now look. And I *said,* I wish Dr. Bimm was the type of—"

"Please. Please stop talking about Fred. It'll ruin everything. The only way it could be less sexy is if you started talking about one of my aunts." He managed to shove down his jeans and underwear, then nearly tripped as he tried to close in on Barb. "Fred's fine. Hey, you don't know where I can find a hot older woman to play stern schoolteacher, do you?"

Barb had a hand over her mouth, trying in vain to stifle her giggles. "You're going to fall and give yourself a concussion."

"A small price to pay," he said, and then he *did* trip, falling into her. She held him for a moment, then toppled to the rug beneath his greater height and weight. She groaned as the breath whooshed out of her lungs. "Barb? You okay?"

"You're going to pay for that," she said, twining her fingers in his hair and wrenching his mouth toward hers.

"I certainly hope so," he murmured and kissed her, cupping her right breast as he did so. "For hours, I hope."

"That's more up to you than me," she said into his mouth, then squealed as he pinched her.

Thirty-five

Thomas Pearson, M.D., Ph.D., and BIHSYDWTMW (Boy In High School You Didn't Want To Mess With), pulled up to Fred's opulent rental house

(man, this place really isn't her)

and killed the engine. As if seeing Fred wasn't stressful enough, today he had to contend with the captain. Man, if anybody but Fred had asked . . .

It was so stressful, in fact, that he tended to leave Fred's place at dawn and sulk in the Starbucks down the street. And he didn't have a key, which meant waking the house when he returned. Maybe Fred would answer, possibly nude . . .

He tried to shove that out of his mind as he approached the front door. Fred wasn't his, was never his, would never be his. She was going to marry Artur, and who could blame her?

Artur could show her a world he never, ever could. The guy was a prince, for God's sake. And could know a side of Fred that Thomas could never relate to—Fred was, after all, only *half* human. She would be cheating herself and her father's heritage by starting a relationship with plain ordinary human Dr. Pearson, and Thomas knew that perfectly well.

Also, he was a fucking coward.

He rapped on the door.

Yep, a coward, a yellow-belly asshole, most definitely, yes, sir, and yes, ma'am, no argument, no question. How many times had he scuttled out of town because he knew he wasn't good enough for her? And when Artur moved in, how many times had Thomas fled the fucking *country* so he wouldn't have to watch the courtship close up? Knowing, always knowing, that whether he stayed or left, the end result would have been the same.

(but you didn't even try you didn't even)

He ignored the irritating inner voice. His father's voice, so quick to point out shortcomings, so quick to spot weakness.

Jesus, he'd even tried to substitute Tennian for her, and that had worked for about eight whole seconds. It was stupid of him and horribly unfair to Tennian, and it hadn't taken him long at all (eight seconds, in fact) to determine that he and Tennian would only, always be friends. *Just* friends. To her credit, Tennian had never tried to push it further

(Why would she? When she, like Fred, could have any man?)

and he was grateful for that.

He'd been gone on Fred even before he knew she was a mermaid—sorry, Undersea Folk. If Artur hadn't killed the sadistic fuck who'd shot her, he would have taken care of it himself. As it was, jamming his knife into her shoulder to get the bullet out was the hardest thing he'd ever had to do.

So hard, in fact, that he had avoided her more or less regularly ever since. Because if he felt that way on such short acquaintance, how might he feel—how much would it hurt—to fall even *more* in love? What if he had to hurt her *again* to save her?

He still had nightmares about it. Fred, shot. Artur, holding her down so he could dig out the bullet. Fred, screaming.

Screaming.

He pounded harder. That was no way to be thinking. That was past, it was done, and he was here now because she needed his help and, by God, he was going to do everything he could to—

A yawning Jonas opened the door. "What? D'you know what time it is? Jeez."

"It's oh-eight-twenty," Thomas replied, "and the captain will be here at oh-eight-thirty."

"Seriously?"

"You can set your fucking watch," he said glumly. "And good morning to you, too."

"Not a morning person, so kindly drop dead and disintegrate into a thousand tiny pieces." Jonas stepped back so Thomas could enter.

Thomas liked Jonas a lot. In another world—a world where he could be around Fred every day without destroying himself or ruining her life—they could have been best friends. Jonas did not take himself at all seriously, a quality Thomas greatly admired. He also loved Fred—a quality Thomas could relate to.

But, even though they weren't best friends, he was fond enough of the guy to poke him in the gut as he passed him.

"Keep your hands off my rock-hard abs, shithead," Jonas said warmly.

"Rock hard? For a second I mistook you for the Pillsbury Doughboy. Hee-*hee*!"

"Lies," Jonas yawned, "from a teeny, envious mind."

That was a little too close to the truth, even if Jonas didn't know it. "Is Fred up?"

"Up and in the pool since oh-God-thirty this morning. She's been sulking on the bottom of the deep end for the last hour or so."

"Great." Oh, Lord, she would be in her tail, her glorious, gorgeous, amazing tail, and her unbelievably fine tits would be bare and her taut stomach would—"Uh, could I have some coffee?" *To throw in my face so I can keep my mind on business?*

"In the kitchen." Jonas stretched. He was wearing Opus the Penguin pajama bottoms and nothing else. "I guess I better get dressed if your dad's on the way."

"Why? You don't have to be there."

"What? And miss meeting The Thing That Spawned Thomas Pearson? No chance, pal."

Thomas laughed. His father would assume, as nearly everyone did, that Jonas was gay. When, in fact, Jonas was merely the most metrosexual fellow on the planet. Well, that was fine. Anything that irritated the captain was fine.

"Hey, will you give me an address where you actually pick up mail?" Jonas asked on his way back up the stairs. "We have no idea where to send the wedding invitation."

"Send it care of my publisher," he suggested. A navy brat, Thomas felt itchy if he was in the same place more than nine months. Funny, since when he was a kid he swore he'd pick one spot and never move again. He'd moved eighteen times since he became the legal drinking age. "They can always track me down. I'll e-mail you their address."

"Great, Priscilla." Jonas yawned and continued up the stairs. "See if you can haul Fred out of the pool, will ya? And Artur's gonna be here any minute."

"No doubt," he muttered and went through the sliding door and down the stairs to the pool.

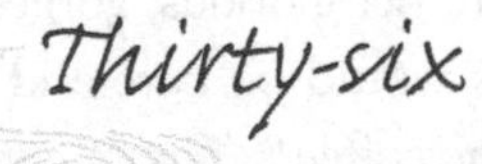

Thirty-six

Yup, there she was, at the bottom of the pool. But she wasn't sulking in the deep end. She was swimming back and forth, back and forth; it was almost hypnotic. She was so strong that it took just a few flicks of her tail to carom to the other end of the pool—which was Olympic-sized. Facedown. Back and forth. Flick. Flick. Turn. Back and forth.

She was thinking about something. Thinking hard. He almost

hated to disturb her, but the captain would need to talk to her and Artur.

He knelt and lightly slapped his palm on the surface of the water. He could barely hear the splash, but she flipped over at once, spotted him, and shot to the surface.

"Morning."

"Hi," he replied, then realized his voice had actually cracked. Christ, he always felt sixteen years old when he was around her. He coughed. "Hi," he said in a much more baritonesque tone.

She bobbed out of the water, crossed her forearms on the cement, and rested her chin on her left wrist. "Say. I never thanked you. For yesterday, at the aquarium."

"No big."

"It was a 'big.' To me."

He shrugged. "Can't blame you for not wanting to show your boobs to a bunch of tourists, although, if I can offer a professional medical opinion, they're probably the third-finest set in the country."

"Third?" she cried with mock outrage, and splashed him. "You dog. How much research have you done in this field, exactly?"

"I almost went into plastic surgery," he lied, and grinned down at her. "Listen, sorry to interrupt your ruminating—"

"Oooh, someone's been using Word a Day toilet paper again."

"Off my back, *doctor.* The Captain's going to be here any minute."

She was staring at him thoughtfully and he noticed, again, that her eyes were the color of creamy jade. He had heard her refer to them as "the hideous tinge of Brussels sprouts" and wondered, for the zillionth time, why beautiful women never knew they were beautiful.

"You did it again," she said after a long moment.

Tell me, tell me she's not reading my mind.

"Did what?" he asked with feigned lightness.

"Called your dad 'captain.' I call my dad Farrem, but I've known him less than a week."

Thomas shrugged and started to stand. Quicker than thought—

than his eyes could even track—one of her hands shot out and grasped his wrist with the strength that never, ever failed to surprise him.

She could snap my wrist without breaking a sweat. But she would never. And she doesn't even know how marvelous that makes her on a planet where you can get knifed for the five-dollar bill in your pocket.

Artur will tell her, he tried to comfort himself. *He'll tell her how great she is every day.*

"I didn't realize," she admitted. "When Artur and I thought about asking you to call your dad. I didn't know you didn't have a, um, loving-type relationship."

He shrugged. "How could you?"

"But you called him anyway."

"Sure."

She shook her head and smiled and released his wrist. Thank God, because his fingers were starting to lose all sensation. "You're too good, Thomas. You were a dope to let Tennian go."

"There was never anything to let her out of," he explained (again). "Ask her."

"No chance . . . she might bring that Wennd girl around again."

"Oh, my God," he said, staring up at the sky. "The eyes. The hair. Could you believe it?"

"I know! I felt like El Frumpo just being in the same room with her. Did you believe how shy she was? She was actually nervous to meet us. Us! And we're completely harmless!"

Thomas, who had a somewhat more objective view of Fred and her gang, said nothing.

"Speaking of difficult fathers, I had a really cool conversation with mine," she said and laid it out for him in about five minutes.

"So he got rich? He owns a fleet? And multiple houses on land?" Thomas shook his head, smiling. "Not bad for the traitor of his people."

"Tell me. And he's getting out of town pretty soon, too. He's worried that him being around will be a constant goad to the old guard. That it'll threaten my throne, if you can believe it."

"Thirty years is a long sentence."

"And it's not over yet. He's still banished from Undersea Folk society. But even the king couldn't banish him from land. But I think you're forgetting something. Thirty years is nothing to a UF. It's a Sunday afternoon. It's a sick day."

"Point," he admitted. He glanced at his watch, and she noticed.

"All right, I'm coming." She started to heave herself up and Thomas handed her the robe on the lawn chair, politely (and reluctantly) averting his eyes as he did so. He'd seen her breasts a few times, but only when she had a tail. "I better throw some clothes on before 'the captain' gets here."

"That would be nice," he agreed.

Thirty-seven

Captain Pearson pulled up to the unbelievably showy mini-mansion and shut off the car. He glanced at his watch: oh-eight-thirty.

He got out. Marched up the walk. Rapped precisely three times on the front door, automatically making sure his slacks and shirt were neat, his shoes shined. His hair, military short, needed no adjustment, despite the mild breeze.

His boy had called and he had come.

The boy never called.

The boy was all he had of his dear wife, cruelly snatched away by breast cancer forty-two months and eighteen days ago.

The boy did not like him and was quite correct to feel that way.

He, Capt. James T. Pearson (ret.), decorated veteran of the Vietnam conflict, had been a shit father.

He hoped to have a chance to make up for the past. For his carelessness and close-mindedness and cruel comments. Because his wife had been right all along, and he was just a stubborn old man who had made too many mistakes.

The door opened, and there he stood. His boy, tall and strong and handsome—so handsome! With (oh, God) his mother's eyes staring out at him.

Book smart, too, plenty smart—a doctor! Two kinds of doctor, actually. And he wrote silly stories for the fun of it and even though it was just a hobby, the boy had turned it into a seven-figure-a-year income. In his spare time! The captain had tried to read one of the stories and didn't care for it, but plenty of other people sure seemed to. He had researched the romance—what did they call it? The romance genre. He'd been astounded to discover it was a billion-dollar industry . . . and his boy had cleverly tapped into it.

Whenever he had to fly somewhere, he always checked the airport bookstores and was always pleased to find one or more of the boy's stories on a shelf.

Once, it had seemed so vitally important that the boy serve his country. It seemed like a slap in America's face when the boy had gotten a scholarship and gone to medical school. He had not spoken to the boy for many years.

He had thought the boy frivolous and silly and maybe, maybe even a coward.

He was a stupid old man.

"Hello, Captain."

And, even though he was stupid, he would never show the boy how much it hurt to be called captain by the only son he would ever have . . . the only living reminder of his wife. Because he had it coming, all that and more.

How arrogant he had been to think that he would never have to pay for his sins. That the past didn't have teeth.

"Good morning, Thomas. May I come in?"

"Yes, sir."

The captain followed the boy into a large room that seemed to be a combination kitchen/dining room/living room. An exuberant blond fellow was fairly bouncing down the stairs, heading straight for them.

"Hey, hi there!" The man—compact and muscular, with a friendly smile—extended a hand. "I'm Jonas Carrey, I'm a friend of your son's. It's great to meet you."

The captain shook hands. "Hello, Mr. Carrey. I'm James Pearson."

"So, you really unleashed the thing that is Thomas upon the world? And you own up to it and everything?"

The captain was startled into laughter and, from the look on the boy's face, he wasn't the only one who was startled. "Yes, Mr. Carrey. I freely admit to it. He is my son. Fortunately, he takes after his mother."

The boy raised his eyebrows.

"It's Jonas, Captain Pearson. Thomas said you earned about a thousand medals in Vietnam, and led men into battle, and you were always the last one in retreat, and you saved a whole bunch of soldiers." Mr. Carrey actually gasped for breath after this recitation.

The captain, shocked, glanced at the boy, who shrugged. He had no idea Thomas *ever* spoke of him, much less in complimentary terms he did not deserve.

"I did what I could for my country," he replied carefully. "That's the best any soldier can hope for."

"Spoken like a man used to kicking ass. I like you, Captain Pearson, despite the fact that you fathered Thomas, here, who's irritating in almost as many ways as my friend Fred. If you're in town long enough, you ought to come to my wedding."

What an interesting and—yes, it was true—odd man. Wedding? Jonas had seemed so bouncy and, er, overly friendly, the captain had assumed . . . Well, it wouldn't be the first time he was wrong about one of Thomas's friends.

"You're very kind. Perhaps I will, if my schedule allows."

"Lots of cake," Jonas wheedled. "You want some coffee?"

"Please."

Jonas bounced toward the kitchen, leaving the captain alone with the boy.

"You're looking well," he said after an uncomfortable silence.

"Thank you, sir."

"I was surprised to hear from you."

"No doubt, sir. Thank you," the boy said formally, "for coming so quickly."

"I was intrigued." Inwardly, the captain cursed himself for lying. Or at least not telling the whole truth. Yes, he had been intrigued. But he would have come no matter what the boy's request.

"Have you—have you had a chance to visit your mother's grave recently?"

"Yes," the boy said distantly.

"She, uh, always liked irises. Maybe sometime, we could—"

"Hi," a female voice said, and the captain glanced over the boy's shoulder.

Ah. The famous Fredrika Bimm. A doctor, like his boy. But not a *real* doctor—she was a scientist.

A damned good-looking one, too. The hair—such an unusual color! And green eyes—true green, not hazel. Tall and slender, neatly dressed in a button-down shirt and khaki shorts. Bare feet. There was something fresh and vital about her, something he couldn't help responding to, even though he was an old man.

He wished, again, that his poor wandering boy would settle down in one place and find someone to love, start a family. The boy deserved more family than he currently had: which was, of course, just the captain.

"Dr. Bimm," he said and tried not to wince when she shook his hand. *Holy hell, she's strong!* This was his first experience with a mermaid, though they'd certainly been all over the news lately. He'd been following the stories quite carefully. The military applications alone were so exciting, it was—

But then, that was why he was here, wasn't it?

"Captain Pearson. Thanks a lot for coming. We're just waiting on Prince Artur and then we can get started."

"The one who wanted the meeting is late?" he said, more sharply than he intended.

And then the lovely Dr. Bimm ripped him a new asshole.

"Yeah, well, *Captain*, we don't all run our empty, meaningless lives by a clock. Some of us, *Captain*, have families and loved ones to think about and those loved ones often throw wrenches into our schedules. Some of us, *Captain*, have entire kingdoms to worry about, as opposed to spending all of our time, hmm, I dunno, ignoring our only son."

The boy's eyes actually bulged. "Jesus, Fred!"

The captain laughed. And laughed. And finally had to sit down and hold his sides, because they ached so from such unaccustomed glee.

Thirty-eight

Fred eyed Thomas's father with thinly veiled suspicion. He looked like a typical military hard-ass, and from the moment she saw him she could guess how it had been between Captain Kick-ass and a son who had no interest in a military career.

Correction: a son who wrote romance novels and had no interest in a military career.

It made her ashamed for how much she took Moon and Sam for granted . . . for her occasional embarrassment at their hippie ways. Well, Moon would have lit herself on fire before trying to direct Fred's choice of career. Fred could have turned tricks and Moon never, ever would have cut off contact.

Funny. Funny to think that Moon and Sam had protested at Vietnam rallies in the sixties. Trying to end the war. Trying to get men like Pearson out of the jungle and back with his family.

Men like Pearson, who would have sneered at Moon's bell-bottoms and Sam's beard. Who would have called them fools for loving peace more than loving serving their country.

Yes, she could guess how it had been. It made her admire Thomas all the more for sticking to his choice, for denying his father's wishes and going his own way.

It was just another version of stage mothering, that's what it was. Or fathers pushing their sons into football so they could relive their long-gone glory days.

In a phrase, irritating beyond belief. She recalled a line from one of her favorite novels, *The Prince of Tides.* "Fuck the fathers. They should know better."

And wasn't that the truth.

Still. She could have chosen her words with a little more care. It was too bad she'd lost her temper a little.

Well. A lot.

And then he'd laughed. And laughed. And laughed!

So now Fred had no idea what to think, and she didn't like the feeling one bit. She didn't even know she was going to say it until it was out. And, like so many other things she said, once it was out, there was no taking it back.

There were so many things, she thought, staring at her now-present fiancé, you couldn't take back.

She couldn't deny it felt good to stick it to the old man—the thought of this guy not appreciating someone as wonderful as Thomas was fucking *infuriating*—but realized instantly that she'd antagonized their only source of military intelligence.

Amazingly, he hadn't minded.

Weird.

Really quite weird.

And then Artur had arrived, and she had to focus on the matter at hand.

The captain, to his credit, shook hands with Artur while looking him straight in the eye and *not* looking over-awed, as most people did when they met the imposing prince. They'd all had a seat at the big dining-room table.

Jonas had made coffee, put out platters of scrambled eggs and toast and jars of jelly, and had sat unobtrusively at the end of the table (most unusual!).

"Good sir, I am grateful you have come." Artur, who loved surface-dweller food, had a pile of scrambled eggs on his plate that resembled a yellow pyramid, three pieces of toast, and two cups of coffee. "My king has a problem and we need your assistance."

The captain, sitting ramrod straight in his chair (his spine didn't even touch the back!), nodded. He took a sip of his coffee and replied, "So my son implied. What's the trouble?"

Artur laid it out, quickly and precisely. The captain's eyebrows arched a few times (and how he looked like Thomas when he did that!) but he seemed to readily accept telepathy, missing Undersea Folk, the king's astonishing telepathic range, and how he and Artur discovered the problem. Fred was slightly amazed.

"I do not mean to impugn your honor by implying your government may be involved," Artur said carefully, "especially as Thomas has explained to me what a great warrior you were for your people."

Again with the eyebrow arch. Another glance at Thomas. And Thomas shrugged, something he was doing a lot with his father around. He was hardly saying anything at all—major-league unusual.

"But perhaps you may have some ideas about where we may look. Or perhaps you may strongly feel we are going in the wrong direction and can share that with us so we waste no more of your time. My people, and my father, would be grateful for any assistance you can give us, in whatever form that may be."

The captain smiled. It did amazing things to his craggy face: the years fell away. He had the same dimple Thomas did. His eyes, arctic blue, actually seemed to thaw. "Prince Artur, you will be an excellent king. I've rarely heard such potentially dangerous questions posed so diplomatically."

Artur inclined his head.

"You should see him juggle bowling pins," Jonas piped up from the end of the table, chomping on toast slathered with roughly an inch and a half of jelly.

Fred smirked in his direction.

"But I'm afraid our government would never, and has never, had anything to do with kidnapping, unlawfully detaining, or killing any of your people."

"Not the good people who brought us Fat Man and Little Boy," Fred said mockingly. "Or Agent Orange, the nuclear submarine, Japanese-American internment camps, the Thompson submachine gun, the long-range bomber, land-based ballistic missiles, or the B-52."

Thomas was actually covering his eyes. "Fred," he groaned.

Fred couldn't have stopped if someone had stuck a gun in her ear. "Of *course* the government isn't up to no good. Perish the thought!"

The captain quirked an eyebrow at her and the corner of his mouth turned up. "Why do you hate America, Dr. Bimm?" he asked pleasantly.

She threw her hands up in the air. "Oh, don't even start with that crap, Captain!"

"You look about the same age as my son. Hmmm. Let me guess: your parents were hippies? Antimilitary? Vietnam War protesters?"

"*Are* hippies," she corrected. "And yes. And yes."

"In other words, they were free to protest their government's actions because the military secured that freedom for them."

"Children," Jonas said around a mouthful of eggs. "Play nice."

"Quite right, Jonas."

"Sorry," Fred muttered.

"Quite all right, Dr. Bimm. As I was saying, my government has not harmed or unlawfully detained any Undersea Folk. Not for military applications, not for border skirmishes, not for money, not for oil.

Not for anything. I regret the loss of your people, but my government is blameless."

"I see." Artur was silent for a moment. "I am sorry to have wasted your time, Captain."

"It was no trouble. I was glad for the chance to see my boy again."

Thomas choked on his coffee. Fred had to pat him on the back when his face turned an alarming shade of purple.

"And, of course, I made a stop yesterday to visit some cronies at Sanibel Station—the naval base they have just down the road?"

"Sanibel Station?" Fred repeated, startled.

"There's a naval base on this teeny island?" Jonas asked.

Fred had no idea how to answer him. The navy often allowed marine biologists (or consulted with them) on various projects, and so Fred and Thomas, during their years of education and fieldwork, both had a working knowledge of most naval bases in the country.

And Thomas, of course, was the son of a naval officer. From the look on his face, he'd never heard of Sanibel Station, either.

"Well, perhaps I'm mistaken." The captain shrugged. "I'm getting old. My memory isn't what it used to be."

Thomas snorted into his coffee.

"Perhaps it's called something else. Or perhaps it's some*where* else. But regardless, it was nice to talk to some old friends. One of them—" The captain laughed, a freeing, joyful sound. "He's a sentimental idiot."

"That's . . ." Fred paused. "So sweet."

"Oh, he's always talking about how I carried him on my back through ninety yards of rice paddies to the chopper pickup. What crap! I keep telling him he's got the wrong guy. On paper, I was sixty miles away. That's what my orders said, anyway." He shook his head, still snorting laughter. "Like I said, he's an idiot. But it was nice to talk to him, all the same. Trading war stories. Finding out what former squad members have been up to. Silly old man stuff." Pause. "And it was very nice to see my son."

Thomas was staring at his father as if the man had sprouted a bathtub faucet from his forehead. For that matter, so was Fred.

The captain stood. Artur and Thomas stood. Fred and Jonas remained seated, Jonas because he was still chomping away, and Fred because her brain was working furiously to figure out just what the hell was going on.

"It was nice to meet you, Prince Artur."

"And you, Captain Pearson. I see now where Thomas gets his warrior spirit."

The captain shook his head. "No. He's his mother's son. For which I thank God every night." They shook hands, surface dweller–style.

Fred had to stand up and smack Jonas on the back. He really ought to stop eating until the captain left, she thought.

"Good to see you, son."

"You, too, sir." Thomas stuck out his hand.

And the captain put a fat file folder in it, with classified and eyes only and project jammer stamped all over it in red.

Then he smiled.

Hugged his son (who was standing, frozen, and Fred feared he would drop the folder, or faint, or both).

Left.

Thirty-nine

"Uh," Jonas said. "What just happened?"

Thomas had dropped the folder on the table and started to sit. If Fred hadn't shoved the chair over, he would have landed splat on the floor. They were all staring at it.

Bulging with papers.

EYES ONLY.

CLASSIFIED.

"I can't believe he did that," Thomas murmured.

"I know!" Fred said, wide-eyed. "If it gets out that he gave us this, it'll be his ass!"

"I meant hugging me."

"Also extremely shocking. And just when I'd made up my mind that your dad was a dick."

"Fredrika," Artur reproved. "Do not speak so of such a warrior."

"Have you actually *met* me, Artur? For God's sake. So. Thomas, your dad made this happen." She pushed the folder over to him. "Why don't you do the honors?"

After a few seconds, he flipped open the folder. Passed chunks of paperwork around (the thing was two inches thick; it would have taken one person a week and a half to get through it).

They began to read.

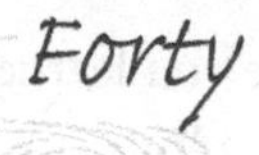

Forty

King Mekkam came through the door. He didn't knock and get invited in. He didn't open it and walk through. He *burst* through the door and chunks of wood went flying everywhere.

Fred groaned, mentally kissing her security deposit good-bye.

"I came at once, my son."

"We noticed," Jonas said, big-eyed.

"What is so urgent? Are you all right?"

King Mekkam looked like a slightly older, grayer version of Artur.

They were even the same height. And, though the man was over a century old, he had the broad chest and shoulders of a lumberjack. His ruby-colored eyes glittered and he carried himself with an aloof dignity that proclaimed his royal blood far more efficiently than something so silly as a crown.

"We have had a fascinating visit from Thomas's sire," Artur replied.

"Fascinating isn't the word," Thomas muttered, rubbing his temples as if he were getting a headache. "Surreal. *Twilight Zone*–esque. In fact, it's possible that was an alien robot and not my father at all."

"You'd better have a seat, Mekkam," Fred said. "We've got lots of stuff to tell you."

The frown lines on his forehead disappeared and he smiled. "Fredrika!"

"You, uh, sound surprised to see me."

Mekkam shook his head, clasped her hands, then raised them to his mouth and kissed them. "I have not had an opportunity to tell you how very pleased I am that you are joining my family. I look forward to your mating ceremony and to many pups."

"Pups?" Jonas repeated. "Oh, God. This is too good. Pups?"

"They call being pregnant 'in pup,'" Fred explained, resisting the urge to strangle her friend. "So I'm guessing mer-babies are pups."

Jonas laughed harder.

"I hate you," Fred commented. "So much."

"But now, back to the matter at hand. What have you learned?"

They had reassembled the file and showed it to the king.

"What is Project Jammer?"

"It seems you have a few traitors in your midst, Mekkam," Thomas said heavily. "Some Undersea Folk apparently sought out a clandestine branch of the navy, a base called Sanibel Station that hardly anyone *in* the navy knows about. I imagine it's their version of Black Ops."

"Black Ops?" King Mekkam asked.

"It's usually a secret branch of the military, secret because there's often a question of ethics or legality involved," Thomas explained.

"Our governments aren't supposed to send assassins or perform non-FDA-regulated experiments or think up new bioweapons or stuff like that, but of course they do. Everyone's government does. Black Ops exist so the government of whatever country is running the team has total deniability."

"Lots of sneaky stuff gets done that way," Fred added. "Among other things, research into unconventional warfare."

"Like telepathy," Jonas said.

Mekkam was silent. Then, "My . . . my people? Have done this? Gone to your military and . . . what, precisely?"

"Shown them what they can do, telepathically. Given them tissue samples. Submitted to experiments."

"But . . ." Mekkam looked so devastated, so horrified, Fred could hardly look at him. "Why?"

"So the navy could help them increase their telepathy," Thomas said, very quietly.

"You mean the people who disappeared . . . they did so . . . willingly? They allowed themselves to—" The king paused. Then a large fist slammed onto the table, which obligingly cracked. Everyone pushed their chairs back, but it only cracked down the middle; for the moment, it held together. "Then they are planning something. They are—" Shocked, he looked at Fred. "We were wrong. It isn't your father."

"No," Fred admitted, making no effort to hide her relief. "But it's probably some or all of the youngsters who sided with him during the coup. The ones who weren't banished, who apologized and made nice with everyone and pretended Farrem led them astray."

"And like a fool, I believed them!"

This time, the table broke under the blow. Fortunately, Jonas had cleared all the dishes while they were waiting for Mekkam to arrive.

"They probably meant it at the time," Jonas suggested, nervously eyeing the eight-foot table, now two four-foot tables. "So why wouldn't you have believed them? But after a while, they probably got to thinking . . . wondering if things could be different . . . and I'm betting you're not the kind of guy who spies on his people's thoughts just for funzies. So how could you have known?"

"No, no, I would never—" Mekkam sounded furious and bewildered, a frightening combination to watch. "I merely—I mean I don't *spy* on them like a filthy—"

"Mekkam, there's no way you could have seen this coming," Fred said gently. "You got rid of the problem. The youngsters apologized. Nobody talked about Farrem anymore. That was that . . . for years and years."

"But why now? Why would they start disappearing from my mind in the last six months?"

"That's what we haven't been able to figure out," Thomas admitted. "Some of this report is pretty dense, and there are charts that Fred and I have to figure out. Some of it even appears to be in code. What we know so far is that some of your people have been working with the naval equivalent of a Black Ops team—probably a tit for tat."

"Pardon?"

"In return for giving the navy brain-tissue samples, for letting doctors run tests on them, for basically being guinea pigs so the navy—that one, small, secret branch of the navy—can help them increase their telepathy, they've probably been running missions for the government."

"There's no way *any* government would have turned them down," Jonas added. "Fred warned you from the beginning that we, as a species, are incredibly nasty to anyone even slightly different. If the someone slightly different *volunteers* for, say, vivisection . . ."

"Now here come men and women who can breathe underwater," Thomas said. "They're incredibly strong. They're incredibly long-lived and they age unbelievably well. You could send a man out with seventy years of combat experience, and he'd get carded if he tried to buy booze. Good stamina. Incredible swimmers—they're mermaids and mermen, for God's sake. The stuff of legend. And best of all, most wonderful of all, they're *telepaths*. And here comes a bunch of them willing to be experimented on if the navy will help them augment their innate abilities." Thomas paused to let this sink in. "Jonas is right. There's not a government on the planet who wouldn't have jumped at the chance."

"But why? Why do this?"

Fred paused. Surely the king *knew.* He was many things, none of them a fool. She put it down to shock. And she was sad for him. This was very likely a direct result of the Undersea Folk letting the world know they existed.

"Why try to make themselves stronger? Why disappear off your radar?" Thomas paused, then went on as gently as he could. "You've got another coup on your hands, Mekkam."

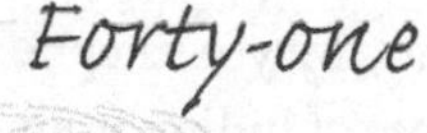

Forty-one

"How can we find out who they are?" Mekkam demanded.

Fred and Thomas exchanged glances. "Um," he began. "That's a little tricky. Other than storming a secret naval base on Sanibel Island, I don't have a clue. And with all respect, Mekkam, I don't think you want to go to war with the United States Navy. Which means the United States." He paused. "We fight dirty. We fight to win."

"Fat Man and Little Boy," Fred muttered. She didn't dare mention Hiroshima . . . Mekkam was having a bad enough day.

"I cannot sit back and wait to be attacked. If it were only my life, I would not mind. But I must think of my son—of our future queen—and my people."

"Ack!" Fred choked. "Please, *please* don't factor me into any of this. Artur and the Undersea Folk, absolutely. But I can take care of myself. Please don't worry about me. You've got enough problems."

"Do not underestimate your father's people, Fredrika. News of your betrothal has spread from mind to mind at the speed of thought. You would make an excellent target."

"Big deal, she's been hearing that since the third grade," Jonas scoffed. "Usually from me."

"Don't forget, Mekkam, I have zero trouble hanging out on land indefinitely. Any UF who comes after me is risking major dehydration. I'll be safe as long as I stay out of the water."

"I recommend moving to the Sahara," Thomas said. "Today."

"I'll help you pack," Jonas offered.

"I'll help you help her pack," Thomas added.

"Everyone calm down. And nobody's touching my things. Listen, we've agreed storming the naval base is baaaaad. Right?"

Nods all around. Except for Mekkam. Mekkam's gaze was fixed on her. She wondered when he was planning to blink.

"Well. These guys, whoever they are, they've disappeared off Mekkam's radar, right? Maybe *specifically* his radar. Maybe they've been augmented, or whatever, strictly for the purpose of hiding from Mekkam's telepathy, maybe the whole royal family's telepathy."

"Yes, yes, my Rika. We know this."

"We've surmised it," Thomas corrected. "We don't *know* shit."

"Well. Who's the most powerful telepath after the royal family?"

Dead silence.

"Who would these guys never *dream* of being a threat because he's been banished for decades?"

Finally, from Artur, "He will never help us. We made his name unspeakable. We banished him to a friendless life, to die alone. We—"

"Yeah, yeah, I know all about it. But I've been talking with him—you remember, he's sleeping here at night—and he's fine with it. Well. Not *fine*. But he's older now, you know, and he's sorry. He's had years and years to think about his mistakes. And in the interim he's made an entirely new life for himself. Believe me, Artur, my father would *leap* at the chance to help you guys."

"Leap?" Mekkam said doubtfully.

"Like a frog on cocaine," Fred confirmed. "But if you want his help, we need to ask him *now*. He's leaving any day. He's afraid that if he sticks around it'll cause trouble for me."

"That is . . . thoughtful," Artur admitted. "I will say, the Farrem I knew was not remotely thoughtful."

"You want to talk to him?"

"Yes, Fredrika. I do."

"Then you can do it in about an hour." Fred glanced around at the group. "He told me last night he was seeing to some business this morning; he was headed for a FedEx drop-off. Payroll or some such crap; I wasn't paying much attention. But we're supposed to have lunch today." She glanced at the clock on the far wall. "In sixty minutes."

Thomas stood. "I think we've got some hamburger left in the fridge. I can fire up the grill."

"I shall catch some fish," Artur said, also standing. "I detest sitting around waiting. Join me, Rika?"

"Ah, no, thanks, Artur." On the off chance her father showed up early, she wanted to make sure she was here. Who knew how the meeting would go without her? It could end up a cluster fuck. Or worse: more of the furniture could get broken.

Forty-two

Fifty-five minutes later, her father walked through the large hole that was once her front door. "Fredrika, are you well? What in the king's name happened here? Did you—"

He saw the group waiting for him and stopped short.

The king cleared his throat. "Greetings, Farrem."

Farrem couldn't have looked more amazed if the king had kissed him on the mouth. "G-greetings, my king. Prince Artur. Thomas. Jonas. Fredrika." He paused and took another step into the house. "May I ask what is going on? Has someone been hurt? Fredrika? Is your lady mother all right?"

"My lady mother and Sam are at SeaWorld for the day, thank God. We need your help, Farrem. Do you have some time? Can you talk to us for a little bit?"

"Certainly." He eyed the broken table and sat down in an empty dining-room chair without comment.

As they explained the situation and showed him bits from the classified file, Farrem's eyes got wider and wider.

"But this is my fault!" he cried, shoving the file away from him as if it were hot. "They *must* be some of my old followers. And they never would have—would have let surface dwellers *do* things to them if I hadn't—if I—" He looked up at Mekkam, stricken. "My king, I am so very sorry. Count on me. I will do whatever you require to make amends."

Mekkam, who had been sitting stiffly (as stiffly as Artur . . . both of them looked as flexible as mannequins), relaxed slightly. "I thank you, Farrem. Our people will be most grateful for your help. But . . ." He seemed to struggle with the words, then coughed them up. "But you are not responsible for what youngsters decided to do once they attained a few years. Our society has ever been about free will."

"Hey, so is ours," Jonas whined.

"You are kind, my king. But my debt is great. I am grateful for the chance to pay it off." Her father smiled grimly. "Including the interest."

Forty-three

"What in the name of the king happened to your door?"

"Funny how people keep using *that* phrase," Jonas sighed.

Tennian and Wennd were standing in the hole where the door used to be, and Fred figured it was about time to find a gallon of Off! and pour it over her head.

Tennian shook her head as if trying to come back to herself. "Forgive me, my king, the door is irrelevant."

"Says the woman who didn't have to cough up a four-figure security deposit," Fred grumped.

"You called and I have come."

"Thank you, Tennian."

"Four figures," Fred reminded them. "Down the drain."

"Oh, shut up and dig into your trust fund," Jonas hissed. "Priorities, dammit!"

"Besides the prince and me, you are the only member of the royal family within three thousand miles. We need your courage today of all days. And I needed to make sure you were safe." The king turned to the beautiful violet-haired mermaid. "Wennd, this is none of yours, young one," Mekkam said gently. "I wish for you to return to the Indian Ocean as quickly as you can."

"I—I was with her when you called, my king."

Fred couldn't help looking at the beautiful woman, but it wasn't the hair or the eyes that had her attention. There was something about Wennd that was bugging her, and damned if she could put her finger on it.

"I want to help," Wennd whispered. "Please let me help. Don't send me away if my people are in danger."

Artur smiled at her. "Very well, Wennd. I should hate to reward such loyalty with dismissal."

What was it about her? Fred wondered if it was something so simple as concern. Wennd was so timid and gentle, Fred wasn't crazy about the thought of her getting hurt. She really had no business here. Things could get nasty.

She wished the king had made her leave.

Tennian, meanwhile, had marched up to Farrem. "It appears you are redeeming yourself," she managed through clenched teeth, hands on hips, staring up into his face. "I am grateful, on behalf of my family, for your assistance. I . . . regret my rudeness earlier."

Farrem laughed, but it wasn't mean. It was a cheery laugh and Fred grinned, despite the seriousness of the situation. "No, Tennian, you do not. But it is kind of you to swallow your ire for the sake of your king."

"Mmph." As a comeback, Fred thought, it wasn't much, but at least Tennian wasn't tackling her father or throwing him through the kitchen window. Progress! "What are we doing?"

"Farrem has kindly agreed to try to locate those who have hidden themselves from me," Mekkam explained. "If he does, and if he can pinpoint their locations, we will form teams and go after them."

"How many of us are in these waters?" Farrem asked.

"Seven hundred sixty-four, not counting the ones I can no longer 'see.'"

Jonas whistled, but Artur shook his head. "A mere fraction. If what we fear is true, and we face war against artificially augmented traitors . . ."

The king nodded grimly. "I will mobilize all the Folk in the area and we will hunt them down."

Fred wondered what that meant. She knew that in general, Undersea Folk abhorred killing one another. It was almost unthinkable.

"One coup in a lifetime is quite enough," Mekkam continued grimly. "I would this one were thwarted before it truly began."

Fred leaned over and whispered in Farrem's ear, "Told you they'd give you another chance if you gave them one. Thirty years was long enough."

"You did tell me," he admitted, *not* whispering, "but I put it down to the naïveté of extreme youth."

"Well, thanks a heap, *Dad*."

"Farrem, if you please," Mekkam asked, except everyone in the room knew it was a royal command. "Please try to locate the lost ones."

Lost ones, Fred thought. That was an awfully generous way to put it.

Farrem nodded and sat back down in the dining-room chair. He leaned forward, resting his elbows on his knees, and closed his eyes.

The room felt . . . Fred didn't know exactly how to describe it . . . it felt *thick.* Charged, even, the way it felt before a kick-ass thunderstorm. And if she could sense that, what must Tennian and Wennd and Artur and Mekkam be feeling?

Cripes, Farrem calling . . . searching . . . it must be like a megaphone in their heads!

Farrem's shoulders started to tremble. His face was hidden in his hands as he concentrated. In seconds he was shaking all over.

Suddenly, shockingly, Wennd's odd, goose-like laugh sounded through the room, making them all jump. And she was just—she was just standing there, holding her stomach and laughing.

And Farrem looked up.

He was laughing, too.

Forty-four

"You really thought I was going to help you. Didn't you, Mekkam?"

Fred clutched the arm of her chair so hard, she felt it splinter beneath her fingers. Too late, she had it. The thing that was bugging her.

"Dammit!" She was staring at the hee-hawing Wennd. "You live in the Indian Ocean. And my father has a house in Perth. Which is on the Indian Ocean." Aarrgghh! She was a fucking marine biologist, she knew her geography, which countries and cities bordered which oceans. They had both dumped a large clue in her lap, and she hadn't suspected a thing.

Moron!

"Nice," Thomas said, his mouth twisting in distaste. "You sent your girlfriend to spy on us."

"Of course I did."

"That 'scared of surface dweller' thing," Jonas said. "Nice act."

"Do not speak to me," Wennd said by way of reply.

Artur was on his feet. "You will address my father as 'my king' or 'Your Majesty.'"

"Actually, that's how you'll address me. If you were going to live through this. Which you won't. Sit down."

Slowly, looking astonished, Artur did so.

"Why do I feel like I came into the middle of the movie?" Jonas asked.

"Because you're a worm," her father replied. He wasn't even mean about it. Perfectly casual, the way Fred would have said, "because you have blue eyes."

"You won't get away with this, Farrem. You didn't before," Fred said. "Also, not to be a nag or anything, but this really isn't the way to win back the royal family's trust."

"Do not speak to me, you stupid girl. I've known anemones that had more intelligence."

"That seems uncalled for," Jonas said.

"I know. I think he needs a nap. He's getting grumpy and he was up late last night, poor tyrannical baby."

"Be *quiet*! To think, a child of mine who can't read, who can't speak our language, much less possess the rudimentary telepathy an *infant* is born with! I cannot believe your mother let you live."

"Yeah, well, she's full of flaws like that."

"I've told Moon and told her," Jonas said, "she just has to step up the baby-killing. But she never listens."

"And by the way, *Dad*—"

"I ordered you not to speak to me."

"—there's more of us in this house than you. Why, exactly, are we not going to rip your treacherous heads off?"

He smirked. "I confess to shock; I thought the prince or the king might ask that. Not you. I wasn't working this morning, stupid. Well, I was, but not the way you think. I stopped by Sanibel Station—very helpful, some of those surface worms—and made sure that Captain Pearson worm was going to leave with the file."

"What?" Thomas asked, his voice dangerously low. "You got my dad involved in this?"

"Not at all. It was just a delicious coincidence that he was going to stop by to try to get information for you. I knew Mekkam would eventually notice something was wrong, and I knew my idiot daughter would have a worm friend somewhere that could help her."

"Did he just call *moi* a worm friend?" Jonas asked.

"No," Thomas said. *"Moi."*

Looking annoyed that the three of them weren't more terrified, Farrem continued, "I made sure one of his worm friends had access to it."

"So we're supposed to believe you *wanted* us to have your super-secret file?" Jonas asked skeptically.

Fred, meanwhile, was wondering why Tennian, Artur, and Mekkam weren't moving or speaking.

A megaphone in their heads. That's why.

"Of course I did! Because I knew even if I *literally* handed you the plan, you'd be too dim to comprehend it. And I knew that what little you could figure out would inspire the stupid girl to suggest they ask for my help."

"I have to admit," Fred said, "that wasn't one of my brightest ideas."

"Like the time you tried to eat two packages of Mint Milanos with Baileys chasers," Jonas agreed.

Farrem hissed through his teeth, appeared to recover his temper, then turned to Fred. "I so enjoyed our little talk by the pool, girl. I knew you were dim, but that conversation confirmed it, even before I realized you were mind blind. I certainly dropped enough hints."

And so he had, Fred realized, cursing herself. When he called her stupid, he wasn't so far off.

Perth.

So you did sort of get your own kingdom, after all.

Just because your father, and grandfather, and great-grandfather had been king, that didn't mean that you should be king.

My gift and my curse.

Your mother's blood is strong in you.

I naturally assumed one of my blood . . . You are your mother's daughter.

Awww. She had disappointed her papa. Oh, the shame of it!

She couldn't have been more thrilled. It was hard not to chortle.

Like a typical James Bond villain, her doorknob dad was still bragging about his clever plan. "So after thirty years, I was again face-to-face with my enemies. And they were kind enough to bring the royal cousin, too!"

Wennd smirked. "She was planning to swim down to La Habana

today. But I kept her in the area." Fred noticed that her normal voice was not a whisper. In fact, it was rather nasal and grating, like Madison when she had a head cold and had eaten too many Mentos.

"Too bad," Fred said.

"What?" Wennd asked, seeming surprised that Fred was speaking to her.

"You're not beautiful anymore," she said simply, and Jonas and Thomas nodded in agreement.

"Your sire told you not to speak."

"Yeah, well, *Dad* hasn't been paying much attention this past week if he thinks that'll shut me up. What's the matter, Farrem? Is something not going according to plan?" Slowly, Fred stood.

Wennd actually took a step backward. "You said they wouldn't be able to move, Farrem. You promised you could control—"

"Quiet," he snapped.

"Tough luck about your daughter being the UF equivalent of retarded. Mind blind, isn't that the phrase? Are you trying to telepathically control me right now, Pop? Because I couldn't help but notice I can think and talk and move without any trouble at all. So I guess I'll be kicking your ass starting right about now."

"Even now," Farrem said, "even now my people are starting to take over. They're subduing any Undersea Folk they can find. None of them will be able to move or speak until I say so. It is through me that my people can control yours, Mekkam! My stupid daughter and her idiot worm friends couldn't break the codes or decipher the charts."

"Well, of course not. The thing was a thousand pages long. They only had it for a couple of hours," Jonas said reasonably. "Way to play fair, ya big pussy."

It really wasn't the time or place, but Fred had to hide a smile. It was her and Jonas and Thomas against the super strong, super quick, super psychotic nutbag (and his super strong and quick henchwoman/girlfriend) who had boned her mother on a Cape Cod beach. And Jonas and Thomas were acting like it was lunch at McDonald's. Nothing extraordinary going on here, no way, nuh-uh.

"If they'd had the sense to understand what I *handed* them," Farrem ground out, "they would have understood my people weren't getting enhanced, they were swimming about the world doing—isn't this a funny phrase?—wet work."

"What's—" Jonas began.

"Assassinations," Thomas said.

"Of course that's what it means." Jonas sighed. "And here I thought they were designing water parks."

"Will you *stop talking*?" Farrem shrieked. They were clearly ruining his gloating supervillain moment by not being terrified. "I paid for my enhancement . . . for the drugs, and the treatments, the *years* of biopsies and operations and experiment after experiment—I paid Sanibel Station with my people. They did the work and I got enhanced. Enhanced enough to hide them from *you*, Mekkam, you pious whale. Enhanced so that you will not move or speak unless *I* wish it."

"Truly inspiring leadership," Thomas commented. "Making the team do the dirty work while you lie around on a Valium drip getting experimented on."

Jonas laughed.

Farrem glared dead into Fred's eyes. "I will kill them if you don't shut them up."

"Like you wouldn't kill them anyway?"

"I'd kill us anyway," Jonas said. "Thomas?"

He nodded. "Oh, yeah. I'd have quit babbling ten minutes ago and killed us, to be honest."

"In fact," Jonas added, "if you're going to keep talking, *would* you please kill us? Right now?"

"Your worm friends think they're funny. Shut them up if you value them in any way."

Fred shrugged. "Believe me, I've been trying for years. But kill them if you can. Problem is, you fucked up, Farrem. Big-time."

"You really are enormously stupid," he marveled. "Even now, you cannot comprehend it is over. I am king. Very soon Mekkam and Artur will be dead. Don't you understand? I can *make* them kill themselves! I won't even have to lift a finger! And you! I can't have you *breeding*."

"Well, I wasn't going to do it right this minute."

"You're disgusting and your deficiencies will die with you."

She was fairly certain no one had ever looked at her with such loathing—not even that waiter at the Hancock Tower Legal Sea Foods.

"You're a freak, a genetic joke. You're not a worm and you're not one of my people. You can't be allowed to breathe for another minute."

"Yeah, yeah, and you're going to ground me and take away my car keys. Can you think of the part of that story you *shouldn't* have told me?" she asked sweetly. She forced her fingers to loosen on the armrests.

She had to keep him on land. Had to. If they went in the water, he'd have the upper hand and it would be all over. And not just for her. She could never take on a full-blooded UF in the water. Certainly not a psychotic one.

And she had to get him out of the house, keep him away from Jonas and Thomas. No hostage-taking today, thank you.

She prayed Dr. Barb wouldn't be back anytime soon, but kept her tone light and teasing.

"Daddy-o? Can you?"

Jonas was waving a hand in the air. "I know, I know! Pick me!"

"Yeah, you should pick him." Thomas yawned. "He always gets picked last."

"Shut *up*!" Farrem said.

"But it's true," Jonas said earnestly. "I do always get picked last."

"The thing you shouldn't have told me is the part about how you're the enhanced one. Not your followers."

Then Thomas produced his switchblade—from where, Fred had no idea. One minute his hand was empty, the next there was a snick of sound and Thomas was holding a knife, turning, throwing it.

Right into Wennd's throat.

Forty-five

Farrem shrieked and clutched his head. He was powerful enough so that his grip on Artur's and Mekkam's and Tennian's minds did not lessen, but hearing Wennd's death screams in his head couldn't have been too comfortable.

Fred dove across the table at him, her momentum carrying them both through the glass patio door. The sound was a thousand teacups breaking at once.

Good. Good. Get the fight away from Thomas and Jonas. And keep Farrem out of the water. If he ever got into his tail form, the fight was over.

And so was everything else.

His fist looped toward her face but she ducked, and then they were rolling across her lawn, Farrem choking and gagging on grass. When they stopped, Fred was on top and the pool was less than seven feet away.

"Your girlfriend's having a real bad day, did you notice?" she asked, then brought her head down and broke her father's nose with a muffled crunch. It hurt her forehead, but not as much as it hurt him, and that was just fine.

He howled and punched out at her, but he was distracted by the blood running down his throat and, she imagined, Wennd's dying screams running through his big, stupid brain. She tried to follow up but he managed to buck her off. He scuttled like a crab, clawing through the grass in an attempt to get to the pool. She leapt forward and caught a handful of his thick green hair, so like hers.

She *hated* her hair. She yanked. Hard. Farrem yowled. A lot.

She dragged him away from the pool. Yep, he was stronger than she was, no doubt. Probably smarter, too, she'd give him that—it was a good plan. Everything had come about the way he predicted it would. It would have worked, if not for the Freak That Was Fred.

But she'd spent her life hiding her mermaid nature, blending with surface dwellers. She'd been raised by hippies, for God's sake. She was a helluva lot more comfortable on land than he was. Banished or not, big houses or not, he still couldn't stay out of the water for very long. And the longer he was out, the weaker he got.

She could stay out of it for weeks, and had.

She yanked harder, a thought

(am I actually enjoying this?)

there and gone before she could catch it. His hair (and some of his scalp) came off in her hand and then he was again getting to his feet, this time heading for the dock.

Too slow. Again. She leapt for him, landing on his back like dear old Dad was giving dumb Daughter a piggyback ride. She grabbed his chin in both hands. And wrenched to the left, hard.

The crack was undramatic, the sound a walnut makes when it's crushed in the nutcracker. But Farrem dropped like a rock.

A big, green-haired, psychotic, dead rock.

She didn't even have time to comprehend she had won—it had been so *fast*! He'd only revealed himself, what? Fifteen minutes ago? But there was no time to understand what had happened because someone from behind yanked her off his body.

She rolled, trying to scramble to her feet to face the new threat

(oh, man, which henchmen is this now?)

only to see Thomas standing over her father's corpse. He brought a foot down on Farrem's rib cage, hard.

"You were dead the minute you called her stupid, motherfucker!

When you said her mother should have drowned her! Your girlfriend's *dead*! You're *dead*! You can't touch her, *ever*! Get up, you piece of shit! Get up so I can feed you your balls!" Another crunch as the left ribs caved in.

"Thomas!" She grabbed him from behind, dodged (barely) the elbow he brought back, and carefully pulled him away from the corpse. "He's dead, Thomas. He's already dead. It's pointless. The prick can't feel a thing. Unfortunately," she added.

"Put me down, please, Fred," he said, perfectly calmly.

She did.

He turned, grabbed her face with both hands, and kissed her so hard she felt it in her knees.

Which, of course, was the moment Artur and Mekkam and Tennian came staggering out the broken patio door.

Thomas pointed to Artur. "And you can't have her, either."

"Holy shit!" Jonas said, peeking around Tennian. "What'd we miss?" Then, "I'm not cleaning any of this up."

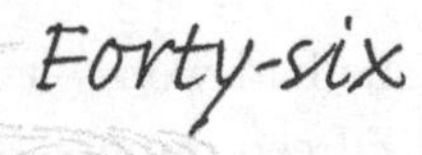

Forty-six

They were all sprawled in various spots in the living room.

"Thank God," Jonas moaned, "thank God Barb was out shopping for a wedding dress."

"Thank God he made the classic Bond villain mistake," Thomas said.

Fred, who was sprawled almost prone, sat up. "That's exactly what I thought!"

"I cannot believe," Mekkam was muttering, "that Wennd fooled me."

"And me," Tennian added. She and Artur and Mekkam were moving very gingerly and holding their heads; it was clear they had crushing headaches. "I'm sorry Thomas killed her; I so wanted that pleasure for myself."

"And Thomas! Way to stud up, man! You threw that knife, what? Eight feet? *Zam*, right into her neck." Jonas shook his head. "How many of those things do you have? And where do you keep them?"

"Enough." Thomas looked grim. "We got lucky. I was aiming for her eye."

"But what was she doing here? Farrem said himself that he was the enhanced one, that he was lending his power to his followers."

"Isn't it obvious?" Jonas asked. Fred scowled, because it wasn't. "He had her here just in case Fred didn't warm up to him. He had no guarantee she'd be friendly—shit, he was probably amazed when she offered him a guest room."

"Not one of your brighter moves," Thomas needled.

"Tell me. And that reminds me. Call the fumigator."

"So she was his 'just in case.' And he made sure the captain had the file," Jonas added, clearly warming to his subject (he'd been a huge *Encyclopedia Brown* fan in elementary school), "because it was the one thing that would make Artur yell for his dad. Once Mekkam got here, it was inevitable that Fred would suggest what she did. Then Farrem had all the royals—the ones in this area, anyway—in one spot. If Fred had been vulnerable to his giant evil brain blasting power, it would have worked perfectly."

"Fortunately," Fred said cheerfully, "I'm defective."

"So are all his followers," Mekkam said, gingerly holding his head. "They died when he died. I felt it. He could no longer hide them from me, and without his protection, they were helpless."

"But he *knew* Fred was—what was it? Mind blind? Why'd he still try it?"

"Because he was sure he and Wennd were more than a match for two worms and a freak," Fred said sourly. "Classic Bond villain mistake number two."

"Fredrika."

"At least it's over," she said.

"Fredrika."

"What?" And then she realized. It was Artur, and he wasn't calling her my Rika, or Little Rika, or any term of endearment.

"Will you step outside with me?" he asked quietly and, with a glance at Thomas, she rose and followed him through the hole that used to be her front door.

They stood in the front yard (Farrem's corpse was still on the back lawn), Artur with his arms crossed over his chest, Fred fidgeting.

"Thomas seemed quite sincere about his intentions toward you when he finished with your father's body," he said, mildly enough.

"Uh, yeah."

"What are your thoughts on that?"

"That I'm a coward."

He smiled. "Hardly."

"I'm not in love with you, Artur, but I like you an awful lot. I think you're awesome. But I can't be your queen." *Among other things, I can't do that to the Undersea Folk gene pool.*

And Thomas wants me. He wants me!

"Part of the reason I said yes was because I planned to spend the rest of my life hiding in the Black Sea. Running away from the messiness of hybrid life. It's a rotten way to start a marriage, never mind a family. It would have been a shitty thing to do to you."

"You were wrong. In your interview, you were wrong."

That was so unexpected, she couldn't immediately process it. "What?"

He took her hands in his, looking down into her eyes. "When you save an Undersea Folk—at least, when you save this one—you do get a wish. I release you from your word. You are no longer she-who-will-be-my-mate."

She wrenched her hands away and flung her arms around his neck.

"Thank you, Artur. Thank you, thank you. I'll always be your friend. And the next time a megalomaniac tries to kill the royal family, you better come get me!"

He kissed the top of her head and hugged her back. "Agreed, Fredrika."

And if he had seemed the smallest bit relieved, she was going to pretend she hadn't noticed. She didn't know if he had fallen out of love with her, or if he had realized that the chase was more fun than the engagement, and she didn't care.

They would always be friends. He was, after all, her prince.

Forty-seven

It seemed like they were cleaning up the mess (it was considered strictly an Undersea Folk matter and, thank God, the nearest neighbor was too far away to have heard anything amiss) for hours.

Mekkam ate six Advil and took charge. Little by little, the bodies were taken away, the damage to her home was repaired (or at least boarded up), and by the time she had the house to herself (and her roommates), Fred was exhausted.

And slightly amazed. Because the Undersea Folk treated her like royalty. Ironic, given that she wasn't ever going to be royalty.

They were anxious about the repairs to her rental—did they meet with her approval? Would she prefer another table? Was it all right if they couldn't replace the patio glass until tomorrow? Because if not, they would see to it that—

The fight, it seemed, had been seen in the mind of all the Undersea

Folk in the area. Farrem had been projecting everything, a sadistic touch to ensure their cooperation, to make sure they knew who was in charge. Knew who had taken over. Knew who was going to kill the king and prince.

Knew who was going to get his neck broken by a half-breed mind blind marine biologist with split ends.

"It's almost a shame you're not engaged to Artur anymore," Jonas whispered to her, watching their deference in awe. "Also, I'm not speaking to you because I really, really wanted to plan a royal wedding."

"Go soak your head," she whispered back.

Amazing! All you had to do to earn their admiration was break your father's neck on your back lawn.

"What a week," she groaned, stumbling into her room. It was two thirty in the morning and she needed a shower in the worst way.

"Say it twice," Thomas said. She heard the bedroom door close and realized with a start this was the first moment they'd had alone all day.

"Sit," he ordered, and, sighing, she obeyed. He *would* go into M.D. mode, of course, even though she was perfectly fine except for a few cuts (from the patio glass) and bruises (from the fight). But she was a fast healer, and he didn't need to poke or prod.

"Thomas, really, I'm—"

"I love you," he said, bending so he could look her in the eyes. She could feel her own eyes widening. "I've always loved you. And I was stupid about it. I thought Artur was the best thing for you and I didn't fight for you and I damned near made the worst mistake of my life. I'm scared shitless you'll get hurt. I'm scared shitless I'll have to hurt you again to fix you—like in Boston.

"But I'm even more scared at the prospect of a life without you. So we're getting married. Right away."

"Are you asking me?" she asked, feeling the bubble of joy spread from her heart all the way into her throat. It was actually hard to talk, she was so happy. "Or telling me?"

"Shut up and kiss me," he said, smiling, and she did. In seconds they were rolling around on her bed, groping and kissing and moaning and clutching.

"Wait, wait," she gasped. "I'm gross. I've still got Farrem's blood under my nails."

"I could use a shower, too." For a moment he looked grim, and she realized the healer was wrestling with the avenging lover. "It's not every day I throw a knife into a woman's neck."

"A woman who helped Farrem plot the deaths of hundreds, at the very least. Or did you think he was going to pick some other ridiculously beautiful woman to be his queen?"

"True enough. Come on." He stood and held out a hand. She took it and he pulled her to her feet. "I'll wash your back."

"That's nice. I'll wash your front."

And so they did, and when they were clean they stayed under the pounding spray, kissing until their lips were numb, soaping breasts and balls and buttocks, running slick hands all over slick flesh, gliding, sliding, and Fred was actually having trouble determining where one of them stopped and the other began.

And then, ah, God, he was lifting her, and entering her, and she was arching her back and meeting his thrusts, her fingers were digging into the heavy muscles of his shoulders, and at the height of her orgasm he kissed her on the side of her throat and she thought, *Home, home, I've never really felt like I belonged anywhere but right this minute I'm home, oh, thank you, God, I'm home at last.*

Epilogue

"This dress itches."

"Quit bitching, Fred."

"And this bouquet has made me sneeze twice."

"I mean it, Fred."

"And I'm hot. It's fucking ninety degrees out here and I'm in a floor-length dress!"

"So is Barb, so shut your hole."

"When is this thing going to *start* already?"

"It has started. You'd just rather be off somewhere banging Thomas."

"As a matter of fact, I would."

"Disgusting," Jonas said smugly, adjusting his bow tie. "You two are like monkeys. *Loud* monkeys."

"Look who's talking! How many scenes of debauchery have I walked in on? At least we've got the decency to keep to our bedroom." *And our shower. And the hot tub. And the pool when everyone's asleep. And—*

"I get that you haven't had sex in, what? Eight years?"

"Jonas," she warned grimly.

"But you two are going to hurt each other if you keep trying to make up for lost time."

"Jonas, I'm five seconds away from hanging you by your cummerbund. I'll get the electric chair, of course, but it's a small price to pay."

"Wait!" Jonas cocked his head as the tempo of the music changed. "That's your cue. Go, go!"

"Why are you even back here?" she demanded. "The bridesmaids are supposed to be back here." The other two had already gone, and hallelujah.

"To make sure you don't head for the hills." He gave her a rude shove in the middle of her back. "Now get going! I'll duck around the side and pop out in front."

"Great. It's not a wedding, it's a fucked-up magic show."

"Sparkle, Fred, sparkle!" Then, before she could pummel him, he had darted away.

She stomped down the aisle, recognizing several guests: Artur, Tennian, Mekkam. Her mother and Sam. Colleagues from the New England Aquarium, including *(oh, God)* Madison.

The captain, in full dress uniform, sitting beside Thomas. They both smiled at her as she passed them and Fred marveled at the change in her fiancé's father. The man had seriously mellowed after his wife's death. He'd certainly been nice enough to *her*, even going so far as to give Thomas his late mother's wedding and engagement rings to present to Fred. Fred had been proud to accept the engagement ring and, in another month, would be wearing the wedding ring as well.

Even though she'd been wearing it for over a month, she couldn't help being distracted by it now and again. It was a nice piece of jewelry, a platinum band with a half-carat diamond setting, but that's not why she caught herself staring at it during inopportune moments.

She loved what it represented, that was all. Almost as much as she loved the man who had given it to her.

She tipped him a wink, and prayed Jonas wouldn't notice she had refused to wear the silver heels he'd picked out for her.

Barefoot, she padded up the aisle to take her place beside Dr. Barb, who was looking dazzling in a cream-colored dress Jonas had selected. Dr. Barb looked exhilarated and intimidated and thrilled, all at once.

As the music reached its crescendo, she leaned in and whispered to the bride, "By the way, I'm withdrawing my resignation."

"What resignation?" the bride whispered back. "And you'd better not be late next Monday."

Real romantic, that's what it was.

Fred buried her face in her bouquet and snorted laughter into the white roses.